Henry Warwick Cole

Saint Augustine

A Poem in Eight Books

Henry Warwick Cole

Saint Augustine
A Poem in Eight Books

ISBN/EAN: 9783337206659

Printed in Europe, USA, Canada, Australia, Japan

Cover: Foto ©Andreas Hilbeck / pixelio.de

More available books at **www.hansebooks.com**

SAINT AUGUSTINE.

ST. AUGUSTINE'S TOMB AT PAVIA

SAINT AUGUSTINE

A POEM

IN EIGHT BOOKS

BY THE LATE

HENRY WARWICK COLE, Q.C.

TOLLE LEGE; TOLLE LEGE.

MURRAY AND GIBB, EDINBURGH,
PRINTERS TO HER MAJESTY'S STATIONERY OFFICE.

THE POETS are—

"The only truth-tellers now left to God;
The only speakers of essential truth,
Opposed to relative, comparative,
And temporal truths; the only holders by
His sun-skirts, through conventional grey glooms;
The only teachers who instruct mankind
From just a shadow on a charnel wall,
To find man's veritable structure out
Erect, sublime,—the measure of a man!"

ELIZABETH BARRETT BROWNING.

PREFATORY NOTE.

T HE widow of my dear friend, the author of the following poem of *St. Augustine*—herself not unknown
to literature as the author of *A Lady's Tour round Monte
Rosa*—has requested me to introduce to the public this
posthumous work. The circumstances under which it is
published will prove, I hope, a sufficient apology for not
declining the task.

The author had for several years devoted much of his
leisure to the study of the life of St. Augustine, and
cherished the hope of perfecting his study when he should
find a more convenient season. This convenient season,
however, never arrived, for he died, after a very brief
illness, on the 19th of June 1876.

His career at the Bar is so well known in the profession,
that it would be superfluous in the writer to speak of it
here; but he cannot forbear mentioning the fact, that out
of thousands of cases brought before him as judge of the
County Court at Birmingham, scarcely a single judgment
that he gave was ever reversed. His careful work on the
Domicil of Englishmen in France bears evidence also to
his accurate knowledge of International Law.

A lover of truth, of judgment, and of equity; of eminent modesty, fairness, and discretion ; of considerable natural gifts, improved by assiduous labour and persevering study ; of great capacity for business, and conscientious toil in the fulfilment of every duty,—the author of *St. Augustine* yet found time to cultivate the serious bias of his mind, and took intense pleasure in pursuing those studies, to which his brief leisure was by his own choice devoted.   The work is now submitted to the public as it came from his pen, after careful revision of the proofs by the Rev. W. J. Batchelor, M.A., of Leamington College.

Had the author been longer spared, his work would have undergone careful and thoughtful correction ; for he was one who spared no toil in perfecting to the utmost of his power whatever he undertook ; and he had mentioned to the writer of this preface, in friendly intercourse, that he was conscious of imperfections in the poem that he should endeavour to remove before its publication.   His sudden removal after only ten days' illness, at the age of sixty-four, left the MSS. in their present condition ; and they are now published as a memorial of the inner and higher life of one of whom it may be justly said, that his motto was DUTY, and his constant practice, LABOUR.

HENRY NOTTINGHAM.

THE SUBDEANERY, LINCOLN,
    February 1877.

CONTENTS.

—0—

BOOK I.

THE NUMIDIAN MOTHER.

		PAGE
I. OSTIA,		5
II. THE ELDEST-BORN,		21
III. THE STUDENT,		26
IV. ROMAN CARTHAGE,		30
V. THE COLLEGIAN,		34
VI. THE MANICHÆAN,		42
VII. THE LOVER,		48

BOOK II.

THE SEPARATION.

I. CONSOLATION IN DESPAIR,		57
II. DEATH AND SORROW,		61
III. SUNSET ON THE DESERT,		67
IV. THE MANICHÆAN BISHOP,		70
V. FAUSTUS ON THE ISLE,		77
VI. TO ITALY,		82

BOOK III.

IN ITALY.

I. ROME AND MILAN,		89
II. THE PREFECT OF THE CITY,		96

		PAGE
III.	THE PURSUIT,	105
IV.	ST. AMBROSE,	107
V.	OSCILLATIONS,	119
VI.	CALLING ON GOD,	122

BOOK IV.

THE CONVERSION.

I.	WORLDLY DISCONTENT,	131
II.	WHAT IS EVIL?	135
III.	PLATO AND ST. PAUL,	144
IV.	SIMPLICIAN,	149
V.	PONTITIAN,	153
VI.	THE CRISIS,	157
VII.	ALYPIUS TO GOD,	164
VIII.	THE TRIUMPH OF MONICA,	171

BOOK V.

CASSICIACUM.

I.	THE ALPINE VILLA,	177
II.	MONTE GENEROSO,	189
III.	THE PSALMS OF DAVID,	197
IV.	LICENTIUS,	208
V.	THE BIRTHDAY,	214
VI.	ANGEL AND SAINT WORSHIP,	223
VII.	THE DEPARTURE,	232

BOOK VI.

THE CHURCH OF CHRIST.

I.	THE BAPTISM,	239
II.	VERECUNDUS,	244
III.	THE DAY OF PENTECOST,	250
IV.	THE CHURCH,	258
V.	OUR LORD JESUS CHRIST,	263
VI.	THE HOLY TRINITY,	275

CONTENTS.

BOOK VII.

THE DEATH OF MONICA.

		PAGE
I.	TO OSTIA,	283
II.	GRACE,	288
III.	WHAT GRAVE?	296
IV.	THE DEPARTURE,	300
V.	THE BURIAL,	308
VI.	CHRIST'S RESURRECTION,	314

BOOK VIII.

THE THREE TEMPTATIONS.

		PAGE
I.	THE WORLD,	319
II.	THE FLESH,	332
III.	THE DEVIL,	363
IV.	MYSTIC BABYLON,	381
	APPENDIX,	387
	LATIN NOTES,	400

ERRATA.

Page 10, note 2, *for* Ecclesiastique *read* Ecclesiastiques

" 21, line 17, *for* wildling *read* wilding.

" 31, note, *for* Blackesley *read* Blakesley.

" 96, line 18, *for* MAXIMIM *read* MAXIMIN.

" 181, line 16, *for* shreds *read* sherds.

" 192, line 15, *for* By fierce *read* By the fierce.

SAINT AUGUSTINE.

———◆———

INTRODUCTION.

L IFE! human life! so bitter and so sweet!
　　So sweet to fools, so bitter to the wise;
Life! tedious oft, but oftener far too fleet,
　　Thy close here longed for, there a rude surprise;
Life! which none sane presumes to cast away,
Though some, in pain, for thy departure pray.

Life! thou enigma few can understand,
　　And fewer fashion to a noble end;
Life! whose brief glories all men, mean and grand,
　　Condemn at heart, although their tongues commend,
Which art so poor yet rich, so false yet fair,
And worth scant praise from true lips anywhere.

Life! precious gift! but now prosaic grown,
　　When viewed impatiently by careless eyes!
Yet doth the humblest human life e'er known
　　Contain deep pathos, which close hidden lies,
Till love, by labour, bid it stand confest;
Life! always seeking, never finding rest!

Let us now study thee, O Life! in one
  Who, fifteen hundred years since, took chief part
In work which had at that time to be done ;
  Unveil the inmost secrets of his heart,
And watch the struggles of his mighty soul
As he pressed on to reach a destined goal.

Founder was he of that theology
  In modern times called Protestant, which stands
As a firm bulwark against heresy,
  And strict exclusion from the Church demands,
As things incongruous with its Author's plan,
Of lies, corruption, and the guile of man!

Perchance such study,—in an age like this,
  Greedy of gain, mechanical, and slow
To strive for better things than worldly bliss,—
  May warm some minds to an unwonted glow,
And rouse them, conscious of a nobler aim,
To call on GOD, not sigh for wealth and fame !

SAINT AUGUSTINE.

———•———

BOOK I.

THE NUMIDIAN MOTHER.

BOOK I.

———

I.

OSTIA.

NOT battles, sieges, and the pomp of war,
    Nor heroes slain with garments rolled in blood,
Nor ladies weeping for their lovers lost,
Are now our theme ; but struggles of man's soul
In the wild sea of error tempest-tost,
The rescue of a captive chained by sin,
A mother's tears, despondency, and joy,
Spiritual strivings of a holy saint,
His meditations when by GOD'S grace saved,—
These are our topics, which to thoughtful minds
And noble loving hearts will worthy seem.
    In the fourth century, towards its close,
When Christianity had just escaped
From persecution, and had gained at last,
Despite fierce Pagan hatred, that success
Which is the rightful privilege of truth ;
When, though at times assailed by Arian foes,
The Church rose up, a structure beautiful,
Amidst the ruins of a crumbling world ;
When men had just renounced their ancient creed,
But hardly learnt their new one ; when true faith
Was daily vexed by novel heresies

Which Alexandrian subtilty conceived ;
When o'er the enervated Roman race,
And the great empire which its sword had won,
But which Imperial cowardice now ruled,
Rude Gothic hosts hung like a thunder-cloud
To burst ere long, and from the lofty Alps
Swiftly descend to deluge Italy ;—
In such an age, when all was insecure,
Did human genius, touched by GOD'S own fire,
Emerge from darkness, to delight the world,
Give strength to love, stability to faith,
And be for centuries a radiant light,
Guiding men's footsteps on the road to heaven.
   On a calm eve, at this momentous time,
A group of travellers was seen to stand
Above the shifting sands of Ostia,
Watching the glories of the setting sun.
To ignorant observers they appeared
But ordinary men, like those who oft
Came there and went, whose names were heard no
    more ;
Yet they, ere long, would prove themselves to be
The world's true salt, to savour it anew.
One of the group was worthier than the rest :
He had the greatest, highest intellect
Of all who then the human race adorned.
They had arrived from Rome some days before,
And tarried now, close to the Tiber's mouth,
Until a vessel could convey them back
To Carthage. Noble Africans they were,
And of that nation which had erst strived hard
To gain earth's empire, and as rivals fought
So many and such doubtful wars with Rome.
Simple and unassuming their attire,

As became laymen of their quality ;
And their demeanour, during the few days
In which they, in the church at Ostia,
Had joined in worship, had been so devout
As to inspire a kind of reverence
In all who with them there had knelt to GOD.

   Of the six persons who composed the group,
One was a lady, clad in robes of white,
Which hung with fulness round her wasted form,
Without embroidered hem or golden fringe.
Although not far advanced as yet in years,
She was so thin and pale, that her sweet smile
Could not from an attentive eye conceal
How much, in former days, some brooding grief
Had tried her faith and agonized her heart.
Her name was MONICA. Beside her stood
One on whose arm she leant so tenderly,
That he must be her son. Thirty-three years
Had now elapsed since he—her eldest-born,
The object of her fervent, ceaseless prayers—
Had first beheld the light, and known her love.
AURELIUS AUGUSTINE, though still young,
Was grave and pensive ; elegant of form,
But statelier in his air than in his height.
His strength was less of body than of mind ;
His smile and every feature of his face
Betokened keenest sensibility,
Deepened by pure refinement of the soul.
His voice, though weak, was musical and clear ;
His large, black, flashing eyes would look men
    through,
But scared them not; for in their brightest gleam
Was an expression of such tenderness,
That all whose searching glances met his own

Gazed unabashed, by sympathy sustained.[1]
He was in structure strong, yet delicate,
Bright-eyed, small-handed, and with feet as swift
As those of the Numidian antelope,
Which over rocky barriers bounds with ease.
His moods would vary, as great clouds will change
From bright to dark, then back to bright again.
Taciturn oft, because in thought absorbed,
Or timidly in deep reserve entrenched ;
Then would he when disturbed imploring look,
As fain to say, could he to do so dare,
" Ah ! stir me not ; in silence lies my strength !"
Yet, when the impulse moved him, and he spake,
His speech would flow in language eloquent,
Each word selected by fastidious choice,
And all in fittest places deftly set ;
Then, if opposed, his arguments would roll,
From the mere presence of abundant thought,
Like the resistless spring-tide of the sea,
Passing accustomed bounds and barriers old.
In controversies hard he took delight,
And in their thorny coverts loved to dwell.
His mind was like a spacious crucible,
Which swings at white-heat over blazing fire,
And in whose deep revolving vortex piled
Are seen, commingled in disorder rude,

[1] There is an ancient portrait of Augustine at Milan, which represents him, as he appeared before his conversion, in a Manichæan dress, when professor of eloquence in that city. Although this portrait cannot be 1500 years old, it gives, at all events, Augustine's traditional appearance. " Il ritratto celo presenta vestito in una forma, che in volgo dice Manichæa, ma veramente propria, o di quei tempi, oper lo meno de' pæsi Africa ; né è molto dissimile da quella ché anco ne' nostri giorni si costuma generalmente in Levante. Il colore è vermiglio tendente al fosco ; la fronte stessa ; lo sguardo penetrante si, ma dolce e sospeso ; la struttura del corpo restreita e gentile."—Bugeaud, *Hist. de Monique,* p. 190, n.

Collected substances of strangest sorts,—
Other men's thoughts and doubts, his own as well,
Fancies and facts, observed phenomena,
Figments of air by speculation bred,
More solid reasons culled from history,
With deeper truths by revelation told ;—
These, in confusion tumbled, sometimes seemed
Hopeless of order and congruity ;
But as the fire of genius scarched them through,
And skill controlled what driving force impelled,
The crude conglomeration fused at last,
And from the molten mass came forth pure gold,—
The dross expelled, the precious ingots gained ![1]
Although by nature gentle, loving, mild,
And ever courteous, he in truth's cause proved
Daring and brave.   Therefore, when JEROME once,
By learning overweighted, sanction gave
To what ORIGEN carelessly had said,—
Declaring of ST. PAUL that he had erred
In his Epistles, wherein he relates
What PETER did, when he and BARNABAS
"Walked not uprightly," and received rebuke,—
Whereby the Holy Scriptures were accused
Of being false, AUGUSTINE proved him wrong !
Then rose up JEROME, terrible in wrath,
To smite the young aspirant who presumed
To cross his path, and rushed to close with him,
Like a huge grisly bear of cubs bereft,

[1] These precious ingots are more plentiful in Augustine's letters than in his more elaborate treatises. An English version of his Letters, or rather the greater number of them, has just been published, and will be found of deep interest, notwithstanding that the translator has omitted much which Possidius rightly thought worth preserving. *Letters of St. Augustine, Bishop of Hippo*, translated by the Rev. J. S. Cunningham, M.A. Edinburgh, 1872-5.

Trying to catch him in his sinewy arms,
And out of him compress the gasping life
By strength prodigious.   But AUGUSTINE stood
Undaunted by his fury, stepped aside
To let the onset pass, then nimbly leapt
On his assailant,—not as DAVID did,
When from their Syrian foe his lambs he saved,
To slay him straight,—but fast to pin him down,
Until, with rage extinguished and spent force,
He was content to own himself o'ercome.[1]
Then peace ensued, age no more youth despised,
And from their contest noble friendship sprung.
Again, when ZOSIMUS, the Pope of Rome,   ·
Not then supposed to be infallible,
Egregiously mistook the heresy
Of the Pelagian, sly CŒLESTIUS,
That compound strange of advocate and monk,
And would, by an usurped authority,
Have spread his error widely through the Church,
AUGUSTINE manfully the Pope withstood,
Appealed unto the Emperor for aid,
And, with assistance of the temporal power,
Stopped rash presumption's ignorant career :
Then forced he the false step to be retraced,
And made the humbled prelate change his tone,
Disown false teaching, and accept the truth ![2]
None who AUGUSTINE viewed as on this day,
With placid face beside the Libyan sea,
Could have foreseen how soon, when he should go

[1] Aug. *Opera*, Epist. 39, 28, 40, 67, 68, 72, 73, 75, 81, 82, also 180 (to Oceanus).   See also Jerome, *Opera*, Book i., against the Pelagians and Cyprians ; and Epist. 70 (to Quintus).

[2] *Cathedra Petri*, by Thos. Greenwood, Q.C., vol. i. pp. 283-292. *La Vie de Saint Augustine*, par De Tillemont ("Memoires Ecclesiastique "), tom. xiii.   Paris, 1710.

Unto Numidia for some few years
To gather up his strength in solitude,
His name, till then unheard, would loudly sound,
To echo for all ages through the world!

Tagasta comes to me in dreams;
    White shine her walls,
Green are her groves, and clear her streams
    And waterfalls;
Each night to beckon me she seems;
    Her sweet voice calls!

Give me the pinions of a bird,
    Hither to fly
Swifter than a courser spurred!
    Else will I cry,
While anguish deepens every word,
    Oh, let me die!

" Be patient, ADEODATUS," gently said
The voice of MONICA ; " dost thou not know
That till the ship be freighted we must wait?"
At this the lad turned round, and thus addressed
His father's brother, who stood close behind :
" To-morrow thou must take me then to see
Old Tiber's mouth, through which ÆNEAS came
When he from Carthage sailed for Italy,
And steered his gallant ships to Latium.
Let us start early, that we may arrive
Just at the time which VIRGIL has described,
When there the sea to redden first begins
With the sun's rays, and from the lofty sky
AURORA, saffron-hued in rosy car,
Brightly shines forth, while suddenly subside

The winds, and every zephyr dies away!"
"Agreed," NAVIGIUS said; "with thee I'll go."
He was of nature sweet, complying, mild,
Averse to angry looks and hasty words;
Throughout his life he had on MONICA
Lavished the deep affection of a son,
Followed her good advice, her will obeyed,
Believed as she had taught him when a child,
Nor by a thought or act once caused her pain;
Yet seemed he not one-half so dear to her
As his more gifted brother, for whose sake,
When he through wilfulness had gone astray,
Her sleepless eyes had oft in tears been bathed!
   The other two of this distinguished group,
EVODIUS and ALYPIUS, were both born
Within Tagasta, their friend's native town.
Younger than he, yet had their happy lives
In school and college days with his been passed.
EVODIUS, the child of parents rich,
Had from his infancy been reared with care,
Nurtured in honour, taught to speak the truth,
And trained to use his wealth for public ends,—
Best proof of true nobility of soul;
Strict in his morals, yet most tolerant
Of others' failings, all men loved him well.
He had from earliest youth with eagerness
The study of philosophy pursued,
As some would woo a mistress; then, misled
By admiration for AUGUSTINE, who,
Himself in error, caused his friends to err,
He had embraced a heresy which soon
Made him a sceptic.   Shortly afterwards
He left his native Africa for Milan,
Where he obtained an office of high rank

And of great value in the Emperor's Court.
At Milan he attended oft to hear
ST. AMBROSE preach, and was so much impressed,
That he ere long the Christian faith embraced,
And was baptized.   When, in his turn, AUGUSTINE
Also to Milan went, EVODIUS
Renewed with him their intimacy old,
And their close friendship strengthened every hour ;
But when AUGUSTINE, by GOD'S saving grace,
Became a convert to the Church of CHRIST,
And, wishing to devote his life to GOD,
Resolved to pass his days in Africa,
That he might work secluded from the world,
EVODIUS his post at Court resigned
To go back with him ; cheerfully gave up
Unto the poor whatever he possessed,—
His wealth, his time, his strength, his ceaseless prayers,
Exchanging luxury for poverty,
Eating scant food, but thinking glorious thoughts,
And striving on this earth to realize
Some foretaste of the bliss which is to come.
He knew not then that GOD had pre-ordained
That he himself a shining light should prove,
And die ere long a bishop and a saint !
  But dearer to AUGUSTINE was ALYPIUS.
He was a scion of the noblest house
In all Tagasta ; ever wise though young,
Virtuous as wise, and tolerant as true,
His form, though small, was hardened into strength
By firm resolve to combat toil and pain.
His friendship for AUGUSTINE had become
The passion of his soul.   He loved him first
When they were schoolboys ; loved him even more
When they at Carthage passed their time together

In their bright college days, so full of hope,
Audacity, and error ; loved him yet
With an increasing love, when, later on,
AUGUSTINE, as Professor, had commenced
To lecture on the art of eloquence ;
And as a pupil to his class he went
Despite his father's wish, who entertained
A fellow-townsman's narrow jealousy
Against AUGUSTINE and his early fame.
AUGUSTINE then reclaimed his youthful friend
From too great passion for the Circus games ;
Taught him to search for wisdom and love truth,
Embrace philosophy, and hold her fast.
Then did these two stray hand in hand together,
Through all the devious paths of human thought,
Preferring those which promised novelty,
Till they became entangled in a maze
Of error, which deceived them.   Finally,
After a separation of some years,
They met by chance in Italy once more,
And tried old studies on a wiser plan ;
The errors of their early youth abjured,
Searched through the Scriptures, weighing what they
    read,
Heard AMBROSE preach in Milan, and at last
Were by his hands on the same day baptized !
They loved each other as two men will love,
Who, meeting shipwreck in some stormy sea,—
Where in a fragile bark they idly roamed
With silken sails, to be in tempests caught,—
Have 'midst great perils given each other aid,
Battled through dangers, and escaped from death,
To reach at last the haven they desired.
Now with a nobler purpose were they bound

Unto their native country back again ;
Never to know a separation more,
Unless of place, but to be joined as one
For the full term of five-and-forty years,
When, weary of this world, its woes and sins,
AUGUSTINE yielded up his life to GOD,
And, bending o'er his face, ALYPIUS
Closed those loved eyes which once had flashed out
    fire.[1]
  Unto them all was ADEODATUS dear,—
A boy whose birth had been AUGUSTINE'S shame,
Whose life was now his solace and his pride !
For though not yet sixteen, his cultured mind
Was clear and strong, his loving heart beat high,
Deep were his thoughts, and eloquent his tongue.
He too at Milan had, by grace, received
Baptism with his father from the hands
Of AMBROSE, and with earnest, ardent faith
Believed what he professed.   He hoped, fond youth !
Before his life on earth should pass away,
To do some labour worthy of reward
In CHRIST'S great vineyard, overgrown with weeds ;
Nor knew in how few months his tender soul,
Unfit to bear the buffets of the world,
Would, by GOD'S mercy, suddenly be called
To leave this vale of tears, and enter heaven !
   Happy was MONICA when she surveyed
This group of those she loved, scanned the bright face
Of ADEODATUS, listened to the tones

---

[1] Augustine, in his Epistle No. 28, cap. i., speaks thus of Alypius and his
friendship for him : " Any one who knows us may say of him and me that
in body only, and not in mind, we are two ; so great is the union of heart,
so firm the intimate friendship existing between us ; though in merit we
are not alike, for his is far above mine."

Of his sweet voice, and joined her sons and friends
In earnest converse, as, brimful of hope,
They planned the active future of their lives,
And sought for means by which to save men's souls,
Glorify GOD, and christianize the world !

They now were sojourning in Ostia,
Full of desire to reach their native land,
And toil there till their work on earth should close ;
Nor could e'en Italy, though passing fair,
Abate the yearning for it in their hearts.
True, the fierce sun casts there a scorching heat
O'er sultry plains, deep vales, and swelling hills,
But every ray which touches fills the soil
With rich fertility ; and though it lies
This day a wild and wasted wilderness,
Let it but feel the hand of industry,
And quickly on its cultured plains appear
The yellow corn, the luscious, cooling fig,
The grape, the olive, and the pomegranate,
In an abundance which makes Italy
Look poor and barren.[1]   The first dwellers there
Were aborigines of Libyan name,
Who roamed about as untaught savages,
Their food the produce of the chase, with fruits
Bestowed by nature, not by culture raised.[2]
Then came the Persians in o'erwhelming hordes,
From far Euphrates and the Syrian shore,
Who on the Libyan and Getulian fields
Settled in swarms, and clustered on the land
As when the east wind from a blackened sky
Deposits locusts.   Their dismasted ships,

[1] L'Abbé Bugeaud, *Histoire de Sainte Monique*, p. 75.
[2] Sallust, *De Bello Jugurth.* cap. xviii., xix.

With keels turned uppermost, afforded sheds,
Which served as models for their herdsmen's huts.
Next came the trafficking Phœnicians,
To found a city greater e'en than Tyre,
Whose roving ships all unknown coasts explored,
From Britain to the west of Africa.
They the best parts and richest regions seized,
And on a peaceful and nomadic race
Their own adventurous character impressed.
Grand their exploits, glorious their history,
Though written by the pens of unjust foes !
Rome finally, when Carthage was no more
Sent thither swarms of needy colonists,
To people cities, cultivate the lands,
And hide old ruins underneath the pomp
Of new imperial magnificence.
This blending of great races promised well :
The Oriental's soul contemplative,
More prone to subtle thoughts than daring acts ;
The mariner's industrious energy,
With hardy limbs to long endurance trained ;
And the determined, persevering will
Which made the Romans masters of the world,
United in one people, who appeared
Destined for greatness. But disorders rose
From a rebellious spirit in the mass ;
All would make laws, but none would laws obey ;
Commotion spread unchecked, and order ceased.
Internal weakness paralyzed the State,
Whose riches tempted foreign plunderers ;
Feebly it languished until trials came,
When helplessly it into ruin fell,
By Vandal fury heaped in massacre,
And burnt by Saracenic fires to dust.

B

These great calamities, then unforeseen,
Were in the womb of time, and caused no fear.
Hope reigned untroubled in exulting hearts,
And Carthage, with its neighbouring provinces,
Still flourished in renewed prosperity.
Therefore the natives of the land might well
Love it above all others, and feel proud
Of the great people who within it dwelt ;
Whose toil and skill had made the region bloom
As a fair garden, and had filled it full
Of stately cities and industrious towns ;—
A race which had of old, in mighty wars,
Fought for supremacy by sea and land,
And had by HANNIBAL, its general,
Taught Pagan Rome the noble art of war,
But should for Christian Rome do even more ;
For by the Carthaginian intellects
Of CYPRIAN, TERTULLIAN, and AUGUSTINE,
Were Rome's proud priests, once strangely ignorant,
Taught the new science of theology ![1]
"Behold !" AUGUSTINE said, "the sun's broad disc
Already dips beneath the western wave.
Let us go home ; for the November mists
From yonder marshes have begun to rise,
And threaten fever." Slowly at these words
They walked along the shore, and reached the town
Wherein they lodged. Then, ere he went to rest,
AUGUSTINE, with a grateful heart to GOD,
Mused on the self-denial which his friends
Had shown to please him, asking only love
From him as recompense ; the noble aims
They had in common ; and the friendship true
Which knit their hearts together : then he thought

[1] *Histoire de Sainte Monique*, par Bugeaud, Paris 1869, p. 76.

How different were some friendships of his youth !
Yet one of them had been so passionate,
That when his friend had died, he, from mere grief,
Had nearly followed ; but the love of GOD
Would now, he hoped, support and comfort him,
Even if he should lose, by some hard doom,
Which might perchance be hanging o'er his head,
One of the friends whose love he needed most :
His mother or his son, or even both !
Then, with his soul directed unto GOD,
His thoughts at last found vent in words like these : [1]

' What trifles once would captivate my mind
    If friends joined in them ! We would sit and jest
Together, do in turns some office kind,
    Read to each other books of interest ;
At times in trivial sports find mirth and joy,
At times in worthier acts our days employ.

" Sometimes, but free from bitterness, dispute
    As one may with himself, and by the aid
Of rare dissensions, sweeter constitute
    Our oft concurrence ; now to teach be made,
And now to learn ; feel absence as a grief,
But welcome presence as of joys the chief!

" Tokens like these, proceeding from the heart
    Of those who love and are beloved no less,
Signs which the face, the tongue, the eyes impart
    With thousand gestures, which love best express,
Would through our souls, like fire through touchwood,
      run ;
The heat thus raised fused many into one.

[1] Appendix, Note A ; Augustine's *Confess.* lib. iv. c. 8, 9.

" This, then, it is, that is so loved in friends!
    Yes, so much loved, that human conscience quails
As self-accused, if it no love extends
    To him who proffers love, or should it fail
When loving to give love, and yet nought seek
Beyond the tokens which of true love speak.

" Hence, should some dear friend die, comes that deep
      woe,
    Those gloomy shadows of o'erwhelming grief;
A heart all steeped in tears, which vainly flow,
    For sweet's to bitter turned beyond belief!
And thus the loss of one, who mourned for dies,
The death of the survivors oft implies.

" Blest is the man, O GOD, who loveth Thee!
    And in Thee loves his friend, and, for Thy sake,
His enemy as well! For only he
    Loveth none dear enough his heart to break,
To whom all creatures, when beloved the most,
Are loved in One who never can be lost.

" And who is He but GOD! our GOD of old!
    GOD who made heaven and earth, and doth them fill;
Because by filling that which doth them hold,
    He did all things create of His mere will.
None loseth Thee, we may with justice say,
But faithless men, who flee from Thee away.

" And whither, when to 'scape Thee they desire,
    Shall such deserters go, or whither flee,
Except from Thee in love to Thee in ire?
    Where in their wanderings can they fail to see
It is Thy law which punishes them now?
Thy law is truth, and truth itself art Thou!"

II.

THE ELDEST-BORN.

ALTHOUGH the age of MONICA fell short
    By two years of threescore, her energies
Were conscious of a premature decay
Stealing upon them surely ; for the path
She through her life had been compelled to tread
Was a hard struggle, one with tears bedewed.
Her parents were of noble family,
Whose wealth had much decayed.   They, at a time
When in Tagasta heresy was rife,
And Paganism flourished as a weed,
Were orthodox and Catholic in faith ;
They shunned society, and lived retired.
The Punic blood which coursed along their veins
Was mixed with Roman, which gave stedfastness
Under affliction, and forbade despair ;
For Roman grafts on Carthaginian stocks,
Like choicest roses upon wildling thorns,
Could bear bright blooms of fragrance unsurpassed.
An old decrepit maid, her father's nurse,
One for religion zealous, but austere
In temper, and a grumbler at small faults,
Taught MONICA in childhood lessons stern
Of self-denial, patience, discipline,
And strict obedience to the laws of GOD.
Thus was she trained to grow in piety :

E'en when a girl she visited the sick,
Relieved the poor, and washed the pilgrims' feet.

If quarrels rose, she stilled their violence,
By sweet looks curing bitter angry words,
And spreading round an atmosphere of peace.
Modest and gentle was she, fair and good ;
As a true worshipper of GOD in CHRIST,
She made her wishes wait upon His will ;
Simple and pure in taste, she never sought
To captivate men's eyes by broidered hair,
Or gold, or pearls, or costly rich attire,
But by good works, and that true ornament,
A meek and quiet spirit, which doth shine,
E'en in GOD's sight, as something of great price.
Her parents, who were needy, wedded her
With unwise haste unto PATRICIUS,
A magistrate of no great dignity
And of small fortune in her native town.
He was of nobler lineage than his wife ;
Was more than twice her age, not half her worth :
A Pagan, neither rich nor very poor.
He haughtily regarded MONICA,
Until he knew her better, as a toy,
To trifle with at times, then cast aside ;
Nor was she even mistress of his house,
For in it lived, and over all bore rule,
The husband's jealous mother, who at first,
Stirred up by wicked servants' whisperings,
Stormed out against her, but at length was won,
By MONICA's endurance and meek love,
To recognise her excellence as true.
Then, when the servants had been punished well
For their false tales, the two became as one,

And lived together in the closest bonds
Of mutual kindness till the mother died.
But MONICA, when mistress of her house
With undisputed sway, was meek and shy.
She sought seclusion, like the violet,
Which under broad green leaves remains unseen,
Though shedding fragrance round it every hour.
The common eye, that stares at garish things,
Noticed her not; but if a gentle soul
Stooped where she grew, and gazed upon her face,
The ravished sight beheld for recompense
Sweetest embodiment of humble joy!
PATRICIUS, from his birth a spoilèd child,
Had, e'er grown up ill taught and unimproved,
With tongue unbridled and with temper harsh;
A man whose life and faith were both impure;
Boisterous and boastful in his moods of joy,
A striker when the wine-cup made him mad;
Yet had he in his heart the precious germs
Of goodness undeveloped, which his wife,
By patience, kindness, skill, smiles, tears, and love,
Tenderly cultured till she made them grow,
Bud forth, and blossom in the light of CHRIST.
Hence, ere their twenty years of wedded life
Came to a close, he left his Pagan creed
And Pagan vices, to obtain through her,
Within the Church, repentance bringing peace,
The cleansing power of the baptismal rite,
A happy deathbed, and a Christian's grave.

 Three children were the pledges of their love:
The younger boy NAVIGIUS was named;
PERPETUA was their daughter; and these two
Repaid with grateful love their mother's care.

She in return showed them that tenderness
For common children felt by mothers kind.
The third, her eldest son, she idolized !
She doated with a love inordinate
Upon AUGUSTINE from his earliest days,
And loved him more than all the world contained,—
More than her husband, more than life itself !
When he was but a babe, she oft would sit
Beside his cradle, gazing on his face,
So calm and beautiful in sleep, until
Her soul by deep-felt joy became entranced ;
But when she recollected what a world
There was without, and that her son one day
Must walk amidst its struggles and its sins,
Her heart misgave her, and with tearful eyes
Looking to heaven, she breathed such thoughts as these :—

MONICA BY THE CRADLE.

Tell me, O GOD, the destiny
   Of this sweet, sleeping babe of mine !
Shall he a mighty warrior be,
   Expert in combats, love, and wine,
Seeking for plaudits as he goes
O'er gory heaps of slaughtered foes ?
     Ah, no ! Ah, no !

Shall he become a statesman wise,
   And rule by policy the world ?
Grasp, as his own, ambition's prize,
   Till, from a dizzy height down-hurled,
He learn how base in treachery
Some men he trusted most can be ?
     Ah, no ! Ah, no !

Shall he as merchant take delight
   To gather piles of shining gold ;
Make gain his god, and wealth his might,
   By care grow prematurely old ;
Hard as the diamond which he sells,
False as the tale he scheming tells ?
        Ah, no ! Ah, no !

Shall he obtain a poet's name,
   Feel first the woes his verse shall tell ;
Find tears for bread, neglect for fame,
   In disappointments taste of hell ;
Live without solace for his soul,
Save the great thoughts that therein roll ?
        Ah, no ! Ah, no !

Shall he, O GOD ! be wholly Thine,
   Strive on this earth to do Thy will ;
Lead others on to paths divine,
   Thy precepts love, Thy laws fulfil ;
Look upwards, nor in troubles faint,
Become Thy child, Thy priest, Thy saint ?
        Yes, yes ! Ah, yes !

III.

THE STUDENT.

AUGUSTINE'S mother taught him carefully,
　　When but a child reclining on her lap,
To place, like her, his faith in JESUS CHRIST ;
But through the custom which existed then,
Or, possibly, to please his Pagan sire,
He was when grown to manhood unbaptized.
Once, prostrated by sickness, he had asked
To have the sacramental rite conferred.
But health returning drove the wish away.
He read all books on which his hands could seize,
Joined seldom in the sports of youthful friends,
Lived quiet and reserved, observing much
But thinking more, to all men sweet and mild ;
Respectful to his father, whom he feared,
But to his mother passionate in love,
Her best companion in her daily walks,
And growing like a plant beneath her hand.
"I will not have him made a milksop here,"
PATRICIUS said, "nor longer let him walk
Tied to his mother's apron-strings : depart
Unto Madaura shall he ; 'tis the nest
Of my progenitors, and in its school,
Renowned for grammar, arts, and eloquence,
He shall be taught what suits a man to know.
If boys there cuff him, let him cuff again !

My small inheritance is in that town,
And when I journey there to take the rents,
I can o'erlook him, learn how he succeeds,
And give him comfort should he such require.
Yes, he shall leave his home, and face the world!"
These words were grievous unto MONICA,
But she submitted, and the young lad went.
It was an ancient town of much repute,
But unimproved by Christianity,—
Corrupt in life and in religion false.
The tender bloom upon AUGUSTINE'S soul
Was there rubbed off; mixed up with heathen boys,
He at his mother's teachings learned to smile,
And, by bad training spoilt, began ere long
To think and talk precociously of vice.
When his school days were finished, and the youth
Had dangers gathering fast around his path,
He came once more to his paternal home,
To pass a useless year in idleness.
There lived he as his own will prompted him,
Exempted by his father from control,
And well assured his mother's blinded eyes
Would never see, in one she perfect deemed,
The failings which their neighbours knew too well.
AUGUSTINE, then by manners dissolute,
Became corrupted, and disdained to shun
The perils which involved his very soul.
When MONICA at length, to her dismay,
Learned what had been from her alone concealed,
She wept with agony, made prayer to GOD,
Implored her son from wickedness to cease,
And gave him counsels motherly and wise.
The more he sinned, the more did MONICA,
Hating the sin, love him who caused her shame.

Yet, from her very weakness, came at last
A strength so great, that by her prayers and tears
AUGUSTINE'S lofty intellect and will
Were both subdued, and after weary years
She led him rescued to the fold of CHRIST.
When MONICA discovered what had long
Been to PATRICIUS known, and in deep dread
Whispered the truth to him in gentlest tones,
Her boisterous husband laughed, and praised the lad.
" He has the right stuff in him," he exclaimed,
" The stuff to make a man of ; and just such
Was I when young, yet what a man am I !
He has been lying fallow here at home
More than twelve months, like ground unfit for use.
Weeds have grown up, whilst I, with scanty means,
Was saving up a little store of gold
To pay his cost at college.   This is done:
Now shall he go to Carthage, and begin
To study logic, law, and eloquence,
And fit himself to be an advocate ;
For such my will is and my purpose wise.
He shall become accomplished in dispute,
Make things dissimilar appear alike,
And like things different ; refute, declaim,
Rely on precedent or principle,
As each the occasion suits ; become astute
To mark the errors of the other side,
And by his answers promptly lay them bare.
When he shall speak, crowds will drink in his words
Exultingly ; the very chatterers,
Who throng the courts to idle out the day,
Will in deep silence hush when he begins.
By him defended, Innocence attacked
Shall foil injustice, and her rights maintain.

By him denounced, shall Fraud and Tyranny
Be made to feel a fitting punishment,
Lashed by his words and withered by his scorn.
Clients shall gather round him in the courts ;
Clients shall wait for him when he returns.
Fame, riches, honour, lofty rank, and power
Shall he obtain, whilst we, his parents proud,
Look on with rapture, his abundance share,
And in the sunshine of his glory bask !
This is my plan, and this shall he perform.
Nay, answer not, for I no answer brook ! "
Then was AUGUSTINE unto Carthage sent,
And with a willing mind he left his home.

IV

ROMAN CARTHAGE.

WHEN SCIPIO triumphed, Carthage was destroyed,
    And he to Rome the famous message sent,
" Obliterate is Carthage."[1]—This was true ;
Her walls and palaces had been reduced
To comminuted dust, her citizens
Slain or as slaves dispersed.   The Roman Senate
Not even then could feel themselves secure,
Until a curse, tremendous in its words,
Had been denounced on any daring wretch
Who ventured fallen Carthage to rebuild.
But CAIUS GRACCHUS loved not SCIPIO,
And by his help the city rose again,
In humbler guise, uplifted from the ground
Like a poor widow.   Colonists he sent
From Rome, a band necessitous and few,
To build her up.   Old MARIUS thither fled
When he, by SYLLA beaten and proscribed,
Became himself a ruin.   When there hid,
In a mean hut beside a reedy marsh,
The Prætor's lictor came to bid him quit,
And asked what message he should carry back
Unto his master, who his presence feared.
The warrior sat some minutes mute with rage,
Revolving in his mind how times were changed

        [1] " Delenda est Carthago."

Since he, when young, had to the city marched
JUGURTHA'S conqueror, and all cried, Hail!
Then, turning to the messenger a face
Terrific by its fierceness and contempt,
Sternly replied : " Go, tell him thou hast seen
MARIUS, an exile, on the ruins here
Of Carthage seated." JULIUS CÆSAR next,
Troubled one night by visions in his sleep
Of weeping armies, on his tablet wrote,
" Colonize Carthage." · That which he began,
AUGUSTUS finished. Commerce did the rest,
And under its benignant influence
The city rose in splendour from the dust,[1]
Though by no battlements encircled round
Till jealous Rome herself by Goths was ta'en.
She teemed with corn from fertile provinces,
And merchandise collected from the world,
Britain's rare tin, and gold from Ophir's mines.
Then on the hill of Byrsa, where erst stood
Fair DIDO'S palace, were again beheld
Structures of beauty and magnificence,
The outside marble and the inside gold.
The temple of CŒLESTIS there uprose,
At whose famed shrine ASTARTE'S priestess oft
Published abroad ambiguous oracles,
Which emperors heard with dread. The tribunal
Of the Proconsul there was held to which
CYPRIAN was dragged in chains, a prisoner,
Doomed, like the BAPTIST, soon his head to lose.
HADRIAN, a mighty builder of great works,

[1] *Recherches sur la Topographie de Carthage*, par M. Dureau de la
Malle, Paris 1835. For the topography of this country, see also *Four
Months in Algeria*, by the Rev. J. W. Blackesley (now Dean of Lincoln),
Cambridge 1849 ; *Carthage and her Remains*, by Dr. N. Davis,
London 1861.

Constructed from the city to the hills
A lofty aqueduct, whose fragments still,
With arch on arch upreaching to the sky,
Inspire awe.   This, though a monument
Prompted by pride, became a precious boon ;
For as AUGUSTINE on his entry walked
Beneath its arches, high above him flowed
Delicious waters, fresh from distant springs,
And to the thirsty city daily brought
Pleasure and health, where languor else had reigned.
AUGUSTINE from an eminence looked round
Upon the city and its swarms of men ;
Cothon, its cup-shaped harbour, and the fleet
Of ships which floated there, secure from storms.
Nor did he fail to fix admiring eyes
On the triumphal arch of PROBUS, raised
In honour of a Roman emperor,
Who by the sword had lived, and by it died.
'Twas he who, as AURELIAN'S general,
Fought and o'ercame, but with unwonted risk,
Palmyra's queen, ZENOBIA the fair ;
And on this coast he the Marmarides
Subdued for ever, killing with his hand
In single combat their distinguished chief,
ARADION, in memory of whom
And of his valour, built he a tall tomb.
But PROBUS unto Carthage did more good
When he its fierce contentions quieted,
Quelled tumults raised by brawling democrats,
And to the city gave that blessing, peace !
Therefore to him the grateful citizens
Raised the grand arch on which AUGUSTINE gazed.
When, with the name of PROBUS on his lips,
As one to him of hopeful augury,

He passed along the city's winding streets,
But knew not how himself would one day find
Another PROBUS, who should prove his friend,
And win the tribute of his love and praise.

V.

THE COLLEGIAN.

SCARCE had AUGUSTINE'S college life begun
    Before his father died, and MONICA
Was left with means too small to bear the load
Of her son's cost, whose course would therefore close.
But help, prepared by GOD, was close at hand.
ROMANIAN was the richest citizen
In all Tagasta, and a relative
Of young ALYPIUS, AUGUSTINE'S friend.
Owner of houses, vineyards, olive-grounds,
He grew in opulence, yet blameless lived ;
Great was his wealth, but greater far his heart ;
Bounteous to others, sparing to himself,
He freely gave to those who were in need,
And gladder felt, when thus he helped the poor,
Than they whose wants his kindly aid supplied.
Throughout his life he strove to make him friends
By the coarse mammon of unrighteousness,
In hope that when he died his soul might hear,
From saints before him gone to Paradise,
A welcome to their everlasting home.
Yet, though so bountiful, ROMANIAN
To stop iniquity could make a stand :
Therefore, when one by long-concocted fraud
Tried to deprive him of a large estate,
He offered firm resistance to the wrong,

And in the courts of law had many suits.
Chicanery foiled him, and at first he failed ;—
Then left he many years his happy home,
His native town and Africa itself,
To prosecute appeals in Italy,
And sue for justice till his cause was won.
ROMANIAN, from AUGUSTINE'S infancy,
Had known and loved him, recognised his worth,
Admired his genius, and now stood his friend.
He knew how poor PATRICIUS had died ;
Therefore, without delay and with no stint,
He tendered help still unsolicited,
Lent MONICA a house, and paid the sums
Required for college uses ; nor content
Was he to give thus kindly a mere shred
Of his superfluous wealth to help his friend,
But to AUGUSTINE offered all he had,—
His house, his purse, his friendship, his advice,—
And tried by exhortations, mixed with praise,
To stir his mind up to a great career.
Thus through ROMANIAN'S cheerful, ready aid,
A widow's pain-wrung heart was comforted,
A young aspirant's path was easier made,
And joy prevailed where grief would else have reigned.

Three years at Carthage did AUGUSTINE stay
In ease and pleasure, while his mother lived
In hope and prayer for him at Tagasta.
Although of this world's wealth her share was small,
She of her want gave freely twice a day
Oblations at GOD'S altar, and bestowed
Alms on the poor ; the sick she visited,
And to the wretched and bereaved would bring
The soothing consolation of her tears.

Meanwhile AUGUSTINE, unto manhood grown,
Gained great applause at college, as his mind
Began with all the arrogance of youth
To make display of misdirected strength.
His fellow-students bowed before his blaze,
Which as it waxed made their poor light wane pale :
He shone among them like a lustrous star,
And sparkled in their eyes with dazzling sheen,
As when ARCTURUS, on a moonless night,
Flames in the front of the bespangled sky.
No college discipline was exercised
To train the students to a virtuous life,
Or e'en to punish flagrant acts of vice :
All were allowed to riot as they chose.
They formed themselves into tumultuous bands,
Which wandered through the city's streets with noise,
Frightening the old, the peaceful, and the weak ;
And hence, from acts upsetting decency,
Were called " Upsetters," [1] nor refused the name.—
Such are the reckless youths, who, when grown men,
Form the fierce mobs in revolutions seen,—
A howling crew of violence and hate,
Ready for plunder, readier for blood.
Of them the abler trade as democrats,
And thrive by fanning every discontent
Until it burst in flames ; loud they of tongue,
But void of wisdom ; burly blusterers,
Who vilify the rich and cheat the poor ;
They rail against and seek to overthrow
Whatever is established, but if called
To plant where they have wasted, lack due sense
To make aught grow that longer can endure
Than JONAH'S gourd.   The best of men like these

[1] " Eversores."—*Confess.* iii. 3.

Can but find out, pounce down upon, and tear
The rotten portions of an ancient state,
Which time hath made decay.   Such are their food,
And on such garbage they like vultures feed,
Discharging thus their only usefulness!
But woe unto that ruined commonwealth
In which such wretches seize on place and power!
Destruction then, like a huge avalanche,
Rolls on unchecked, vile things o'ertop the good,
Rapine is rule, convicts are ministers,
Red-handed murder stands where justice sat,
Order is lost, and anarchy prevails!
Even AUGUSTINE'S eyes were doomed to see
The Circumcelliones rage unchecked,
With rapine waste the fields and fire the towns.
Weak men, disheartened by anxieties,
Pained by the present, by the future scared,
Refused to struggle more against the bad,
Or hold them by repression in their place,
But, taking refuge in mere cowardice,
Fled from a world in which no joy was found ;
Thousands on thousands left their shops and homes,
Turned monks and hermits of the wilderness,
To seek, but vainly, peace in solitude.
Ambitious turbulence then swayed the realm,
And crushed all opposition into dust.
Resistance to its madness being gone,
It turned to try its strength upon itself,
And into fragments split, each part whereof
Could burn and ravage, though it could not rule.
They dignified their crimes by such fine names
As patriotism, freedom, true religion ;
But Arian heresy was their best creed,
Foul Pagan practices their ritual,

Immunity their wish, and self their end!
GOD did not long their shameful ways endure ;
For GENSERIC in Africa appeared,
And found no government his course to check.
Ruin ensued ; the evil and the good
Were mixed together in one gory heap,
For no discriminating hand hath war !
Their scenes of horror are forgotten now ;
One object only lives in history,
The figure of an old, grief-stricken man,
In robes episcopal, with long white hair,
And hands uplifted in appeal to GOD,
Kneeling besieged on Hippo's battlements,
To check fierce Vandals by the strength of prayer.

AUGUSTINE, when at college, took no part
In riots by his fellow-students raised,
Nor deemed, as they, their hatred of all rule
A proof of manly courage. Working hard,
He strove and toiled proficiency to gain
In controversial arts and eloquence.
He had not yet forgot the lessons wise
Taught him in infancy by MONICA,
And hated vice, though clothed in virtue's garb.
At times he turned his mind to muse upon
The self-deceptions and bad faith of men,
And his own relish for sin's blandishments ;
Then, when such thoughts weighed heavy on his
        soul,
Would raise his voice to GOD in words like these [1] :—

" Pride imitates exaltedness, whilst thou
        Alone art GOD exalted over all !

[1] Appendix, Note B ; Augustine's *Confess.* lib. ii. c. 6.

Ambition seeks that we should her allow
   Honours and glory ; whilst o'er great and small
Thou only art in honour, and shalt be
Enthroned in glory through eternity.

" The cruelty of tyrants maketh known
   The wish to govern other hearts by fear ;
But who should fear inspire, save GOD alone ?
   And from His power what thing unto Him dear
Can wrested be or snatched ?   Say when or where
This can be done, or who to try would dare ?

" The false allurements of the wanton sort
   Would love inspire ; but none can so allure
As doth Thy Charity, nor is there aught
   Which can for Love more healthiness ensure
Than doth Thy Truth, which shines before our sight,
Beyond all objects beautiful and bright !

" Man's Curiosity would outside seem
   Study of knowledge by intelligence ;
But Thou hast knowledge which is all supreme !
   With names of Simpleness and Innocence
Do Ignorance and Folly wrap them round ;
But no simplicity like Thine is found,

" Nor doth man's innocence with Thine compare ;
   For that which anguish to the wicked brings
Is their ill conduct, which such fruit must bear.
   Sloth seeking rest to mere indulgence clings ;
But how can any rest true peace afford,
Except that rest which cometh of the LORD ?

" Luxuriousness desires we should her call
　　By such mild language as Sufficiency
And rich Abundance, honoured by us all ;
　　But Thou art Fulness in entirety,
As well as an unfailing, plenteous store
Of Sweetness incorrupt for evermore !

" Profusion but the shadow doth impart
　　Of Liberality ill understood ;
But Thou the liberal Dispenser art
　　Of everything in substance really good.
Avarice would riches her possessions call ;
But Thou, the Maker, dost possess them all !

" Envy for Excellence disputes ; but who
　　Is excellent as Thou ?　Rage vengeance seeks ;
But where is vengeance like Thine, just and true ?
　　Fear takes alarm at every work which speaks
Aught strange or sudden, as if ill were there
For objects loved, whose safety is her care ;

" But how to Thee can anything appear
　　Strange, or what sudden news can on Thee break ?
Or who, though he to try may persevere,
　　Can any separation really make
'Twixt Thee and what Thou lovest ? where shall we
Find safety ever sure, unless with Thee ?

" Grief pines away because she feeleth pain
　　At loss of those she loved with ardent mind,
And, like Thee, no bereavement would sustain :
　　Thus sins the soul that turns from Thee to find
Pleasures, which pure and clean it seeks in vain,
Until it cometh back to Thee again.

" Thus all do Thee perversely imitate,
  Who to a distance far from Thee digress,
And their poor selves against thee elevate ;
  But they, by imitating Thee, confess
That Thou Creator of all nature art,
Nor, from Thee severed, can aught live apart."

VI.

THE MANICHÆAN.

THE brilliant thoughts of CICERO, contained
    In his lost treatise called " HORTENSIUS,"
Charmed the young student, for he read therein
An exhortation to philosophy,
Which gave him higher hopes and purposes
Than merely to excel in eloquence,
And win applause to pamper vain conceit.
He felt aroused and kindled by the love
Of wisdom stirred up in him by that book :
Yet one defect he in it ever found,
For therein was the name of CHRIST not seen,
Nor was the want of Him there told !   Around
AUGUSTINE'S heart his mother's teachings clung
With such tenacity, that no discourse,
However learned, polished, or correct,
Could wholly master him without that Name !
Delighted by the consciousness of strength
Which made him, as he thought, superior
To other men, he for a little while
Turned to the Scriptures, to investigate
What there the prophets and apostles taught.
But to a mind swoln out with arrogance,
The Scriptures were too plain ; he deemed them far
Below the stately eloquence which charmed
In TULLY, and fit only for the minds

Of humbler men, whose dulness he deplored ;
Nor could his self-deceived intelligence
Pierce to the inner meanings, which lie hid
From supercilious eyes.   Therefore ere long
He closed the holy volume in disdain.

There was in Carthage then a sect, whose name
From MANES was derived,—a Persian slave,
Who at the end of the third century
Had fashioned into shape, with plastic skill,
The Oriental dogmas of belief
And a few shreds of Christianity,
Constructing thus a system which combined
The doctrines of the East and of the West,—
The Persian faith which ZOROASTER taught,
The Indian creed of BUDDHA, and the light
Of Christian revelation.   Thus he tried
To solve all problems, reconcile all doubts,
And bring to harmony conflicting thoughts.
There were, said MANES and his followers,[1]
Two great Eternal Principles, from which
All things proceeded.   One of them was Light,
From which came Good ; the other Darkness was,
The source of Evil : from the first came Spirit,
And from the second Matter ; and these two,
Which were antagonistic to each other,
Originated, but did not create,
The Universe, which from their union strange—
A hostile inroad Evil made on Good—
Was bodied forth, and thus of each partakes.
Man's spirit was, they said, an emanation

---

[1] See Dr. Pusey's elaborate Essay on the Manichæan Heresy, Note A to
The Confessions of St. Augustine; Library of the Fathers, vol. i. pp.
314-346. London, 1840. 8vo.

From GOD ; his body, which imprisons it,
From Evil : therefore man is not one made,
But is a particle of Deity ;
And GOD, through CHRIST, endeavours to release
Imprisoned souls, and bring them to Himself.
They, then, who struggle with success against
Their lusts and appetites, will at their death
Be from their sinful bodies loosed, and brought,
When purified, to be again absorbed
In the pure Light of which they all form part ;
But they who fail will be at death consigned
To dwell within the lower animals,
Whose bodies will contain their wretched souls.
As matter was of Evil, they denied
CHRIST'S incarnation, who was of the Light
A phantom only, by appearance seen
Of human nature unto Him conjoined.
The rite of Baptism their sect condemned ;
For water, said they, can contribute nought
To man's salvation, nor can any rite
Which doth at all through matter operate.
The body's resurrection they denied,
As plainly hostile to felicity.
The Scriptures of the Older Testament
They quite rejected ; recognised the New
In part ; but even that was criticised
With freedom which some modern sciolists
Might envy for its deep irreverence.
They would profess to praise austerity,
Condemning all that gives the body ease,—
That gloomy prison of the pent-up soul !
But they, in practice, were so tolerant,
That none was blamed who loved debauchery ;
For man, they argued, sins against his will,

And to compulsion of the Evil yields,
Which in his members and his substance reigns.
By every birth a particle divine
Becomes imprisoned in the bonds of flesh ;
Hence, to increase the number of men born,
Is, by dividing Light, to make its rays
Feebler and scattered.   Therefore they declared
That marriage and concubinage alike
Are in the sight of God repulsive things !
The teachers of this hateful heresy
Were called the "Elect ;" they for themselves pro-
        fessed
Ascetic living, but their followers,
Whom they called " Hearers," were allowed full scope
In gross indulgence,—might, if they desired,
Marry, or live unwedded in plain sin ;
Nay, they might even cultivate the Earth,—
That mass of matter from the Demon sprung !—
Provided they would of its produce give
To the " Elect" with liberality.
This Manichæan doctrine had become
The fashionable form of creed which then.
Prevailed in Carthage, and ere long AUGUSTINE,
A young philosopher of nineteen years,
Was by its specious brilliancy deceived.
The artful teachers of the heresy
Professed that if men followed, they would lead,
By reason's simple, sure, and only way,
To GOD, and rescue them from errors vain ;
Would banish superstition from the mind,
With all its terrors, and with ease explain,
What none else could, Evil's real origin ;
For MANES was, they said, the PARACLETE—
Had known all truth, and had all truth revealed.

As in the days when some great pestilence,
Coming from east to west, corrupts the air,
And, like the Black Death, spreads from realm to
        realm,
Marking its course by desolated towns,
Abandoned cities, and the bones of men,
While from the earth uprises the loud wail
Of nations maddened by their misery ;
So, in AUGUSTINE'S age, this Eastern creed,
Begotten of the Devil to delude,
Diffused itself through Europe, and soon reached
The teeming shores of Northern Africa,
Slaying men's souls in number numberless !
But though it had its triumph for a time
Over AUGUSTINE, who was young and weak,
Yet was he destined in maturity
To rise superior by the strength of Truth,
Resist its course, and quench its baleful fire.

AUGUSTINE joined the Manichæan sect
Soon as its fever reached him, but became
A "Hearer" only ; yet was not content
Merely to learn, for he must also teach !
He spread abroad among his youthful friends
The same delusion which possessed himself,
And dazzled them by expositions false.
Even ROMANIAN, though of riper years,
Caught the contagion.   Young ALYPIUS
Followed his friend, and was deceived like him ;
But, though a "Hearer," lived as strict a life
As if appointed one of the "Elect,"
And bound to make his life and creed agree ;
For he despised indulgence, pain defied,
Nor cared how soon his prisoned soul might 'scape.

But whilst AUGUSTINE gloried in the praise
His converts brought him, GOD'S face turned away,
And he was left some years without a guide ;
Nor could his mother's daily prayers and tears,
Offered to GOD whilst absent from her son,
Save him, when thus abandoned, from a fall,
Amidst the dangers which his folly braved.

VII.

THE LOVER.

AUGUSTINE, when he came to Carthage, found
    A fiery caldron of unholy loves
Seething and boiling everywhere around.[1]
He loved not then, but greatly wished to love :
And from that want, deep seated in his heart,
Hated himself for wanting not enough !
He sought what he might love, longing to love,
But spurning safety and a path unsnared.
Yet, though the famine which within him raged
Was such as only GOD, its proper food,
Could satisfy, no appetite he felt
For sustenance by substance incorrupt,—
Not because therewith filled, but for this cause,
That, being empty, he it loathed still more.
One eve, as he was passing through the streets,
He saw assembled in a Christian church
A concourse large, among whom there might be
Friends of his own, whom he would gladly meet.
Impelled by curiosity, he cast
Some furtive glances through the open door,
And gazed upon the crowd which knelt in prayer.
Whilst thus engaged, a female face turned round
Near where his shadow fell, and on him gazed,
To see who blocked the light ; their quick eyes met

[1] Appendix, Note C ; Augustine's *Confess.* lib. iii. c. 1.

One instant, and the fate of both was sealed!
A crimson blush the damsel's cheek suffused,
And a light smile played swiftly o'er her lips,
As when some zephyr stirs a shining pool.
AUGUSTINE felt a fiery impulse dart
Into his soul, his heart beat high and strong,
And through his veins a thrilling tremor ran.
With sacrilegious thoughts intent, he stepped
Within the church, knelt down beside the girl,
And in that attitude and in that place
Resolved to compass something, which for fruit
Well deserved death, though GOD, whom he forgot,
In mercy gave a lesser punishment,
And only with the scourge chastised his sin.
On the girl's features were the youth's eyes fixed
With ardent gaze, whilst she without reserve
Enjoyed the admiration she inspired.
At last, the service finished, all arose,
And as they left the church, AUGUSTINE saw
That she whose beauty had bewildered him
Was there alone!   He followed where she went,
Walked by her side, addressed her in some words
Which asked her pardon as they praised her charms,
To which she, flurried by the incident,
Briefly replied, but in her sweetest tones.
They reached the lodging where she dwelt, and ere
She entered and had gone, AUGUSTINE gained
Her promise to permit him to renew
Their conversation, should they meet next day
Within the city's gardens, where at eve
The whole world sauntered idly in the cool
To breathe fresh air, and happy friends sought
     friends.
There met they soon, and left to meet again;
                    D

Then, ere a month had passed, AUGUSTINE took
A lodging in the house wherein lived one
On whom he thought all day and dreamed all night.
The maiden was an orphan fair and young,
Whose skilful fingers worked embroidered veils
And golden tissues for rich Roman dames.
Although her parents left her without wealth,
Yet, having learned from them a gainful trade,
She lived in ease, was free from penury,
And had no mistress but her wayward will.
Her thoughts were unsubstantial, light, and vain,
As the fine fabrics broidered by her hands,
But few the golden threads to give them weight.
Her sagest plans, which nicest care had framed,
The slightest passing breath of admiration
Would lift in air, and scatter to the winds.
The young Numidian lover pleased her much,
Because she found him sparkling, brilliant, gay,
And one by those who knew him held as wise.
This she rejoiced to hear, although her mind
Disliked all subjects dull or even grave.
Unstable, volatile, capricious, wild,
Light as a feather, blythesome as a bird,
Untameable as summer's butterfly,
She fluttered on through paths most perilous,
Met good advice with a contemptuous smile,
And drowned remonstrance in her sprightly laugh.
She had no wish to be AUGUSTINE'S wife,
And live the humdrum life of wedded dames ;
But when he wooed, consented readily
To be his mistress, that she might remain
Her own as well, and not on him depend.
Before the year was out she bore a child ;
But in that city's mixed society,

Where the loud laugh of vice drowned virtue's voice,
She felt no shame to walk before the world
As an unwedded mother with her son,
And flaunt her frailty in the light of day.
AUGUSTINE too was then so paralyzed,
So dead in conscience to his state of sin,
That when their son was born, he with delight
Regarded him as a choice gift of GOD,
And named him ADEODATUS [1] in his joy ;
But of such gifts he had this only one.
The mother by her gaiety repaid
The fervent love of an impassioned soul ;
Her very love as lightsome as herself,
Nor could her nature summon strength enough
To answer the emotions felt by him,
Who in her saw the mother of his son.
The sweetness of their intercourse was spoilt
By gall besprinkled on it from the hand
Of GOD, whose goodness ever was at work,
And would, in time, dissolve unholy ties.
AUGUSTINE knew how insecure a thing
Was the fidelity of her he loved,
And wished to keep his young companions off
From any close approach to one so frail.
Her very name was carefully withheld
From mention by his lips, and he would fain
Have spread a darksome cloud of secrecy
Round her existence ; but they found her out.
Called in his absence, were by her received
With joy, which showed itself in merry words,
Were sent away with topics for gay talk,
Invited to return at times unfit ;
Whereby, ere long, the scourge of jealousy

[1] God-given.

Smote on AUGUSTINE'S Oriental heart,
Like a hot brand of iron, burning deep !
His mind was tortured by suspicious fears—
Reproaches made were bandied back again—
Anger to torment added bitterness ;
And thus, 'midst passion, fury, quarrels, tears,
The agony of rapture insecure,
Some years were passed in what the world called
    love !

JEALOUSY.

Exquisite Flower ! I love thee much !
        No other hand
But mine must thee presume to touch ;
        For thou dost stand
From other blossoms wide apart,
Rocked by the beatings of my heart.

Sweet is thy breath and rich thy hues,
        O fragrant Flower !
Tinted by sunbeams, fed by dews,
        Fanned every hour
By zephyrs, thou art lovely grown,
The fairest creature eyes have known !

Yet should a spoiler's hand thee seize
        From off my breast,
And thou some other's eyes should please,
        And be carest
By strangers, it would be my fate
Thy charms to loathe, thy beauty hate !

Thy presence would no longer be,
　　　As now, most dear ;
None then could live abhorred like thee !
　　　Shouldst thou draw near,
These hands would thee far from me thrust,
And my feet crush thee in the dust !

SAINT AUGUSTINE.

———•———

BOOK II.

THE SEPARATION.

BOOK II.

———

I.

CONSOLATION IN DESPAIR.

WORDS cannot tell the grief of MONICA,
     When news from Carthage to Tagasta came
That he, her son, whom she had so much loved,
And whose salvation was the constant aim
Of all her meditations, hopes, and prayers,
Had publicly the Christian faith renounced,
And joined the Manichæan heresy!
News, too, that he, whose genius all admired,
Had in his fall involved the choicest youths
Sent by Tagasta to the schools of Carthage,
And drawn them into errors like his own.
News, too, that he, so young for wickedness,
Lived with a Carthaginian mistress fair,
And had become a father!   News indeed
Of gravest import, nor believed at first,
Until, on coming home, his very mouth
Confirmed its truth, and justified the acts.
Then MONICA bent down beneath the blow
Dealt on her heart by such intelligence,
As one o'erwhelmed ; but soon, with sudden start,
The short-lived impulse of a wild despair,
Drove out AUGUSTINE from her humble home,

As one unworthy!   Then sank on the ground
In desolation, and for hours remained
Lost amidst tears, deep wailings, sighs, and swoons.
When more composed, she offered prayers to GOD,
With supplications and incessant cries,
And wept and groaned, and groaned and wept all night,
Until ere dawn she sobbed herself to sleep.
Then in a vision she conceived herself
To stand upon a narrow rule of wood,
Which held her up ; when, lo! before her came,
In glorious garments of transcendent light,
A beauteous, noble youth, whose countenance
Was full of liveliest joy, and on her smiled.
He saw her tears, and graciously inquired
Their cause ; when MONICA replying said,
She wept for her lost son!   " Oh, vex not thus
Thyself in vain," the gentle youth replied ;
And, pointing to the wooden rule, exclaimed,
" There is he where thou art !"   On looking round
She saw AUGUSTINE standing by her side
On the same rule, and then the vision fled.
When MONICA awoke as daylight dawned,
She deemed the words of such good augury,
That forth she ran to tell them to her son.
He listened to the tale, and wished to prove
That what the angel said meant only this :
That where he was, his mother too should be.
But MONICA exclaimed : " It was not so !
And what the angel said will come to pass,
That where I am, there thou shalt be with me."
From that time, though nine years must first run out
Before the vision proved true prophecy,
She felt assured her son would yet be saved ;
With undiminished fondness took him back

Unto her home and heart, prayed GOD for him,
Wept much, and waited long with patient hope,
Until the promised day at last did come!
What could this weeping, widowed mother do?
The son she idolized would not accept
The easy terms on which unto mankind
Salvation is ensured.   GOD hath done all
That even GOD can do to save lost man,
Unless He take from him conscience, free-will,
Knowledge, and faith, those precious, priceless gifts,
And force him, like a bridled mule, by dint
Of whip and spur, to keep the narrow way
Which leads to life eternal.   But AUGUSTINE
Scorned to inquire in what words GOD had told
In times long past His purposes and will;
Refused to read, as far below his taste,
The Book of inspiration, which contains
A faithful record of GOD'S acts and words.
He wandered, gazing idly on the light
Of meteors, which his fancy took for stars;
And though in darkness, trod with heedless feet
Paths hemmed around by pit and precipice.
Must he then perish? pondered MONICA;
This darling son, so handsome, brilliant, wise!
In a brief hour or two, she weeping thought,
Some fever, plague, or merest accident
Might hurry him away from out this world
To speedy death; and unto what a death!
A death which leads to everlasting woe,
To endless pain, like that produced by fire,
But of a deeper, stronger agony!
Then floods of tears would stream forth from her eyes,
The very earth she walked on was bedewed
With weeping; every day and night she sighed,

Nor found alleviation but in prayer.
One day, despairing and disconsolate,
She sought an ancient bishop of her Church,
Who in his youth had tasted error's cup,
And been a Manichæan, but had since
Waked from his sleep, which else had turned to death.
He then, repenting of his errors past,
Had by great labours in the Church of CHRIST,
And holy living, won a just renown.
Him she entreated to convert her son,
To reason with him, and explain away
Delusions which misled and warped his mind.
But the old bishop steadily refused,
And counselled MONICA to trust to prayer
Rather than refutation, and to wait
Until AUGUSTINE, by his native strength
And by GOD's grace, should burst in two his bonds.
But MONICA became importunate,
Weeping as she was wont ; then thus he spake :
" Go hence in peace ! for it can never be
That one who is the child of tears so many
Can perish !"   Then back went she to her home,
And consolation in that promise found.

II

DEATH AND SORROW.

AUGUSTINE in Tagasta lived four years,
    Watched over by the eyes of MONICA,
And by GOD'S eyes, which slumber not nor sleep ;
But near him, as a shadow on his life,
Was the young nameless girl, who left him not.
He, as professor of the sister arts
Of rhetoric and logic, lectures gave,
Which brought a throng of students to his class,
And all Numidia joined to give him praise.
Except for daily bickerings with her
Whose folly proved too hard for him to bear,
He lived a life of calm tranquillity,
Unruffled by the troubles of the world.
The path he in his progress onwards trod
Looked green as verdure growing on a grave ;
But earthly happiness is insecure,
And when most prized will quickest fly away !

    Among Tagasta's citizens was one
About AUGUSTINE'S age, whom we will call
HORATIO, a name to friendship dear !
AUGUSTINE was accustomed to receive
From other friends respectful deference,
Paid by them gladly, nor by him refused ;
All that they had was his, would he it take.

But none on terms of full equality
Enjoyed, unawed, his confidence and love,—
None but HORATIO, who, from fear exempt,
And with an intellect of highest range,
Grappled AUGUSTINE oft in argument,
And in a friendly contest tried his strength.
If other men were to AUGUSTINE bound
By fascination none could well resist,
He, in his turn, by spell as marvellous,
Clung to HORATIO, and homage paid !
He had no pleasure with his friend away,
Whose simple presence doubled every joy.
Community of tastes, pursuits, and aims,
Equality of age and social rank,
Studies and recreations both had shared,
The offices of kindness interchanged,
And hopes and wishes mutually disclosed,
Had, from their earliest days, compelled their hearts
To grow together on a common stalk,
And now, rejoicing in their union sweet,
They blossomed with the opening flower of youth.
AUGUSTINE in his friend's mind had infused
The errors which bewildered then his own,
And warped him from the straight hard lines of truth
To superstitious Manichæan tales.
Inseparable were they, as if one ;
Nor could AUGUSTINE'S soul endure the want
Of a companionship which every year
Grew sweeter than all sweetness of his life !
But these two fugitives from GOD were soon
To taste of anger they had long provoked ;
A sudden fever on HORATIO seized,
And in prostration low, of strength deprived,
Delirious sank he down.   His family,

Which crowded mournfully around his bed,
Despairing soon of his recovery,
Had him baptized, in hopes that through that rite
His sins, by GOD'S grace, might remission find,
And he be saved.   AUGUSTINE, who sat there,
And never left him, looked on what was done
With a derisive mind; then, when his friend,
Rallying awhile, appeared so much restored
That he was able to be told at last
Of what, while senseless, had been done with him,
AUGUSTINE tried to make the theme a jest,
In expectation of an answering smile!
When lo! to his surprise, HORATIO
Shrank from him as from some vile enemy,
With prompt and startling freedom bade him cease;
Adding, that if he would his friend remain,
He must from language such as that forbear.
AUGUSTINE in astonishment recoiled!
But though he held his peace, and stilled the rise
Of his emotions for a little while,
Fearing to agitate HORATIO,
He inwardly determined to renew
The same attack when health should be restored.
But after some few days, and at an hour
When, absent from HORATIO, he planned
What he would say, and how to answer him,
Back came the fever, and the poor youth died.
What grief then fell upon AUGUSTINE'S heart!
What utter darkness settled on his soul!
His native country and paternal home
Became to him a strange unhappiness.
HORATIO gone, all joys, which he had shared
In happy days with him, now brought instead
Distracting tortures.   Everywhere in vain

AUGUSTINE'S tearful eyes sought out his friend,
But found him not; he hated every place
Because it had not him for whom he pined,
Nor could it say, as when he was alive,
"He comes!" AUGUSTINE communed with his soul,
And asked, "Why art thou so disquieted?"
But she knew not what answer to return.
He grieved for what was lost, and bowed beneath
The sorrow that o'erwhelmed him; misery
Was now his food, and all his joy was fled.
Nor could he hope HORATIO would come
To life again; to no such end his tears
Flowed ceaselessly; he did but weep and grieve,
To find relief in bitterness alone.
Yet painful then as was his wretched life,
He clung to it with more tenacity
Than to his friend, nor would have given it up
Even for him whose loss he so deplored;
For though he loathed to live, he feared to die!
One half of him was dead, the other half
He would preserve, and so half save his friend.
Thus fretting, sighing, weeping, near distraught,
AUGUSTINE bore about a shattered heart,
Which bled at every pore, and knew no rest.
Impatient was his soul that he found not
A place for its relief. No charming groves,
No games, no songs, no garden full of scent,
No costly banquets carefully prepared,
No pleasures of the couch or of the bed,
Not even books or poesy itself
Could the repose his soul required bestow.
The very light was ghastly to his eyes!
Whatever thing was not HORATIO
Was to AUGUSTINE hateful; tears alone

And groans refreshed him; when from these withdrawn,
A load of anguish weighed him to the earth.
He knew that GOD alone could bring him ease,
But unto Him he neither would nor could
Apply for help, for GOD was not to him
More than a phantom then; his only god
Was his presumptuous error, and therein,
Whene'er he offered to discharge his load
To give him rest, it glided through the void,
And with a crash came down upon his head.
Whither, then, in this maze of misery,
Should his heart flee, to sever from his heart?
Whither should he take refuge from himself?
If in Tagasta he should still remain,
Death soon would be his doom! Therefore he left
A place where everything recalled his grief,—
Left the loved region of Numidia,
His mother, native city, and his friends,
And unto Carthage went disconsolate.

AUGUSTINE'S LAMENT.

" Hast thou then gone and left me here,
    With this world's glory passed away,
No solace but the scalding tear,
    Nor rest at night, nor joy by day?
        Oh, come again!

" The sky is torn by tempests dire,
    The sun and moon refuse their light;
The earth looks blackened as by fire,
    The starry heavens shine no more bright!
        Oh, come again!
E

"In vain would I these tears control,
        For death hath doomed thee to depart ;
Mute are those lips which soothed my soul,
        Cold, cold, thy noble, loving heart !
                Oh, come again !

"Where art thou ?   In the grave's embrace,
        Buried from sight, to waste to dust !
Horror were mine to view thy face,
        Yet would I, yea, and see thee must !
                Oh, come again !

"Strange voices reach me from the street,
        I start at sounds that shake my soul,
But hear no more thy coming feet,
        And spurn the friends who would condole.
                Oh, come again !

"Come as a flash in some great storm,
        When common mortals shake with fright ;
Or come a white-clad, gliding form,
        In the deep silence of the night !
                Oh, come again !

"Come, to restore this broken heart,
        To wipe these tearful eyelids dry,
Some cure for anguish to impart,
        Some consolation ere I die !
                Oh, come again ! "

III

SUNSET ON THE DESERT.

WHEN from Numidia AUGUSTINE went,
    Some young companions led him on his way,
But not direct to Carthage. Mounting steeds
Whose swiftness was their nation's chiefest pride,
They scoured the southern hills,—those fastnesses
Which oft had stopped invaders in their course,
And made their armies pause. They looked around
On lofty mountains and on swelling plains,
High, beetling cliffs, and rocky, deep ravines,
With ruined cities sometimes interspersed,
Whose fallen stones neglected paths bestrewed.
Enormous arches overgrown with weeds,
And broken aqueducts, lay useless there,
Like the blanched bones of some huge skeleton
Left by the fabled serpent of the sea,
And stretching many a mile along the ground.
They reached, ere they were tired, the desert's edge,
Sahara's wilderness; nor turned they back
Until its desolation they beheld.
AUGUSTINE, sad, but gathering strength each day,
Observed with interest all objects strange,
Marked how in flocks the red flamingoes flew,
Heard in the night the hungry lions roar,
And marvelled at the brightness of the stars.
But on one eve a glorious sight appeared,

Such as the desert-dwellers oft behold
With mingled adoration, love, and awe,
And none forget who see it, though but once.[1]
The broad horizon of the desert seemed
Wide as the sea ; and from the distant west
Rose tufted cloudlets, radiating up
Until they reached the zenith, and their line
Went deepening in its tints, from pale turquoise
To richest purple.   In range parallel
And with concentric rings, these cloudlets bright
Formed a grand arch against the western sky,
Beneath which shone a clear, pellucid space,
Just where the sun when setting would descend.
Each cloudlet kept its individual form ;
All were distinct, but not in size the same.
They looked like choirs of the angelic host,
Arranged in ranks to hear and to adore
Some word of wisdom from the mouth of GOD.
AUGUSTINE, in a reverie profound,
Moved silently along, as if he feared
The slightest noise might drive the scene away.
When next he looked, the sun below the arch
Had in the open shining space dropped down,
Like a great king upon his golden throne !
Framed thus in fretted gold, its rays intense
Tinted with yellowness the tawny sand,
Which gleamed like fire ; while in the upper air
The cloudlets shone with amber-coloured hues,

---

[1] The following lines, describing a sunset in the desert, were written in Professor Owen's garden at East Sheen. For the appearance of the phenomena here described, and for the language, which has only been altered for the purpose of versification, the author is indebted to a MS. of the Professor, in which that distinguished naturalist noted down at the time, with accuracy and power, what he himself observed in the desert when he was in Egypt.

And glowed in glory with excessive light.
Then the great arch of solid, floating cloud,
Whose burnished surface shone like heated brass,
Deepened to orange.   On each side the arch,
The sky-line showed a thin, transparent green,
Which like a rainbow passed to violet ;
Then a great scarlet radiance from the sun
Extended upwards, fainter as it went,
Until with roseate tinge of tender pink
It reached the zenith, and was lost at once
In deep cerulean blue, darker than night.
Soon the round sun beneath the horizon dipped,
And at the change each colour glowed still more
With richer hues, which faded suddenly !
Then, as AUGUSTINE sighed to think how quick
Such rich effulgence could from earth depart,
There came, emerging from the serried clouds,
The brilliant crescent of the new-born moon,
Which through the sky sailed like a diamond boat.
Then cried AUGUSTINE to his friends with joy,
" Such is the law of transitory things ;
One glory fades, when, lo, another shines ! "

IV

THE MANICHÆAN BISHOP.

HOPE at last came to solace him once more,—
    Hope of some sort, though not of highest kind;
Hope for celebrity and men's applause
In the wide field which Carthage could supply.
There, in the college where he once had learned,
He now as a professor, in the class
Of rhetoric, instructed advocates
To thrust and parry in the war of words.
Thus had ISOCRATES in ancient Greece
Employed his life and gained immortal fame;
And now AUGUSTINE hoped to do the like.
To drown distracting sorrows in his mind,
He cast himself with eager vehemence
Into the study of philosophy,
And wrote a Treatise on the Fit and Fair,
To prove their nature is identical,—
That Fit is Fair, and all things Fair are Fit.
But science most absorbed his earnest thought,
And acted as a wedge, which, by GOD driven,
Broke up the fabric, built of heresy,
Which error had established in his mind.
All books then written on geometry,
On music, or arithmetic, he read,
But in astronomy found chief delight.
He deemed it marvellous, that they who made

Astronomy their study could so well
Track out the course of planets, count the stars,
Measure the heavens wherein they moved about,
And, many years before the time arrived,
Predict eclipses of the sun and moon.
AUGUSTINE'S intellect was so well trained,
That had he lived when science was, as now,
A second revelation made to man
By the Creator, speaking through His works,
He would have mastered it with ease, as when
He, a mere boy, the abstrusest thoughts perused
Of the great Stagyrite, yet nothing found
But what he had discovered long before!
All that the world then knew he quickly learned ;
With wonder and delight he gazed upon
The luminiferous ether,[1] which is held
In space, and doth within itself contain
The nuclei of the stars, heavy and huge,
Which therein, at enormous distances,
Are interspersed, and splashing light revolve.
But though he understood not how it was
That this prevailing substance doth receive
From every star its tremors molecular,
Which it distributes, faster e'en than thought,
As visual light around the universe,
Yet was he able to discern some facts
Which stood opposed, in contradiction clear,
To what the books of MANES had declared ;
For that impostor, in his ignorance,
Had written largely on astronomy,
Which he professed by means divine to teach.
How, then, could these and those be reconciled ?

---

[1] Professor Tyndall's "Constitution of Nature," *Fragments of Science,*
pp. 4, 5.

If MANES were at fault in what is least
In merely physical phenomena,
How could he, in the things far more abstruse,
In what is greatest,—subjects spiritual,—
Be a safe guide to teach men hidden truths?
AUGUSTINE in perplexity applied
For explanation unto the "Elect,"
The rulers of the Manichæan sect ;
But they, unable to resolve his doubts,
Held him at bay, and asked him but to wait
Until their bishop, FAUSTUS, should arrive :
He was, they said, a man of sanctity,
On whose authority his faith might rest ;
Soon would he come and every cloud dispel !
AUGUSTINE with impatience for him longed,
And after some delay the bishop came.
An African was FAUSTUS, meanly born
Of parents poor, and had upraised himself
From such low origin to rank and fame.
Corrupt in life, but eloquent in speech,
He preached of self-denial, virtue praised,
Yet loved the luxury his tongue condemned !
His mind was crafty, plausible, astute,
And, through the errors he maintained, perverse ;
Yet, by a natural gift improved by art,
He had acquired persuasive eloquence.
He spoke not better things than other men,
But things far better said, and thus pleased more.
The draught he offered to a thirsty man
Was but poor drink, although the cup was gold.
His choice and readiness of words were such,
That his ideas, though mean, seemed grand and new.
AUGUSTINE was enchanted when he first
Heard FAUSTUS preach, whose action ever kept

Graceful accord with every word he said.
His choice of language gratified the ear ;
But when his words were done, he left untouched
The void which substance only could make full.
His face was comely, and his stature tall ;
Around his forehead on his temples hung
Locks which had been abundant in his youth,
Though now so sparse ; his eyebrows, strongly marked,
Veiled the sinister glances of his eyes ;
Whilst his thin lips, by a strong will compressed,
Distressed men's sight until his voice was heard.
But when they opened, to some phrase adorned,
Which through their portals passed in courtly guise,
Their ugly leanness ceased to be observed.
He as an orator so much excelled,
That when AUGUSTINE, some years afterwards,
Heard AMBROSE preach at Milan, he confessed
That FAUSTUS much excelled in eloquence.
This bishop, in his sermons, in bland terms,
Blasphemed the Law, the Prophets, and their GOD,
Denied CHRIST'S incarnation, and denounced
As false and worthless the New Testament,
Which proved him wrong. In his hot zeal he wrote
A work against true Christianity,
To which AUGUSTINE, at a later time,
Made long replies. The bishop's future lot
Was not a happy one ; after some years,
In which he spread and flourished in the land
As a green bay tree, persecution came.
It was an age of stern intolerance,
And he, for flagrant heresy condemned,
Was sent by the Proconsul far away
To a small isle, in hopeless banishment.
The Christians who at first had him accused

Felt pity for him, but they vainly tried
By intercessions to avert his doom.

    AUGUSTINE called on FAUSTUS privately,
Told him the things which moved his mind to doubt
And asked him their solution, to no end !
For he soon found him wholly ignorant,
Except of grammar, and a smattering
Gathered from TULLY'S speeches, SENECA,
The Latin poets, and some books composed
By members of the Manichæan sect.
These slender stores he husbanded with care,
And, through long practice, as he daily preached,
Learned to manipulate with so much skill,
That they were pleasant and seductive made.
His eloquence succeeded by the help
Of a clear wit and gracefulness of style ;
But when AUGUSTINE brought him to a stand,
The pressure of the young man's intellect
Was as when iron seeks support from foam.
He asked him which he thought most accurate,—
The fables MANES wrote, or the conclusions
Evolved by science. FAUSTUS candidly
Confessed that he knew nothing of such things,
Nor would he be entangled in a maze,
From which was no retreat and no escape !
Then, quitting topics such as these, AUGUSTINE
Discussed with FAUSTUS one less difficult,—
The art of rhetoric, which both professed ;
But even there was FAUSTUS found at fault !
Such, then, and only such, was their bright light,
The Manichæans' vaunted prodigy !
But this experience of the bishop's worth
Destroyed AUGUSTINE'S confidence, and loosed

The snare of death in which he had been ta'en.
He broke not with the sect at once, though soon
The rupture would arrive, but from that time
He swept their rubbish from his inner mind,
Discarded as unsound their heresy,
Turned once again his thoughts to the true GOD,
The great Creator of the universe,
On whom, in words like these, his voice now called :[1]

" I call on Thee, my GOD compassionate !
   Who hast me made, and wilt not me forget,
Though I forget Thee ! Come, I supplicate,
   Come Thou within my soul, which loves Thee yet ;
Which, Thee to welcome right, Thou dost prepare
By longings for Thee first implanted there.

" Forsake not him who now on Thee doth call,
   And whom, before he called, Thou didst prevent ;
Me to whom Thou didst will it should befall,
   Through Thy repeated warnings, to repent,
That I should hear from far, should turn to Thee,
And call at length on One who first called me.

" For Thou, O GOD, didst all my misdeeds blot ;
   Nor will into my hands wrong things repay,
But hast beforehand all my good deeds got
   As tribute to Thyself, who mad'st my clay ;
For ere I was, Thou wast, nor was I, LORD,
Aught to which Thou existence shouldst accord.

" Yet, lo ! I am, because Thy goodness great
   Did all which Thou hast made me long precede,

[1] Appendix, Note D ; Augustine's *Confess.* lib. xiii. c. 1.

E'en that wherefrom Thou didst me first create :
   Not that Thou hadst of me the slightest need,
Nor as if I so excellent were made
That I, my God, could lend Thee any aid ;

" Nor that I might Thee help, as if Thine hand,
   Wearied in working or unhelped, lost power ;
Nor that I Thee should tend, as some fair land
   Else lacking culture ; but might Thee each hour
Worship and serve, that good to me should flow
From Thee, who me enablest good to know ! "

V.

FAUSTUS ON THE ISLE.

BOUND, as a convict, by this iron chain,
Doomed to work hard, and live on wretched
food,—
Black, bitter bread, whose very sight gives pain,—
Beaten and scoffed at by my gaolers rude,
With all hope gone, and even fortitude.
I drag a body frail about with me,
And ah! still more, a rankling, tortured mind!
Here on this cliff, which overlooks the sea,
Will I a moment's solace strive to find.

Sad is the change that has befallen my lot!
But some few months ago lived I in ease;
Wealth from my converts and applause I got;
All that I did or said would others please;
My lips men sought, as flowers are sought by bees;
Fair women lavished on me favours rare;
Around me eager multitudes would crowd,
Content if on my face their eyes could stare:
No pope so grand as I, no priest so proud!

Accurst be they who meanly me accused,
And led me, chained, to the Proconsul stern,—
A judge who all my blandishments refused,
Nor would his face in pity on me turn,
But sent me to this isle.   Condemned! I yearn

For vengeance, and would gladly all woes bear,
  Could I on them inflict and see them feel
One-half my torment, horror, and despair,
  Or make them writhe beneath the headsman's steel.

I know what impulses this bosom move,
  Nor shrink I to avow my heart's true state,
Which spurns with scorn the Christian's vaunted "love,"
  And revels in the bitterness of hate.
  Great is my anguish, but my soul as great!
Though sorrow, want, and pain be now my lot,
  To all my foes I hurl defiance bold;
Of my resentments I abate no jot,
  But keep them warm till death shall make them
    cold.

Accurst be my accusers, every one!
  Weak, silly fools; not men, but senseless stocks!
May failure disappoint their work when done,
  Derision blast their doctrines orthodox,
  False pastors lead astray their sheep like flocks;
May every wind infectious that breeds pain,
  And all calamities that sharpen grief,
Visit their dwellings, health and honour stain,
  To bring them misery, but no relief.

Their very memory I drive away,
  As something foul and hateful to my mind.
I cannot hope, I cannot even pray!
  My soul and body cruel fetters bind.
  On my past acts I fear to look behind;
This present time is one of unmatched woe,
  The future scares me with unwonted dread;

In doubt and trembling onward must I go
    A few more steps, ere numbered with the dead.

The GOD the Christians worship is not mine ;
    No supplication unto Him I make !
Disgrace would be a name for grace divine
    If shown on me, nor will I such grace take.
    Be it that my salvation is at stake,
Yet will I boldly, though a wretch forlorn,
    Whilst I have strength to reason and reflect,
Maintain my doctrines, and with utter scorn
    The Christian dogmas, creeds, and faith reject.

Unto which GOD shall I for help appeal,—
    The Principle of Evil or of Good ?
The GOD of Goodness may desire my weal,
    But He hath not the Evil One withstood ;
    So mischief overwhelms me like a flood !
Why did not Goodness stop the onslaught made
    By Evil, when creation first began ?
Pleasure had then not been by pain repaid,
    Nor misery have formed the lot of man.

Goodness and Weakness are too much the same ;
    I will not worship One whose power stands checked.
He will not harm me, though I curse His name,
    Because, through His default, my bark is wrecked.
    His altar shall not by my hands be decked :
Unto a greater spirit will I pray,
    When prayers I offer ; even unto thee,
O Evil Spirit ! darkness, and not day !
    Mightier than love, thou god Malignity !

Thou who hast caused me mischief, take it hence ;
    Bear it away, like poison, in thine hands,
To where it may, with action more intense,
    Spread o'er the plain whereon New Carthage stands,
    And as a fire consume it.   Thy commands
Will be obeyed, if thou wilt but decree
    That on my countrymen, who sent me here,
Shall fall the wretched doom endured by me,—
    Famine and chains, disease, remorse, and fear!

That thou wilt punish them I dare not doubt ;
    But much I question if, now I am thine,
Thou from my cell wilt ever let me out,
    Or bid my prisoned soul no more repine.
    Its substance is a particle divine,
Which thou wilt loose not from its fleshly chain,
    But, when by death divorced from human shape,
Wilt fasten in a body once again,
    And thus produce some crocodile or ape.

In what form, when my spirit quits its earth,
    Shall I be found by transmigration strange ?
Shall I receive a serpent's monstrous birth,
    Or, as a wolf, the plains for rapine range ?
    Become a fish, or to a reptile change ?
Or shall I, for my soul-deceiving lies,
    Be made a spider, fierce and fell of mood,
To weave thin cobwebs for unwary flies,
    Pounce on my prey, and suck its vital blood ?

The doom for me reserved looks black and stern—
    The Christian's Hell, if Christian faith be true ;

Else to some hideous creature must I turn,
  When men the grave's dust on this body strew,
  And I a hated transformation rue ;
Yet will I, while I breathe earth's tainted air,
  Groan execrations with my latest breath,
Mutter infuriate ravings of despair,
  And stagger wildly to the gates of Death !

VI.

TO ITALY.

CARTHAGE became distasteful to AUGUSTINE,
  When science, that fair handmaiden of truth,
Had undermined his trust in what was false,
And brought him back to his Creator's feet.
He had no longer patience to attend
Assemblies of the Manichæan sect,
Where FAUSTUS was faith's chief expositor.
Nor at the college, where he held his class,
Could he find comfort; for no discipline
Which the authorities would tolerate
Reigned there, to keep young students within bounds:
Therefore a shameless course they led unchecked,
Of vile, unruly licence, and oft burst
Into the class with tumult, noisy cries,
And frantic gestures; but their lawless acts
Unpunished passed, for custom sanctioned them.
AUGUSTINE could at last no more endure
That by these youths both he and decency
Should be subverted. He had never joined,
When there as student, in such practices;
Nor would he now, as a professor, stoop
To be of rude irreverence the mark.
Therefore he threw up his professorship,
Abandoned Carthage, and to Rome would go.

When MONICA intelligence received
Of his projected journey, she was struck
With horror at the dangers he must run,
And hastened from Tagasta unto Carthage,
To change his plan or else with him depart;
For would she otherwise again behold
Her son, who was the idol of her heart?
When she arrived, she found AUGUSTINE'S ship
Just on the point of sailing; but she threw
Her arms convulsively about his neck,
And held him back by force, to keep him there,
Or make him promise she should with him go.
But that he wished not, for he shrank, when bound
To a strange city in a foreign land,
Upon a scheme untried, to bear aloft
Upon his shoulders any extra weight,
Which might impede his course, and chances spoil.
Therefore to make her calm he temporized,
And threw her off her guard, that he might 'scape.
She walked out with him on the pebbly beach,
Where his ship rolled at anchor; but he feigned
That he must wait to please a timid friend
Who would not sail until the wind proved fair;
For which cause their departure was postponed.
There was a place hard by, where pious hands
Had to the memory of CYPRIAN,
The Carthaginian saint, built on the shore
An oratory, wherein prayers were said
To GOD unceasingly.   In this withdrew
The mournful MONICA, to pray and weep;
But whilst her tears bedewed the very earth
Beneath her down-bent face, and she prayed GOD
Not to permit her son to sail, he went!
AUGUSTINE privily escaped on board,

The wind blew fresh, the sails at once swelled out,
The anchor was uplifted, and the prow
Dashed through the waves and left the port behind.
When in the morning MONICA looked forth,
The ship was gone, and she was left alone !
GOD had refused her prayer, but not her wish ;
For what she had for years entreated GOD
Her son was now to be, and this would come
From that departure thence which she deplored.
Maddened with sorrow, on the yellow sand
She cast herself, full of complaints and groans,
And her maternal love of earthly kind
Was chastened with that scourge so oft its lot.
She dreamt not then how great would be the joy
Which out of this departure GOD would work ;
Therefore she wept and wailed, and in her pain
Appeared the doom inherited from EVE,
For she with sorrow sought and could not find
What she with sorrow had before brought forth.
She railed against her son for treachery,
Loudly accused him of hard-heartedness,
But soon relented, and betook herself
To intercede for him again with GOD.
Then, as he went his voyage on to Rome,
She to Tagasta, sad of heart, returned.

THE SONG OF MONICA.

" O ship ! that dartest forwards in thy course
                So swift, so gay ;
    O sea ! whose waves bear hence that gliding bark
                Midst foam and spray,
    Bring back to me ere long the precious freight
                Ye take away.

"O ship! O sea! to whom I, weeping, trust
  My heart's chief charm,
Guard him I love, support and keep him safe
  From risk and harm ;
Nor let my soul have ever any cause
  For this alarm.

"O CHRIST! whose word can calm the raging sea,
  Bid it be still ;
Whose voice the very winds and waves obey,
  My prayer fulfil ;
Bring to the haven which he seeks my son :
  Be this Thy will !

"And calm, oh, calm this tempest in my mind,
  This dread, this fear,
That I may never see or clasp again
  My son so dear,
Whose absence from me will each hour demand
  A groan and tear ! "

SAINT AUGUSTINE.

———◆———

BOOK III.

IN ITALY.

BOOK III.

I.

ROME AND MILAN.

AUGUSTINE crossed the sea, arrived at Rome,
    And dwelt there in a Manichæan's house.
The Emperor and his Court had ceased to live
Upon the Palatine, but SYMMACHUS,
A learned Pagan, who in Africa
Had been Proconsul, held the reins of power
In temporal things as Prefect ; and the rule
O'er all things which the Christian faith concerned
Was left to DAMASUS, who then as Pope
Lived at the Lateran, in luxury,
On contributions by the faithful made.[1]
AUGUSTINE now gained grace to recognise
ALMIGHTY GOD, but not to understand
GOD'S SON, our Saviour, whom he still conceived
As having been a phantasm of light,
Which never touched the substance of real flesh,
But with its likeness and external form
Was merely shaded, so as to be seen.
CHRIST came, he thought, to do the FATHER'S will,
Rescue men's souls, and lead them back to GOD ;
He on the cross was shown, that He might teach

---

[1] Ammianus Marcellinus, lib. xxvii. cap. 3.

The true condition of the soul, which lies
In matter bodied, bound, and crucified ;
Therefore the death of CHRIST to him appeared
Delusion of the senses, nothing more !
At Rome AUGUSTINE mixed with the " Elect,"
And not with " Hearers " only ; but was shocked
When he, in his friend's house, beheld their life,
And found that they who preached austerity
Followed in secret a licentious course ;
Nor was there one untainted by such sin.
" It is not we," they said, " who sin ; it is
Some other thing to which we are conjoined,
And therefore truly we are free from blame."
AUGUSTINE would have willingly believed
No blame attached to him for wrong acts done,
But conscience filled him with profound distrust ;
And when he saw his Manichæan host
Receive with confident credulity
Such fables as his sect passed off for truths,
AUGUSTINE warned and much discouraged him,
But could not give him true ideas of GOD,
Whom he still fancied as an aggregate
Of physical existences, a mass
Of bodies, and he knew not what besides.
He could not substance spiritual conceive,
Else would he long before have broken off
From doctrines which ensnared his heedless soul.

When safe in Rome arrived, he eagerly
Sought out ALYPIUS, his youthful friend,
Who had, two years before, gone there to learn
The law, and practise as an advocate.
The two young men their former ties renewed
Closer than ever ; but in some few weeks

AUGUSTINE sickened in the Roman air :
Foul, pestilential vapours laid him low,
And brought him fainting to the verge of death.
But if the fever then had done its work,
How dreadful would have been his endless doom !
Once, when a boy, by sudden weakness seized,
He had begged hard for the baptismal rite,
Which only his recovery postponed ;
But now with hardened will and scoffing mind
He took his chance, and met death's frown unawed.
But GOD compassion on his soul bestowed ;
For when he helpless tossed upon his bed,
His mother, at Tagasta, on her knees
Was praying for him with incessant tears.
Although unconscious of his state at Rome,
She never ceased to supplicate and weep ;
And if he then had, unconverted, found
In body and in soul a double death,
The wound that would have pierced her heart was one
No healing could have cured ; she would have lost
The prayers made by her for so many years,
Beseeching and imploring, with one aim,
That GOD would grant to her, not this world's goods,
Not gold or silver coveted by man,
But the salvation of her lost son's soul !
GOD heard her prayers, forgave and saved her son,
Who from that sickness sore rose up restored,
That He who healed his body might in time
Bestow on him a more abiding health,—
And better, since his soul would have the gift.
AUGUSTINE'S project, when to Rome he went,
Was to instruct young students of the law
In rhetoric, and open there a class ;
But like a thread of gossamer, this plan,

When put to trial, snapped ; for though at first
Students came flocking to his lecture-room,
And with decorum listened as he taught,
Yet, when they should have paid, they disappeared !
Just at this crisis, when the teacher's mind
Felt deep disgust, the chair of eloquence
In Milan's school fell vacant, and they sent
From thence to Rome to beg of SYMMACHUS—
Himself distinguished as an orator—
That he would choose and to their college send
A skilled professor.   This he undertook,
And from the candidates AUGUSTINE chose,
Who then left Rome, and left without regret.

Must, then, ALYPIUS once more lose his friend ?
Death had to sever them so lately tried,
And had so near succeeded, that ALYPIUS
Had in despair sent unto MONICA,
To warn and to prepare her for the worst ;
But afterwards, with health again restored,
AUGUSTINE had to him been given back,
Whereby his joy rose brimming to the full.
Now came this change his happiness to spoil,
And take from him the friend whom most he loved,
And one through whom he had himself been saved
From worse disease than fever,—from a spell
Which like a frenzy had possessed his mind.
In the great Flavian Amphitheatre
Were cruel sports still held, from Pagan times
Derived, in which fierce gladiators fought,
And in the dreadful struggles which ensued
Those overpowered were slain.   ALYPIUS,
When first he came to Rome, refused to go
To sanguinary scenes, from which his heart

Revolted in disgust. At last one day,
Some of his young companions, flushed with wine,
Returning from a feast, met him by chance,
And in a frolic seized him in their arms,
Lifted him up, and bore him off by force.
Brought thus, against his will, within a place
Which he abhorred, he sat upon a bench
In moody silence, shutting both his eyes,
That, present bodily, he might in mind
Be absent, and thereby balk jeering friends.
Thus he remained, and kept his purpose firm,
Until a fearful shout arose, which shook
The air, the earth, the very souls of men !
At sound of which, and cries of " Habet," " Habet,"
ALYPIUS started, and with opened eyes
Looked down on the arena, where he saw
The final triumph, as one combatant
Gave the last stroke which pierced another's heart !
Gazing with eyes distended and clenched hands,
ALYPIUS, when he saw the blood, drank in
A horrible delight, felt a strange spell
Subdue him ; then, more frenzied than the crowd,
Stared, yelled, and raved at every incident
Of the atrocious pastime.   From that hour
He, by the fiendish fascination caught,
Attended every show, drew young friends thither,
And by his mad excitement would ere long
Have made sweet mercy foreign to his soul,
Had not AUGUSTINE, just in time, reached Rome,
And, full of horror at such barbarous sport,
Withdrew him from them, and their charm dispelled.
Therefore ALYPIUS felt deep gratitude.
" Shall we then part ?" he cried.   " Forbid, it Heaven !
Such misery as that will I avert,

And give up Rome, to go where goes my friend."
Therefore ALYPIUS to AUGUSTINE clave,
Abandoned Rome, and both to Milan went.

THE SONG OF ALYPIUS.

" In a far isle beyond the sea,
    For men of valour glorious,
Renowned for mountain, turf, and tree,
    The realm of King CARACTACUS,
There dwelt a youth no toil could daunt,
Who made the woods and hills his haunt,
And knew the note of every bird
Whose songs in leafy grove are heard.

" Oft would he sit within a dale
    Where mighty oaks their branches spread,
Hearing a blissful nightingale
    Which warbled sweetly o'er his head :
No day could pass but in that place
He looked around with anxious face,
And listened till his quick ears caught
The notes he loved, the song he sought.

" But when the summer-time was gone,
    And autumn's mists would shortly rise,
The bird's voice lost its thrilling tone
    For want of food and brighter skies.
Soon would she go from Albion's strands,
Seek for a nest in warmer lands,
With outspread wings fly many a mile
To Afric's coast, and cross the Nile.

" But what would the young chieftain do
  Without her song to cheer his heart?
Cold blasts were coming soon, he knew;
  Should he then, like the bird, depart?
Yes, he would leave his woodland dale,
To follow the sweet nightingale;
And when at last he heard her voice,
His heart should leap, his soul rejoice!

" ' Go where thou wilt, I follow thee!'
  The fond youth cried to that loved bird;
' My life a dull, dark blank would be
  Unless thy tender voice I heard.
No space of earth shall part us twain;
I follow, and we meet again!
Yes; though I journey many a mile
To Afric's coast, and cross the Nile.'"

THE PREFECT OF THE CITY.

BEFORE AUGUSTINE turned his back on Rome,
    He called on SYMMACHUS to give him thanks,
And found him seated in an inner room,
Attended by his lictors.　The old man
Embraced him kindly, but his feeble arms
Trembled through age while resting on his neck.
" I have selected thee to go to Milan,"
The Prefect said, " and given thee preference,
Although thy tongue hath brought from Africa
Some faults detected by nice Roman ears ;
These thou must remedy, though unto me—
An African Proconsul in past times—
They bring back happy memories of old.
Thy parents I remember, and thy town
Tagasta, with its gently sloping hills,
And corn-fields waving in the evening breeze.
I have heard well of thee, and prize thee much.
Young MAXIMIM, thy pupil, hath confirmed,
By boundless admiration for thee felt,
The good opinion I myself have formed.
In me thou seest a Roman advocate,
Who practised once the art which thou dost teach,
Gaining some honour until office came,
Which made my duty more to act than speak.
I am, as thou dost know, of the old school

And old religion, out of fashion now!
Yet have I well upheld against the world
My place and power, and still them safe retain.
At Milan thou wilt meet another man,
Who, like myself, was advocate and prefect,
But, being in the superstition bred
Which now prevails, and liking what he learnt,
Hath undergone the strangest transformation,
And from a lawyer hath archbishop turned!
I saw him lately, when he came to Rome
At a large gathering of the Christian prelates
About some point of doctrine—what, I heed not.
I found him—something which I deemed not all—
A man of noble bearing, good and wise.
When I, to please my friends who still prefer
Rome's old religion, asked the Emperor
To let the goddess Victory once more
Have in the Senate-house her statue back,
As in the ancient times, AMBROSE alone
Withstood me boldly, and our purpose balked.
But though his creed I hate, I love the man!
Friends have we always been, and are so still."

AUGUSTINE, as the Prefect spoke, looked up
With curious eyes, and saw before him stand
A tall old man, with grizzled hair and beard,
A massive chin, large eyebrows, deep-sunk eyes,
With lofty forehead, rough and weatherworn;
Like a grand oak, firm rooted in the earth,
Though tempest-torn about the limbs and crest.
Upon his shoulders hung, as white as snow,
The graceful toga; for he loved the dress
Which Roman senators in days of yore
Had in the Forum worn, when CICERO

G

Harangued the people surging like a sea.
Nothing new-fangled suited SYMMACHUS:
He worshipped the old gods of heathen times,
Kept to the customs of his ancestors,
Resisted innovation as a plague,
Spurned novelties, and walked in ancient ways.
He now, with flowing courtesy, received
The young aspirant who had pleased him most.
They had long talk of Carthage, and the men
Of greatest note there in the days gone by;
How some had thrived, some failed, some passed away
After a flash of short prosperity,
Which want of prudence into ruin turned.
As every name was mentioned, SYMMACHUS
Drew from his active, teeming memory
A store of anecdotes and shrewd remarks,
Showing keen observation, but no trace
Of any glance which touched the inner life.
He asked AUGUSTINE of his parents, heard
With sorrow that PATRICIUS was dead;
Then, as that name brought back a crowd of thoughts,
He, smiling on his youthful friend, thus spake:
"Thy mother MONICA, I knew her well!
A meek-faced dame, who drank her wine by sips;
A prodigy of chastity and truth,
Devoted to her husband, but by friends
Of virtue frail more laughed at than admired;
For your good father was a votary
Of VENUS, that great goddess, whom we serve
With open adoration and fit rites.
Yet would your mother to PATRICIUS
Display such sweet and loving constancy,
That such a wife, at times, I envied much,
And would, methought, have granted him for his

Any of mine, who oft for playing false
I have divorced, to take ere long another,
Fairer, but no whit truer than the last!
She, though a Christian, I could tolerate,
Though never felt I much complacency
For Christian men,—who should, I think, be
    men,
Rough, ready, strong, fierce on the battle-field,
First in all feuds, revenging every wrong,
Contented with the faith their fathers held,
And worshippers of VENUS, MARS, and JOVE.
The hooded monks who crawl about old Rome
Like swarms of beetles, muttering senseless prayers,
Deceiving women by their solemn looks,
And preaching peace to men whose trade is war,
Move my abhorrence! Their vile novelties
Will undermine this empire's wasted strength,
Unnerve the warrior's arm, make dull his sword,
And turn our eagles into bleating lambs!
Then will those fierce barbarian hordes of Goths,
Which swarm around our frontier everywhere,
Like packs of starving wolves eager for prey,
Come down upon us, dire revenge to take
For centuries of violence and wrong.
That which thy countryman, great HANNIBAL,
Failed to effect when Rome adored the gods,
A meaner foe, now that the gods are fled,
May easily accomplish ; and the cause
Will be that weakness, miscalled tolerance,
Which let the Christian conflagration spread
From dwellings poor to palaces and shrines,
When we had strength to stamp it out at once,
And might have made a quick extinguishment
Had there been will to shed sufficient blood."

"That method hath been tried," AUGUSTINE said,
" Too often tried, but signally it failed ;
Even when Christian men in Rome were few,
The cruel NERO could not root them out.
And if you dread that Rome may taste of fire
Because the hands which should defend her walls
Are idly telling beads in monkish cells,
Remember that in NERO'S Pagan days
She fell a prey to devastating flames,
And smoked in ruins, not by Christians caused."
"True," answered SYMMACHUS, "yet soon again
She rose in more resplendent loveliness,
Blessed by the gods !   But if you talk of fire,
These eyes of mine have seen, in these our days,
Rome burning like a furnace, with red flames
Lighted by Christian hands !   Some years ago,
When Pope LIBERIUS died, the priest who now
Lives in the Lateran in regal pomp
Claimed to succeed him ; but some men said nay,
And started an opponent, who, like him,
Coveted power, as priests will ever do :
Both aimed at wealth whilst preaching poverty,
And sought to stifle influence by force.
The streets of Rome were thronged by Christian mobs,
The partisans of one side or the other,
Who surged and stormed with unexampled rage,
Forgetful of the meekness they profess,
But would have others practise.   DAMASUS
Did nothing to restrain the violence
Of his supporters, who from shouts and cries
Soon had recourse to blows ; these were returned,
And Pagan eyes beheld Rome's gutters run
With Christian blood, which Christian hands had shed !
No sound of hymns was heard, but clash of swords,

Shrieks of the wounded, groans of dying men;
The torch completed what the tongue began!
Street upon street in Rome blazed forth with fire,
Houses and palaces sank down in flames,
And the whole city might have been a wreck
Had not our Pagan soldiers rendered aid
To quell the riot and a truce compel.
Then o'er the bloody corses of the slain,
And in the lurid light of burning streets,
Stept DAMASUS to mount ST. PETER'S chair.[1]

[1] Ammianus Marcellinus, a Greek Pagan, but of acknowledged truthfulness, was living when this contest between Damasus and Ursinus took place in the year 367, and gives the following account of it in his history :—

"Damasus and Ursinus, heated with an extraordinary ambition for the episcopal seat, were so fierce in their contention, that on each side the quarrel proceeded to wounds, and even to death. Inventius (Prefect of Rome), not being able to stop or compose the difference, was compelled to retire into the suburbs. Damasus overcame in the contest the party opposing him. It is certain that in the Basilica of Sicinninus, where there was an assembly of the Christians, 137 were killed in one day; and it was a good while before the exasperated multitude were brought to good temper. Nor do I deny, considering the pomp and wealth of the city, that they who are desirous of such things are in the right to contend with all their might for what they are fond of; since, having obtained it, they are sure of being enriched with the offerings of matrons, and will ride in chariots, and be delicately clad, and may make profuse entertainments, surpassing the tables of princes. But they might be happy indeed, if, despising the grandeur of the city, which they allege as an excuse for their luxury, they would imitate the life of some country bishops, who by their temperance in eating and drinking, by the plainness of their habit, and the modesty of their whole behaviour, approve themselves to the eternal Deity and His true worshippers as men of virtue and piety" (lib. xxvii. cap. 3). Dr. Lardner, in whose work the above quotation is to be found (vol. viii. p. 56), observes as follows :—"What Ammianus here says is very true. Damasus was Bishop of Rome after Liberius; and Socrates says (*H. E.* t. iv. cap. 29), that in the contention between Damasus and Ursinus many were killed. And he observes that the ground of the contention was not any heresy or difference of opinion, but only which of them should be bishop;" and Sozomen, in the very words of Ammianus, says, "This contention proceeded to wounds and death." "It is," adds Dr. Lardner, "plain from Ammianus, that at that time the bishops of Rome lived in great splendour, and that this contention about the bishopric was a scandalous thing."

Yet he whose course began in fire and blood,
Now seeks to be Rome's lord, proclaims the reign
Of peace on earth, displays his pompous self
As fittest representative of peace,
And tries by intrigues with the Emperor
To filch from out my hands the temporal sway,
And make e'en me subordinate to him !
What can exceed the arrogance of priests ?
Men now call every Christian bishop pope ;
But soon the bishop here will claim that name
As his alone, and try to make the rest
His humble slaves, as he would fain make me.
But while I check his efforts by main strength,
They, subtler far, will be content to yield,
Hoping in turn to rule o'er other men,
And gain what most they love, rank, pelf, and power.
Ye gods ! whom, in the days when Rome was great,
MARCUS AURELIUS, that philosopher,
Worshipped, as had his fathers in old time,
Have ye deserted us for ever now ?
We hoped when JULIAN was Emperor,
That ye again, descending from Olympus,
Would have renewed our Roman glory gone,
And driven these black-frocked gentry from the earth
To the Cimmerian darkness of deep hell ! "

The Prefect paused awhile, as lost in thought,
And stood with drooping head and downcast eyes,
Pondering on painful themes. AUGUSTINE smiled
At earnestness for things whose days he knew
Had passed for ever ; then by gentle words
Essayed to calm the rage he could not quell.
He even ventured to express a hope
That Christian practice might ere long become

Consistent more with Christian principle ;
Then, though some men might lose, the world would
    gain !
But SYMMACHUS impatiently replied :
" Say, what advantage would befall the world
If temporal power were ta'en from one like me,
And placed in hands like those of DAMASUS,
The weakest but the craftiest of priests ?
One who, inflamed by coarsest vanity,
Kindled by adulation's fetid breath,
Proclaims himself to be a demi-god,
Yet hath no nobler method to secure
Remembrance among men of his poor name
Than having it inscribed in letters large
On every public structure throughout Rome ![1]
Mean is the man who seeks immortal fame
By scrawling texts on walls he did not build !
Well may'st thou wish to live in Rome no more,
Where evil, like a reeking mass of filth,
Grows fouler every day, and yet must grow !
Better art thou in Milan than with us.
There VALENTINIAN, our Emperor,
Holds his gay court, but, boy-like, acts as bids
JUSTINA, his proud mother, who again
Is but the tool of eunuchs, whom all hate !
But go thou there, and good luck go with thee ;
Push on thy fortunes with thy utmost skill !
From ground once gained advance to conquests new ;
Nor slacken pace or pause through doubts or fear.
But when unto admiring crowds thy voice
Explains the noble art of eloquence,
And tells of those great orators whose fame

---

[1] " Who builds a church to God, and not to fame,
    Will never mark the marble with his name."—POPE.

Will live for ever, do not thou forget
That, e'en in days degenerate as these,
Some few have at the bar obtained renown,—
Lesser than theirs, 'tis true, yet something still.
And thou, perchance, among the list wilt name
Thy friend, the Roman Prefect, SYMMACHUS."

III.

THE PURSUIT.

WHEN Monica intelligence received
      Of her son's fever, she was still engaged
In praying at Tagasta for his soul;
But, terrified to think that he might die
In distant Rome without a mother's care,
She gathered hastily what little wealth
PATRICIUS had left, sold off her goods,
And with the slender proceeds sailed at once
In the first vessel bound for Italy.
Her only daughter, young PERPETUA,
She had bestowed in marriage long before,
Deeming the wedded life, though often tried
By pain and sorrow, happier on the whole
For woman than much-praised celibacy.[1]
This daughter she with tears and sobs embraced;
For something whispered they would meet no more!
Then went she quickly by herself to pray
Beside the grave where slept PATRICIUS,
And where a place had been for her reserved.
She gazed thereon in silence mournfully,
For who could tell what might not her befall?
NAVIGIUS, her younger son, she took

---

[1] Perpetua many years afterwards became a widow and the superior or abbess of a convent of nuns in Africa. There is still extant a most singular letter said to have been written to her by Augustine. *De Vita Eremitica*, Augustine's *Opera*, tom. i. p. 1380.

As her companion ; then, devoid of fear,
Trusting in God, sailed boldly o'er the sea.
But ere they reached the land great storms arose ;
The vessel, tempest-shook, began to leak ;
The mariners by fear grew paralyzed,
And safety seemed too desperate for hope.
But when they thought to let the good ship sink,
A vision came to MONICA in sleep,
Announcing she should certainly arrive
Without disaster whither she was bound.
Then she arose and comforted the men,
Told them her dream, gave courage to their hearts,
And stirred them up to so much energy,
That they, by great exertions, saved the ship :
Thus Italy was reached, and Ostia gained.
Impetuous in her search, she rushed away
And entered Rome ; but when she found the house
Wherein her son had dwelt, he thence had gone !
Baffled and breathless, she was not cast down,
But deemed the news of his recovery
An ample recompense for all her pains ;
Nor did she hesitate to follow him
O'er rugged paths across the Apennines,
Through league on league of lengthened weariness.
At last, with heart whose courage never failed,
She distance, toil, and obstacles o'ercame,
Arrived at Milan, hurried through its streets,
Found her son out, and clasped him in her arms!

IV.

ST. AMBROSE.

AUGUSTINE, when to Milan come, received
From AMBROSE, the Archbishop, welcome warm,
Because he as professor was to teach
In the forensic schools, and AMBROSE once
In early life had been an advocate,
And first in that way had distinction won.
But though by a strange chance, which GOD wrought
    out,
He then abandoned the civilian's state,
To leap in one week from the Prefect's chair
To the Archbishop's throne, he often thought
On what he once had been, and how he rose.
He was untainted by the mean desire
To kick the ladder down up which he climbed,
And stop their way who would like him ascend ;
But he with loving heart and helping hand
Favoured the faculty he once adorned.
His reputation at the bar was marked
By honour, learning, and intelligence ;
Nor did he ever stoop to any act
Of a base kind to win a wrongful cause ;
He scorned to touch the tools which some men use
To turn the path of justice from its course.
No shifty child of artifice was he,
No glib adept in plausibilities ;

But an industrious, truthful, honest man.
His statements, ever clear and accurate,
Commanded the judicial confidence ;
His courtesy and friendliness of soul
Made rough things smooth, not smooth ones harsh
     and rough.
His mind went straightway to the point whereon
The controversy turned, and this he touched
With such persuasiveness, as suited one
Not often eloquent, but always wise.
The darkest labyrinths of Roman law,
Which then were tangled as an Indian wood
(For great JUSTINIAN had yet to come),
His industry had thoroughly explored ;
None better knew its intricate details,
Or with a wider scope could grasp the whole.
His progress had been rapid ; for, conjoined
With merit, influence had helped him on.
He soon, as an Assessor of the Court,
Acted judicially, and won with ease
The reputation of a learned man,
Whom neither favour, prejudice, nor fear
Could bias in his judgment.   When he rose
To be Liguria's governor, he ruled
That province with such perfect gentleness,
That men recalled the memorable words
Of the Proconsul PROBUS, who had said,
When there he sent him, knowing well his worth,
" Go thou and rule the subjects of this land
More as a bishop than a governor."
That wise command was faithfully fulfilled.
Next was he, when a vacancy occurred,
Made Milan's Prefect, where he lived in state,
Honoured by all, feared only by the bad.

He was distinguished less by massive strength
Than by variety of precious gifts ;
And thus the world in him beheld at once
A poet, lawyer, judge, philosopher,
Musician, statesman, orator, and priest,—
A man of action, and a man of thought !
His eyes were fixed not on himself, but looked
Outwards upon the world which hemmed him round :
And this he strove not to control as if
He were the centre, and all else mere tools
To push his purposes and serve his ends ;
He rather strove to do the will of GOD,
And make his own a will subservient,
Deeming himself an atom on the earth
Inseparably joined to CHRIST in heaven !
How strange the chance which made him an archbishop,
When still a catechumen unbaptized !
In this way did the incident occur :
When AMBROSE had arrived at thirty years,
A vacancy arose in Milan's see ;
According to old usage, bishops then
Were nominated by the general voice
Of all the faithful—not, as now, by choice
Of an official, who wields patronage
Sometimes to serve GOD'S cause, oftener his own.
Yet had this ancient method drawbacks grave,
For factious broils in scandalous excess
Arose among the citizens ; some sought
To choose a candidate of Arian views,
Whilst others wished one strictly orthodox.
From week to week had this dispute gone on
Increasing, and the clamours which were made
Grew louder and more violent each day.
At last, in the Basilica, the flock

Assembled to decide whom they should choose,
But difference made all choice impossible ;
And the contending parties stormed so loud,
And showed such fury, that their rage would soon
Have led to bloodshed.   AMBROSE then appeared,
As Prefect of the city, to appease
The fierce disorder, and addressed the crowd
With words which fell like oil upon the waves,
Making all smooth ; with so much eloquence,
Sweetness, and dignity he calmed their minds,
That, when he finished his address, there came
Such silence o'er opposing multitudes
That not a whisper stirred.   Then suddenly
The sweet voice of a child twice cried aloud,
"AMBROSE for bishop !"   At the second cry,
Moved by some impulse, the assembly rose,
Italian fervour sparkling in their eyes,
To echo it, and clap their eager hands :
All then with one acclaim confirmed the choice.
AMBROSE, astonished, would have fain withdrawn,
And vainly tried by many an artifice
The grave responsibility to shun ;
But nothing could resist such evidence
Of his election by the voice of GOD :
He was compelled to yield.   Thus, in one week,
By baptism and prayer and solitude
Receiving short and hasty preparation,
Became he their archbishop, and ere long
Displayed his fitness for the sacred charge.
He knew the world in which he had to act
Was full of learning, piety, and love ;
Was able to maintain the cause of GOD
With emperors and princes ; abler still
To comfort the afflicted, aid the weak,

Strengthen the strong, and lead to heaven the flock
O'er whom he stretched his crook episcopal.

From the first hour that AMBROSE and AUGUSTINE
In friendly converse met and talked together,
Each by clear insight recognised with ease
The greatness and the goodness of the other ;
Nor did the saintly AMBROSE fail to gain
The young man's cordial sympathy and love.

Besides ALYPIUS, there gathered soon
Around AUGUSTINE, in his new abode,
EVODIUS and the rich ROMANIAN,
With many other young Numidian friends,
Drawn to him as the magnet draws the steel.
Among the number was NEBRIDIUS,
One who possessed extensive tracts of land
Near Carthage, an ancestral heritage ;
And for AUGUSTINE entertained such love,
That when news came to Carthage that in Milan
His friend was settled, he at once there went,
Leaving behind his lands, his house, his slaves,
His neighbours, mother, and his native air,
That he might with AUGUSTINE recommence
The search for wisdom. He to find true life
Sighed, as AUGUSTINE did, but once, like him,
Misled by Manichæan tales, had veered
And wavered in opinion. He would bring
To every subject which engaged his thoughts
Acuteness and untiring industry,
But, at this time, was most of all intent
To test the basis of religious faith ;
And when he put a question difficult
On some great point, hated a brief reply.

NEBRIDIUS and AUGUSTINE'S other friends
Enjoyed so much their intercourse renewed,
That they considered how they might pursue,
Free from all change or check, through their whole
          lives,
The search for wisdom which engrossed their thoughts.
ROMANIAN, the richest, then proposed,
With all the fervour of unselfish love,
That they should form a small society
Apart from the great world in which they dwelt,
And own and use, as common property,
Whatever each possessed ; thus might they live,
Even on earth, as angels do in heaven !
But though they longed with equal earnestness
To realize the project, it was found
Unsuited to the changeful life of man
In all its stages and contingencies,
And was abandoned, not without regret.

　　AUGUSTINE mingled with the crowds which flocked
To hear great AMBROSE preach the word of GOD
On every Sunday ; but he thither went
To study eloquence, and not to pray,—
To hear the preacher, but neglect his theme ;
Wishing to learn not what, but how he spake.
Yet soon became he conscious that he heard
No babble of the rhetorician's art,
Like that which still in FAUSTUS he admired.
Then, as he listened, sometimes came the thought,
Not oh, how eloquent ! but oh, how true !
He read again the Scripture narrative,
And studied the Epistles of SAINT PAUL
With eyes fresh opened and a candid mind,
Pondering upon them without prejudice.

Next he began within his heart to feel
The presence of GOD'S Spirit, silently
Melting the icy bonds which held him chained.
But a great sin, condemned by GOD and man,
Still kept him in subjection, and shut out
All hope of progress whilst its taint remained :
For, 'midst the friends arrived from Africa
To gather round him, was the mother frail
Of ADEODATUS, who had brought her boy
To make her welcome by the father sure.
But how with such a tie could he be free ?
How become clean whilst by pollution stained ?
Or how consistently could he accept
The Christian gospel, which condemned his life ?

Such was AUGUSTINE'S state when MONICA
Arrived at Milan.   First by mildest words,
Softest persuasions, gentlest influence,
She severed the connection she deplored,
And sent the weeping, contrite cause of sin
Back to her native Carthage as a nun ;
Nor spared she her own son, but cut from him
Her who, for fifteen years, had shared his life,
By severance rude tore sternly soul from soul,
And shed his very heart's blood for his cure.
Next unto AMBROSE sped she, full of hope,
To beg his intercession spiritual,
And make him promise to convert her son
By warnings wise and strength of argument.
But such were not the weapons AMBROSE used :
His was the winning, soft, convincing style,
Which through the heart attains the intellect,
And melts by warmth, but shatters not by force.
Upon his lips, whilst he was yet a child,

II

Lighted a swarm of bees, which, when they went,
Left their rich honey in persuasion there,
Giving perpetual sweetness to his speech.
Yet when necessity arose to chide
The cruelty of tyrants steeped in crime,
His gentle nature could display due strength,
And even fierceness. This he boldly showed
When THEODOSIUS, the Emperor,
To Milan came with hands yet stained with blood
Of Thessalonian Christians vilely slain,
And wished, without repentance, in that plight
To enter the Cathedral. AMBROSE dared
To meet and stop him at the very porch,
Bade him go back, nor bring defilement there,
But wait until contrition for his sins
Had made him worthier to worship GOD ;
The awe-struck Emperor obeyed and went !
Again, when MONICA in Milan dwelt,
Twice did the brave Archbishop valiantly
Defend GOD'S house, committed to his charge,
From desecration, and his flock protect ;
For when the evil, haughty Empress-mother
Required that he should unto her resign,
For Arian priests, favourites of her Court,
One of his churches, and demanded this
In her son's name, denial AMBROSE gave,
Although JUSTINA'S eunuch minister
Threatened to shed his blood and take his head.
To whose face AMBROSE sternly made reply :
" May GOD permit thee to perform thy threat,
That I may suffer death by thy base hands !
Then each will act the part that best suits each ;
I as a bishop, as an eunuch thou !"
Muttering deep curses slunk away the wretch,

Who wished to strike, but dared not risk the blow.
Soon afterwards an Arian courtier-priest
Called himself bishop of the see of Milan ;
On which the Empress a tribunal named
To judge 'twixt him and AMBROSE, whom she then
Commanded to appear and prove his right.
But AMBROSE, as an ancient jurist, knew
That this tribunal was not based on law,
But malice only, and refused the court
As wanting jurisdiction. He withdrew,
Therefore a sentence that he be deprived
Was passed against him ; but an uproar rose
Throughout the city of so fierce a sort,
From those who looked on AMBROSE as their father,
That none dared try to seize upon his church
Or harm his person, though his life was sought.

On these occasions AMBROSE took his stand
Within the walls of his Basilica,
Staying there night and day, amidst the crowds
Of Christian people, who begirt him round,
Standing in throngs before the doors, to form
A living barrier and oppose attack.
Night after night in sleepless watchfulness,
Aroused by agonies of frantic fear,
The mighty city in convulsions rolled ;
Nor was within it peace or safety felt
Until the Empress her aggressions ceased,
Brooking the thirst she longed to slake in blood.
'Twas in these vigils, while expecting death,
That AMBROSE, full of harmony and love,
First introduced the chant antiphonal,
And by sweet hymns of ceaseless praise to GOD
Lightened the weight which nine long days and nights

Had else made wearisome to worshippers.
AUGUSTINE in such vigils oft took part
When waiting on his mother, and beheld
How great was AMBROSE and how great his cause ;
Heard the sweet hymns which echoed to the roof ;
And witnessed, with emotion and respect,
The Bishop's courage, and his piety ;
Nor could he quench contagious sympathy,
Which spread from heart to heart and reached his
    own.
Though AMBROSE thus at times could rouse himself
To check the violence of haughty foes,
Sweet was his speech and gentle his kind voice
When winning souls to CHRIST.   Unto AUGUSTINE
He spake not controversially at all,
Nor tried by such a mode to teach him truth.
It was his favourite, frequent apothegm,
That not by dialectics was GOD pleased
To save His people !   He perceived at once
That a mind strong and subtle as AUGUSTINE'S
Could not be catechized to orthodoxy,
But must be left by progress and by time
To grow and clarify ; as doth a stream,
Which, bubbling forth, disturbed by mud and ooze,
From deep morasses in an Alpine wild,
Increases as it flows towards the sea,
And shines so bright at last, that its green banks
Are mirrored on its surface smooth and clear.
Therefore, though MONICA would send her son
To the Archbishop with her messages,
And take him oft to talk with him alone,
Hoping that from their converse might arise
Something of moment, yet, in that reserve
Which fences great minds round like mail of proof,

AMBROSE would silently remain unstirred;
Nor would he yield him to her eager wish,
But waited till the time to speak should come.
AUGUSTINE longed to tell the saint his thoughts
On subjects that were boiling in his heart,
But feared to trespass idly on the time
Of one who had no leisure and scant rest.
Thus through one year it seemed no step was
    made;
And save that in the church AUGUSTINE heard,
With the Archbishop's flock, the gospel read,
Listened to sermons and Ambrosian chants,
To swelling anthems and to thrilling hymns,
He had from AMBROSE neither hint nor aid;
Yet when he felt the beatings of his heart,
And pondered on the struggles of his soul,
Conscious became he that within him dwelt
A mighty Presence, until then unmarked!
Wanting in faith, he sought no help in prayer;
But sometimes in the stillness of the night,
When the bright stars were shining o'er his head,
And burning thoughts compelled some utterance,
He gazed around the earth, looked up to heaven,
And with clasped hands thus found relief in words:
"O TRUTH for whom I seek, whom most I love!
To whom in perturbations of my soul
I ever turn, regard thy votary!
Enlighten thou and guide my mind aright;
Save me from error and the lies of men,
And take me to thy bosom as thy child!"
Thus all unconsciously he prayed to GOD;
For GOD is Truth, and Truth soon heard his prayer.
Prayer is the life-breath of the soul;[1] without it,

[1] For this thought I am indebted to the writings of Canon Ryle.

Though men in name be Christians, they are dead
In sight of GOD, who, until asked by prayer,
Declines conferring His most precious gifts
On creatures who through wilfulness are dumb ;
But they who pray obtain the things they ask,
If what they ask be good, and not a snare.

V

OSCILLATIONS.

A CRISIS now impended, and AUGUSTINE
    Was oscillating, like a pendulum,
Each day from doubt to faith, from faith to doubt.
The watchful MONICA beheld her son
With deep solicitude, nor stayed her tears,
Nor ceased the prayers she offered up to God.
Such prayers were not superfluous ; for his life
Had scarcely yet through thirty summers run,
And the hot sun of Africa had mixed
His blood with fire,—a fire yet unsubdued.
Unto a fervid worshipper, like him,
Of all that in this world is beautiful,
The witching smile and beaming eyes of woman
Were as a spell, and his enamoured soul
Seized greedily the cup which passion drained.
If friends reminded him of chastity,
He answered in displeasure, for his mind
Pondered in anger over thoughts like these :
" What ! shall my mouth no more press woman's lips ?
My arms embrace no more her tender form ?
Shall I abandon kisses and sweet sighs,
Nor feel caresses which to mine respond ?
Shall I resign the solace sweet of youth,
The glowing raptures of supreme delight ?
And why ?   Because some misanthropic priests

And dull fanatics cry upon me, Shame !
My soul, indignant, spurns the hateful thought !"
Then, throwing off restraint and modesty,
He for some few sad months plunged deep in sin,
Revelled in pleasures of unhallowed love,
And deemed such pastime, could it but endure,
The full perfection of all human bliss.
But soon he found that sin upon the soul
Acts as doth poison on the heart and blood ;
And in his hours of pain and lassitude
Trembling he stood, aghast at thoughts of death.

Sin and Sorrow.

"Why with terror do I start ?
  Why consumes thus care my heart ?
    E'en when all around rejoice,
      Conscience speaks, I hear her voice !
  Need I stop to question whether
  Sin and sorrow go together ?

" If pleasure lures I rouse me up,
  With mad joy snatch her Circe cup ;
    Regardless whom it may displease,
      Rashly drain it to the lees !
  Soon, too soon, pangs tell me whether
  Sin and sorrow go together !

"Who will allay these racking pains,
  Wash out the poison from my veins,
    Soothe me to rest, assuage my fears,
      Bring back sweet peace, and dry my tears ?
  Hard to me the lesson whether
  Sin and sorrow go together !

" Canst Thou, O CHRIST ?   Wilt Thou do this ?
  Pardon my sins, their dread dismiss,
    Give me Thy grace, and by Thy might
    My spirit to Thyself unite ?
  Aided thus, need fear I whether
  Sin and sorrow go together ? "

VI.

CALLING ON GOD.

THE mind of MONICA had long foreseen
    The dangers into which her son might fall,
And had for him arranged, with his consent,
An advantageous, honourable marriage
With a young girl, whose budding charms required
But two short years to ripen ; but alas!
AUGUSTINE now o'erwhelmed her with dismay,
For he both sinned and gloried in his sin !
He had adopted as his own the creed
Of EPICURUS, and declared one day
In confidence unto his nearest friends,
That for the chief of all philosophers
He EPICURUS held.   " Suppose," he said,
" We were immortal, had the faculty
To live in ceaseless pleasures of the sense,
And had no terror lest they should be lost,
Should we not then be truly happy men ?
And what besides could we as men require ?"
But though ALYPIUS loved and honoured him,
He could not from his mouth such creed accept,
But back recoiled in horror, and became
Himself for once the teacher of his friend.
His own young life was one of purity,
Which made his nature's lower principles
Subservient to the higher, and his flesh

Yield to the dictates of the soul within;
Nor could privation, toil, or any ill
Which tortures the frail body, win from him
A groan or sigh.   Despising luxury,
He walked barefooted through the winter's snow,
And gloried in his conquest over pain.
Now full of tenderness he struggled hard
To do a friendly office to AUGUSTINE,
And wean him from his habits sensual.
Therefore, although his face with crimson glowed
To talk on such a topic, he began
With mild remonstrances, and begged his friend
To try a life as chaste as was his own.
He urged on him the dignity of man,
The priceless worth of unstained purity,
And placed before his eyes, in contrast plain,
The low debasement of lasciviousness.
"Say," he exclaimed, "is there in all the world
Aught we call pleasant, but it brings to us
In future days a grateful afterthought,
Except this lust, whose memory is shame.
A dog, a swine, a fly may do such acts,
And care no more about them; but can we?
Do they not taint the blood, degrade the mind,
Harden the heart, and leave their votary
Only the rubbish of a ruined life,
The mouldering fragments of good gifts misused?"
This and much more ALYPIUS would say,
With frequent iteration; but although
He used no higher argument, nor named
The heinousness of sin by GOD abhorred,
Yet was AUGUSTINE with contrition moved.
He made confession that his life was wrong,
But urged in his excuse that he had now

Become by length of habit so confirmed
In loose indulgences which he despised,
That all attempts to break his sinful bonds
Must needs be useless. "No," he would reply,
"'Tis an infirmity I cannot cure;
Others, like you, that greatness may achieve,
But I, by this disorder of my flesh,
Which is so sweet to me, am firmly bound:
So must I drag through life my heavy chain,
Dreading the hand which fain would set me loose,
For fear its friendly touch might vex the sore."
He dreamt not that he had within him powers
That would develope in heroic strength,
But felt as doth an Indian sybarite,
Who, fed on cates, in gorgeous garments clad,
Reclines on silken cushions, fanned by slaves,
Cooling his thirst with draughts of sweetened wine,
And hath no energy to will or move;
Yet if he do but leave the sultry plains
In which he slumbers out his useless days,
And in the pure air of the mountain heights
Freshness inhale, will feel his limbs expand
With manly strength, unknown to them before,
And, to his own amazement, may perform
Feats which before impossible appeared!
AUGUSTINE, through his friend's remonstrances,
And those of deeper urgency which came
From MONICA, who never ceased her care,
Began to rouse himself, and tried once more
To be no longer passion's loathsome slave.
Preparing thus his heart, by purity,
To be a dwelling fit for holy thoughts,
He mused on the immensity of GOD,
The microscopic littleness of man,

Great only in unbounded selfish pride ;
Then, starting at his insignificance,
Dreaded lest he might in presumption fall,
Should he, in spite of his unworthiness,
Venture with lips unclean to speak GOD'S name.
Yet, taking heart at the encouragement
Given to all who to their Maker come,
And offer prayer or praise, he let his voice
Shape into words like these his fervent thoughts : [1]—

"Great art Thou, LORD, and worthy of our praise !
  Great is Thy power, Thy wisdom infinite ! [2]
Man would to Thee his adoration raise,
  Though of Thy creatures but a portion slight,—
Man who, by his mortality within,
Beareth about a witness of his sin.

"A witness also that Thou dost with might
  Resist the proud.[3] Yet man to praise Thee wills,
Though of Thy creatures but a portion slight :
  Through Thee, to praise Thee, real delight him
    fills,
Because Thou mad'st us for Thine own to be ;
Restless our heart until it rest in Thee !

"Grant me, O LORD, to know and comprehend
  Whether man turned to Thee should first of all
Call on Thee, or make praise to Thee ascend ?
  Should know Thee first, or first upon Thee
    call ?
But who unknowing calls ? If so, one's lot
Might be to call Thee that which Thou art not.

[1] Appendix, Note E ; Augustine's *Confess.* lib. i. c. 1, 2.
[2] Psalm cxlv. 3, cxlvii. 5.   [3] 1 Peter v. 5.

"Or wouldst Thou men should call, that know they
    may?
  But how shall be their calling on Him made
In whom they have believed not?   How shall they
    In Him believe without a preacher's aid?[1]
Who seek the LORD shall praise Him ; for who seek
Shall find, and, having found, His praises speak.[2]

"Thee will I seek whilst on Thee, LORD, I call,
    And will thus call, believing ; for to me
Hast Thou been preached.   On Thee, Thou LORD of
    all,
    My faith now calls—faith given to me by Thee ;
Through Thy Son's incarnation first inspired,
And through Thy preacher's ministry acquired.

"But what mode shall I, GOD to call, embrace,
    Who is my GOD and LORD, since doing so
I call Him in myself?   What fitting place
    Is there in me that GOD therein should go,
Who made both heaven and earth?   LORD, is there
    aught
Within me to contain Thee when thus sought?

"Do heaven and earth, Thy creatures, wherein me
    Thou madest also, Thee in them contain?
Or since what is would not without Thee be,
    Does all that is contain Thee?   Since, again,
I am, why ask Thee in me to repair,
Who would not be wert Thou not present there?

"I am not yet in hell, but there Thou art,
    And Thou art present if to hell I go ;[3]

---

[1] Rom. x. 14.   [2] Psalm xxii. 26.   [3] Psalm cxxxix. 7, 8.

I should not live, O GOD, in life bear part,
    Unless Thou in me wert ; nor should life know
Did not my very life in Thee subsist,
From whom, by whom, in whom all things exist.[1]

" Thus be it, LORD, e'en thus !   Whither shall I
    Call Thee in me, when I in Thee abide ?
Whence to me canst Thou come ? Where, far or nigh,
    Beyond both heaven and earth, shall I then hide,
That there in me my GOD may come to dwell,
Who said, ' The heavens I fill, and earth as well ' ? "[2]

[1] Rom. xi. 36.   [2] Jer. xxiii. 24.

SAINT AUGUSTINE.

———•———

BOOK IV.

THE CONVERSION.

BOOK IV.

———

I.

WORLDLY DISCONTENT.

"ALYPIUS," said AUGUSTINE once in grief,
    "Thou friend in whom my spirit can confide,
To ease its load and give its pain relief,
    Mine inward torments do not thou deride
If I disclose them ; rather strive with care
To cure a secret sore to thee laid bare.

"My heart is swoln with sullen discontent
    At the unjust allotment with which GOD
Hath to mankind His gifts unequal sent,—
    Giving this man a staff, to that a rod ;
Heaping abundance on one favoured head,
But to another grudging daily bread.

"See yonder courtier, who drives proudly by
    With four white horses, which his menial leads,
And scans us angrily with haughty eye,
    Lest we should spoil the prancing of his steeds ;
In golden chariot is his stately seat,
While we on foot must trudge through mud and heat.

" That silly scion of a haughty stock,
    With vacant mind in offuscated brain,
Stands on prosperity as on a rock ;
    Changes of fortune threaten him in vain !
To wealth and grandeur is the booby born,
Yet through his life will nothing earn but scorn.

" A hundred slaves attend to do his will,
    Honour and rank cast lustre o'er his life ;
Daily of choicest cates he eats his fill,
    His nights are solaced by a beauteous wife ;
Unruffled are his pleasures, he has learned
To spend that gold the toil of others earned.

" His marble palace in its gilded halls
    Contains of precious things a wondrous store ;
What glowing pictures decorate his walls !
    What godlike statues strike the soul with awe,
In his majestic parks and gardens trim !
Though the world wail, its clamours reach not him.

" Sweet airs of music from the Lesbian lyre
    Around his ravished senses softly play ;
Of silken raiment is his gay attire,
    Voluptuously he dallies with the day ;
Nor he alone, but thousands do the same,
Born, like himself, to opulence and fame.

" But I, less favoured, live a life of toil,
    Wear coarser garments, eat of humbler food ;
Desires ungratified my best days spoil,
    Modest my dwelling, and my chamber rude :
I cannot with my time do what I list ;
Upon a scanty stipend I subsist.

" No horses, slaves, or chariots are mine ;
    No loving wife converts to bliss my pain ;
In sadness and privation I repine,
    A lot so hard excites my own disdain !
What good to us do talents rare supply,
If in neglect we live, and in want die ?

"Oh that some happy chance would cast on me
    A splendid fortune and a princely name,
Landed possessions, with nobility,
    Exalted rank, and old ancestral fame !
That I in grander scenes might then take part,
And gratify the longings of this heart ! "

ALYPIUS listened to his much-loved friend
    In blank astonishment, and heard his voice
Express fond wishes truth could not commend,
    Misled by thinking he could e'er rejoice
In pleasures by the vulgar mostly sought,
Or be content with joys by money bought.

"What !" said he to AUGUSTINE ; "thinkest thou
    Sordid delights could ever satisfy
The nobler yearnings which inspire thee now,
    Or chain to earth thine aspirations high ?
Were all thou longest for on thee bestowed,
Sad would thy soul be, heavy thy life's load !

" One flash of light which genius can impart,
    One grand conception in a wise man's head,
One gentle movement of a loving heart,
    Or tear for woe of others kindly shed,
Is worth ten thousand times such meaner things
As rank of princes and the pomp of kings !

" The strength of vigour spiritual is love,
　　And love to life gives dignity and worth ;
Love with emotions great the heart can move,
　　Love lifts to heaven the humbler things of earth ;
Love lives when beauty dies, love soothes pain's smart,
Ennobles joy, and purifies the heart !

" Grant that yon scornful noble, who just now
　　Shot like a falling star across our eyes,
Is richer than thyself and me,—wouldst thou
　　Have with his wealth the failings we despise,
His narrow intellect, his feeble brain,
His selfish vices, and his projects vain ?

"Wouldst thou exchange with any wretch like him
　　Thy tender feelings for his heart of stone,
Thy insight clear for his perceptions dim,
　　Thy love for his, which heeds himself alone ?
Estates when large bring troubles which annoy :
Let other men possess and us enjoy !

" Better, far better art thou in a state
　　To which no affluence brings corruption's taint,
Where no ambition tortures thee with hate,
　　Envy is absent, and temptations faint,
Than if thou hadst what worldly wealth contains,—
A heap of treasure with a load of pains ! "

" True, true ! " AUGUSTINE cried.　" I own thee right !
　　No more my voice unjust complaints shall raise.
'Tis shame in luxury to seek delight ;
　　Contented with my lot, its worth I praise ;
Henceforth I render, as I kiss the rod,
Good-will to man, and gratitude to GOD ! "

II.

WHAT IS EVIL?

AUGUSTINE ceased not now to meditate
    On GOD, unto whose kingdom, by slow steps,
His feet, delayed so long, at last approached.
Time, which in this world dominates o'er all,
But which Eternity will swallow up,
Was soon to bring forth fruits then unforeseen.
Great are Time's conquests over strongest wills!
They are but poor philosophers who think
Eternity is elongated Time;
For Time is a created thing of GOD,
With no existence recognisable
Except in minds created: it will cease;
The Future then be one great Present tense![1]
Time is the very breath of human life,
But of Eternity an incident;
It once was not, and once shall cease to be.[2]
AUGUSTINE craved for something yet unknown:
He could not live without some sort of creed;
The vacuum in his heart must be filled up
By some belief, however false and vain.
Therefore, when other men were sound asleep,
He, as his wont for years before had been,

---

[1] Augustine, *Op.* iv. 6. c., 839 A.
[2] Augustine's *Confess.* lib. xi. c. 13.—Dr. Pusey's Preface to *The Confessions*, Lib. of the Fathers, vol. i. p. xxvi.

Observed the planets and the shining stars,
Trying by methods of Astrology
To gain foreknowledge of events to come.
He read, with half-credulity, the books
Of Divination, and essayed to solve
Problems too hard for their pretentious lore.
He calculated his own horoscope
And that of others, to forecast their lives ;
But soon, by observations nice, and facts
Carefully gathered from the most adept,
Discovered the imposture of an art
Which makes the ruling star at time of birth
Determine if the child beneath it born
Shall thrive or fail, and gives a like career
To ESAU and to JACOB !   This result
NEBRIDIUS hastened by his sharp disdain
Of the whole art, as something plainly false.
But serious warnings more prevailed, erst given
In earlier days at Carthage from the mouth
Of old VINDICIAN, a wise, bright man
And good physician, who when but a youth
Had made Astrology and Divination
The business of his ever active life ;
But finding them a lottery of chance,
Had cast the whole aside, and been content
To work less wonder, but to do more good
As a disciple of HIPPOCRATES.

Such were the trifles which amused the mind
And occupied the leisure of AUGUSTINE,
While a great crisis hung above his head ;
And he played with them, as a child might play
With toys and flowers.   He long had shaken off
The rags and tatters of his old belief,

Whose doctrines yet command in various forms
The faith of Eastern nations, and had sought
A refuge among those who gravely taught
That nothing can be known with certainty,
And had made unbelief itself their creed !
CARNEADES was founder of this sect,
Which called itself the NEW ACADEMY :
He and his chief disciples taught mankind
That nought external is by us perceived,
Nor can the faculties of man attain
More than subjective probability ;
That nothing therefore can be understood,
Nor ought, for certain truth, to be believed :
Yet they professed throughout their lives to seek
For truth's similitude ; but as they all
Confessed they knew not truth itself, 'tis clear
They could not even its similitude
By any token recognise, when found !
AUGUSTINE did not long remain content
With creed so vain ; nor was he ignorant
That not the striving after, but possessing
Truth makes man happy, and that happiness
Is found in GOD alone ; for only he
Who is in GOD, and in whom GOD doth dwell,
Is worthy to be thought a happy man.
But when he had dismissed the heresy
That evil as a principle had lived
Like GOD eternally, this question next
Disturbed distractingly his brooding mind—
Whence then did evil come ?—Nor could he rest,
Or give his searching intellect repose,
Until that problem should by him be solved.
Free-will, some told him, was the source of ill,
And GOD's just judgment caused our suffering ;

But this could not convince him at that time.
For is not pain an evil?   Did not pain
Exist before man's evil will did wrong?
Was there not death already, ere man's sin
Brought death into the world?—a penal death!
Not death which is the solacer of pain,[1]
The sweet relief of speechless agony,
The hope of the afflicted, nature's balm,
The weary pilgrim's rest, desired so long;
But an avenging, endless chastisement,
The heritage of sin when unatoned!
Whence then was evil?   Who created it?
Was it the Devil?   Whence then did he come,
Seeing the good Creator angels made
With their whole nature good?   All creatures sure
Were good in the beginning, nor was aught
Of evil then.   How therefore did it come?
This problem tortured him by day and night.
In after years he tranquillized his mind
By thoughts like these: The angels have, as we,
Free-will, and they while they still clave to GOD
Were good and happy; but when any turned
From GOD to something else, and clave to that,
Then, though the thing they sought was itself good,
There was deflection, and the choice then made
Of the inferior for the true Supreme
Was the first fault, from which all evil rose,

---

[1] In his Epistle to Cæcilianus (*Epist.* cli.) Augustine says: "What harm can result from the death of the body to men who are destined to die some time? Or what do those who fear death accomplish by their care but a short postponement of the time at which they die? All the evil to which mortal men are liable comes not from death, but from life; and if in dying they have the soul sustained by Christian grace, death is to them not the night of darkness in which a good life ends, but the dawn in which a better life commences."

And pride, else quite impossible, began.[1]
Man, being tempted, fell : not so the angels ;
They fell without temptation, and must bear
For greater sin a greater punishment.
Sometimes on themes like this he pondered long :[2]
The holy, blessed angels of the LORD
Know what they are in present happiness ;
But have they a foreknowledge of the state
To which they may in future time be changed ?
If so, how was it ever possible
For SATAN, even when an angel good,
To have enjoyed complete felicity,
Knowing, as in such case he must have known,
His great transgression, which would one day come,
And his prodigious, endless punishment ?
At other times he sought to reconcile
Free-will in man with GOD'S omnipotence ;
But in his efforts met but small success,
For who shall things inexplicable solve ?
Man's will is free ; yet how can it be free
When circumscribed by hard necessity ?
It may select an object of its choice
Just as it likes, and round the same revolve,
As doth the moon when with the earth she moves ;
But to the object is the subject bound.
And as the moon is by the earth compelled

---

[1] Augustine in his Epistle to Dioscorus (*Epist.* cxviii.) says : "The first sin, *i.e.* the first voluntary loss, is the mind rejoicing in its own power, for it rejoices in something less than would be the source of its joy if it rejoiced in the power of God, which is unquestionably greater." In an earlier passage in the same Epistle he says, speaking of men : "When the mind is elated with joy in itself, as if in good which belongs to itself, it is proud." In his work on Free-will he says : "Pride produces averseness to wisdom ; whence, however, this averseness, but that he whose good is God would be his own good to himself, as God is to Himself?"—*De Lib. Arb.* iii. 24.

[2] Augustine, *Opera, Epist.* lxxiii. sec. 7.

To gyrate round her orbit ; and the earth,
So potent with the moon, is by the sun
Drawn through attraction ; and the sun itself
Forms of another universe but part,
Unto whose laws it is subordinate :
So must created will—though free to act
Within the narrow limits of its scope
(Except when paralyzed, because of sin)—
Submit to be controlled by higher laws ;
For GOD'S will over all things must prevail !
Questions like these disturbed AUGUSTINE'S rest,
And raised a tempest in his troubled soul,
Which was devoured by dread lest he should die,
And leave unsolved such points insoluble !
His eager eyes round all creation swept,
And in the sight of his impassioned spirit
He set the universe, the sea, earth, air,
All mortal beings, heaven, the dwellers there,
The blessed angels, and the saints of GOD ;
He viewed them in the mass and in detail,
And found them, in the whole and every part,
Environed, interpenetrated, filled
With the Creator's presence, plainly seen !
Whence then came evil ?—This he could not tell.
And yet, though baffled in his search, he found
Some truths worth knowing ; for he recognised
That GOD existed, though by fools denied ;
Hath substance which unchangeable remains ;
That He takes care of and doth judge mankind.
Moreover, growing wiser at this time,
He now believed that GOD, in CHRIST His Son,
And in the Holy Scriptures, hath set forth
The way of man's salvation to that life
Which is the life to be when this is done.

Yet was no answer found to his demand,
Whence cometh evil? Therefore arrogance
Gnawed at his heart, which teemed with pangs hid
    close
In the deep silence of his inward soul;
Nor to his friends his agony he told:
But when, in after years, he understood
What meant the heavings which disturbed his breast,
The gnawings and the sighings of his heart,
He recognised that pain, when sharp and keen,
May teach humility to haughty minds,
And be an instrument that brings forth good.
Great was the conflict in his soul! He looked
Outwards upon the world, and hoped to find
In its phenomena solutions clear,
And learn therefrom the secret things of GOD;
But looked without success. Then next he turned
His eyes within himself; what there he saw
Let his own words, addressed to GOD, explain:[1]

" Admonished to return to mine own heart,
    I entered there; for, as Thou wast my guide,
I could do this, by help Thou didst impart:
    I entered, and my soul's eye there descried,
Above itself, above my mind's own height,
The lofty presence of all-changeless Light!

" Not common light which eyes of flesh can see,
    Nor of such kind, though filling wider space,—
Light rendered clearer by intensity,
    And by mere magnitude pervading space;—
Not such I saw, but Light of other sheen,
Distinct from every species elsewhere seen.

    [1] Appendix, Note F. Augustine's *Confess.* lib. vii. c. 10.

"But not above my spirit was that Light,
　　As oil o'er water spreads, o'er earth the sky;
Yet than myself 'twas loftier, for its might
　　Created me, and I did lower lie
Because made by it.　He who truth doth see
Knows this, and knowing knows eternity!

"Love knows it also.　O eternal Truth!
　　True Love, beloved Eternity!　O Lord,
By day and night I sigh for Thee in sooth:
　　When I first knew Thee, Thou didst grace accord
What I beheld as true to recognise,
But not to know myself, who used these eyes.

"Thou didst my glances weak beat to the ground,
　　Fiercely within me shining, and I shook
With love and terror; for myself I found
　　Far off from Thee, whom I had erst forsook,
And in a region all unlike to Thine:
But then I heard, from loftiest realms divine,

"Thy voice thus speak: 'I am the bread of men:
　　To manhood grow, and thou shalt on me feed,
But shalt not me assimilate, as when
　　Thou eatest food for flesh; for thou indeed
Shalt into me be changed.'　Then I began
To know how Thou, for sin, dost chasten man.

"My soul Thou mad'st to waste away apace
　　As doth a spider.　Is then truth, I said,
Nothing, because in no fixed finite space,
　　Nor through space infinite, it lies outspread?
Then didst Thou, calling from the distant sky,
Thy great name, 'I AM THAT I AM,' reply!

" I heard as only hears the heart, nor more
    Had room for doubt ; and easier would it be
That I should heap up reasons by the score
    To doubt my life, than doubt the certainty
That TRUTH exists, which plainly is surveyed,
When understood by things which have been made." [1]

    [1] Rom. i. 20.

III

PLATO AND ST. PAUL.

WHILE thus AUGUSTINE in dejection pined,
    Chewing the cud of undigested thoughts,
There came into his hands a little book
Written by PLATO, which had some years been
Translated from the Greek by VICTORIN,
Whose work and the example of whose life
Were destined to bear fruit of precious worth !
AUGUSTINE'S mind, as he perused the book,
Seemed to perceive each page diffuse around
The sweetest perfumes of Arabia Felix,
Which in his senses kindled burning fire.
He found enchantment in its wisdom pure,
In thoughts profound which soothed and charmed
    his soul.
And from that hour all human greatness, power,
Desires for glory, dreams of worldly bliss,
Lost their dominion o'er him, and looked poor
In the bright light which gleamed before his eyes.
He saw, or thought he saw, obscurely shown,
That PLATO had a knowledge of the truth
That the Divine Eternal Word or Logos
In the beginning was, and was with GOD,
Made all things, and without Him was nought made ;
But that the human soul is not that light
Which lighteth all which cometh in the world,

Though bearing witness to it.   Yet AUGUSTINE
Read not in PLATO that the Word of GOD
Was here made flesh, and dwelt with mortal men ;
Nor aught of CHRIST'S humiliation deep,
Or glorious resurrection after death ;
Therefore his mind remained dissatisfied.
He knew by science physical that GOD
Is the Creator of an universe
Governed by laws, whose sequence hath no change,
Though individually terrestrial things,
As well as persons, alter every hour.
These laws, by GOD established from the first,
And called the Laws of Nature by some men,
Who by that phrase would gladly GOD ignore,
Inexorable are !   Therefore the man
Who shall the least of them infringe, must bear
The penalty imposed on such an act.
All reparation is impossible
Where Nature reigns, for force, when exercised,
Persists for ever ; every act we do
Outlives us, and its consequences still
After our deaths roll onwards without end.
As Nature is, so too is Nature's GOD !
Therefore when man, by disobedience
To laws by Him imposed, committed sin,
There was no remedy that could be found
In the established order of the world :
Hence the whole human race, in sin involved,
Had perished irretrievably, unless
A power as great as that which all things made
Had by a method of omnipotence
Evolved, from boundless love, a wondrous plan
For ruined man's salvation, who, thus helped,
Hath been redeemed,—a feat impossible

K

Except by One Almighty and Divine !
AUGUSTINE therefore, even when misled
By error, clung tenaciously to CHRIST,
By whom alone could sinful man be saved
From penalties which else must follow sin ;
Nor could he be content with any book
In which the name of CHRIST was nowhere seen.
Hence PLATO ceased to please his fancy long,
And he, in search of something of more worth,
Perused again the writings of ST. PAUL.
Then saw he all the things, once deemed too hard
And contradictory to other texts,
Vanish away, to vex his soul no more ;
As he became accustomed to the style,
So often rude, discursive, and abrupt,
He found in the Apostle of the Gentiles
The noblest human teacher man hath known.[1]
At first a persecutor fierce was he,
But, struck to earth, fell down in mid career,
To hear from CHRIST'S own lips, whose face he saw,
Remonstrance and command. From that same hour,
Despising shame, privation, suffering,
Shipwreck, and chains, the violence of men,
The perfidy of friends, and fear of death,
He worked with energy, excelling ar
Other apostles. He was not content
To labour only for his countrymen,
But had a wider purpose, grander hope,
And sought to save the universal world !
He from humiliation's lowest depths
Passed through each separate stage which hath been
        trod
In Christian progress by the human soul ;

[1] Abbé Bugeaud, p. 341.

And, caught up into Paradise at last,
To the third heaven, in silent wonderment
Heard mystic words unspeakable by man,[1]—
Words which a man may venture not to breathe ;
And then, although condemned on earth to drudge,
No sigh or groan he uttered, but with faith
Fought the good fight, finished his work, and next
Bent down his neck to meet the headsman's sword.
Who can refuse ST. PAUL his confidence ?
For never could a man so true as he
Palter or feign or sanction any lie ;
Nor could an intellect as clear as his
Be made the silly dupe of knaves or fools !
The basis of his life was truthfulness !
His nature open, simple, plain, and bold ;
And when ST. PETER, his inferior
In knowledge, wisdom, courage, faith, and love,
Forsook, for fear of men, strict duty's path,
And wished upon the Gentiles to impose
A burden which he knew they should not bear,
ST. PAUL withstood him. Nothing DAVID wrote,
No, nor ISAIAH, nor beloved ST. JOHN
(Poet, apostle, highly privileged
On Jesus' bosom sad to lean his head
At the Last Supper, and in Patmos Isle
To write from visions the Apocalypse),
Doth in majestic thoughts or strength sublime
Excel ST. PAUL'S Epistles.[2] In them now
AUGUSTINE read to learn how needful were,
For the redemption of lost, fallen man,
The deep humiliation, pains, and death
Of the Incarnate Word, our Saviour CHRIST !
Nor these alone, but he perused as well

---

[1] 2 Cor. xii. 4.   [2] Abbé Bugeaud, p. 311.

The other Scriptures with new interest,
Commenced with trembling to rejoice in GOD,
Learnt there that GOD will not a troubled spirit,
A broken and a contrite heart, reject:
He read of One, lowly and meek in heart,
Who calls to all who labour, "Come to me,
And I will give you rest."   But how then come?
He heard the call, and saw the land of peace,
But could not reach it!   To attain the way,
He must receive direction in his course,
And found at last the man to give him aid.

IV.

SIMPLICIAN.

SIMPLICIAN was an ancient Milanese,
  Who from his earliest youth had worshipped GOD
With singular devotion, and had passed
A life renowned for Christian excellence.
Standing aloof from this world's vanity,
Too great to feel ambition, and too small
To be himself a cause of jealousy,
His days were marked by holiness and peace.
He was the model of a Christian priest.
But though he practised true humility,
Some great events threw lustre o'er his life ;
For by his hands was AMBROSE, his loved friend,
Baptized, and AMBROSE afterwards addressed
SIMPLICIAN as his father ! Yet the father
Succeeded to the son ; for when at last
AMBROSE was taken from this world, SIMPLICIAN
Was made Archbishop, full of grief and age.
Unto this venerable man of GOD,
Who had with AMBROSE oftentimes remarked
The piety of MONICA, with hopes
That she some day would find her prayers avail,
AUGUSTINE went, well knowing what rich stores
He had of choice experience, and could show
The path best fitted for his steps to trace.
To him his history AUGUSTINE told,

And all the troubles of his tortured mind,
To which SIMPLICIAN gave attentive ear.
But when AUGUSTINE mentioned he had read
Some books of PLATO and his followers
Through VICTORIN'S translations, the old priest
Expressed his joy, because their tendency
Leads to belief in GOD and in His Word.
Then, to persuade AUGUSTINE to be bold,
And learn to imitate a noble life,
He spoke of VICTORIN : " I knew him well
In days gone by.   An African by birth,
The learnèd VICTORIN obtained renown
By teaching rhetoric in Rome, and thus
His case bears close resemblance to thine own !
He had perused and pondered in his mind
The noblest writings on philosophy ;
Had the instructor been of senators,
And gained among them a repute so great,
That for his merits and to please his friends
A statue was, within the Roman Forum,
Raised to his honour.   He belief professed
In the divinities of Pagan Rome,
To whom the old nobility were still
Firmly attached.   With them he oft partook
In sacrilegious rites of heathen gods,
And, in the Forum, would maintain their cause
With lofty eloquence, 'midst plaudits loud.
But, at a later era of his life,
When age had calmed the tumult in his heart,
And early prejudice had lost its sway,
He, who read every work of interest,
Perused the Holy Scriptures carefully,
And in the depths of his capacious mind
Stored up their teachings with a silent tongue.

Convinced at last by study and by thought,
Which GOD'S grace made effectual in his soul,
He one day, in the closest confidence
Of friendship, whispered thus : ' Already now
Am I a Christian ! ' In reply I said,
' Until I see thee in the Christian's church
I cannot so esteem thee.' ' Do, then, walls
Make Christians ?' smiling answered VICTORIN,
And went his way ; but kept outside the church,
Fearing the enmity of Pagan friends,
Whose champion he, in years gone by, had been.
But waxing braver as his faith increased,
He one day unexpectedly appeared,
Exclaiming, ' Come ! go with me to the church ;
I wish to be a Christian ! ' There we went,
And he was soon baptized,—Rome wondering,
The Church rejoicing, and its enemies
Gnashing their teeth with rage which he despised ;
Nor did he shrink from public declaration
Of his new creed in sight of all the world,
Disdaining any private, secret mode,
Though such was offered him. When he appeared,
As is our custom, standing up on high
Upon a platform, JESUS to confess
In face of the whole Church, a whisper ran
Throughout the multitude assembled there,
Who joyed to see so great a proselyte ;
While shouts of ' VICTORIN ! ' repeated oft,
And echoed back again, proved how they prized
His fortitude and boldness. After that,—
When the apostate JULIAN ruled in Rome,
And made a law forbidding Christian men
To teach the liberal sciences, or train
Young men in rhetoric and eloquence,—

To persecution yielding, VICTORIN
Resigned the chair of his professorship,
Which gave him bread, went forth into the world,
To do and suffer for the cause of CHRIST ;
Nor for one instant felt irresolute
To bear his Master's cross, until he died !"
AUGUSTINE listened to this history
With interest, made deeper by the fact
That VICTORIN his predecessor was ;
But when he heard the sacrifice thus made
For true religion's sake, AUGUSTINE fired
With wish to imitate him.   When he left
To go back to his home, he sighed and sighed
To think how he, by his own will, was bound
As by an iron chain ; yet he resolved
To shake it off, not now, but presently !
He felt conviction of the truth, but longed
For some delay ere he acceptance made :
" Anon, anon !" he said ; " wait but a little ;
Not now, not now, but presently I come !"
And thus he stood, pausing irresolute,
As doth a naked boy in early spring
Beside a fresh, cool stream, in which he longs
To plunge and swim, but, being faint of heart,
Stands idly there to shiver on the brink.

V.

PONTITIAN.

THE wise SIMPLICIAN had merely told
   A simple story, used no argument ;
But this best helped what AMBROSE most desired.
The crisis, long delayed, would surely come !
After some days a friend of MONICA,
Her noble countryman PONTITIAN,
One of the Emperor's officers of rank,
By a like method brought about the end.

  Upon a day when all were from the house
Except AUGUSTINE and ALYPIUS,
PONTITIAN called, a visit there to pay ;
And as they talked, he on the table saw
A book AUGUSTINE had but just laid down.
He took it up, and found, to his surprise,
No work on eloquence, philosophy,
Or any theme its owner had to teach,
But PAUL'S Epistles ! Then PONTITIAN
Smiled on his friend, and testified delight ;
For he himself had been baptized long since.
AUGUSTINE having told him that the book
Was one which he had studied with much care,
PONTITIAN spoke of the Egyptian monk,
ST. ANTHONY, a poor unlettered man,
Who learned the Holy Scriptures by the aid

Of memory alone when they were read,
And had, by meditation hard and long,
Attained to understand them and expound.
He lived secluded in a desert cave,
Shunned every kind of human intercourse,
Passed all his days and nights in praise and prayer,
Disdaining to partake of sleep or food,
Except the scraps for sustenance required.
He thought to look on women was a sin,
Fled from them, though they greatly reverenced one
Of such austerity and holy life.
The strange example he in this way set
Had prompted thousands—men, youths, widows,
    maids—
To leave their homes, business, and families,
And in the desert, as poor hermits, dwell.
His imitators had become ere long
So many, that great cities, once much thronged,
Had but the rubbish left of citizens
To do the needful work of daily life,
Plough, sow, reap, spin, and learn the art of war,
To keep barbarian hordes at distance safe.
But then this desert-dweller, ANTHONY,
Gained so much reputation, that the world
Eager became to follow in his steps :
Among them some now canonized as saints,—
JEROME, for learning accurate renowned,
And for moroseness ; EPIPHANIUS
And EPHRAIM, with others of less note.
"An author of repute," PONTITIAN said,
"Hath written now *The Life of Anthony,*
Which Christians, with consent unanimous,
Declare a monument of piety !"
Whilst speaking thus of ANTHONY, PONTITIAN

Bethought himself of two old friends of his,
Who, through the mere perusal of that *Life*,
Had changed their own ; and thus he told their tale :
" At Trèves, in Gaul, beside the blue Moselle,
The Roman Emperor his court amused
With the Circensian games.   I, who was young,
And three companions, courtiers of high rank,
Went to some public gardens, which extend
Close to the city walls : we walked in pairs ;
And as one friend and I went on together,
The other two, while rambling, found a hut
In which dwelt certain Christians.   They sat down,
And one of them, to pass away the time,
Took up a book, *The Life of Anthony*,
And read some pages ; but, as on he read,
His bright eyes kindled, and the thought occurred
That he too might himself resign the world,
And pass his future days in serving GOD.
He looked towards his listening friend, and said :
' Tell me, I pray, what wish we to attain
By our exertions from the Emperor ?
What aim we at ? and wherefore serve we him ?
Can our best hopes at court rise any higher
Than to become an emperor's favourite ?
And in that prospect what is there not frail,
And plentiful in perils ?   Thus indeed
By perils we to greater peril come !
And when ?   Within what time do we get thither ?
But if I wish to be a friend of GOD,
At once I can, and lo, the time is now ! '
Then he perused again the little book,
Felt a great change pass through him inwardly,
And travailed in the pains of a new life.
The world fell from his eyes in flaky scales,

And waves of passion tossed about his heart ;
Then, having formed at last his firm resolve,
He spake thus to his friend : 'Loose have I burst
From our vain hopes ; GOD only will I serve :
Yes, from this hour and place will I begin.
But if thou likest not to imitate,
Oppose me not !'   His friend did not oppose,
But to him clave, and promised to partake
The glorious service and the rich reward.
When, then," PONTITIAN said, "my friend and I
Came to the hut to find and bring them home,
Reminding them the day was now far spent,
And urging quick return, they both declared
Their settled purpose, and requested us
Not to oppose if we refused to join.
But we bewailed ourselves because too weak
To make so great a sacrifice of self,
Congratulated them on their resolve,
And begged their prayers.   So with hearts lingering
Upon the earth, we to the palace walked ;
But they remained, with hearts fast bound to Heaven.
And their affianced brides, when the news came,
Also, as virgins, gave themselves to GOD."

VI.

THE CRISIS.

SUCH was the story of PONTITIAN,
 Which having told, he left ; but left behind,
Upheaving strongly in AUGUSTINE'S soul,
A tempest of contrition and of shame.
He could no longer turn his back upon
His selfishness and gross impurity,
Which looked him in the face, that he might see
How crooked, spotted, foul, and ulcerous
Was one who called himself Philosopher !
Long had he known the fact which met his eyes,
But made belief as if he saw it not,
Winked at it and forgot it.   But this time,
No such device being possible, he stood
A mute, repentant, self-confuted man !
Shaking with horror, shrinking in dismay,
He with a troubled mind and countenance
Turned round, and thus unto ALYPIUS spake :[1]
"What ails us ? What is this ? What didst thou hear ?
Behold, unlettered men start up and take
The heavens by storm, whilst we who vaunt ourselves
Upon our learning, being void of heart,
Wallow in flesh and blood ! Are we ashamed
To follow others who have gone before,
But feel no shame in taking not one step ?"

[1] *Confess.* lib. viii. c. 8.

ALYPIUS silently surveyed his friend,
And in his dewy forehead, burning cheeks,
Eyes which flashed fire, colour which came and went,
And in the thrilling accents of his voice,
Saw even more than what his words revealed.

A little garden was behind the house,
Secluded in the deepest privacy :
Thither AUGUSTINE rushed to breathe the air.
ALYPIUS followed close upon his friend,
Nor would forsake him in that painful hour.
In a far corner of this garden fair
They sat them down, and there AUGUSTINE rolled
In agony of mind, tearing his hair,
Beating his forehead, clasping round his knee
With his convulsive fingers, for he willed
To do such things, and did them ; but to make
A covenant with GOD, and to will that
With thoroughness and resolution firm,—
Not with a will half-minded, tost about,
Where one part rises as another sinks,—
He had not power to do ; yet to himself
With earnestness he said, " Now be it done ;
Be it now done ! " Yet as these words he spoke,
A horror, against which he vainly fought,
Held him in doubt, but could not master him,
Or drive him from the purpose in his mind.
Voluptuous female forms, as VENUS fair,
Of beauty ravishing and full of charms,
Floated before his eyes, plucked at his sleeve,
And whispered softly to his willing ear,
" What ! dost thou cast us off ? shall we no more,
No more be with thee ? see thee not again ?
But from the moment thou dost us renounce,

Is this and that unlawful, yea, for ever!"
About to leave, he lingered for one glance,
Felt doubtful of his strength to burst away,
And said within himself, as was his wont,
"Dost thou then think thou canst without them do?"
These words, erst said with firmness, came forth now
But weak and faint; then turning himself round,
He saw, as a conception of his mind,
The noble form of CONTINENCE, most chaste,
Serene, and gay, though free from levity.
She beckoned him to come, bade him not doubt,
And stretched forth to receive and to embrace him
Her holy hands, full of the multitudes
Of good examples, troops of men and maids,
Grave widows, aged virgins, children born
To her, a fruitful mother, through the LORD,
Her husband, in the New Jerusalem.
But when she saw AUGUSTINE hesitate,
She smiled upon him with derisive smile:[1]
"Canst thou not do," she said, "what these poor
　　youths,
These maidens can? Nor can they in themselves,
But rather in the LORD, who is their GOD:
He gave me unto them. Why dost thou stand
Within thyself, and thus not stand at all?
Now cast thyself on GOD, nor fear that He
Will take Himself away, that thou mayest fall.
Cast thyself on Him, fearless as a man,
And He will thee receive and will thee heal."
AUGUSTINE blushed, for still he heard the sound
Behind him of insidious whisperings,
Which held him in suspense. But CONTINENCE
Seemed thus to speak: "Stop fast thy very ears

[1] Augustine's *Confess.* lib. viii. c. 11. Note G in the Appendix.

Against thine unclean members of the earth,
That they who whisper may be mortified.
They tell thee of delights ; but not of such
As doth the law of GOD, thy Lord, allow!"
Thus in his heart a controversy waged
Of self 'gainst self, but no word yet he spake.
ALYPIUS, in silence, waited by.
AUGUSTINE next, after profoundest thought,
Drew from the very bottom of his soul,
And piled up in a heap before his eyes,
All his oppressive misery ; whereat
A storm arose within him, and a shower
Of tears rained down, as from a thunder-cloud ;
At which ashamed, but needing their relief,
He left ALYPIUS, to find a place
Where he alone might in seclusion weep.
ALYPIUS saw the tears and heard the sobs,
But as his mind divined AUGUSTINE'S wish,
He sat still, in amazement, where he was.
AUGUSTINE tottered with unequal steps
Deeper within the garden's leafy shade,
And there, beneath a fig-tree's spreading boughs,
Cast himself down, and gave full vent to tears.
Floods gushed out from his eyes, that they might be
A sacrifice acceptable to GOD ;
And unto GOD, who heard, he weeping spoke
Words inarticulate, which tried to say,
"And Thou, O LORD! how long—how long, O LORD!
Wilt Thou be angry?   Shall it be for ever?
Remember not our old iniquities!"
For still he felt that these yet held him fast ;
Therefore these words of sorrow he sent up
To GOD : "How long, how long?   Say, shall it be
To-morrow and to-morrow?   Why not now?

Why end not, from this hour, my sins unclean?"
Thus was he speaking, full of grief and tears,
In sharp contrition, bitter to his heart,
When lo! from the adjoining tenement,
Wherein the widowed MONICA abode,
He heard a child's voice sing aloud some words!
What voice? what child? 'Tis bootless to inquire.
We know that AMBROSE, to instruct his flock,
Had written solemn hymns and noble chants,
Which by their beauty and their novelty
Charmed every heart, and lived in every mouth;
We know that MONICA took great delight
To teach the youthful choristers to sing,
As once she taught ROMANIAN'S youthful son;
We know that words, melodious as a chant,
Sung by a little child in sweetest tones,
Fell then upon AUGUSTINE'S listening ears,
Turned his attention from his misery,
Calling it outwards, soothing every sense,
And calming the fierce tempest in his mind.
But whether the soft sounds his ears then heard
Came from a child or from some high-strung chord,
Touched by GOD'S hand within his swelling heart,
Cannot be told.   Suffice it to be known
That in those thrilling tones of harmony
He heard some words like these borne through the air:
"Take up and read; take up and read!"[1]   Till then
Never had words like these by him been heard!
Then instantly, with altered countenance,
AUGUSTINE rose, and wondering in his brain
What they could mean, interpreted them thus,—
That by GOD'S will he should the Scriptures take,
Open the book, and see what met his eyes.

[1] 'Tolle lege, tolle lege.' *Confess.* lib. viii. c. 12.

He, in the *Life of Anthony*, had read
How that that saint, while yet a careless youth
Of less than twenty summers, coming once
Into a church in which was being read
The Holy Gospel, felt an admonition,
As if these words, then heard, were said to him :
" Go hence, and quickly all that thou hast sell ;
Give to the poor, and thou shalt then in heaven
Treasure possess ; and come and follow me." [1]
By those few words, as by an oracle,
Was ANTHONY converted unto GOD. .
AUGUSTINE shortly walked back to the place
Where he had left ALYPIUS ; for there
He had laid down beside his wondering friend
ST. PAUL'S Epistles, when he went away.
He seized them, opened, and in silence read
The sentences on which his eyes first fell ;
Wherein the Romans solemnly are warned,
" That not in chambering or wantonness,
Nor yet in strife or envying they should live :
But the LORD JESUS CHRIST now put ye on ;
Nor make provision for the flesh, that ye
Thereafter may the lusts thereof fulfil." [2]
He read no more, nor further would he read,
Nor needed so to do ; for instantly,
As by a light serene, within his heart
All doubts and darkness were dispelled away.
He shut the volume, marking first the place ;
Then to ALYPIUS with calm countenance
He told what had since leaving him occurred.
ALYPIUS asked that he might see the text
AUGUSTINE had thus found : he showed it him ;
Then looking lower on the sacred page,

[1] Matt. xix. 21.   [2] Rom. xiii. 13, 14.

ALYPIUS read and pointed out these words :
" Him that is weak in faith receive ; "[1] which he,
Applying to himself, then begged AUGUSTINE
To make excuse for one behind in faith.
But to ALYPIUS—a noble soul,
Prepared for what is good by being good,
And loving what is true—this incident
Gave strength ; and as he had no secret sins
To make strict self-denying practices
Appear repulsive, had heard AMBROSE preach,
Had searched the Scriptures long with candid mind,
And had in MONICA beheld displayed
The fairest pattern of a Christian's life,
He felt no great reluctance to embrace
A faith to him so suited.   Time alone
Was wanted for his cure.   He had observed
The agitation of AUGUSTINE's soul,
Not as an unconcerned spectator might,
But as well knowing that what shook one heart
Must move the other, and that both would swim
Or sink together in the surging waves.
Therefore—though still in doubt on some great points,
Yet yielding on the whole—he joined AUGUSTINE
In a firm resolution to devote
Their lives, possessions, labour, health, and strength
To the advancement of GOD's truth on earth ;
And from that hour the two, whom love made one,
Held on with constancy their chosen course.

[1] Rom. xiv. 1.

VII.

ALYPIUS TO GOD.

" ALMIGHTY GOD and HEAVENLY FATHER! deign
　　To look down on Thy servant who now prays ;
Forgive my doubts should they return again ;
　　Guide my weak feet, which stumble in Thy ways ;
　　Short is my span of life, Ancient of Days !
And, if not succoured now, when tempest-tost,
My barque must founder, and my soul be lost.

" Outside me is infinity of space,
　　Whose vastness strikes my wondering soul with awe !
Yet to such men as would behold Thy face,
　　And nearer to Thee, as they worship, draw,
　　Space is an antechamber, nothing more,
Unto Thy presence !　Where, then, stands the gate
Through which men pass to find Thee ere too late ?

" I did not ask, O GOD, this life of mine ;
　　'Twas Thy free gift ; yet must I use it well.
On one side open stand heaven's courts divine,
　　Upon the other yawn the jaws of hell !
　　The path I ought to choose I cannot tell :
Give me Thy aid, or my dark erring mind
May rush on ruin, and perdition find.

" The blessed angels who surround Thy throne,
　　And see Thy face, have no place left for doubt ;

They know by sight, truth has become their own,
    Temptation and delusion both shut out;
    But we on earth, who long to be devout,
Feel a hard strain, which faith and virtue tries,
And wander in an atmosphere of lies.

" A judgment by the angels we refuse:
    They would condemn at once man's guilty state.
Thine, Thine alone, O GOD! we humbly choose,
    For err Thou canst not; Thou dost feel no hate,
    Knowest our pleasures small, our sorrows great;
Love is Thine essence, mercy is Thy joy,
The hand which made will pause ere it destroy.

" Temptation, like a vulture o'er our heads,
    Swoops down to seize us for its struggling prey;
Thy choicest gifts, misused, become instead
    The means for our debasement and decay;
    Beauty itself is but a snare! nor may
The man who sins come pleading at Thy feet,
' The woman gave me of the tree to eat.'

" Hard lot! hard life! Why were we made at all?
    Why out of nothing didst Thou us create,
If we, when living, are to sin and fall?
    Better shouldst Thou our race annihilate,
    Than let us turn to wretches worthy hate,
Creatures of lust and crime, who but offend,
Doomed to be SATAN'S children in the end!

" Hark! voices summon me to praise and prayer
    Within Thy church; but why, unless to please

My friend, should I as worshipper go there?
    Here will I stay, and on my bended knees
      Make known my troubles, nor from tears will cease,
Until my burden, grievous to be borne,
Shall win at last Thy pity or Thy scorn.

" How, GOD! shall I, who am a feeble man,
    Stricken in doubts and hardened by distrust,
Accomplish feats which others bolder can,
    Doctrines accept which zealots say I must,—
    Believe that GOD, Thy Son, our weeds of dust
Put on as flesh, and lived upon this earth,
Handled and seen, as one of human birth?

" That it to truthful men seemed so to be,
    Who then recorded fond mistakes believed,
Is something comprehensible to me;
    Sires next their sons would teach what they received,
    And thus the Church's work be half achieved.
But though Thou shouldst consume me inch by inch,
I scorn from reason and its use to flinch.

" I am a pencilled ray of reason's light,
    Environed by the gloom of darkness sheer;
What I believe must shine by that ray bright,
    Be to my senses plain, my judgment clear,
    And tested without prejudice or fear:
I would prefer a thousand deaths to die,
Rather than, terror-struck, accept a lie!

" Yet will I not, as an audacious fool,
    Affirm the little I can see is all!

Reject Thy teachings with presumption cool,
   Highest philosophy my madness call,
   Shutting mine eyes to what must soon befall ;
In wisdom try to match myself with Thee,
Or with my fingers span infinity!

" The light I see by hath in Thee its source,
   And all I have is but Thy gracious gift ;
From Thee proceed my intellect and force :
   Therefore to Thee will I mine eyes uplift
   With reverential awe, nor wildly drift
Into confusion worse than chaos old,
Led by no guide but rashness ever bold.

" Thy thoughts are not like ours, nor is Thy plan ;
   The way which we would choose is not oft Thine :
We deal with finite things as best we can ;
   Thy methods, like Thy nature, are Divine.
   What wonder if Thy will then should combine
Incongruous things, and by Thy heavenly might
The infinite and limited unite ?

" All things to Thee are possible !   This earth—
   A mass of molecules fashioned into form—
To Thy creation owes its wondrous birth,
   Its laws and being, motion, sunshine, storm :
   The breath and life-blood which my body warm
Have the same source ; all are by Thee upstayed ;
Thou out of nothing hast this something made.[1]

---

[1] Lucretius repudiates the notion that God ever created anything out
of nothing : "Nullam rem e nihilo gigni divinitus unquam " (lib. i. 150).
Augustine, however, says : "Nihil nascitur si non id operetur Deus"
(tom. iv. 1888 D).   "Creatura non Dei naturæ, sed de nihilo facta est"
(iii. 157 B).   "Creaturæ ex nihilo factæ, non de Deo" (viii. 783 D).
In his letter to Dioscorus (*Epist.* cxviii.) Augustine thus expresses himself :

" But what if that which we as something know,
   This universe of matter and of mind,
Be but ideas, which from Thy substance flow,
   And are, like Thee, eternal ?[1] We must find,
   Whilst we to Thy creations of all kind
Are in relation placed, that till Time end
All things on Thee and Thee alone depend.

" The atheist's dogma never could me please,
   That this great universe, with its fixed laws,
Is but a crystallizèd congeries
   Of atoms, self-existent,[2] which no cause
   Intelligent hath made ; nor do I pause
In casting forth as false, what some have said,
That life a function is of matter dead !

" Thou art the well of life, O GOD ! the source
   And origin of our vitality ![3]
From Thee all creatures take their active force ;
   When Thou withdraw'st Thyself they cease to
      be ;
   All things exist and live and move in Thee,—
Light, sound, and weight, ocean's resistless dash,
The spark electric and the lightning's flash.

" The mind infers that the one reason why things suffer loss, or are liable
to suffer loss, is, that they were made out of nothing ; so that their property of being, and of permanence, and the arrangement by which each
finds even according to its imperfections its own place in the complex
whole, all depend on the goodness and omnipotence of Him whose being
is perfect, and who is the Creator able to make out of nothing not only
something, but something great."

[1] Augustine, however, says : "Creatura non est de Deo consubstanti-
alis aut co-eterna" (iii. 157 C).

[2] Lucretius : "Animam ex atomis esse scribit." Augustine, *Opera*,
viii. 107 A.

[3] Ps. xxxvi. 9.

" Of Thy ideas small is the group we scan,
     But in them progress, as a law, seems plain :
Creatures to germs succeed, to brute beasts man,—
     Man, who on earth would as a tyrant reign,
     Supreme though wretched,—would with efforts
       vain
Strive to become life's centre, that his will
Should be the rule for others to fulfil.

" Thou workest hitherto :[1] CHRIST told us so ;
     And in Thy works Thy methods are displayed.
Just as men's thoughts, by an induction slow,
     Go step by step from where they last have stayed,
     From old creations are they new ones made.
When CHRIST five thousand men with five loaves
       fed,
He used existing loaves to make the bread.

" When Thou the Jews, that hard but sacred race,
     Didst add on to the family of man,
Their birth did not, as ADAM'S had, take place,
     But from two withered stocks their life began,
     And vital force through dried-up channels ran :
'Twas so with JOHN THE BAPTIST'S wondrous birth.
When CHRIST'S way to prepare he came on earth.

" Even when CHRIST took flesh it was the same !
     It was not made of tissues flashed anew
From elemental atoms, but it came
     From MARY'S womb, wherein as flesh it grew,
     And from her substance pure its increase drew.
Thy Spirit, working where the germ was laid,
From virgin-flesh CHRIST'S precious body made.

[1] John v. 17.

" How shall my soul, lost in bewilderment
    At what it cannot question or explain,
But which to look into it feels intent,
    In philosophic calmness sink again ?
    I had supposed most things to me were plain,
And by me understood ; but lo ! appear
Problems unsolved, where once I thought all clear !

" I, who have read the Scriptures with a mind
    Darkened by prejudice, disturbed by doubt,
Deaf to their teachings, to their beauties blind,
    Yearn now their inner meanings to find out,
    And will that task attempt, with purpose stout :
I would their secrets in my soul revolve,
Their truths discern, their hardest problems solve.

" O Heavenly Father ! teach me as a son ;
    Dispel the doubts which spring from human pride.
With all my soul I say, ' Thy will be done ! '
    Let me to that conform, be that my guide !
    JESU ! who once didst on this earth reside,
Return, and visit my poor aching heart,
Thy presence by Thy Spirit to impart.

" In the great flood of light which Thou must cast
    Within my soul when she shall hear Thy voice,
Reason may find its ray lose brilliance fast,
    Yet, through illumination new, rejoice.
    Behold, I wait ! My soul hath made her choice ;
I clasp Thy knees, and beg Thy help divine ;
Oh, save Thy servant, for his heart is Thine ! "

VIII

THE TRIUMPH OF MONICA.

THE widowed MONICA was deep in prayer
    In the seclusion of her humble room,
When thither came AUGUSTINE and his friend,
Good tidings to announce, and told her all !
She had been pondering on the Bishop's words,
Which had predicted, twenty years before,
That through her tears her son would yet be saved.
She had recalled her vision of the youth
Who erst had told her that the rule of faith
On which she stood, her son should stand upon :
But hope was sick by being long deferred ;
And if her trust in GOD had not been strong,
She had sunk down, and died in her despair.
The glorious career which she, when young,
Full of maternal pride in her bright son,
Had in imagination for him planned,
Had vanished long.   No more she looked to see
In him the splendid champion of the Church,
A priest of doctrine true and practice pure,
The arbiter of councils, prop of thrones,
A holy bishop, theologian sound,
Maintaining truth and quelling heresy ;
But, in her resignation to GOD's will,
She had come down to wishes of less height,—
Would gladly now have seen him plodding on

In the more beaten paths of human life ;
Seen him the husband of a happy wife,
With children clasping him around his neck,
Born of his flesh and in his faith bred up ;
One thriving in the world, of honoured name,
The first in some small section of mankind,
Famous on earth, a doorkeeper in heaven !
But now, when from his lips she heard the course
He had marked out, with will which would not change,
Heard him renounce for ever ancient sins,
The honours, glories, and delights of men,
Ambition, worldly ties, and vain desires,
She felt as if she bore him once again,
And in the travail of her tender soul
Passed from sharp agony to boundless bliss !
In the first fervour of her ecstasy,
She gave Him thanks who able is to do
Even above what we can ask or think,
Who had beheld her tears, heard all her groans,
And turned at last her mourning into joy.
Her soul swelled out in triumph as she now,
With exultation in her eyes, declared
The prophecy fulfilled, the vision true !
That night she sang and prayed, and prayed and sang,
To calm the rapid beatings of her heart,
Till with these words on her exulting lips
She sank to slumber, softly as a child :—

MONICA IN TRIUMPH.

" O swelling heart, which feel'st as thou wouldst burst,
          Be still, be still !
Wilt thou not calm ? Wilt thou not put to rest
          Thoughts which thee fill ?

Then let thine exultation have its vent,
      For 'tis GOD'S will.

" O mighty joy that leapest in my soul,
      Lift up thy voice !
To GOD give praise, who this hath brought about
      Of His free choice ;
And in His mercy, which transcends all hope,
      Rejoice, rejoice !

" O Thou who hearest prayer, and dost prayer grant,
      Give heed to mine!
Let the good seed which Thou this day hath sown,
      With power divine,
Grow every hour and strengthen ; for its life
      Is Thine,—yea, Thine ! "

SAINT AUGUSTINE.

———•———

BOOK V.

CASSICIACUM.

BOOK V.

—•—

I.

THE ALPINE VILLA.

THE noble VERECUNDUS of Milan,
   One of the richest of its citizens,
Was loved by all, and well their love deserved.
He for his wealth cared little, but thought much
Of science, literature, philosophy,
And of his friends who, like him, made such things
Their special study and supreme delight.
Beyond all else he prized exchange of thoughts
And social intercourse of man with man.
Few who knew VERECUNDUS knew if he
Were Christian, Pagan, or had no belief;
But all might know that on him lightly sat
Whatever as religion he professed.
His thoughts were chiefly fixed upon the world
In which he lived, nor heeded he much else :
The present, not the future, was his goal.
All his endeavours were to make this life
A time of social pastime, elegant,
Refined, and cheerful,—one which should exclude
From sight and memory, as troublesome,
The misery which looks us in the face,
And oft will linger near though bid to go.

M

He had been married to a Christian wife,
Though not himself a Christian, and he knew,
By the example of her love and truth,
How beautiful is piety of soul ;
But he would view it—as a connoisseur
Scans a fine picture by a master's hand—
With admiration, yet without a wish
To do himself the like.   His wife he loved
As the most precious jewel of his heart,
Whose worth he knew and valued.   Thus he lived
In the full noontide of prosperity,
A pleasant, intellectual epicure ;
Nor felt he troubled, though his wife and friends
Warned him that night must surely come at last
To change his sunshine into endless gloom.
He had a villa, Cassiciacum,
Which, at the distance of two easy days,
Stood on a mountain's side, whose base immense
Parted two lakes, and by its chestnut trees
Cast a deep shade to veil the summer's sun.
This Alpine villa, built of finest stone,
Arranged in nice proportions, was adorned
With stately porticoes and marble halls ;
Had eating chambers, darkened during day ;
Large baths constructed with consummate skill ;
And, as its greatest charm to studious minds,
A library with precious books well stored.
Luxuriant vines were festooned round the grounds,
Stretching from tree to tree, and on them hung
Delicious grapes, mantled with purple bloom ;
The fig-tree yielded shade and luscious fruit,
Whilst flowers of glorious hue rejoiced the eye ;
The light, pure air, which brought refreshment there,
Came cooled by Alpine snows, which clothed the sides

Of Monte Rosa, seen from heights above.
Stillness and solitude were undisturbed
In that choice region of sweet privacy,
Save by the lowing of the yellow steers
Which brought the golden harvests slowly home,
The chirping of the grasshopper, or song
Of birds which warbled in the thickets near.
On the adornment and the perfecting
Of this abode, to which he oft retired,
Had VERECUNDUS lavished wealth and taste,
To make the place an earthly paradise:
But though he loved its rural beauty well,
He loved still more the city of his birth,
Her spacious streets and splendid palaces;
For there he found, what most he prized on earth,
The conversation of instructed men,
And round his festive board, open to all,
Gathered the poet and philosopher,
The soldier hardened by the toils of war,
The sculptor, painter, rhetorician famed,
The subtle Greek from far Byzantium,
And every man for intellect renowned.
Surrounded thus, and living up the lore
Extracted from their lips, adding his own,
The honeyed treasure of a studious life,
He felt his bliss complete, and little cared
For rural joys, irksome by solitude.
Therefore, as soon as summer's heat was past,
He left his villa on the breezy hill
And back to Milan hurried, though the sun
Yet blazed resplendent in a cloudless sky.
For two whole years had he AUGUSTINE known,
And loved him with sincerity of heart.
Although his age mature was twice his friend's,

Their sympathies in equal course flowed on ;
Each to the other had without reserve
Disclosed his inmost thoughts on questions deep,
The hardest problems of philosophy ;
And VERECUNDUS hoped that with some help
He might himself acquire a fame as great
As any sage of the Academy,
Whose creed was unbelief, and wisdom doubt.
On his return to Milan he sought out
AUGUSTINE, to renew their old pursuits,
But found great change !   The fashions of the world
Charmed him no more; the pleasures of the flesh
Were put away as hateful or unclean ;
His former theories were broken toys;
His rhetorician's chair had been resigned,
And much of what was called philosophy
Had lost its former value in his eyes.
He had continued for the briefest space
To teach his class ; but every day his work
Felt more distasteful, and he had in prayer
Called upon GOD to grant deliverance.

THE RECOIL.

" GOD ! who canst grasp immensity,
    Reckon the stars, encircle space,
Yet dost, with deep intensity,
    Regard man's microscopic race ;

" To Thee alike are great and small,
    Substance to Thee casts shadow none ;
Thou hearest if an atom fall,
    Thy will when told at once is done.

"Kingdoms and empires weigh with Thee
  No more than doth the meanest wight ;—
Turn then Thy searching eyes on me,
  And in my weakness show Thy might.

"The work which late I loved so well
  Looks now repulsive to mine eyes ;
Shall I, for money, wisdom sell,
  And teach young lads to fashion lies?

"Shall I to labours condescend,
  Ignoble, wearisome, yet hard,
Which aim at victory for end,
  But truth and justice disregard?

"My soul rejects with strong recoil
  This strife of tongues, this war of words !
In mercy save me from a toil
  Which splits my shrivelled heart to shreds.

"Guide Thou me on Thy narrow road
  For the few days Thy will allots ;
Oh, ease my shoulder of this load,
  And free my hands from making pots !"[1]

Much vexed was VERECUNDUS at this change ;
To him his friend's conversion seemed a plague,
Which had but spoiled a great philosopher,
Ruined a stately, noble intellect,
And quenched its blaze in hopeless fantasy.
First, in his soul's exceeding bitterness,
He uttered caustic words in courteous speech,
Mixing remonstrance with entreaties kind,

[1] Ps. lxxx.

And striving, by his breath, the sparks to raise
Of an ambition only just put out.
"What!"—said he—"wilt thou barter foolishly
Immortal glory and exalted praise
For the mean prospects of a Christian's life?
A life of poverty and self-restraint,
Of vigils, watchings, fastings, prayers, and tears,
Fit for weak woman, not for lofty man!
Wilt thou desert a friend who loves thee well,
Abandon studies we together made,
Renounce the pleasures of congenial minds,
And treat as a delusive, vain conceit,
PLATO'S great thoughts and TULLY'S eloquence?"

AUGUSTINE listened with composure mild
To his friend's words, who warmly pressed his hand,
And gazing in his eyes with earnestness,
Looked for some sign that not in vain he spake.
"Fear not," AUGUSTINE said, "that we henceforth
Shall cease our mutual interchange of thought,
So sweet to both, nor think I can forsake
The study of philosophy in truth;
Old subjects we will stedfastly pursue,
But in a wider field, with brighter light.
Let us no longer sit, as PLATO says,
In a dark cave, beholding at its mouth
The passing shadows of reality;
But let us to the light of day go forth,
The light of truth, the light which GOD Himself
Reveals to them who ask Him; let us there,
By aid which He hath promised and will give,
Resolve the mysteries of human life,
Trace the real purport of man's history,
His origin divine, his fatal fall,

Seen everywhere in degradation vile,
And learn by what great scheme, which GOD alone
Could have achieved or planned, man yet again
May rise far nobler than he was before,
And be a blessed, happy saint in heaven!
Topics like these will give us ample scope
For talk and meditation, and will bring
Results less barren of reward for toil
Than speculations whose best end is doubt!"
Then in few words AUGUSTINE told his friend
What conflicts had long struggled in his heart,
What wretchedness had weighed upon his soul,
And the conclusion he had firmly formed.
"But do not think," he said, "that I shall act
From a mere impulse that may soon subside;
The baptism I covet to obtain
Will not on me for six months be conferred,
And the whole interval shall I devote
To study of the Scriptures, careful thought,
Unceasing prayer, and Christian practices—
But under the direction of no priest.
Myself, assisted by GOD'S Holy Word
And Spirit, if by grace unto me given,
Will test the groundwork of the Christian faith,
Study its doctrines, weigh its evidence,
And look on truth as GOD shall give me light.
Behold, as earnest of my stedfastness,
And proof that headlong haste impels me not,
I, after my conversion, still endured
For full three weeks the daily drudgery
Of teaching striplings how to wrangle best,
Though conscience sickened at the dreary task,
And, through enfeebled health, each word I spoke
Tortured my lungs, whose strength hath lately failed.

Right glad was I when to relieve me came
Vacation of the Vintage, and at last
I could withdraw for ever from a toil
Which felt like degradation. Now I go
To strict seclusion, with some much-loved friends,
Who there with me will ponder o'er the theme
On which depends the future of our lives."
"Go where?" said VERECUNDUS. "If thou goest
Far from the concourse of this busy town,
Go to the mountains, seek fresh air and shade ;
But where can such be found of finer kind
Than at my villa, Cassiciacum?
Go there, and take with thee thy troop of friends ;
Deem it thine own ; the house and all it hath
Are placed at thy disposal ; go at once !
Would I could with thee go, but business here
Keeps me in Milan."   Urgently he pressed
AUGUSTINE to accept the proffered boon,
Nor ceased until to importunity
AUGUSTINE said, "I go," and thither went.

Escaped from Milan's narrow, noisy streets
Unto the silence of an Alpine hill,
AUGUSTINE, when he came there, breathed again !
Within the many chambers of the house,
And in its spacious halls, reigned sweetest peace.
He paced the gardens, wandered through the groves,
Gazed from the terrace, whose commanding height
Gave prospect of the smiling vales below ;
Examined every tree, shrub, herb, and flower;
Watched every butterfly, whose gorgeous wings
Shone brilliantly with variegated hues,
Richer than gold, more azure than the sky.
He paused to hear the humming of the bees,

Which sucked out luscious honey from the flowers ;
Still more the warbling of the tiny birds,
Which at short intervals poured forth their song.
He breathed with eagerness the balmy air,
And watched each change of sunshine and of cloud ;
Then, lying prone upon the fragrant turf,
Beneath a chestnut's deep and ample shade,
He let the zephyrs play about his brow,
And in a dreamy state, half sleep, half wake,
Revelled in happiness before unknown !
Thus through some sultry hours, in leisure calm,
He idly trifled, wiser in such rest
Than if at work.   Then, leaning on his arm,
He looked around, gazed upwards on the sky,
And mused upon the varied incidents,
The errors wild, hard labours to no good,
Wayward caprices of the intellect,
And total disregard for years of GOD,
By which his life had chequered been so long.
He thought upon the patient watchfulness
And prayers of MONICA ; the mercy great
Of Him whose grace, at last made manifest,
Had saved him from the sins he thus confessed : [1]

" As a fit sacrifice, O GOD, now take
    Confessions unto Thee, which I proclaim
By action of that tongue which Thou didst make,
    And urgest to confess unto Thy name.
To all my bones Thy healing gifts afford,
And let them say, ' Who then is like Thee, LORD ? '

" Not that one who confesses doth Thee tell,
    As Thee instructing, what his motives are ;

[1] Note II in the Appendix ; Augustine's *Confess.* lib. v. c. 1, 2.

For no closed heart can eye like Thine repel,
　No human hardness can Thy hand debar :
All melts as Thou in love or wrath dost bid,
　And from the heat thereof is nothing hid.[1]

" Let my soul praise and truly thus love Thee,
　Mercies confess, and thus Thy praise resound ;
For from such praise cessation none can be :
　No silence in Thy whole creation round,
Nor in the spirit of all human kind,
Which turneth to Thee, speaking by the mind ;

" Nor in things living or corporeal,
　Which speak by minds which thereon meditate.
Thus soars in Thee our soul ethereal,
　Rising from weariness disconsolate,
On things Thou madest leaning, lest she fall,
And passing on to Thee who madest all !

" For with Thee is refreshment and true might,
　But restless evil men from Thee depart ;
They flee, but Thou dost keep them in Thy sight,
　Darkness dividing with such wondrous art,
That lo, all things—which also them include—
Are beautiful, though they be base and rude.

" How can such creatures do to Thee despite ?
　In what respect can they discredit throw
Upon Thy government, so just and right
　From heaven above to humblest things below ?
Whither fled they when flying from Thy face ?
Where undiscerned by Thee found they a place ?

[1] Ps. xix. 6.

"They fled to see Thee not, who saw them well ;
  Blind, they against Thee stumbled, for Thou ne'er
Thy creatures dost desert : wrongly they fell,
  Rightly were pained ; from mildness fled in fear,
Stumbling against Thy righteousness were caught,
And fell in paths whose roughness they had sought.

"They know not Thou art everywhere, art He
  Whom space cannot encompass, who alone
Art present e'en to them who far from Thee
  Remove.   Then let them turn to seek Thy throne ;
For not as they their Maker would evade,
Dost Thou forsake the creatures Thou hast made.

"See them now turned to seek Thee, when, behold,
  There art Thou in their hearts !—in every heart
Of them who to confess Thee shall make bold,
  Who cast themselves upon Thee in their smart,
And in Thy bosom let their tears fall fast,
After their rugged paths in life are past !

"Gently their tears Thou wipest, yet they weep ;
  For even tears to them now joy afford,
Since Thou, O GOD, whose counsels are so deep,—
  No man of flesh and blood, but Thou, O LORD,
Their Maker !—dost their ruins build again,
And art the consolation of past pain."

Thus mused AUGUSTINE, as in constrast strong
He viewed GOD'S goodness and the lives of men,
So careless and ungrateful, till they turn
To seek that goodness, and to find its worth.
But when he rose and walked thence to the house,
The recollection how he once had strayed,

An alien unto GOD for many years,
Struck with remorse his heart.   But the new change
Experienced now inspired him with delight ;
And, with his eyes upraised, his voice again
Spake unto GOD these breathings of his soul : [1]

" Beauty of all things beautiful ! who art
      So ancient and so new ! too late, too late
I loved Thee ; yet Thou wast within my heart,
      Whilst I, outside, sought Thee beyond its gate,
And, like a shapeless monster, in despair
Crashed through that beauty Thou hadst made so fair.

" With me Thou wast, but I was not with Thee ;
      Things which, if not in Thee, were not at all,
Kept me aloof from Thy proximity :
      Then didst Thou unto me in mercy call
With loud acclaim, and thus Thy voice at last
Burst through my deafness by its piercing blast.

" In flashes and in splendour didst Thou gleam,
      And all my blindness scatter.   Odours fine
Didst Thou emit in ever plenteous stream ;
      I drew in breath, and panted to be Thine !
I tasted,—thirst and hunger on me flowed ;
Thou touchedst me, and in Thy peace I glowed ! "

[1] See Appendix, Note K ; Augustine's *Confess.* lib. x. c. 27.

II.

MONTE GENEROSO.

IN Cassiciacum, besides the charms
    Lavished thereon by art and nature's hands,
Were pleasures greater; for AUGUSTINE brought,
To be companions in his sojourn there,
His happy mother and his thoughtful son;
ALYPIUS also, his devoted friend,
And two young relatives, LASTIDIAN
And RUSTICUS, with whom had also come,
To join them in their studies for a while,
LICENTIUS, ROMANIAN'S only son;
Also TRIGETIUS, one who erst had felt
A passion for the soldier's daring life,
Had heard, with joy that could not be repressed,
The clang of arms, the measured tramp of men,
And the trump's clangour, but had tried their charms,
And soon, disgusted by war's cruelty,
Had sheathed his sword, and no more would shed
    blood.
He found employment fitter to his taste
In studying the records of old Rome,—
The terse descriptions of wise TACITUS,
The PATARINIAN'S looser history,
And the exciting, caustic narrative
Of him who knew and wrote of CATILINE.
Older than his young friends, TRIGETIUS knew,

Though not yet twenty, history so well,
That by his conversation on that theme
He seemed a veteran of old research.

At Cassiciacum the inmates scorned
To dream away in idleness their lives :
With strictest care their time was parcelled out,
And every hour had its appointed lot,
For work, repast, talk, exercise, or prayer,
Discussion, meditation, rest, and sleep.
But not so every day ; for routine dull
Was banished oft, and then with lightsome hearts
They wandered up and down the neighbouring vale.
Now MUGGIO called, and from its shallow stream
Dragged the shy fish entangled in their nets,
Or from its sloping and enamelled banks
Plucked fragrant cyclamen, each root of which
Offered the culler twenty purple flowers.
At times they climbed the mountain's grassy top,
At foot of which their Alpine home was built,
And gazed entranced upon the glorious view
Spread out, as some great chart, before their eyes.
Far to the south, beyond the river Po,
Whose stream at sunset glowed like molten gold,
And shone with many affluents as bright,
Arose the line of Alps named Maritime,
Barring the way to Rome like a huge wall.
In the wide interval, the level plains
Of Northern Italy outstretched were seen,
Dotted with countless cities, full of wealth,
Swarming with cattle, rich in corn and wine.
The Adriatic washed the eastern shores,
Faintly discerned by lines of dark-blue mist ;
Whilst on the west, far as the eye could reach,

When turning from the cloudy Apennines,
Appeared stupendous mountains in the air,
Like sentinels who watched the plains below,—
The sharp, white, distant top of Monte Viso,
The snowy slanting peak of Grivola,
The spreading ranges of Grande Paradis,
And the untrodden summits near Mont Blanc.
Then turning round towards the nearer west,
And looking o'er a region occupied
By lakes and mountain ranges linked in chains,
AUGUSTINE and his friends beheld the form
Of that tall mount, which, when from Milan seen
At misty evening by the setting sun,
Turns to the blushing colour of the rose
Which gives its name. Outspreading towards the
    north,
On the right side of this conspicuous mass,
Was seen Helvetia's brood of giant sons,—
The Matterhorn, diminished to a peak,
The bell-shaped Dôm, and splendid Bernese range ;—
Whilst in the north, and trending to the east,
The Susten and the Tödi blocked the view,
Where o'er a silent wilderness of snow
The lammergyer wheeling seeks his prey.
Glimpses were even caught betwixt two hills,
Through a long vista stretching many a league
In hazy distance towards the distant east,
Of Tyrol's pride, the stately Dolomites.

AUGUSTINE shuddered at these wastes of snow,
Regions of rock, and dreadful avalanche,
And gazed with more delight on the fair lake
Beneath his feet, where PLINY in old times
Lived in his Roman villa, whose remains

Still make the traveller from Como pause,
To view a hallowed spot to science dear.
Nor was his pleasure less as he beheld
Thy lake, Lugano ! though he never dreamt
That from thy banks, after a thousand years
Had made his fame increase throughout the world,
Would spring a race of sculptors, who, taught first
As masons working on thy marble rocks
To use the chisel with consummate art,
Would, by BONINO, sculpture his own tomb,[1]—
That gorgeous monument, in beauty wrought,
The glory of Pavia ! where at last
His mouldering bones, conveyed from Africa,
And from their sojourn in Sardinia
By fierce Saracens expelled, would find
That peaceful, happy rest, so long withheld !

But when the sun, down-dipping in the west,
Admonished travellers to gain their homes,
Back they returned upon their former steps.
The younger ones ran gaily on before ;
AUGUSTINE and ALYPIUS walked behind
With steadier pace, in converse close engaged.
But ere they reached their Alpine home, the night
Came like a quick surprise ; then in the sky
Shone out the rich abundance of the stars,
And earth and heaven combined to yield delight.
AUGUSTINE, sated with the beautiful,
Revolved within his mind the things just seen,
Pondered their meaning, and in thought inquired
If the great universe in which he lived,
The things which formed his own environment,
Or the full sum of such existences,

[1] As to his tomb, see Appendix, Note α.

Were GOD Himself or creatures made by GOD?
Then, when once more at home, and all but he
Had sunk to sleep, and stillest silence reigned,
He trimmed his lamp, and full of fervent love
To GOD, whose nature he desired to know,
Breathed forth these words before he closed his eyes :[1]

"Not doubtingly, but with conviction sure,
    I love Thee, LORD! Thou didst mine heart within
Pierce by Thy Word, and with affection pure
    I love Thee! heaven and earth and all therein
So bid me, and by warning words refuse
To all who love Thee not the least excuse.

" In olden time Thou saidst, as well we know,
    Thou wouldst have mercy on the man on whom
Thou wouldst have mercy, and compassion show
    On whom Thy will is that compassion come :[2]
Else heaven and earth, this globe, the starry spheres,
Would vainly tell Thy praises to deaf ears.

" But what then is it that I really love,
    When Thee I love? Not beauty, which we see,
Of form corporeal ; not such charms as move
    From harmony of time ; not brilliancy
Of light, whose gladness to the eye belongs ;
Not the sweet melodies of varied songs ;

" Not odours fragrant, wafted from bright flowers,
    Diffused from richest spikenard of great price,
Or breathed from spices culled in Orient bowers ;
    Not manna, honey, not the mad delight

[1] See Appendix, Note I.; Augustine's *Confess.* lib. x. c. 6.
[2] Rom. ix. 15.

N

Of limbs in whose embrace the flesh would be :
Not these I love, when I, my GOD, love Thee !

" And yet some kind of light and melody,
    Sweet fragrance, food refreshing to the sense,
And something of embracement I descry
    When I love GOD, who is the light intense,
The music, perfume, food, and fond embrace
Of all that in my inner man hath place.

" There to my mind shines light no space can bound,
    Sounds melody no time can e'er repress,
Smells scent no breeze can scatter or confound,
    Tastes food no eating can make any less,
Clings fondness no satiety sets free ;—
And this I love when I, my GOD, love Thee !

" What then is this ?   I questioned first the earth,
    Which promptly answered me, 'I am not He ;'
As likewise did whatever there hath birth.
    I asked the ocean's deep abyss, the sea,
All creeping things of life ; and they confessed,
' We are not GOD ! above us make your quest.'

" I asked the winds which stormy tempests swell,
    And, in reply, at once this answer got,
From both the air and all which therein dwell :
    ' The Grecian sage [1] was wrong ; GOD I am not !'
I asked the sun, the moon, the stars, the sky,—
' Nor we the GOD ye seek,' was their reply.

" I said to all the things which circling fill
    Those inlets to my brain, my senses five :

[1] Anaximenes.

' Ye say of GOD, ye are not He ; but still
  To give some notion of His nature strive.'
Then all, at this request, did answering state,
With mighty voice, ' He did ourselves create ! '

" These questionings were but the thoughts which burned
  In mine own mind ; the answers all things gave
Were but their beauty.   Next myself I turned
  Unto myself, and said, ' Reply I crave ;
Tell me what Thou art ! ' when at once began
And as soon ceased, this sole response : ' A man ! '

" Lo, here I have at hand two things, though weak,
  My body and my soul,—one placed outside ;
One inward : then by which should I GOD seek,
  Whom I to find had through my body tried,
Far as in quest, from earth to heaven's extremes,
Mine eyes could send, as messengers, their beams ?

" The inward best can task like this surmount ;
  For unto it, as judge and president,
All messengers corporeal bring account
  Of the replies from earth and heaven sent,
And from all things therein, which loudly state,
' We are not GOD ; He did ourselves create.'

" What knowledge thus mine inner man did find
  Was to the active ministration due
Of that which is outside ; for I, the mind,
  These things by fleshly senses only knew.
I asked again the mighty mass of earth :
' I am not GOD,' it said ; ' He gave me birth.'

" TRUTH at last said to me, with voice serene,
    ' Nor heaven nor earth, nor any creature made
Of matter, is Thy GOD : their nature e'en
    Tells this to all who see what stands displayed.
A mass it is, a mass without a soul,
Whereof each part is less than is the whole.'

" Therefore, my Soul, to thee I henceforth say :
    ' Thou art my better part ! because I know
Thy body's mass, which else were senseless clay,
    Thou quickenest into life that cannot flow
To flesh from flesh, which is itself a clod ;
Then, O my soul, thy life of life is GOD ! ' "

III

THE PSALMS OF DAVID.

AUGUSTINE had from Milan gone in haste,
    Without a visit unto AMBROSE paid,
The news to tell, or any word of thanks.
He wished not to disclose so soon the change
Wrought on his heart by grace, nor his resolve,
By the same grace, to give his life to GOD.
He craved, before such purpose was declared,
A leisure time for meditation calm,
For reading, careful study, and deep thought,
Whereby to make assurance doubly sure.
Perchance, while thus at work in his own way,
He cared no priest should lead him on his road—
Not e'en SIMPLICIAN : therefore did he speed
Without such guidance to the Alpine hill,
Nor found there what he took not when he went.
But now, when settled in his new abode,
He, full of reverence, to AMBROSE sent
A brief epistle, asking his advice ;
And AMBROSE courteously to him replied,
Advising the perusal of ISAIAH,
Because, of all the prophets, he the best
Foreshowed CHRIST'S coming, with the gospel's truth,
And that the Gentiles should be called to GOD.
But when AUGUSTINE tried to read that book,
He found himself not yet advanced enough

To study prophecy ; therefore he laid
The book aside, as one for future use.
Yet was he at no loss, for MONICA—
Who through so many years had tasted grief,
Wept unconsoled, yearned hopelessly for hope,
And had at last felt wild, exulting joy—
Knew well where all emotions of the soul,
In every phase, were in GOD'S Word expressed.
"Go thou, my son," she said, "and read the Psalms."
A woman's wisdom gave that good advice,
And what he sought in DAVID'S Psalms, he found.

This son of JESSE was a shepherd lad,
Who, on the rocky hills of Palestine,
Tended his father's sheep.   There many a night,
While so engaged, he scanned the firmament,
And, like the old Chaldeans, noted well
The rise and motion of each shining star,
And all the changes which the seasons bring ;
But saw, with rapture to their hearts unknown,
The glory of the heavens made bright by GOD !
DAVID, a younger son, learned discipline
Imposed by elder brothers, who beheld
With envy aspirations of a mind
Unlike their own.   As he increased in years,
His courage grew incapable of fear ;
And trusting in his GOD for needful help,
He slew, one day, a lion and a bear,
Which came to tear the flocks o'er which he watched.
With a smooth pebble, chosen from the brook,
And a mere sling, he smote GOLIATH'S brow,
When the rude giant, clad in steel of proof,
Defied the King and hosts of Israel.
Promoted to the Court, he took his place

At the King's table, sang upon the harp
The songs of Sion, felt a tyrant's frown,
And strove by music to allay that rage
Which made him hold his life within his hand.
Soon, by his wondrous nobleness and grace,
Won DAVID the affection of the Prince,
And in the lasting love of JONATHAN,
Greater than that of woman, found how true,
How fervent, is the friendship of a man!
Behold him next a trembling fugitive,
Driven from Court, a price set on his head,
SAUL and his spearmen thirsting for his blood!
Forlorn he wandered o'er the barren hills,
Knew hunger, thirst, and human wretchedness,
Dwelt in the wilderness, was hid in caves,
And, in his misery, at last became
The captain of a fierce and outlawed band.
An exile next amongst the Philistines,
He wailed his lot, because compelled to dwell
With Mesech, and abide in Kedar's tent:
Yet, mindful still of the eventful day
When SAMUEL poured on his anointed head
The holy oil, and hailed him as the King,
He waited patiently with trust in GOD.
This prophecy fulfilled, he wept the fate
Of JONATHAN and SAUL, who in their lives
Were lovely, and whom death did not divide.
Then as a shepherd good he led the flock
Of Judah and the tribes of Israel,
And ruled them prudently with all his power:
He in the council chamber, judgment hall,
And on the field of battle toiled and fought,
Partook of dangers, sat in dignity,
Planned laws for Judah with AHITHOPHEL,

Who, wise, but full of falsehood, ate his bread,
Reclined upon his bosom, and then schemed,
Like JUDAS, to betray him.   Yet more wide
And varied was his life's experience:
For when KING DAVID lay in glory's lap,
And, enervated by prosperity,
Let from his housetop wandering eyes peer forth,
To view the beauty of his neighbour's wife,
From which adultery and murder sprang,
He heard the stern rebuke which NATHAN gave,
Felt cruel visitations of remorse,
Saw his child die, and learned that on his head
A stroke retributive should one day fall,
Although GOD'S mercy then withheld his death.
Long after, by the parricidal act
Of ABSALOM, his son, whom most he loved,
Chased from Jerusalem, he fled in shame,
Was cursed by SHIMEI'S evil, bitter words,
And rescued only by the bloody point
Of JOAB'S spear, which pierced his loved son's heart!
Then, in Jerusalem again a king,
He watched with wonder, which increased each day,
The growing wisdom of young SOLOMON,
His son and his successor, in whose arms
He, when his time was come, gave up the ghost.
Instructed, chastened, tried, and purified
By such vicissitudes, the soul of DAVID
Drew in with eagerness, as his life's breath,
The inspiration of the Holy Spirit;
In deep prayer heard at times that still, small voice,
Known to the prophets and vouchsafed to him;
Then, as each great event which marked his life
Filled him with grief or joy, he eased his mind
By the outpourings of his soul in song,

And gave expression in impassioned words
To all emotions which had stirred his heart.
Nor did he speak of themes which touched himself,
Or his own people only, or his day,
But on the wonders of futurity
His rapt and daring soul presumed to gaze!
He saw in visions sure, and prophesied,
The great MESSIAH'S reign,—beheld Him come
To bring salvation to a sinful world:
First as a Man of Sorrows, known to grief,
A worm, no man at all, the scorn of men,[1]
The outcast of the people, mocked, despised,
Whose hands and feet they pierced, and, staring on Him,
Parted his very garments as their spoil,
And for his seamless vesture cast their lots;[2]
Next, as the King of Glory saw he Him,
And heard Him, on the day which yet shall come,
Calling the world from the sun's rising up
Unto his going down,[3] that He may judge
His people, and Himself may testify
Against thee, Israel! for He is GOD,
Even thy GOD, and thee will He reprove![4]
But to the righteous and His chosen saints
DAVID beheld Him GOD'S salvation bring;
And, when entranced in spirit, plainly heard
The FATHER thus to JESUS CHRIST declare:
"Thou art my Son; upon this day have I
Begotten Thee; desire, and I will give
To Thee the heathen for Thine heritage,
And the earth's utmost parts for Thy possession:
Thou with an iron rod shalt bruise Thy foes,
And break them, as a potter's cup, to sherds."[5]

---

[1] Ps. xxii. 6.   [2] Ps. xxii. 16, 17, 18.   [3] Ps. l. 1.
[4] Ps. l. 7.   [5] Ps. ii. 7, 8, 9.

Hence, in the Psalms which DAVID wrote, are found
Something to soothe or satisfy the wants
Of every human soul, in joy or woe;
And the emotions he hath there expressed
Are deep as truth, and varied as his life.
AUGUSTINE with ALYPIUS read the Psalms,
Each verse of which to MONICA was known,
Lived in her heart, and trembled on her lips.
If they should pause at some obscurity,
She was their wisest, best interpreter:
Her stores of Bible knowledge and deep thought,
Which had for years been hidden from the world,
She now brought forth, to help and please her son.
Domestic duties could no more suffice
To occupy her time; she gave commands,
And let domestics do the things which erst
She, as a humble housewife, had performed.
Now, when her son was seated with his friends
For some discussion on a point abstruse,
She in the grave assembly took her place,
And, with an air modest and matron-like,
Gave oft assistance to the argument;
Upon the darkest questions would she throw,
When others were at fault, the clearest light;
It seemed as if a change had lifted her
Higher than earth, and somewhat nearer heaven,
So that illumination from within,
Like that which angels know, brightened her thoughts.

But comfort greater and intenser joy
AUGUSTINE felt, when he perused the Psalms
In his own chamber, with the world shut out.
His soul was tempest-tost, like DAVID's soul,
And felt a whirlwind passing o'er its waves.

For fear he trembled, then with hope took fire;
Thrilled with delight, and shuddered with dismay.
His memory recalled the hideous time
When, as a Manichæan, he had scorned
Words which the Psalms now plainly spoke to him,
And in deep sorrow intermixed with rage
He thought upon that sect, which claimed him once.
Aloud unto himself would he rehearse
Verses which touched him most, and utter them
With voice and countenance whose changes showed
How vibrated his heart to every sound.
In the fourth Psalm he found coincidence
With his own case, as others may with theirs :
"Hear me, oh, hear! Thou GOD of Righteousness,
Whom now I call! Thou hast at liberty
Set me, when I was troubled. Hear my call!
Have mercy on me ; hearken to my prayer!"
This took he to himself; then on he read :
"O sons of men! how long will ye blaspheme
Mine honour, have in vanity delight,
And after leasing seek?" This, too, he felt
Had once applied to him ; for he in lies
Had sought for truth, and found but vanity,
Though GOD had magnified His Holy One,
And raised Him from the dead, and set Him down
At His right hand, whence He would surely send,
As He had promise made, the Comforter,
Spirit of Truth! But though already sent,
AUGUSTINE long had known Him not ; but now
He heard, and trembled at the solemn words.
Then in his chamber, angry at himself,
He communed with his heart till he was still,
And until gladness, put there by the LORD,
Made him once more rejoice ; for now he felt

His corn and wine and oil had all increased,—
Not by additions to his worldly goods,
Which time would waste away, but by the Spirit,
Eternal, simple, self-same, and divine!
Nor did the Psalms alone now occupy
AUGUSTINE'S thoughts; his large and searching
    mind
Grasped the whole Scriptures; viewed them part by
    part,
Then as a whole found continuity
Where dull men saw confusion; for his eyes
Were opened to behold the brilliancy
With which they shine when lightened by GOD'S
    light.
In no self-confident, presumptuous mood
He laboured hard, yet would he fain behold
Not the mere surface only, meanings plain,
Discernible by all who seek for truth,
Which babes may understand, though often hid
From those who in the world are counted wise:
He sought to penetrate to greater depths,
To learn the inner, secret mysteries,
The hidden things of GOD.   Then for GOD'S aid
In such an enterprise, by which he hoped
To gain more strength to help his fellow-men,
He prayed upon his knees, and used these words:[1]

"O LORD my GOD! give ear unto my prayer,
    And let Thy mercy hark to my desire,
Which, like a sea, is tossed about with care,—
    Not for myself alone, but doth aspire
Some work of love fraternal now to do;
Thou seest within my heart that this is true!

   [1] See Appendix, Note M; Augustine's *Confess.* lib. xi. c. 2.

" In sacrifice to Thee would I bestow
    The humble service of my tongue and thought ;
Then give what I to Thee may offer : lo,
    I am a needy one, possessing nought,
But Thou art rich to them who on Thee call,
And bearest, safe from care, the cares of all.

" Do Thou my lips then strictly circumcise,
    Inside and out, to free them from the bane
Of every kind of rashness and of lies.
    LORD, let Thy Holy Scriptures aye remain
My pure delights ; but let me not believe
Delusions from them, nor thereout deceive !

" Hearken, O LORD ! spread forth Thy mercy wide ;
    O LORD my GOD, Thou of blind eyes the light !
Strength of the weak ! who straightway art, when
      tried,
    Light e'en of them who see, and the true might
Of them most strong ! Heed now my soul in woe,
And hear her crying from the depths below ;

" For to such depths did not Thine ears incline,
    Where should we go or whither cry, O GOD ?
The day is Thine, the night is also Thine ;
    Our moments fly away at Thy mere nod.
Grant, then, such space as ample leisure brings,
To meditate on Thy law's hidden things.

" Shut not to them who knock ; Thou didst not will
    That all in vain should secrets so obscure
Have written been, which many pages fill.
    Have not these woods their harts, which, there
      secure,

Retire from view, range, walk about, and feed,
    Lie down and ruminate on grassy mead ?

"Perfect me, LORD, and these dark things reveal!
    Thy voice to me is joy, Thy voice is bliss
Beyond the fulness men from pleasures feel.
    Give what I love, for I do love ; and this
Is Thy gift too !   Never Thy gifts forsake,
Nor Thy poor, thirsting herb tread down and break.

"All that I shall within Thy Scriptures find
    Will I to Thee confess ; when reading, hear
The voice of praise ; imbibe Thee when my mind
    The wondrous things of Thy law shall see clear,[1]
As, full of thought, it doth a survey take
From that Beginning, in which Thou didst make

"The heaven and earth,[2] unto the endless reign
    Of Thy Jerusalem, with Thee to rest
In everlasting joy when built again.[3]
    Have mercy on me, LORD ! hear my request ;
For things of earth do not my thoughts entice,
Nor gold and silver, precious stones of price,

"Nor rich apparel, honours of the great,
    Official power, pleasures the flesh doth give,
Nor e'en things needful to the body's state
    And for this pilgrimage in which we live :
For these shall all be added, us to bless
Who seek GOD'S kingdom and His righteousness![4]

"Behold, O LORD, wherein is my desire ;
    The wicked tell me tales of base delight

---

[1] Ps. cxix. 18.   [2] Gen. i. 1.   [3] Rev. xxi.   [4] Matt. vi. 33.

Which are not of Thy law.   O heavenly Sire!
   See in what aim my wishes all unite!
Father Almighty! look down from above,
See, and with favourable thoughts approve!

" Let it Thy pleasure be, I Thee implore,
   That in Thy mercy's sight such grace I find,
That when I for admission knock, the door
   Of entrance may be opened to my mind,
So that the inner meanings it may see
Of revelations full of mystery.

" This I entreat Thee by our LORD, Thy Son,
   E'en JESUS CHRIST, ' the Man of Thy right hand,' [1]
The Son of Man, whom Thou, our GOD alone,
   Established for Thee hast, by Thy command
Our Mediator with Thyself to be,
By whom Thou didst us seek who sought not Thee.

" Thou didst us seek that we Thyself might seek,
   Thy Word might seek, by which Thou madest all,
And me among them ;—of Thy Son I speak,
   Only-begotten! through whom Thou didst call
Unto adoption all men who believe,
And wilt among them me, as one, receive.

" Through Him who sits at Thy right hand I sue,
   Who intercedes for us ; [2] in whom, so meek,
All treasures wisdom hath, and knowledge too,
   Close hidden are!   Him in Thy books I seek.
Of Him wrote MOSES, who did see His day ;
Himself said this, and Truth the same doth say !" [4]

[1] Ps. lxxx. 17.   [2] Rom. viii. 34.   [3] Col. ii. 3.   [4] John v. 46, viii. 56.

IV.

LICENTIUS.

HOW sweet the days at Cassiciacum!
　　Refreshing to a worn and weary man!
How soothing to a soul which yearned for rest!
But serious thoughts did not alone prevail,
Nor were such thoughts congenial unto one
Who sojourned there; for young LICENTIUS,
Gay as a blithesome lark upon the wing,
And volatile as finest essences,
Diffused the spell of cheerfulness around.
ROMANIAN loved him warmly as his son,
Yet saw in him too great vivacity,
Which only careful training could subdue.
The grateful MONICA had spent long hours,
When this bright youth was still a little child,
In watching o'er his mind's development,
And carefully instilling in his soul
Those lessons which, when learned in infancy,
Are not forgot in manhood, but will cling
Around the hardened hearts of sinful men.
As he grew older, tutors of repute
Had him in charge, and taught him what they knew.
Thus nurtured in the learning of his time,
The youth attained proficiency in Greek,
Read the best authors, and to memory
Committed passages of choicest kind;

Which oft, at dinner, he would thunder forth,
And look around, ambitious of applause.
At other times he sang, with sweet, clear voice,
Lines from a choral strain of SOPHOCLES,
And struck the cythera with skilful hand.
He wept o'er VIRGIL'S page, wherein he read
Of Carthage, which he loved, and DIDO'S woes.
He had the poet's mind, the eye of fire,
The strong, impetuous beating of the heart,
The piercing insight nature gives at birth,
The storm of passion and the gush of words
From soul emotional and thoughts intense.
Encourage him, and straight would from him flow,
Upon the impulse of a moment's birth,
Words improvised, well marshalled into verse,
And sometimes fashioned by a ready wit
To keenest shafts of pungent ridicule.
But oftener would he warble strains of love,
Although ALYPIUS frowned to see a youth
Of sixteen years on such a theme employed.
Behold him now, at mid-day, when the task
Of irksome study was at last fulfilled,
To which AUGUSTINE held him closely tied,
With all his young companions !   Prone he lies
Upon a thymy bank with languid limbs,
Intent on some strange fancy in his brain :
Pensive his face, from which are banished smiles,
So wont to lurk about his dimpled cheeks
And play upon his lips.   He hung his head
As if some grief oppressed him by its weight,
And musing with a melancholy mien,
Lingered in silence till his friends should speak.
" What ails LICENTIUS ?" said RUSTICUS.
" What ails thee, youth ?" was echoed by them all.

O

He motioned with his hand that they should cease,
And seat themselves around him in the shade ;
Then seized his lute, touched mournfully its strings,
And thus in tones disconsolate began :

> " Light be thy slumbers, love !
>   Pleasant thy waking !
> May grief thine heart ne'er move,
>   Throbbing and aching !

> " And when thou liest down,
>   Gentle sleep wooing,
> Stern may she never frown,
>   But grant thy sueing.

> " So shalt thou never know
>   How lone is night,
> How seethes the burning brow
>   Till day's slow light ;

> " When, every fond wish dead,
>   Back on the past
> Looks the eye for pleasures fled,
>   While the tears flow fast ;

> " And the heart, of life weary,
>   Sick'neth with sorrow,
> Shrinking from the future dreary,
>   Hating the morrow ! "

But here ALYPIUS could no more restrain
His anger at such trifling. " Stay ! " he cried ;
" Hast thou nought better than a love-sick song
For men of decent gravity and sense ?

Hast thou no hymns like those at Milan taught?"
"Check not the youth," AUGUSTINE smiling said,
" Nor tread a violet beneath thy feet."
But MONICA rose up to kiss the lad,
And laughed outright as thus she questioned him :
" Oh, sweet LICENTIUS, art thou then in love?
Yea, that thou art! and well I know with whom ;—
A Milan beauty, often seen by thee,
The merry daughter of VICENTIUS,
Thy elder by two years! LIVIA, I ween,
In making sport of thee, hath touched thy heart.
But grieve not thus, for time will heal the wound."
LICENTIUS blushed, nor let his eyes meet hers,
But thrust his lute aside, and hastily
Fled from the garden to the chestnut woods ;
There cast him down upon a shady bank,
Buried his burning face in violets,
And listened to the sighing of the wind.

Three days and nights AUGUSTINE writhed in pain,
Sharply afflicted by a raging tooth,
Until such torment he no more could bear.
Speechless, he wrote on tablets his request,
And, by his wish, his mother and his friends
Knelt down with him, and offered prayer to GOD,—
Deep, earnest prayer for merciful relief.
When they arose his agony had ceased!
Their prayer was heard, the mercy asked for gained!
But other pains were not so promptly quelled,
Such as from little bickerings arose
Among the young, not yet by discipline
Framed to forbear from jealous, angry taunts.
TRIGETIUS and LICENTIUS oft engaged
In controversies, with the noble aim

Of finding truth by dint of argument;
While, as an umpire in their difference,
AUGUSTINE sat, and noted down their thoughts,
At times assisting by a wise remark.
One day, when thus employed, TRIGETIUS
Made an assertion rash, which drew on him
AUGUSTINE'S blame, at which repentantly
He begged what he had said might be erased;
But this LICENTIUS earnestly opposed,
Wishing that his opponent's fault should stand
Recorded for his permanent reproach.
This drew upon him a rebuke so sharp
That the youth blushed, at which TRIGETIUS
Laughed in derision, and enjoyed his shame.
AUGUSTINE then in sorrow urged them both
To seek for truth alone, not victory,
Nor by dissensions aggravate his cares.
Tears stopped his words; LICENTIUS, in amaze,
Inquired what they had done to give him pain.
"What!" cried AUGUSTINE, "would you introduce
Into philosophy itself, wherein
I find a life of consolation true,
Vainglory and low envious jealousy,
By which I see you both are borne away?
But if I cure you of this malady,
Say, will you not in indolence subside,
Because the ardour which impelled you on
For reputation is extinct? must he
Who one defect removes make others grow?"
"We will, as you shall see," LICENTIUS said,
"Correct beforehand our deficiencies;
Pardon us now, and from the tablets strike
All this affair." "No, no!" TRIGETIUS said;
"Let it remain to be our punishment.

That reputation which attracts us now
May drive us from her, as if with a scourge!
No one but friends these notes will ever see."
LICENTIUS gave consent, and peace ensued.

V.

THE BIRTHDAY.

"THIS is your birthday, son," said MONICA
    One morning to AUGUSTINE.[1] "You have
        lived
Thirty-two years. May GOD be pleased to grant,
Through all your years to come, a happy life."
"But what is life, and what is happiness?"
Inquired AUGUSTINE, looking towards his friends,
Who all were there except ALYPIUS.
"See," he continued, "how the rain pours down,
Drenching the earth. We will not work to-day;
But the November clouds and cold east wind
Forbid a pleasant ramble. Let us sit
Within the house, and every one explain,
As best he can, what is a happy life."
"Agreed!" his friends exclaimed. Then when their
        meal,
Simple, but thankfully received, was done,
They all assembled in the spacious hall
Used for the baths, where, seated at their ease,
With MONICA to share in their discourse,
They entered on the argument at once.
First they discussed the complex state of man,
Composed of soul and body; next, what food
Is fit the soul to nourish. "Knowledge, is it?"

----
[1] *De Beata Vita;* Augustine's *Opera*, tom. i. 488.

Inquired AUGUSTINE. "Plainly is it so,"
Replied his mother ; " for I do believe
The soul can nourished be by nothing else,
Except by understanding and by knowledge."
With this TRIGETIUS was not satisfied ;
He thought the soul possessed two kinds of food,
And if some souls were nourished by the truths
Which knowledge gave, some others found their food
In errors, vanities, and mere illusion.
This led to long discussion, and AUGUSTINE
Showed that TRIGETIUS was clearly wrong,
Since errors and such like can nourish none,
But make the soul which feeds upon them poor,
Empty, and barren, with all vigour gone ;
And therefore MONICA was right, to think
That truth alone was fittest food for man.
AUGUSTINE next inquired, "Do we not wish
For happiness ? Then tell me, is not he
Happy who hath whate'er he doth desire ? "
"If that be good which he doth wish and have,
Happy is he," made answer MONICA ;
"But if the thing he wishes for be bad,
Then, though he have it, is he wretched still."
AUGUSTINE, smiling, lifted up his hands.
"O mother," said he, "thou hast climbed at once
The highest summit of philosophy ;
For in like words to those thou just hast used,
Hath TULLY, in HORTENSIUS, declared
The same great truth." Then opened he the book
And showed the passage, while the others looked
With wondering eyes on one who with them sat,
Despite her sex, as some illustrious man.
But her delighted son with fondness gazed
Upon the fountain whence such wisdom flowed.

Then they pursued the question, What can make
Happy the soul of man?   Can riches, health,
Glory, or beauty, any things like these?
But these are changeable, they fade and die,
And if we have them, how can they be kept?
"Yet," said TRIGETIUS, "there are many men
So fortunate, possessing all these things
In such abundance in this life, that though
The things are fragile and most apt to fade,
Nothing which they desire fail they to have."
TRIGETIUS then, by some hard questions pressed,
Must needs admit that he who feeleth fear
Cannot be happy, and that he who loves
Aught good must feel so, if he may it lose;
And therefore he who lives, and doth possess
Such transitory things, cannot be sure
Of being any way a happy man.
But here AUGUSTINE'S mother intervened:
"Even," said she, "if such a man be sure
Of no loss of such things, yet by them all
He cannot possibly be satisfied;
Therefore he too tastes misery, for he
Hath indigence to make him ever so."
"What!" said AUGUSTINE, "if he hath good things
In full abundance circling him around,
And he can place a limit to his wants,
And what he hath can thoroughly enjoy,
Contented with no pleasure in excess,—
Doth he not seem to thee a happy man?"
"No," answered she, "for such things do not make
His happiness; but all the bliss he hath
Comes of the moderation of his mind."
"Well said!" exclaimed her son; "no better words,
Nor from thee any other suitable,

Could have proceeded.   Yes ! if any man
Wishes for happiness, let him obtain
That which when gotten doth for aye remain,
And no ill change of fortune takes away.
But GOD alone hath such an attribute ;
And therefore only he hath happiness
Whose soul hath GOD."   To this they all agreed.
"Then who," AUGUSTINE asked, "think ye, hath GOD?"
" He who lives right," LICENTIUS answering said,
With the impetuous eagerness of youth.
" He," said TRIGETIUS, "who doth do the acts
Which GOD would have him do."   To which reply
LASTIDIAN for himself gave full assent.
Then one, the least in the assembly, spoke,—
Young ADEODATUS, prematurely wise :
"That man hath GOD," he said, " who doth possess
A spirit in him from uncleanness free."
Here MONICA, who was content before,
Expressed her preference for this ; and all
Gave their assent by silence or in words.
Then, after seasoning their long discourse
By pleasantry, in which LICENTIUS
Had the chief share, but even MONICA
Scorned not to join, they full of joy and smiles
Came to an end, and all retired to rest.

On the next day, soon after they had dined,
The conversation was again resumed,
In the same place and in more serious mood.
AUGUSTINE asked his son, what man it was
Who had, he thought, a spirit not unclean ?
"One who lives chastely," ADEODATUS said.
" But in what sense dost thou mean chastity ? "
"That man is truly chaste," rejoined the youth,

" Who strives with all his might to reach to GOD,
And, having reached, cleaves unto Him alone!"
AUGUSTINE marvelled at the lad, and wrote
Upon his tablets what had thus been said.
Then he began, with kindly playfulness,
To use admissions from the younger ones,
By which to catch them in a tangled net,
Adroitly framed by the logician's art.
"LICENTIUS," he said, "thou hast declared
That he hath GOD in him who liveth right
According to GOD's will ; and thou, TRIGETIUS,
He who performs such acts as GOD approves ;
But tell me, doth not he who seeks for GOD
Fulfil both these conditions ?   Thou, my son,
Hast said that he alone a chaste soul hath
Who strives to reach to GOD, and hold Him fast;
But can a soul impure seek GOD at all ?"
Then, when the youths showed some embarrassment,
And laughed to find themselves entangled thus,
AUGUSTINE'S mother helped them by these words:
" Who liveth well hath GOD propitiously ;
Who liveth ill hath GOD, though as a foe ;
And he who seeks but hath not yet Him found,
And hath Him not as friend or enemy,
Is yet not wholly of GOD destitute."
" But is not GOD propitious," said AUGUSTINE,
" To one He favours ?   Favours He not him
Who seeks Himself ?"   To this all answered " Yes."
" Then let us," said he, " sum up the result
In these few words, that he who hath already
Found GOD, hath GOD propitious unto him,
And happy is ; that he who only seeks
Hath GOD propitious, but hath not attained
To happiness as yet ; but that the man

Who doth by vice and sin cut off himself
From GOD, is noways happy, nor doth live
Even with GOD propitious unto him."

    By conversation on such themes as these
They occupied the leisure of two days,
Nor yet were satisfied without a third.
The clouds, which till that morning heavy hung
O'er Cassiciacum, had disappeared ;
Then, prisoners no more within the house,
They sallied from it, full of joyfulness
The sun to feel, the balmy air to breathe.
They to the sheltered fields below walked down,
Where, seated in a safe nook at their ease,
They recommenced and finished their discourse.
They had before discussed the state of those
Who GOD possess ; also the state of such
As seek Him : now the conversation turned
On those who have Him not, and therefore live
In indigence of soul and misery.
But are all miserable men in want ?
Must all who want needs be in misery ?
May not a man live free from any wants,
Possess in rich abundance all good things,
Yet be in misery, because he fears
The loss of what he hath ?—Questions like these
Were now the topics, and AUGUSTINE helped
To sift them thoroughly in various ways :
He pointed out that want resolves itself
Into not having, not in fear of losing
That which one hath ; the man who fears to lose
Is wretched though he want not anything,
Therefore not all who are in misery want.
"Yet know I not, nor can I understand,"

Said MONICA, "how we can separate
In any manner misery from want,
Or want from misery ; for the rich man
Who hath abundant wealth, nor more desires,
Doth yet, because he fears his wealth to lose,
Want wisdom ; therefore, if we call one poor
Who wanteth gold and money, may we not
Call him who wanteth wisdom just the same ? "
Again all present gave her words applause ;
But none was so much pleased to hear her speech
As was AUGUSTINE, who had come prepared
To read from writings on philosophy
The same conclusion she had just expressed.
" See ye not," said he, " that it is one thing
To have stored up and ready for our use
Doctrines of numerous and varied kinds ;
But different far is it to have a mind
Which, like hers, waits on GOD with diligence ?
For whence come these things we in her admire,
Unless from Him ? " Then young LICENTIUS,
Who dearly, like a son, loved MONICA,
Cried out with joy : " Undoubtedly, no words
Could have been truer said or more divine !
For no one can have greater indigence,
Or be more wretched, than the man who wants
Wisdom itself; but he who wants not wisdom
Can want for nothing ! " Thereupon began
Another argument, and they discussed
Wisdom and folly, and the ways of each ;
Nor came they to an end until AUGUSTINE
Explained what Highest Wisdom really means.
For what can properly be wisdom called,
Except GOD'S Wisdom ? And we must admit,
Upon authority divinely true,

The Son of GOD to be Himself none other
Than that same Wisdom! He is GOD the Son!
"I am the Truth," He said : "then by this Truth
Whoever comes to GOD may thus have GOD.
All other men, however much of wealth
They have from GOD, never have GOD Himself.
In Him alone the soul is satisfied
In fullest plenitude ; a happy life
Is lovingly and wholly Him to know,
By whom alone we into Truth are led,
In whom we then in Truth do Truth enjoy,
Through whom we are united to Himself ;
And these three demonstrate to candid minds
One GOD, one substance!" But when MONICA
Heard that, her memory a line recalled
Of an Ambrosian hymn, and she cried out,
"Assist our prayers, O Holy Trinity!"
Then added, "This, without dispute, is then
The happy life,—one perfect, unto which
We surely can, as thither we haste fast,
Be onwards led by a well-grounded faith,
A lively hope, and fervent charity!"
All then in GOD rejoiced, and gave Him thanks.
"Ah, would," TRIGETIUS said, "we in this mode
Could daily celebrate a natal feast!"
"The plan to do so everywhere is this,"
Replied AUGUSTINE ; "only let your heart
Betake itself to Him who is our GOD!"
Then, having ceased from further argument,
They, separating, went to seek repose.

LICENTIUS SINGS.

"Philosophy! men praise thee well,
And I with thee content might dwell

Secluded in a hermit's cell,
O'er books to pore ;
But, Poesy ! the truth to tell,
I love thee more !

"'Tis noble to be grave and wise,
Gaze round the world with thoughtful eyes,
Solve problems hard without surprise,
Grand themes rehearse ;
But sweeter far to breathe the sighs
Of love in verse !

" Let others follow sages great,
Sit at their feet with looks sedate,
With them theology debate.
It may be wrong,
But early I prefer, and late,
The poet's song ! "

VI.

ANGEL AND SAINT WORSHIP.

AUGUSTINE worshipped GOD without a priest,
    Long as he dwelt at Cassiciacum.
Was this by accident? or was it choice?
He scrupled not to speak to GOD direct
Into His ear, without interpreter;
He uttered praises, supplications, prayers,
And boldly told the troubles of his soul.
But could a mind, well trained and keen as his,
Pass by, through inadvertence, topics great,
Which have at all times occupied men's thoughts?
He felt that want, which many others feel,—
Want of some intermediate agency
To act between his sinful soul and GOD.
His memory told him how PATRICIUS
Had, when a Pagan, thought the sea, the streams,
The mountains, hills, and dales, the groves and meads,
Peopled by tutelary deities,—
By tritons, dryads, nymphs, and goatish fawns;
That he had deemed the purple vintage due
To BACCHUS, the inebriate God of Wine,
By whose great name he daily swore his oaths;
That CERES ruled the harvests, PAN the fields,
NEPTUNE the sea, and JUPITER the sky:
To them PATRICIUS would libations pour,
Pay tribute to them of his flocks and herds;

And if he anywhere a temple saw
Raised up in honour of some deity,
Who there obtained especial reverence,
He would kneel down beneath its spacious vault,
Pray at the shrine, and try the oracle.
Yet on this darkness of his blinded mind,
A glimmer faint of something far above—
An unknown but supremest Deity,
The one Great Cause and Highest Principle—
Would flash at times and give uncertain light ;
But if a Pagan could such glimpse obtain
Of the Great Truth, yet worship fifty gods,
Might not a Christian, fainting on his way,
Assistance ask of one less awful than
The LORD JEHOVAH ?   For to trembling men
GOD is too terrible! e'en when, as CHRIST,
He hath vouchsafed to lay His glory by,
And humbly clothe Himself in human flesh :
For shall not CHRIST one day to judgment come ?
To whom, then, should AUGUSTINE have recourse ?
Were there no Angels, blessed Virgin, Saints,
To whom a frightened sinner might apply
For mediation with a GOD incensed ?
Might not AUGUSTINE, if he called on them,
Obtain a speedier answer to his prayers ?
Why, then, not try?   What doubts could hold him
    back ?
First, he bethought himself of GABRIEL,
Who in GOD'S presence stands, who came to MARY
To tell glad tidings to her guileless ears,—
The birth of Jesus, to be born of her !
Might not an Angel of such dignity,
So near the throne of GOD, if asked by prayer,
Make intercession for a votary ?

But then the VIRGIN, though a prophetess,
And speaking as the HOLY GHOST her moved,
Had never bent to GABRIEL her knee,
But listened to the message which he brought,
And praised GOD only in undying words.
Next he remembered how ST. JOHN himself,
When in the spirit carried up to heaven,
And made a witness of the things to come,
Had turned him to the angel who poured out
One of the seven vials, and essayed
Twice at his feet to fall and worship him,[1]—
Once when the sights beheld inspirèd joy,
And once when they bewildered him with fear.
But then ST. JOHN, on each occasion, heard
The angel's quick rebuke, who to him said,
"See that thou do it not, for I, too, am
Thy fellow-servant; turn and worship GOD!"
But then, if angel-worship were forbid,
Might not one call upon the holy saints,
The stones which build up New Jerusalem,
The house of GOD, the living limbs of CHRIST?
But how can saints once dead such calling hear?
For what is death? what severance doth it make?
Where, after death, do souls of men depart;
And where is ABRAHAM'S bosom, where they sleep?[2]
Doth not their death withdraw them from this world
To rest in peace until the judgment day,
Take from them consciousness of earthly things,
Of human acts and wishes, crimes and prayers?[3]

---

[1] Rev. xix. 10, xxii. 8, 9.

[2] That the souls of the pious rest in Abraham's bosom, see Augustine's *Opera*, iv. 375 B. They have no body, iii. 507 C.

[3] "Proinde fatendum est nescire quidem mortuos quid hic agatur, sed dum hic agitur: postea vero audire ab eis qui hinc ad eos moriendo pergunt; non quidem omnia, sed quæ sinuntur indicare, qui sinuntur etiam ista

MOSES, whose burial-place was never known,
ELIJAH, who in chariot of fire
Was carried up to heaven, were both beheld
Transfigured on Mount Tabor, and displayed
Their bodies changed to substance glorious,
As in the twinkling of an eye our own
May one day be ; but then, did even they
See the apostles, who with fear saw them ?
No word, at all events, to them they spake ;
For CHRIST in glory sight and thought absorbed.
At the great resurrection of the just
Our souls will find themselves once more conjoined
Unto a body incorruptible,—
Not one like that in which we prisoned, live,
But one raised up in glory and in power ;
And such a soul, to such a body joined,
Will come in correspondence once again
With the material universe, from which
It is by death withdrawn, and in that state—
Corruption and unwieldiness both gone—
May in an instant like the lightning pass
From heaven to earth, traverse the Milky Way,
Circle around or dart athwart the stars.
What means the body's resurrection, then,
But correspondence once again renewed
Between the soul which lives and outward things,
By a fresh gift of substance corporal ?
Can He who gave that once give it no more ?
If He so promised, will He not perform ?
But can an unembodied human soul
Have cognisance of words which flesh and blood

meminisse et quæ illos, quibus hæc indicant, oportet audire."—*De Cura pro Mortuis Gerenda ;* Augustine's *Opera,* tom. vi. 882 C, D. "Defuncti per naturam propriam vivorum rebus interesse non possunt."—*Ib.* 884 A.

Address to it ?[1] Can saints in true peace rest
If they must hear the tales of human woe ?
Yet hath the hand of Providence at times
Performed great miracles by bones of saints,
When men were honouring their memory.
Surely, if bones of saints can do so much,
The souls which filled them once so full of life
May do still more, and mediate with GOD !
Prayers made for man, when offered up to Him
By living saints on earth to sorrow doomed,
Are the choice incense which the angel throws
Upon the altar placed before GOD'S throne.[2]
But can the prayers of saints in heaven be gained
By supplications framed by fleshly lips ?
And can such supplications be e'en heard ?
Nay, why should we suppose them requisite
To supplement the perfect work of CHRIST,
Who sits at GOD'S right hand and intercedes ?
GOD'S court is holy ; at the throne of GOD
CHRIST mediates ; none less than He prevails ;
Nor is CHRIST sluggish to require a goad.
In heaven no private influence exists,
As in the courts corrupt of this world's kings ;
And to suppose it possible, involves
Conceptions gross, compounded of earth's clay.
The prayers of saints on earth, by gold unbought,

[1] Augustine's *Opera*, iv. 1741 A.   Although Augustine thought the
saints in heaven could not hear words addressed to them on earth, he is
apparently inconsistent in one of his sermons, where, addressing St. Stephen
and St. Paul, he says: "Ambo modo sermonem nostrum auditis ; ambo
pro nobis orate."—*Sermo* 317 ; Augustine's *Opera*, v. 1869.   But this is
said with the kind of meaning which the Psalmist had when he calls on
the mountains, etc. to praise God, and which Bishop Heber had when he
wrote his hymn to the Star of the East, "Brightest and best of the sons of
the morning."
[2] Rev. viii. 3.

Are precious, as an exercise of faith,
And "avail much," as Scripture hath declared.
But faith, like hope, in heaven is realized ;
And hope, if seen, is no more hope at all ;[1]
Love, love alone eternally abides!
Why invoke saints who cannot hear when called ;
And, if they could, can no effective kind
Of mediation make ?   For, without CHRIST,
Their utmost efforts can accomplish nought.
To call on saints and angels, in CHRIST'S place,
For intercession, which by Him is made
Spontaneously, and not at others' call,
Is but to turn from GOD to seek vain things.
AUGUSTINE pondered long on thoughts like these,
But never knelt to or invoked the saints.
E'en to the martyrs, said he, build we not
Temples as unto gods, but only build
Memorials of them, as revered dead men
Whose spirits live with GOD ; nor do we raise
In those memorials altars unto them,
Nor thereon offer any sacrifice
To them at all, but to the only GOD,
Their GOD and ours, to whom is worship due ![2]
All worship, taught he, should be GOD'S alone,[3]
Though men should give the memory of saints
Honour, to faith and suffering justly due.
The saints and angels will not hope allow
To be in them reposed ;[4] it makes them sad.[5]

---

[1] Rom. viii. 24.   [2] Augustine's *Opera ; De Civ. Dei*, xxii. 10.
[3] " Nec colimus, nec colendum docemus, nisi Deum unum."—Augustine's *Opera*, tom. viii. 545 B.   Elsewhere he says, " Sancti honorandi sunt, non adorandi" (1265 A).   Again he says, " Sancti homines, similes angelis, nolunt se ab homine pro Deo coli et adorari."
[4] " Sancti et angeli non permittunt spem in se collocari."—Augustine's *Opera*, iii. 36 B.   [5] *Ib.* v. 336 D.

From this he never swerved, and when some years
Had passed, and he in good time had become
A priest and bishop of the Christian Church,
He, noting down to edify the world
Some truthful records of his thoughts and life,
Did thus, in his confessions made to GOD,
Express the ripe convictions of his soul : [1]

"Whom could I find my soul to reconcile
    To Thee, O GOD ?   Should I for this draw near
To angels ?   But for them, of prayer what style,
    What sacraments are fit ?   Many, I hear,
Struggling to come to Thee, though much delayed
By their own weakness, have this trial made ;

"But have then fallen, in their course profane,
    In curious visions of extravagance,
Being deemed worthy of delusions vain ;
    For they, high-minded, did by proud pretence
Of learning seek Thee, swelling out the breast,
Rather than smiting it for sins confessed !

"By means of hearts which their own semblance share,
    They drew friends to them who in pride delight,
Conspirators, the powers of the air,[2]
    By whom they were deceived through magic might,
A Mediator seeking, whose work done
Might purge them of their sins ; but found they
        none !

"For it was SATAN, self-transformed to be
    An angel of the light ; [3] and much it pleased

[1] See Appendix, Note N ; Augustine's *Confess.* lib. x. c. 42, 43.
[2] Eph. ii. 2.   [3] 2 Cor. xi. 14.

Proud flesh that he from carnal flesh was free,
 For they were sinners, mortal men diseased !
But Thou, O GOD, whom they by pride would win,
Immortal art, and wholly without sin.

"A mediator GOD and man between
 Should something God-like have, and something
  show
As shared with manhood ; lest if both ways seen
 As human, he from GOD should too far go ;
Or if both ways divine, should too far be
From man, and then no mediator he.

"That mediator, then, so counterfeit,
 By whom, according to Thy secret plan,
Pride merits the delusion it doth meet,
 Hath one thing, namely sin, along with man,
And fain would seem as if he did possess,
Along with GOD, this other thing no less ;

"That as he is not clothed, like men below,
 In weeds of flesh, nor breathes mere mortal breath,
He might himself as one immortal show !
 But since the wages due to sin are death,
He hath with man such wages in the end,
And therefore, with him, is to death condemned.

"Whereas the Mediator true and right,
 Whom Thou, in secret mercy, hast displayed
Unto the meek, and sent here that they might
 Learn, by the pattern His example made,
Like humbleness,—that Mediator who
'Twixt GOD and man makes mediation true,—

"The Man CHRIST JESUS,[1] here appeared between
    Us mortal sinners and that Righteous One
Who is immortal, and He thus was seen
    Mortal with man, with GOD His righteous Son !
So that, because the wage of righteousness
Is life and peace, He might, mankind to bless,

"By righteousness to GOD joined ever fast,
    Make void that death of sinners justified,
Which He had willed, along with them, to taste.
    Hence was there of Him vision clear supplied
To holy men of old, that they might see
By faith CHRIST'S passion, which was yet to be ;

"And thus be saved, like us who call Him LORD,
    By faith now it is past: for He as man
A mediator was ; but, as the Word,
    To be aught mediate He never can ;
For equal to and GOD with GOD is He,
Both, with the Holy Ghost, one Deity ! "

               [1] 1 Tim. ii. 5.

VII.

THE DEPARTURE.

ALYPIUS, when at Cassiciacum,
  Was ignorant of some doctrines of the Church,
Nor could he, with his friend's rapidity,
Which never slackened, some deep truths attain ;
But every day, he, with AUGUSTINE'S aid,
Discussed them with increasing earnestness.
Nor were objections wanting ; for it chanced
That they had left NEBRIDIUS behind
In Milan, to give VERECUNDUS help ;
Who, for the love of knowledge, not for gain,
Taught grammar as a science ; but their friend,
Though absent from them thus against his will,
Felt keenest interest in all great themes
Which then absorbed the thoughts of them he loved.
NEBRIDIUS, wishing much to learn the truth,
Claimed from AUGUSTINE, by the strictest right
Of friendship, such assistance for himself
As he felt need of, nor would be denied.
Therefore, to gain the help which he required,
He sent by every post a string of points,
Inquiries, doubts, and subtle questionings,
To all of which he asked a full reply.
AUGUSTINE, therefore, sometimes groaned to find
What labour this imposed, although ALYPIUS
Gave his best aid to make the labour less,

And then, whilst helping thus, oft helped himself
To clearer insight into points obscure.
NEBRIDIUS, earlier than them all, had gained
Sufficient insight into truth to see
The strong objections which beset the creed
Of MANES, and had proved it to be false.
This was at Carthage: now he earnestly
Pressed for solution of some doubts which worked
Upon his mind, and asked to have them cleared.
Whenever an epistle to him came,
Giving AUGUSTINE'S answers, he would take
And read it, line by line, to VERECUNDUS,
Who felt at first some lack of interest,
But presently, when forced to understand
And made to listen by NEBRIDIUS,
Began to manifest a zeal like his ;
Nay, would on some occasions lay aside
His much-loved PLATO, to peruse the works
Of the evangelists, and analyze
The life and doctrines of the great ST. PAUL.
But GOD would shortly reunite the friends
Severed so long ; for winter now was gone,
And Easter near,—the time the Church had fixed
To baptize all who should receive the rite,
And, by its water made regenerate,
Have their repentant souls cleansed free from sin.
To Milan, then, to claim this holy rite,
They must depart from Cassiciacum.
They left it as one leaves a cherished friend,
Looking behind with longing, heavy hearts,
And thinking much of happy moments gone ;
For in its spacious halls and gardens fair,
Its groves and fields, a pleasant time had passed
For all ; but it had to AUGUSTINE brought

Invigorated health, a faith confirmed,
The comforting extinguishment of doubt,
The birth and nourishing of glorious hope !

　As the long cavalcade to Milan went,
AUGUSTINE paused to view the house once more,
Before it passed for ever from his sight.
He caught one precious glimpse, then looking up
Beheld the mountain on whose side it stood,
And thought of VERECUNDUS, his kind friend,
Who gave him such a refuge, where to find,
Safe from the fever of the world, repose !
"O GOD," he cried, "I pray Thee to requite[1]
With the eternal joys of Paradise
The friend who lent us Cassiciacum.
Forgive his sins on earth, and let him climb
Thy mountain rich, which yieldeth curds and milk ;
Let Thine own mountains, which shall be revealed
Above all mountain-tops, afford him strength
By its rich stores of grace, which flow like milk
Fresh from a mother's inner self : and thou,
O Mountain ! upon which our eyes now gaze,
Whose grassy crest our feet so oft have trod,
Stand as our friend's memento through all time,
And be his GENEROSITY thy name ! "

　In silence they proceeded on their way ;
But soon the prattle of LICENTIUS,
Which nothing could restrain, brought back their
　　smiles.
"Shall we not see at Milan," he exclaimed,
"Good VERECUNDUS and NEBRIDIUS,

[1] See Appendix, Note O ; Augustine's *Confess.* lib. ix. c. 3.　See also
Dr. Pusey's Note N in *Lib. of the Fathers*, vol. i. p. 159.

Besides my father, who so loves us well ?
The maiden, too, whose name is LIVIA,
Who sings sweet songs, and sings them best with me!"
"Well said," replied AUGUSTINE ; "yet methinks,
Except for LIVIA, less would be thy joy.
True, we shall see the friends thou nam'st, and more,
Whose absence we have felt when far away :
Let us look back no more, but onwards go!"[1]

LICENTIUS SINGS.

"O mountains! glorious in the sunshine's glow,
Around whose crests twine wreaths of driven snow,
Upon whose sides the firs and flow'rets grow,
          Take our farewell !
For friends far distant call us, and we go
          Thy charms to tell.

"O mountains! when in early morn the flush
Of rosy light shall o'er thy summits rush,
Fleeting and tender as a maiden's blush
          At love's first breath,
Think how we oft have on thee gazed, in hush
          Silent as death!

"O MONTE ROSA, of yon Alps the queen !
Think with what joy we have beheld thy sheen,
In the bright flashes of the stars serene :
          From no brave heart

---

[1] In a Letter of Licentius, written to Augustine when the latter had returned to Africa, he wrote thus: "Oh that the morning light of other days could with its gladdening chariot bring back to me bright hours that are gone, which we spent together in the heart of Italy, and among the high mountains, when proving the generous leisure and pure privileges which belong to the good !"—Augustine's *Epistles*, No. 26, sec 4.

Shall the remembrance of thy peaks, once seen,
      Ever depart.

"O God! who mad'st these mountains by Thy word,
  And through their excellence our souls hast stirred
  To give Thee thanks, by Thee so gladly heard,
      Receive our praise,
As now we unto Thee, for gifts conferred,
      Our eyes upraise!"

SAINT AUGUSTINE.

BOOK VI.

THE CHURCH OF CHRIST.

BOOK VI.

I.

THE BAPTISM.

TO Milan now returned, with soul prepared
   By prayer and study for the holy rite
Which should admit him to the Church, AUGUSTINE
Gave in his name, in Lent, to be baptized.
ALYPIUS also, and young ADEODATUS,
Were with him joined as "Seekers;" and the three
Submitted with devout humility
To the Archbishop's discipline and rules.
AMBROSE rejoiced to see such converts come
To seek the waters which regenerate,
And, under his directions, they were lodged
Near the Cathedral, to be exercised
By close examination, which should prove
That in the Christian faith their views were sound.
AUGUSTINE, full of deepest interest,
Listened to those who taught and catechized,
As doth a traveller among the Alps,
Who, having soon to cross some glacier
At peril of his life, inquires of those
Acquainted with the pass the surest way.
For he must be prepared, when once baptized,
To go unto the Table of the Lord,

And venture boldly, with a thankful heart,
To eat CHRIST'S body and to drink His blood.
That which he erst as dull and irksome felt
In things which appertain to piety,
Brought now delight, nor could he have enough
To sate him, as in thought he fed upon
The wondrous sweetness present in his soul,
When he considered gratefully how deep
GOD'S councils are to save the human race.
The hymns and canticles sung in the church
With harmony of voice and heart, in words
AMBROSE had written and to music joined,
Touched to the quick AUGUSTINE'S tender soul,
And, as he listened, oftentimes he wept.
The voices of the white-robed choristers,
Reaching his ears, flowed in them like a stream ;
The truths they sang were in his heart distilled,
And from that source devout affections welled,
O'erflowing in their course ; thus tears ran down,
And in those tears true happiness he felt.

At length the day arrived, or rather night,
For upon Easter Eve, between the hours
Of evensong and matins, as was then
The ancient usage, the baptismal rite
Was by the hands of AMBROSE ministered
Unto ALYPIUS, AUGUSTINE'S son,
And to AUGUSTINE'S self, within the church.
Thus, at the time when CHRIST, whom he adored,
Rose from His tomb in heavenly glory clad,
To quit the earth and take His seat in heaven,
AUGUSTINE from this world's corruptions passed
Into a higher life ordained by GOD.
Upon a sign by the Archbishop made,

He turned his face towards Jerusalem,[1]
Looked to the Light so long to him unknown,
Which, like the sun, now rose within his soul,
And in the holy cleansing font thrice plunged,
Saying the form of words the Church prescribed.
Then AMBROSE, after prayer, standing upright,
Poured water on his humble, bent-down head,
And spake aloud the sacramental words
Which CHRIST commanded ere He left the earth.
Next, with a napkin girt about his loins,
And kneeling down, he washed AUGUSTINE'S feet.
The new-made Christian then they wrapped around
In a white tunic reaching to the ground,
Which typified his innocence restored.
This tunic MONICA herself had made ;
And when with triumph she beheld her son
Arrayed therein, her eyes wept tears of joy,
And in her heart she Hallelujah ! cried.
Then as AUGUSTINE to the altar moved,
To kneel before it and receive the bread,
Which is, to every thankful worshipper
Who eats with faith, the very flesh of CHRIST,
She knelt beside him full of love and joy,
And in that blest communion tasted heaven.[']
They drank, too, of the cup, which was not then
Withheld from any ; for no haughty priests,
Puffed up by arrogance of fleshly minds,
Had superseded then the plain command
Which CHRIST gave, saying, " Drink ye all of it ! "
Nor had presumptuously reduced the words
Into this form : " Drink some of you ; not all !
Drink clerics only, not the laity."
AUGUSTINE'S mouth received the bread and wine,

---

[1] Abbé Bugeaud, pp. 431, 432.　　　　　[2] Matt. xxvi. 27.

Which to his soul became CHRIST'S flesh and blood.[1]
O mystery of mysteries divine !
Great through transcendent force of simple truth !
Perverted by the proud who long for pomp,
But to the meek and humble full of joy !
This bread, which looks but ordinary food,
Is CHRIST'S own body when received with faith !
This wine we drink in deepest thankfulness,
His blood of the New Testament to man !
Therefore, who worthily such food receive
Become thereby incorporate with CHRIST,
Part of His body mystical.   Safe thus
From hidden perils of engulfing hell,
Though wide its open jaws to suck souls down ;
For how can we, part of CHRIST'S precious limbs,
Writhe in hell's torments or perdition know ?
Tradition, of all witnesses the worst,
Hath testified that when the sacrament
Had been administered, ST. AMBROSE stood
Beside the altar, looking up to heaven,
And from his lips burst forth triumphantly
The first lines of the anthem called TE DEUM ;
At sound whereof AUGUSTINE instantly
Chanted the second verse, as one inspired.
AMBROSE then sang the third ; and thus the two,
Chanting alternately verse after verse,
Jointly composed that glorious song of praise.
Music, at all events, was there, and words
Sung by sweet voices trained to harmony.
As soon as AMBROSE and AUGUSTINE ceased,

---

[1] In his Epistle to Boniface (*Epistle* xcviii.) Augustine uses these important words : "Sicut ergo *secundum quemdam modum*, sacramentum corporis
Christi corpus Christi est, sacramentum sanguinis Christi sanguis Christi est,
ita sacramentum fidei fides est."

The congregation rose with one accord,
To give GOD praise in the triumphal hymn
Which saints in glory sing before His throne :[1]

"Worthy is the Lamb once slain,
   Riches, wisdom, strength, and might,
To receive as His again !
   Honour, glory are His right.

"Blessing, blessing, is His own !
   Blessing, honour, glory, power,
To Him who sits upon the throne,
   And unto the Lamb for ever !"

[1] Rev. v. 12, 13.

VERECUNDUS.

AMONG the crowd in the Basilica,
　　Who thronged there when this baptism took
　place,
Were many of AUGUSTINE'S chosen friends :
NAVIGIUS, his brother, who long since
Had, when in Africa, received the rite ;
EVODIUS, who recently in Milan
Had done the like ; NEBRIDIUS, who wished,
And would ere long, but still held back in doubt ;
ROMANIAN, and his son LICENTIUS,
Who lovingly beheld the touching sight,
And in AUGUSTINE'S act their own foresaw ;
SIMPLICIAN, who in sacerdotal robes
Assisted AMBROSE, and rejoiced to see
CHRIST'S wandering sheep brought safe into the fold.
But one was there, a looker-on, who gazed,
Pleased though distracted, softened yet distressed,
And saw the weeping joy of MONICA
With sympathizing eyes filled full of tears.
He had been ill ; the pallor of his face
Made friends exclaim, " How art thou, VERECUNDUS ?
Hath thy late fever not yet left thy veins ?
Abide not here, but get thee home to bed."
He answered with a sigh, but not with words,
And still sat there in silent wonderment.

But when the hymn of triumph sounded loud,
And all the congregation, rising up,
Chanted such notes as made the roof resound,
He whispered to his wife : " Quick, go we home ;
Give o'er thy hymn, and lend a helping arm."
Then, by her loving outstretched arm sustained,
He tottered through the crowd, reached the fresh air,
Entered his house, and on a couch sank down.
He made his hand a shade to guard his eyes
From the sun's light, just gleaming in the east.
His slaves and freedmen, with officious zeal,
Crowding around, were waved off by his hand ;
None but his wife remained, who at his feet
Sat in deep silence, by him most desired.
Thus for some hours he lay, as in a trance,
Buried in thought, bewildered with amaze,
But hoping that AUGUSTINE soon would come,
To calm by sympathy his restless soul.
They had met much of late ; for, when AUGUSTINE
Returned to Milan, he had called at once
To render thanks for Cassiciacum,
And they had talked together long and oft ;
But as each interview approached its end,
AUGUSTINE could not, when he wished, depart,
For VERECUNDUS was importunate
Until he promised soon to come again.
It seemed as if the heart of his sick friend
Yearned for AUGUSTINE with increasing love,
And life its savour and delight had lost
Unless his face were seen and his voice heard.
"When will he come to me," sighed VERECUNDUS,
" To soothe these feverish doubts which vex my soul ?
When will his presence gladden me, like hope ?
Why, when thus restless made by some disease,

The fate of other men as well as mine,
Find I no comfort in philosophy?
None in my wealth, which seems to me like dross?
None in my reputation or my rank?
None in the empty pleasures of this world?
What means this change, which from my sight blots out
The roseate hue which once suffused my life?
Is it because I feel within me pain?
I, as a Stoic, spurn the thought with scorn!
Stretch these poor aching limbs upon the rack,
And I could smile with grim indifference.
Is it because some strange presentiment
Of death keeps whispering within my heart,
Giving the lie to friends, whose lips declare
How soon, all illness gone, I shall be well?
When, then, did I fear death, whom I defy?
Lo, calm as TULLY, when he held his neck
Outstretched to meet his slayer's bloody sword,
Would I hold mine, nor flinch when came the blow!
I know no dread of pain, no fear of death;
Yet, in disquiet, roll I on my couch
And groan within myself, disconsolate.
I hate this pride of wealth, this pomp of power,
The plaudits of the crowd in which I live,
The pageantry of state, once so desired!
I would as soon eat earth for daily bread,
As comfort seek in things so vain as these.
Nor, when I turn to books I prize the most,
Taste I the balm I need, but cannot find!
No more the classic grace of CICERO,
VIRGIL's heroic and immortal verse,
Or the refinement HORACE ever shows,
Bring to this aching, anxious bosom peace.
Great ARCHIMEDES' skill might lift the earth,

But cannot lift my heavy, weary heart.
The sculptured forms of PHIDIAS, once so prized,
Chill, like the marble chiselled by his hand.
No longer SOPHOCLES enchants my mind,
Or ARISTOPHANES provokes a smile ;
Not even PLATO can my thoughts command !
Are eloquence and poetry then dead ?
Is wit extinguished, and is art a toy ?
Science a cheat, philosophy a dream ?
Or doth some craving want possess my soul,
Which, until satisfied, makes all else pall ?
But want of what ?   Is there, then, anything
I cannot have, if I but name the wish ?
Alas! I wish for nothing in the world
That is not mine.   My wife, who slumbers there,
Heavy with grief and sleep, my love returns ;
My friends with earnestness reciprocate
All my affection, nor is one untrue ;
The great AUGUSTINE bears me in his heart.
Yet even friendship, as bestowed by me,
And in full measure rendered back again,
Fills not the void, which, like a dark abyss,
Yawns in my soul, and will not let me rest.
Peace, O my soul! I cry, but peace comes not ;
A haggard fury stares me in the face,
And bids me banish every hope of peace
Until this dark abyss, however deep,
Is by the presence of some mightier power
Filled with a substance, to which adamant
Is in comparison as soft as down !
Who, then, will close this void I cannot fill ?
Where shall I find the substance I require ?
Its nature, from its use, should be divine ;
The person whose it is must needs be GOD.

GOD, then, I long for, as the thirsty hart
Desires the water-brooks ; not GOD as shown
In the abstractions of man's intellect,—
Not GOD as one who is but possible,
The sickly dream of speculative thought !
But GOD, a being certain, personal,
Who loves me tenderly, demands my love,
Knows all my sorrows, pardons all my sins,
Can ease my burden and will bring me peace !
This is the GOD I need, but have not found,
Because I wilfully have shut my ears
Unto His voice when He hath loudly called,
And closed mine eyes, which would not see His light.
For years have I rejected with disdain
His written revelations made to man :
And what excuse found I for doing this ?
This was my plea, my soul to justify,—
That men are liars so egregious,
And their most solemn words so often false,
That any evidence from them received,
Of miracles in mercy wrought by GOD,
Hath such far stronger probability
Of being rather fictions or mistakes
Than proof of a departure from the course
Observed in Nature's uniformity,
That I must needs such evidence reject !
Thus have I held it quite impossible
That GOD, who made, can speak to one like me
Except by methods I to Him prescribe.
Not proof derivative, but proof direct
Have I insisted on, as due from GOD !
But is such insolence a just excuse ?
Can I—should my reliance rest on this—
Escape, if I neglect as I have done

CHRIST'S great salvation?   True indeed it is
That men oft lie; for even I myself
Lie to myself by pretexts such as these,
Which conscience tells me to be false and vain.
Is not my presence here miraculous?
Was it not out of Nature's former course
When on this earth, peopled with brutish things,
At last came man, that standing miracle?
Hath GOD not given, as His choicest gifts,
This reasoning soul, this searching intellect,
Truth to discern, though sometimes made obscure
To give faith trials?   Can I not detect
All tainted lies, however much disguised?
I can; yet must not for mere lies mistake
Imperfect statements which are based on fact.
My conscience, if truth dwells within my heart,
Becomes a touchstone for eternal things,
A great discriminating faculty,
Enlightened by GOD'S Spirit present there.
Shall I then bury and not use GOD'S gifts?
Behold, a span of life for me is left!
This still is mine, and this alone is mine,
To do with as I will for some short days.
Wake, then, my soul!   O sleeping fool, arise!
Shake off thy drowsiness while yet 'tis day!
Night soon will come, in which all things are dark.
Rouse in their potency thy faculties,
Grapple with this transcendent theme for thought;
Nor faint at toil, for GOD will give thee strength.
Kneel, stubborn knees! and thou, O tongue so dumb!
Call on thy Maker for His promised aid."

III.

THE DAY OF PENTECOST.

THE happy MONICA had left the church,
    Leaning upon her baptized, Christian son,
And, thus supported, slowly wended home ;
Then, after pressing him to her full heart,
Fulness no words could utter, she retired
To her own chamber's inmost solitude ;
There in thanksgiving raised her soul to GOD,
And found a sweet relief in floods of tears.
For fifty days she waited what would come ;
For GOD, she knew, would something bring about.
In this same interval AUGUSTINE framed,
In concert with his friends, a rule of life,
Which should thenceforth bind all with one consent.
The pomp and pleasures of fair Italy,
Which had aroused ambition in their hearts,
They would resign, seek out Numidia,
The birthplace of AUGUSTINE and of those
Who should, as his companions, cross the sea.
Yet would they not, as then the hermits did,
Even great JEROME, flee to solitude,
And in a desert shun the haunts of men ;
But strive in Africa to realize,
For nobler objects and a better end,
The project they in earlier days had planned,
Had tried a little, and with pain resigned :

They would, as laymen, in some house reside
Amidst the very thickest throngs of men ;
But they who lived there should, as in the days
Of earliest Christian faith, all things enjoy
In common ; nor should any one affirm
Aught as his own, and not his brother's too.
To this they added something weightier still :
Their worldly goods, except some needful things,
Should be sold off to feed the sick and poor,
Whom their own hands with daily care would tend.
In sacred studies they their lives would pass,
Nor banish science and philosophy,
The liberal arts, whose influence elevates
And brings increased refinement to the mind :
Yet would they in the Scriptures daily search
To find a reason for their faith, and strive
By fastings, prayer, almsgiving, praise, and love,
By patience, chastity, and poverty,
With strict obedience to GOD'S holy will,
To bring their bodies into full subjection,
But not like raving maniacs torture them ;
Would try to make their swelling hearts become
A habitation for GOD'S Spirit fit,
And thus, by discipline of highest kind,
Their very inmost nature sanctify,
Prepare themselves to combat heresy,
Confute the false, assist the ignorant,
And in the mighty struggles of the world,
Where truth and error fight for mastery,
Cast such decisive weight to make truth win,
That centuries to come should still have cause
To recollect their names, and efforts bless !
Thus would they live and strive, and live to strive :
And though they ever laymen would remain,

If left to follow what themselves desired,
They would, by suffering, bear the cross of CHRIST,
And for their fellow-men work hard and long.
In this their rule were they so moderate,
That by no vows should any man be bound ;
And though celibacy they would profess,
As fittest for them, yet if any one
Should afterwards in marriage wish to live,
Which is a holy state by GOD much blessed,
He was at liberty their house to leave,
And act as he proposed,—a liberty
Which some years later good NAVIGIUS took,
Although AUGUSTINE's brother, and became
The happy father of two daughters fair.
AUGUSTINE was much urged to be a priest,
And ordination from the holy hands
Of AMBROSE take ; but firmly he refused,
And for two years to come that danger shunned,
Until compulsion wrung from him consent.
Well might he hesitate to undertake
The priestly office, by temptations tried,
And for its grave responsibility
Reluctance feel ; though not yet in his age,
Nor until mediæval ignorance
Had darkened knowledge and disfigured truth,
Was any priest, who knelt to be ordained
By hands episcopal, compelled, as now,
To hear the declaration to him made,
That he and all priests—though no few may be
Foolish and false, faithless and truculent—
Have power on them by the rite conferred,
As if each individual were the Church,[1]

---

[1] The words, "Whose sins," etc., which, in the service for the ordination
of priests, are addressed to them by bishops of the English Church, were

Sins to forgive to men or sins retain.
To some, not all, of His disciples, spake
JESUS the words which such great power bestowed,
But not until He first had on them breathed
His breath divine, to give the Holy Ghost.[1]
E'en doubting THOMAS no such breath inhaled,
Unless he caught it when he gasping cried,
With hand in CHRIST'S side thrust, "My LORD, my
    GOD!"
Faithless no longer, but at last believing!
Well might AUGUSTINE shrink to hear it said
That by his hands were miracles performed,
Which no external evidence confirmed;
And he, by promptings of proud thoughts, induced
To predicate of bread material,
When in the sacrament once consecrate,
That which the senses plainly contradict.[2]
Albeit CHRIST, whose meaning men pervert,
Declared His words were "spirit" and were "life,"[3]
Well might AUGUSTINE shrink to be a priest,
And a divine commission thus receive,

not used in any ordination service of any church until about 1000 years after the birth of Christ (Martine, tom. ii. p. 317; Palmer's *Antiquities of the English Ritual*, vol. ii. p. 305, note). Their introduction in the tenth century is attributable to the ignorance and presumption of the mediaeval clergy of the Church of Rome. No small part of the evil now so actively at work in the minds of some of the English clergy may be traced to the arrogance engendered by these words having been addressed to them by the bishop, in a manner not warranted by Scripture. How much better would it be, if the words are to be retained in the Ordination Service at all, that they should be mentioned historically only, according to the method adopted in the latter part of the consecration prayer of the Holy Communion!

[1] John xx. 21, 23.

[2] "Non quod videtur, sed quod creditur, pascit," Augustine's *Opera*, v. 813 C, D. "Eucharistiæ sacramentum, etsi necesse est visibiliter celebrari, oportet tamen invisibiliter intelligi," iv. 1522 A. "Spiritualiter manducetur, spiritualiter bibatur," v. 924 B. "Eucharistia corde manducanda, non dente premenda," iii. 1984 C.   [3] John iv. 63.

Which, if accepted, cannot without sin
Be like a cast-off garment laid aside![1]
Well might he hesitate to join a class
Too greedy oft for place and precedence,
And apt to lord it over frightened flocks,
Rather than be their humble minister,
As CHRIST was, when, to give example good,
He, like a servant, knelt and washed the feet
Of His disciples, in amazement lost !
Well might AUGUSTINE shrink to be a priest,
Whom SATAN fishes for, with pride as bait,
To catch him fast in superstition's net,
And drag him through the sacerdotal mire ;
Or, if he pause to dally with the snare,
Whirl him along the current of conceit,
Where speedily, by quicksands swallowed up,
He sinks in heresy and unbelief,
Or, cast on shifting banks, a scarecrow lies,
For storms a pastime, and by wise men shunned !
Yet worthy are the ministers of CHRIST
(Whether, as bishops, they the flock o'ersee,
Or humbly serve the smallest cure of souls)
Who dedicate their lives to work for GOD,
For Him, and not for sacerdotal power !
How beautiful upon the mountains are
The feet of them who there the gospel preach,
And bring glad tidings of good things to man ![2]
How blest the eloquence with which they strive
To save lost sinners, for whom JESUS died !
Each generation forms a glorious link
In the unbroken chain, which from the age
Of the apostles reaches down to ours.

[1] Augustine's *Opera*, v. 2403 A, 3166 D, 3172 A.
[2] Isa. xlii. 7.

No gift of tongues, no miracles are theirs!
But CHRIST is with them now, and so will be
To the world's end ;[1] they have authority
To preach the gospel, and administer
The sacraments, which CHRIST Himself ordained.
On them His blessing rests, and on their work!
Woe, then, to all who shall their words despise!
Though men who hate the very name of CHRIST
Hate them, and their best acts calumniate,—
Though heartless worldlings leave them in neglect,
Without one smile of kind encouragement,
Great still is their reward laid up in heaven.
They sow good seed in faith for time to come ;
This, ripened by the Sun of Righteousness,
And reaped by hands appointed thereunto,
Will yield rich sheaves, which in the lap of CHRIST
Gathered shall be, when He, at the great day,
Shall call them, "of His Father, blessed ones,"
And bid each "Enter thou in thy Lord's joy."
E'en in this world shall they some solace find
For toil and disappointments, in the love
Of many faithful hearts, which judge them right ;
The praises of the noble, wise, and just
Shall yield them honour, poor men pay them thanks,
Sorrow forget her sighs on them to smile,
Sin flee with superstition at their sight ;
And when they die, a shower of unfeigned tears
Shall, like the fertilizing rain of spring,
Drop on their graves, and consecrate their dust.
The rule of life they planned was suitable
For such an age as that in which they lived :
Society was then corrupt and base,
Sick with intolerable taint of sin!

[1] Matt. xxviii. 19, 20.

Therefore pure minds, which from contagion shrank,
Yearned for a refuge from its contact vile.
To some it seemed less horrible to dwell
In solitary caves and deserts wild,
As hermits, than to live where they must hold
Companionship with open wickedness!
E'en men of courage, who refused to flee,
Lest evil unopposed should larger grow,
Desired with earnestness when in the world
To live apart, though living in its midst,
And in a close, select society
To practise virtue and to worship GOD.[1]
They unto MONICA their project told,
And she at once approved of it with joy;
For well she knew that if they trod that path,
The future, which belongs to GOD alone,
Would many things evolve, not then foreseen;
And in the hands of GOD their plans she left.

But when the DAY OF PENTECOST arrived,
AUGUSTINE joined again with MONICA
In the great sacrament by CHRIST ordained;
Then after he had gone, as was his wont,
To visit VERECUNDUS, and discuss
Deep things of GOD, hid often from the wise,
But unto babes revealed, his mother sat
Alone within her chamber, rapt in thought.
The sacred bread which cometh down from heaven[2]

[1] In a letter to Count Boniface (*Epistle* clxxxix.), Augustine, at a later period of his life, thus expressed himself: "Since it is necessary in this life that the citizens of the kingdom of heaven should be subjected to temptations among erring and impious men, that they may be exercised and 'tried as gold in the furnace,' we ought not before the appointed time to desire to live with those alone who are holy and righteous, so that, by patience, we may deserve to receive this blessedness in its proper time."

[2] Bugeaud, p. 441.   See Appendix, Note I'.

Had filled her full of such satiety,
That common food to nourish human flesh
Revolted her, and one whole day and night
She passed in a continued abstinence,
Until all consciousness of earthly things
Departed for a while. Thereby set free,
Her spirit, at a bound, sprang up on high ;
Bright angels held her in their circling arms,
And lifted her from earth ! She gazed around
In glory at the opening scenes of heaven,
And looked, with eyes which blenched not at the sight,
On heaven's brightness and on CHRIST her spouse ;
She saw the wedding garments all prepared
To clothe her for the great festivity,
Which should unite her unto Him she loved,—
Raiment of needlework and cloth of gold !
She saw the virgins who should follow her,[1]
To be her glad companions as she went
To enter the great palace of the King ;
She heard His voice, the voice of her Beloved,
Who from His garden called to her to come
And gather lilies ; told her she was His,[2]
Placed a bright golden crown upon her head,
And said His eyes, which looked upon her face,
Had pleasure in her beauty. " Then make haste ![3]
Haste, my beloved ! " His thrilling voice exclaimed,
" And be thou like a roe or a young hart
Upon the spicy mountains of the East."
Then MONICA awoke, and looked around
Upon the sordid, common things of earth ;
But knew that she ere long would be CHRIST'S spouse,
And pined to see the coming of that day !

[1] Ps. xlv. 14, 15.　　[2] Cant. vi. 2.　　[3] Cant. viii. 14.

IV.

THE CHURCH.

" LISTEN," exclaimed ALYPIUS to AUGUSTINE,
     " Unto some lines which young LICENTIUS,
Full of enthusiasm for the Church
We have just joined, hath in her honour made."
Then read he out unto his friend these words :

  "O Church ! which art so bright and glorious ;
      Great mother, hail !
  Thy matchless beauty is beloved by CHRIST,
      Nor will it fail ;
  Against thee striving shall the gates of hell
      Never prevail !

  " In the resplendent robe of righteousness
      Art thou arrayed,
  And by the hands of Him whom thou dost love
      Was that robe made :
  Take courage amidst perils, nor of foes
      Be thou afraid !

  " Like a great tree shalt thou with branches wide
      O'erspread the earth,
  In every nation and in every clime
      Display thy worth ;
  Nor shall there of the fruits which thou dost bear
      Be any dearth.

"And yet as a lone widow art thou left
    Till CHRIST'S great day,
When He shall come to wipe from every eye
    All tears away,
And in His kingdom place thee as His queen,
    With Him to stay.

"Oh, be that coming soon ! that we who are
    Thy members all
May in Thy glory also have our share,
    And at His call
Soar up to heaven with an impetuous flight,
    Which fears no fall ! "

AUGUSTINE listened, and then smiling said :
" One of the poet's figures I approve ;—
The Church indeed is like a fruitful tree,[1]
An olive of the noblest, choicest growth,
Whose trunk and root are even CHRIST Himself.
May many useful limbs spring from this tree,
With countless branches spreading far and wide,
To bear abundant foliage and good fruit,
That all who need may food and shelter find !
But to the Church must evil one day come ;
For time and wicked men will work such harm,
That e'en the grandest limb of all the tree,
Which, from its size and nearness to the trunk,
Might seem to some to be the tree itself,
May, in the course of ages, so much waste
By rottenness, that from its hollow core
No bud will blossom and no green leaf grow,
Nor any living thing spring forth and thrive,
Except the fungus, product of decay !

      [1] Augustine's *Opera*, iv. 2133; ix. 836 A.

The Church is like the moon, for she will wax
And she will wane.   She too may be eclipsed,
Until her light seem gone ; when lo, again,
High up in heaven her glorious orb appears !
The Church may also be with truth compared
Unto CHRIST'S body,—temple, city, house,
Of which He is the Head, is its Indweller,
Its Sanctifier, King.[1]   The Church is built
Not upon PETER, but on CHRIST alone ;
SIMON confessed that JESUS was the CHRIST ;
Therefore the LORD said to him : ' Thou art PETER ;
And on this stone, which thou hast now confessed,
Namely, on me, Son of the living GOD,
Will I build up my Church ; that is, on me
Thee will I build, not build myself on thee.'[2]
The Church is therefore built on CHRIST Himself ;
And wondrously is her construction framed !
She is within and also is without !
Some men who, bodily and to the eye,
Are mixed up in her unity, are still,
By their bad, evil lives, from her cut off,
And separate therefrom !   Many who seem
Outside the Church are yet within her bounds,
And some who seem within only seem so ;

---

[1] "Cum autem corpus Christi est et templum, et domus, et civitas : et ille qui caput corporis est, et habitator domus est, et sanctificator templi est, et rex civitatis est."—*Enar. in Psalm.;* Augustine's *Opera,* tom. iv. 2099 D).

[2] "Hoc autem ei nomen, ut Petrus appellaretur, a domine impositum est : et hoc in ea figura, ut significaret Ecclesiam. Quia enim Christus petra, Petrus populus christianus. Petra enim principale nomen est. Ideo Petrus a petra, non petra a Petro ; quomodo non a christiano Christus, sed a Christo christianus vocatur. *Tu es* ergo, inquit, *Petrus ; et super hanc petram* quam cognovisti, dicens, *Tu es Christus, Filius Dei vivi, ædificabo Ecclesiam meam :* id est, Super me ipsum, Filium Dei vivi, ædificabo te, non me super te."—*Sermo* lxxvi., Augustine's *Opera,* tom. v. 595 D, 596 A ; *Sermo* cclxx., tom. v. 1604.

For bodily alone are they within,
But spiritually without do they abide.[1]
None who are avaricious or do ill
Really belong unto the Church of CHRIST ;[2]
Nor will they, as her members, reign with Him.[3]
Wherever GOD is feared and duly praised,
There is the Church ;[4] and to the Church belong
All faithful men who hitherto have been,
Who now are, or who shall hereafter come :
CHRIST is the Head ; the Universal Church
His body is, and we that body form.[5]
The Church is catholic, throughout the world
Diffused without exception ; nor unless
She were so spread would she be catholic.[6]
She is not hidden or invisible,
Cannot in truth be hid ; but ever stands
Clear and conspicuous to the eyes of all.[7]
The Church alone from CHRIST receives the power
Sins to remit ; to her the keys are given,
As once to PETER :[8] by no single man,
But the whole Church, then, are the keys received ;
For PETER truly did but represent

[1] Augustine's *Opera*, tom. ix. 271 B, C, 272 B,C ; iv. 1729 A ; ix. 218 B, 219 C, 220 C, 286 A.

[2] *Ib.* tom. ix. 210 C, 211 C, 218 B, 219 A, B.

[3] *Ib.* tom. vii. 941 B.

[4] " Ubicumque timetur Deus et laudatur, ibi est Ecclesia Christi."—*Enar. in Psalm.;* Augustine's *Opera*, tom. iv. 141 C.

[5] " Si ille caput est, nos membra sumus : tota Ecclesia ejus quæ ubique diffusa est, corpus ipsius est, cujus est ipse caput. Non solum autem fideles qui modo sunt, sed et qui fuerunt ante nos, et qui post nos futuri sunt usque in finem sæculi, omnes ad corpus ejus pertinent ; cujus corporis ipse caput est, qui ascendit in cœlum. Quia ergo jam novimus caput et corpus, ille est caput, nos corpus."—*Enar. in Psalm.;* Augustine's *Opera*, tom. iv. 866 A, B.

[6] Augustine's *Opera*, tom. ii. 178 A ; ix. 1623.

[7] *Ib.* tom. ix. 578 A. [8] *Ib.* tom. vi. 379 C, 439 C.

The Universal and United Church,
When CHRIST said to him, ' Unto thee I give ; '
And gave to all, but not to him alone.[1]
CHRIST promise made that He would found the
    Church
Upon a stone or rock : that stone is CHRIST !
The Church is figured only in ST. PETER ;[2]
But so it was in NOAH'S ark,[3] by EVE,[4]
By the great flood,[5] and e'en by JEPHTHA'S daughter.[6]
The Church is like to MARY, for the Church
Brings forth and is a virgin.[7]   Here she is
Not without sin and error.[8]   May she have
In every nation under heaven a branch,
Pure, spotless, orthodox, and be a guide,
A teacher true, and mother to mankind ! "

[1] " Has enim claves non homo unus, sed unitas accepit Ecclesiæ. Hinc ergo Petri excellentia prædicatur, quia ipsius universitatis et unitatis Ecclesiæ figuram gessit, quando ei dictum est, *Tibi trado,* quod omnibus traditum est."—*Sermo* ccxcv. ; Augustine's *Opera,* tom. v. 1756 B, C.

[2] " Petrum vero apostolum Ecclesia unicæ *typum.*" — *Sermo* lxxvi. ; Augustine's *Opera,* 595 C.

[3] Augustine's *Opera,* tom. ii. 1036 B ; iv. 63 B, C.

[4] *Ib.* tom. i. 1099 C ; iv. 2043 B.   [5] *Ib.* tom. iv. 1634 D.

[6] *Ib.* tom. iii. 958 D.   [7] *Ib.* tom. v. 1368 D.

[8] *Ib.* tom. v. 1255 C, D ; i. 35 A, 66 C, 95 C.

V.

OUR LORD JESUS CHRIST.

ALYPIUS had in error once supposed [1]
    That Christians, orthodox and Catholic,
Believed that GOD had been so clothed with flesh
That only GOD and flesh, but not a soul,
Were in CHRIST found ; nor did he understand
A human soul was unto CHRIST ascribed.
But from this heresy AUGUSTINE strove
To wean him, and at last successful proved.
Then was he by his friend's instruction taught
That GOD, the Word, man's nature had assumed,
And, in a wondrous fashion of His own,
Had sublimated it in CHRIST, GOD'S Son ;
So that He who that nature humbly took,
And what He took, was in the Trinity
One of the Persons ; for no Christian saith
That CHRIST is only GOD, or only man ;
But that He is the only Son of GOD,
Begotten of the Father,—One who is
Without beginning, and before all time ;
Also true man, and was, when full time came,
Of human mother born. ALYPIUS learnt,
By the same aid, freely on him bestowed,
That CHRIST'S humanity, whereby He ranks
Inferior to the Father, doth not work

[1] Augustine's *Confess.* lib. vii. c. 19.

To derogate from His divinity,
Whereby He to the Father equal is.
Others may be partakers of GOD'S Word,
Having the Word of GOD, yet none but He
Can properly be GOD'S Word!   This Word
Was JESUS named, and of Him it was said:
"The WORD was flesh made, and among us dwelt." [1]
ALYPIUS next began to understand,
That though one kind of wisdom is create,
There is another which existed ere
Creation was, and is the very same
Which of itself thus spake through SOLOMON,
Ere CHRIST had come: "The LORD did me possess
In the beginning of His way, before
His works of old.   I, WISDOM, was set up
From everlasting, e'en from the beginning,
Or ever earth existed ; when there were
No depths was I brought forth." [2]   This Wisdom true,
This Wisdom uncreate and everlasting,
Is GOD the Son.   AUGUSTINE taught him so,
And gave this exposition upon CHRIST :
From the most early times of fallen man,
CHRIST'S coming hath been preached,[3] and everywhere
Throughout the Holy Scriptures is it made
The very central fact of prophecy ; [4]
So that the men of old, by GOD inspired,
Who did, before His coming, CHRIST behold
By faith, might thereby like ourselves be saved,
Who, now that He is gone, believe on Him ; [5]
For to the ancient fathers and ourselves
Is CHRIST the same ; [6] but in the ancient law

---

[1] John. i. 14.   [2] Prov. viii. 22.
[3] Augustine's *Opera*, ii. 417 A ; ix. 1362 D.   [4] *Ib.* ii. 738 A.
[5] *Ib.* iv. 403, 670 C.   [6] *Ib.* v. 2025 A.

He shows as figured only;[1] in the New,
As one whom, though the Word of Life, men saw
With their own eyes, and handled with their hands.[2]
CHRIST'S incarnation was a work performed
By the whole Trinity,[3] which made His flesh;
Though that, when made, to Him alone belonged.[4]
He came to us, impelled by love; no cause
Had He to come, except lost man to save:
For if all wounds and sickness are removed,
No cause for medicine to heal exists.[5]
Because of ADAM'S fall was CHRIST'S descent;[6]
GOD became man that man might GOD become.
That a mere servant should into a lord
Be turned, the LORD received a servant's form.[7]
But yet our sins, and not our merits, led
CHRIST down from heaven, to come upon the earth;[8]
Unless, indeed, the Word of GOD had deigned
Man to be made, the fallen human race
Could not have been redeemed from sin and death:
Man then had perished![9] CHRIST, when on the earth,
Humbly partook of man's mortality,
That man in His divinity might share.[10]
CHRIST put on flesh, lest man in carnal things
Should be absorbed;[11] but He was never man
In such a way that He e'er ceased to be
The only one begotten Son of GOD,[12]
And equal unto GOD, although GOD'S Son![13]
He is the Son of GOD, and Son of Man:[14]
The former, since by nature He is so;

[1] Augustine's *Opera*, vi. 64 D.   [2] 1 John i. 1-3.
[3] Augustine's *Opera*, v. 366 B, 1413 B.   [4] *Ib.* v. 444 A.
[5] *Ib.* v. 1208 A.   [6] *Ib.* iv. 1948 B.   [7] *Ib.* v. 2170 A.
[8] *Ib.* v. 1206 B, 1383 A.   [9] *Ib.* ii. 1321 B; v. 1142 B.
[10] *Ib.* v. 1299 B.   [11] *Ib.* ii. 1321 B.   [12] *Ib.* x. 1580 C.
[13] *Ib.* v. 874 A, B.   [14] *Ib.* viii. 318 C, D, 333 A.

The latter, since He did, in time, by grace,
Assume that character upon the earth.[1]
CHRIST is the Word and man,[2] and GOD and man.[3]
No greater gift could GOD on men bestow,
Than that His Word, by which He all things made,
He should establish as their Head, and them
Make fit for being members unto Him.[4]
As man, though soul and flesh, is but one man,
So GOD and man in CHRIST is only one.[5]
For not a demigod, as GOD in part
And man in part, is CHRIST, but very GOD
And very man ; one person, and not two.[6]
He, through the Spirit, did receive a soul,
And through the soul, a body ; if He had
Received a soul alone, we should not be
Members of CHRIST except as to our souls.[7]
CHRIST's flesh was true, and was from MARY ta'en ;[8]
True, though it was not sinful flesh like ours,
But of the likeness of our sinful flesh.[9]
His body, flesh, His wounds and scars, were true.[10]
CHRIST's weakness came of power ;[11] He suffered thirst
And hunger, since to suffer them He deigned,
But not because they forced Him so to do.[12]
He of men's evil things partook, that He
Might give to man His own things, which are good.[13]
CHRIST was conceived by MARY without taint
Of concupiscence ;[14] for through grace alone,
Believing, she conceived,[15]—not carnally,

---

[1] Augustine's *Opera*, viii. 967 B.   [2] *Ib.* iii. 2150 D.
[3] *Ib.* iv. 584 B ; v. 271 B, 618 A, 683 A, 717 C.   [4] *Ib.* iv. 1286 D.
[5] *Ib.* v. 1202 B, 902 C.   [6] *Ib.* v. 1734 B; vi. 430 B, 995 B; viii. 318 D.
[7] *Ib.* v. 1119 C.   [8] *Ib.* v. 2110 D.   [9] *Ib.* v. 1075 B.
[10] *Ib.* viii. 370 C, D, 486 C.   [11] *Ib.* vii. 575 D.
[12] *Ib.* v. 1238 B.   [13] *Ib.* v. 858 D.
[14] *Ib.* ii. 1032 C ; iii. 431 D.   [15] *Ib.* v. 1047 B.

But by the Spirit.[1]   He was mortal born,
To banish death;[2] He took mortality,
That immortality He might bestow;[3]
He shared our death, to give to us His life![4]
He came to raise souls from iniquity
And bodies from corruption,[5] so that we
Might place our faith in GOD, and He might give,
After a life of faith, eternal life![6]
CHRIST punishment endured, but never sin,
That He might blot out sin and punishment.[7]
CHRIST, and CHRIST only, had in life no sin.[8]
He had no concupiscence,[9] else had He
Not cured it in ourselves.[10]   Although no sin
He did, yet was He for our sakes made sin.[11]
He made our sins His own, that He might make
His righteousness the righteousness of man.[12]
CHRIST only among men could boldly say,[13]
"Which among you convinceth me of sin?"[14]
But none replied.   He took on Him our flesh;
Not its iniquity, but took flesh clean
And without spot,—took from the Virgin's womb,
That He might offer it as something clean,
For the unclean, to GOD.[15]   He neither had
Man's sin original, nor any sin
Done by Himself.[16]   He proved Himself to be
GOD by His words and works, that so He might
Be known as GOD and man.[17]   CHRIST from the Word
Was never separate or deposed, not e'en

[1] Augustine's *Opera*, vi. 364 B; iv. 965 B.   [2] *Ib.* v. 1436.
[3] *Ib.* v. 870 A.   [4] *Ib.* v. 869 D.   [5] *Ib.* iii. 1949 D.
[6] *Ib.* iv. 2331 A; iii. 2137 C, D.   [7] *Ib.* v. 1193 C, 1748 B.
[8] *Ib.* iii. 843 A.   [9] *Ib.* x. 1868 C.   [10] *Ib.* x. 1136 B.
[11] *Ib.* vi. 368 A.   [12] *Ib.* iv. 136 B.   [13] John viii. 46.
[14] Augustine's *Opera*, iv. 663 C.   [15] *Ib.* iv. 2270 A, 2402 A.
[16] *Ib.* v. 1047 D, 1185 C; x. 1930 B.   [17] *Ib.* iii. 1997 A.

In the humiliation of His death.[1]
He was of royal and of priestly race,
The Son of GOD, and also DAVID'S son
According to the flesh ;[2] born in Judea,—
But not to Jews alone, for He was born
The Jews and Gentiles in Himself to join.[3]
The law was by a servant, MOSES, given,
And made men guilty ; pardon by a King,
By CHRIST, whose pardon made the guilty free.[4]
CHRIST was made poor that He the poor might fill,
And of His poverty make many rich.[5]
Mercy occasioned CHRIST'S humility,
Not want of power.   He emptied out Himself
By taking what He was not, not by losing
That which He was.[6]   Small, and of no repute,
He, as one poor, came forth in human flesh,
That He, in that same flesh, when raised again,
Might, as one mighty, pass the gates closed fast.[7]
Because of the enormous sin of pride,
GOD came in deep humility, that He
Might bring almighty medicine from Heaven
For souls afflicted by such great disease.[8]
CHRIST, who made angels, was Himself made man,
That man might angels' food be given to eat,
Which is the body and the blood of CHRIST.[9]
The mark of CHRIST is His humility !
He wishes not to see His glorious star
Shine on the forehead of His faithful ones,
But His cross only.[10]   Who this cross despise
Are proud, and very far from saving health.[11]

---

[1] Augustine's *Opera*, iii. 2258 C, D ; iv. 10 A.   [2] *Ib.* viii. 653 A, 367 D.
[3] *Ib.* iv. 1494 A.   [4] *Ib.* iv. 490 B.   [5] *Ib.* iv. 1489 B.
[6] *Ib.* v. 717 A.   [7] *Ib.* v. 1382 C.   [8] *Ib.* iv. 125 A, 300 C.
[9] *Ib.* v. 1304 C.   [10] *Ib.* iii. 1699 D.   [11] *Ib.* v. 869 B.

CHRIST'S miracles are such as, by GOD'S aid,
Others have worked ; but these are all His own,—
That he was of a virgin born, arose
The third day from the dead, and into heaven
Ascended.[1]   CHRIST for us doth proffer prayer
Because He is our Priest ; He prays in us
Because our Head ; to Him our prayers are made
Because He is our GOD.[2]   Since He is CHRIST,
He too is man, and, for that reason, weak ;
And because weak, must pray ;[3] but, as GOD'S Word,
He neither had to whom He prayer could make,
Nor cause for making prayer.[4]   CHRIST prays as
    CHRIST,
And gives what He doth pray for ;[5] and He prays
That He may teach to pray ; as also He
Suffered, to teach how suffering should be borne.
He, after death, was raised, to teach mankind
The hope of resurrection.[6]   JESUS CHRIST
By JUDAS was delivered up to death ;
But by GOD also![7]   That which JUDAS sold,
And the Jews bought, the Christians have acquired.[8]
CHRIST yielded up Himself unto the Jews,
That He, by those who knew Him not, might do
What was His will ;[9] Himself the author was
Of His own cup, the cup of which He drank.[10]
Unrighteous men desired His unjust death,
Which a just GOD permitted.[11]   CHRIST refused
To punish them who pierced Him, that to us
He might, when we are most distressed, teach peace.[12]
CHRIST suffered as a man, but not as GOD,

---

[1] Augustine's *Opera*, ii. 608 C.   [2] *Ib.* iv. 1287 A.
[3] *Ib.* iv. 190 D.   [4] *Ib.* iv. 191 A.   [5] *Ib.* v. 1394 B.
[6] *Ib.* iv. 758 C.   [7] *Ib.* v. 1801.   [8] *Ib.* v. 1923 D.
[9] *Ib.* iii. 2413 B.   [10] *Ib.* iii. 2414 B.   [11] *Ib.* iv. 862 A.
[12] *Ib.* iii. 2418 C.

Though He is rightly called GOD crucified ;[1]
And death may justly be ascribed to Him,
Though His Divinity could never die.[2]
CHRIST, on the cross, taught that no form of death,
However shameful, should inspire dread :[3]
He held His peace in anguish, underwent
With patience, insults, spittings, mockings, blows,
For our example ;[4] would not leave the cross,
Because He from the sepulchre would rise ![5]
His side was opened, that all men by that
Might enter, as within an open gate ;
And thence flowed blood and water, that in one
Might be our cleansing, and our great redemption
Be in the other,—for His blood washed out
The sins of men.[6]   His death was of His will
Spontaneous, not of mere necessity.[7]
In that which constitutes a man, CHRIST died,
And man is raised to life by what is GOD's.[8]
CHRIST was not mortal by mortality
Of His own substance, but by that of ours ;
And, in like manner, we immortal are
Not by our substance, but by His alone.[9]
CHRIST's death slew death ;[10] and by accepting death
He overcame him.[11]   He too by His cross
Conquered and slew man's adversary fierce,
The Devil, and became our only King.[12]
Unless He, owing nothing, had all paid,
He from our debts had not delivered us.[13]
That which CHRIST's passion figures is a Lamb

[1] Augustine's *Opera*, ii. 906 B.   [2] *Ib.* iv. 491 B.
[3] *Ib.* vi. 269 A.   [4] *Ib.* iv. 364 B, 1378 B.
[5] *Ib.* iii. 1819 B.   [6] *Ib.* vi. 1029 A ; v. 1844 A.
[7] *Ib.* iv. 1316 C ; v. 1936 D.   [8] *Ib.* iv. 2092 B.
[9] *Ib.* iv. 2342 C.   [10] *Ib.* v. 1436 B.
[11] *Ib.* x. 300 C.   [12] *Ib.* iv. 2401.   [13] *Ib.* v. 1076 A.

Slain as a sacrifice.[1]   He was a priest,
Who, when He found not in this world aught clean
Which He might offer, offered up Himself![2]
The blood of CHRIST did the whole world redeem :[3]
He purchased all His brethren with the same,
Made the condemned acceptable, brought back
Those sold, did honour to poor men oppressed,
And vivified the dead ;[4] nor shall a man,
Redeemed by blood so precious, perish.[5]   He
Bought, by the greatness of the price He paid,
The universal human family.[6]
His blood, which can remit the sins of all,
Was shed in such a fashion that the same
Can even take away the very sin
Which shed that blood.[7]   It doth ensure salvation
To them who wish for it ; but unto them
Who shun to take it, punishment alone ![8]
CHRIST hath done more than He did promise make ;
And now it is far more incredible
That what is dead should die eternally,
Than that a mortal man should live for aye.[9]
CHRIST, by His soul, descended into hell,[10]
Into the place of torments, even where
Sinners are crucified by cruel thoughts.[11]
He some of them relieved, and loosed their pains,[12]
Though whom He loosed it would be rash to say.[13]
CHRIST penetrating to the depths of hell,
And thence arising as death's Conqueror,
Worked a great miracle among the dead.[14]

---

[1] Augustine's *Opera*, vi. 481 B.   [2] *Ib.* iv. 2120 B.
[3] *Ib.* iv. 142 C, 144 A, 1484 B, C.   [4] *Ib.* v. 1194 D.
[5] *Ib.* v. 1628 A.   [6] *Ib.* v. 1818 C, D ; iv. 1508 C.
[7] *Ib.* iii. 2324 D.   [8] *Ib.* v. 1974 A.   [9] *Ib.* iv. 2388 B, C.
[10] *Ib.* ii. 1019 A, B.   [11] *Ib.* iii. 509 B.   [12] *Ib.* v. 538 B ; ii. 860 D.
[13] *Ib.* ii. 858 B, C.   [14] *Ib.* iv. 1330 D.

CHRIST'S resurrection was reality,
Nor could it be deferred,[1] nor His flesh kept
For the last resurrection, which shall come.[2]
He raised Himself, and Him the Father raised ;[3]
For by the Father was He raised as man,
And by Himself as GOD.[4]   He had the power
To lay His life down, and He had the power
To take it up again.[5]   CHRIST on the cross
Displayed His patience ; in His resurrection
He showed His power.[6]   None, before CHRIST, from death
Ever arose to live eternally.[7]
When His disciples thought they saw a spirit,
He reprehended them.[8]   He with them talked
After His resurrection, to confirm
Their faith ;[9] partook with them of meat and drink,—
Not of necessity, for He was free
From thirst and hunger,[10] but he ate and drank
To manifest thereby His power and love.[11]
His resurrection is the hope of ours ![12]
His death is good to teach us not to fear,
His resurrection to excite our souls,
And in us to awake Faith, Hope, and Love ![13]
CHRIST, after He had risen, left the world,
To build our faith up, so that when He was
Absent in body, we might turn our thoughts
On His Divinity.[14]   He did ascend
To heaven, that His disciples might no more

[1] Augustine's *Opera*, ii. 642 D.   [2] *Ib.* ii. 650 C.
[3] *Ib.* v. 1822 A.   [4] *Ib.* iv. 500 A, 759 C, D, 1747 B.
[5] *Ib.* v. 1821 D.   [6] *Ib.* vi. 971 D.
[7] *Ib.* iv. 2003 C, 2079 D.   [8] *Ib.* v. 1447 A, B, 1448 C.
[9] *Ib.* v. 1568 D.   [10] *Ib.* iii. 2243 C.
[11] *Ib.* v. 831 A, 1770 C.   [12] *Ib.* iv. 2078 B.
[13] *Ib.* iii. 432 A, 844 A, B.   [14] *Ib.* v. 1443 A, 1571 B.

Remain in carnal things ;[1] nor till He went
Could come the Holy Ghost, whom He would send.[2]
The glory of CHRIST'S victory appeared
And was completed in His resurrection
And His ascension ; for those certain facts
Support our faith.[3] They unto CHRIST are joined
Who wish, like Him, ascension into heaven ;[4]
And there His body is, in that same state
In which it was on earth, when it above
Ascended 'midst the clouds, a holy thing
Which never has nor shall e'er see corruption.[5]
CHRIST, as a man, hath His eternal seat
In glory with the Father ; but as GOD,
He everywhere exists, here and above.[6]
He is a King and Priest, the mighty LORD
Of angels and of men ;[7] yet is as well
Victor and victim, priest and sacrifice.[8]
To eat His body and to drink His blood,
In the great sacrament which He ordained,
Is in Him to abide.[9] He who believes
In CHRIST doth thereby eat of living bread.[10]
Belief in CHRIST is coming unto CHRIST ;[11]
And such belief is the sole gift of GOD,
A gift predestined ere the birth of time.[12]
CHRIST is the only Mediator true
'Twixt GOD and man, nor should we other seek :[13]
He mediates as man, and not as GOD.[14]

---

[1] Augustine's *Opera*, v. 1569 A.
[2] *Ib.* v. 1603 B.
[3] *Ib.* v. 1564 A ; iii. 26 D.
[4] *Ib.* iv. 1998 B.
[5] *Ib.* ii. 1164 B, C, 1167 A, B, C.
[6] *Ib.* vi. 960 B.
[7] *Ib.* vi. 73 B, 482 C.
[8] *Ib.* i. 328 B ; vii. 411 A.
[9] *Ib.* iii. 1987 A, B, 1988 D, 1991 C.
[10] *Ib.* iii. 1970 C, 1978 A.
[11] *Ib.* x. 1361 B, 1419 C.
[12] *Ib.* i. 45 A ; iv. 191 C, 1388 A, 2131 A ; v. 374 C, 627 A, 859 A, 1734 A, 2095 D ; vii. 368 A ; x. 582 D.
[13] *Ib.* vii. 369 C.
[14] *Ib.* iii. 2295 C ; iv. 1672 A ; vii. 369 C.

S

He is the Way, the Truth, the Life.[1] Whilst He
Is with the Father, He is Truth and Life ;
And He, when flesh He takes, is made the Way.[2]
He is the only way unto salvation ;[3]
Nor can that way belong to us, unless
We of His body and His blood partake.[4]
As no man dies except in ADAM, so
None comes to life again except in CHRIST,
Who is our Saviour, Hope, Redeemer, GOD![5]
CHRIST hath two comings into this our world :[6]
The first to save, the second one to judge![7]
One hidden, and one brightly manifest.[8]
CHRIST, as a judge, shall come in form of man
To judge the whole world, for which world He paid
The price in full.[9] He then will show Himself
As fire upon the judgment-seat, to give
Light to the righteous, but to wicked men
Eternal judgment.[10] All who love the LORD
Should love His coming, and His day desire![11]

[1] Augustine's *Opera*, iii. 37 B, 1937 C, 2257 C.   [2] *Ib.* iii. 2042 B.
[3] *Ib.* i. 245 D ; ii. 762 C.   [4] *Ib.* ii. 762 C.   [5] *Ib.* x. 228 C.
[6] *Ib.* iii. 1608 B, 1712 A, 2000 C, D, 2068 A, D.
[7] *Ib.* iii. 2053 D, 2055 A.   [8] *Ib.* v. 135 B, 140 D.
[9] *Ib.* iv. 1484 B, C.   [10] *Ib.* iv. 949 C.   [11] *Ib.* iv. 2351 C.

VI.

THE HOLY TRINITY.

" GO, teach all nations,"—gave the LORD command
  To His apostles,—"and them, in the name
Of Father, Son, and Holy Ghost, baptize."
Thus, in St. Matthew, read ALYPIUS.
Not in the "names," but in the "name," thought he;
Then is the GOD these words describe but One,
And yet they designate the Trinity!
What means this mystery of Christian faith,
From which the intellect of man recoils?
Can there be one, and one be three, in heaven?
Whereas on earth, where time and space prevail,
Arithmetic exclaims, Impossible!
Yet that and logic are but tools of thought
For finite things, and have no larger use.
If, then, man's reason shall such instruments
Seek to apply to what is infinite,
Must they not lead him to conclusions vain,
And reason's self become irrational?
If GOD hath in the Scriptures clearly told
That which by revelation, as sole means,
The human mind can ever truly know,
Shall man, when he accepts GOD's solemn words,
Recorded by the prophets of old time,
By the apostles and saints testified,
And plainly by evangelists confirmed,
Complain or feel surprise, because, forsooth,

His feeble mind could not have guessed the truths
Which they declare, nor can his faculties,
Even when told, their fulness comprehend?
But if the intellect of man falls short
When it would grasp what is beyond its scope,
Is language better?   Must not language fail
To body forth in words which are precise
That which e'en thought imperfectly conceives?
True, " Father, Son, and Holy Ghost" are words
Which best express, although by metaphor,
Relations centred in the Deity,
And the three Persons which are yet one GOD ;
But they, being words of human origin,
Can but approximate to aught divine.
What just conception could we form of GOD,
If His eternal nature in itself
Had no such wondrous multiplicity ?
Is difficulty gone, if we believe
The Deity uncomplex singleness ?
Nay, is there not in such a view of GOD
A difficulty greater?   For was He,
In the beginning, ere creation came,
Infinite loneliness ?—self, only self ?
Is, then, that love, whose very name is GOD,
Something which never met and cannot know
An equal love responsive to itself,—
Can GOD's love only be made manifest
By condescension to created things ?
Till their creation did no love exist ?
GOD is of love the very principle ;
But, as the name implies, eternal love
Must from eternity have always had
Some person or some thing which it could love ;
Nor can we else conceive that it could be.

Therefore, although a personality
That is divine and infinite must needs
Differ from human personality,
Yet neither thought nor language can express
With more exact precision what is meant
Than " person " does ; and we may well believe
As self-consistent,—what we know by faith,
Through revelations GOD hath deigned to make,—
That love which language only can describe
As that felt by a father for his son,
And love a son doth for his father feel,
Have both had being from eternity.
Each unto man is separately known :
The Son as sent, the Father sent of none ;
But since GOD'S essence, which we substance call,
Is one and indivisible, the link
Which doth unite these persons is a third,—
The Holy Spirit, even Love itself,
Who in His known relation to mankind
Stands as the Paraclete, the Comforter,
Our Advocate who pleads for us with GOD
More tenderly than mother for a child,
And intercedes with groans unspeakable.[1]
ALYPIUS revolved these subjects long
Within his mind, and had his faith confirmed
By conversations on them with AUGUSTINE,
To whom in this momentous argument
No point was new nor less than fully known.
The doctrine catholic and orthodox
Was one AUGUSTINE had with zeal embraced ;
For only some few years before his birth
Had ATHANASIUS left this troublous world,
Wherein he, as a Christian bishop, met

[1] Rom. viii. 26.

With persecutions, deprivation, scorn,
Imperial malice, and fierce Arian hate ;
But, faithful to the definitions true
Embodied in the creed which bears his name
(Though now, as cast in shape by later minds,
Marred by storm-water of intolerance),
He all endured, and triumphed in the end.
He was an obstacle to heresy
Harder than iron, stronger than a rock ;
Tumultuous waves burst over him in vain ;
Man to his heart struck far less awe than GOD.
He was of daring thought and ardent faith ;
The truths he taught he fearlessly maintained
With earnest soul, immoveable and firm.
Though tyrants menaced,and though courtiers scowled,
Force could not turn nor threats dismay his mind.
He left a great example, which AUGUSTINE
Regarded with admiring reverence,
Due to his doctrine and his saintly life.

AUGUSTINE told ALYPIUS that to him
The Trinity appeared as in a glass
Darkly, although he fully recognised
That this same Trinity is GOD Himself.[1]
For GOD the Father did in the beginning
(Which word, He saith, refers unto the creature
Whom He created) make both heaven and earth
In JESUS CHRIST, His Son, who is to Him
Equal and co-eternal ; for He is
The Father's Wisdom, and of Him begot.
Moreover, in the Scriptures it is said
That at creation "on the waters moved
The Spirit ;"[2] and ST. PAUL hath testified [3]

---

[1] Augustine's *Confess.* lib. xiii. c. 5.   [2] Gen. i. 2.   [3] Rom. v. 5.

That in our hearts is shed abroad GOD'S love
By the same Holy Spirit to us given.
" Therefore, behold ! " exultingly he cried,
" The TRINITY, who only is my GOD,—
The Father, Son, and Holy Ghost, the true
Creator of all things which are create !
But," added he, " this further must we grant :
GOD'S nature in the Trinity by few
Is understood, though many it believe.[1]
The Greeks unto the Trinity assign
One essence and three substances, but we
One essence or one substance (for these words
Are but equivalents) and Persons three.[2]
Within the Holy Trinity exists
One will, one power, and one majesty ; [3]
Its total nature is immutable,
Nor can it possibly be different.[4]
At man's creation, doubtless, there appeared
In the Creator a plurality
Of persons, and, with certainty no less,
The singleness of the Divinity ! [5]
Something in man exists, by means whereof
Whatever of the Trinity is told
(Although ineffable its nature be),
And in whatever way, is capable
Without mistake of being understood; [6]
Yet is there Unity in Trinity,
And Trinity in Unity as well." [7]

O GOD ! who dwellest in the highest heaven
Invisible, incomprehensible,

[1] Augustine's *Opera*, iii. 347 A.   [2] *Ib.* viii. 1310 A, 1313 A.
[3] *Ib.* iii. 1944 C.   [4] *Ib.* viii. 964 C, D, 966 D.
[5] *Ib.* v. 889 D.   [6] *Ib.* viii. 976 C, D.
[7] *Ib.* i. 356 D, 1128 A ; v. 1261 D ; vii. 449 C, D.

Forgive us men, made but of earthly clay,
When we presume in controversies hard
To use concerning Thee such terms of speech
As " Substance " and as " Person," and suppose
We know our meaning when our words declare
How or from whom the Holy Ghost " proceeds."
Forgive us when from terms like these we try
To make deductions by our reasoning,
And in set phrase define the Infinite !
But oh, still more forgive our insolence,
When, full of pride at what we thus have done,
We on our shrinking fellow-men turn round,
And thunder in their ears the awful threat,
That they who hold not the same creed as ours
Shall no doubt perish everlastingly ! [1]

[1] This must be the desire of most reasonable men who have studied
controversies which have taken place on the subject of the Trinity among
the orthodox members of the Church of England themselves, of which a
summary is given in that most able work, *The History of Religious Thought
in the Church of England since the Reformation*, by the Rev. John Hunt,
London 1870-1873.

SAINT AUGUSTINE.

———

BOOK VII.

THE DEATH OF MONICA.

BOOK VII.

I.

TO OSTIA.

"FAREWELL, great city!" cried AUGUSTINE'S
  voice,
When, having out of Milan's streets emerged,
He and his friends had reached the road to Rome ;
For there they first must go, and afterwards
Take ship from Ostia for Africa.
"Farewell, my friends, whom here I leave behind,"
Continued he with tears ; "ROMANIAN,
NEBRIDIUS also, shall I see ere long,
For they will come to meet us at Tagasta ;
But never will the hand of VERECUNDUS
With friendly pressure greet again mine own,
SIMPLICIAN smile on me, or these ears hear
The voice of AMBROSE winning souls to GOD :
No more in this world shall I them behold !
But in the world to come, should they go first,
How warm will be their greeting, when, with toils
Finished on earth, we reach Jerusalem
Which is above, and these in glory see
Where the saints dwell, and CHRIST for ever reigns !
Be this our consolation and our hope."

With slow and toilsome journey they crossed o'er
The wooded Apennines, on whose sides dwelt,
'Midst silence and privation,—far withdrawn
From human duties, work, affections, cares,—
Many a solitary anchorite,
Who tried to rival in austerities
The monks of Egypt, and become, like them,
The talk and wonder of the gaping world.
But though that novelty had not yet borne
Evil, which time would as its harvest reap,
And such an abnegation of the laws
Of beings, whose creation GOD called good,
Had some attraction by its scorn of pain,
Yet from AUGUSTINE not one word it drew
Of admiration or approving praise ;
Nor did he or his friends, from what they saw,
Alter the rule which was to guide their lives.

At Rome, AUGUSTINE made but briefest stay,—
Only a few short weeks,—in which he tried
To aid the contributions to be made
To pay expenses back to Africa,
By getting in some slender debts, long due,
But shamefully withheld by students false.
Baffled and vexed by their dishonesty,
AUGUSTINE lost all patience, and exclaimed :[1]
" These men are base ! and pardon me, O LORD,
If, since I suffer by them, I perchance
Hate them e'en more than I should hate, because
They do what is unlawful ;—base they are,
To Thee unfaithful, and they love alone
Unstable trifles of the passing hour,
With filthy lucre, which the hand besmears

[1] *Confess.* lib. v. c. 12.

Of them who grasp it. Lo, this fleeting world
They hug, but Thee despise who dost abide,
Callest them back, and will forgive man's soul,
Though stained by sin, when it to Thee returns.
Such bad and crooked men loathe I and hate ;
Yet would I love them could they be improved,
And would prefer the learning which they get
To money which they save, and Thee, O GOD,
Prefer to learning ; for Thou art the Truth,
The full completeness of most certain good,
And purest peace ! "   Whilst thus to GOD he
     made
Complaint concerning men who would, ere long,
Be punished by the sword of ALARIC,
Sad news arrived from Milan ! VERECUNDUS
Had suddenly expired ! but not before
He had, with much contrition for the past,
And full of blessed hope, his faith declared
In the LORD JESUS, had been then baptized,
Eaten with thankfulness the flesh of CHRIST,
And entered the communion of His saints.
Therefore the news, though sad, brought to AUGUSTINE
Comfort, where else he had been unconsoled ;[1]
And he was able thanks to render GOD
For mercy shown not only to his friend,
Who rested now in heaven, but to himself,
And all who erst at Cassiciacum
Had that friend's hospitality enjoyed ;
For they must needs have been o'erwhelmed with
     grief,
And agonized with pain, too great to bear,
If VERECUNDUS, when he left this world,
Had not been numbered in the flock of CHRIST.

[1] *Confess.* lib. ix. c. 3.

Therefore resignedly their heads they bowed,
And all, with one accord, to GOD gave thanks.

Rome did not long detain them on their way.
A vessel, as they heard, would soon depart
From Ostia for Carthage : there they went,
And found the ship which had, two years before,
Amidst great perils of the winds and waves,
Safely brought MONICA to Italy.
It now was floating idly in the port,
Taking in cargo, slowly brought on board.
Therefore in marshy, sickly Ostia
Were they detained, hoping each day to sail.
There first we met with them, when on the shore
They watched the sunset, listening to the waves,
But not without presentiment of ill.

MONICA IN PRAYER.

" O CHRIST, dear LORD, our SAVIOUR and our GOD !
    Assuage our sorrows, and dispel our fears ;
Give us the comfort of Thy staff and rod,
    As we walk weeping through this vale of tears ;
Until our feet this pilgrimage have trod,
    Be Thou our guide, and one our cry who hears !

" Behold, what perils we must pass along !
    What stumbling-blocks obstruct our narrow way !
What snares, which to the Evil One belong,
    Would catch our feet or lead our steps astray !
In gloom and darkness sadly sounds our song,
    As we wait longing for Thy promised day.

" When to illume our path shall Thy star shine ?
  When wilt Thou glimpses of Thy truth afford ?
When shall our eyes behold Thy face divine,
  Unveiled at length, to be by us adored ?
Long have we waited for that voice of Thine ;
  Then come, come quickly, JESUS CHRIST, our
    LORD !"

II.

GRACE.

An Epistle from Nebridius.

"UNTO Augustine and our other friends,
  Beloved in God, Nebridius greeting sends:
Augustine's letters have I lately read
With grateful heart; for they to me have given
Comfort 'midst grief for Verecundus dead.
But from these topics will I pass at once
To others, which embarrass me with doubts
Craving solution, which I pray Thee give.
I fain would understand and gladly praise
God's moral government and justice, shown
Unto His creatures, above all to man,
Did His omniscience and omnipotence
Not raise obstructions insurmountable!
For how can I, when I survey this world,
And mark the misery which here prevails,
Contrive by reasoning to reconcile
The contradictions which perplex my mind,
And almost drive me to admit again
That no small share some Evil Being had
In the creation, goodness to oppose?
For how could God, whom we with awe regard,
As Wisdom, Love, and Justice infinite,
Create a hell, and, next, mankind create,

With the foreknowledge sure and the intent
That there the greater number needs should go,
To pine for ever, and in torments wail?[1]
GOD foresaw all, yet acted as He did!
Can a created being think or act
But in conformity to principles
Established at creation for his rule?
The wolf seeks blood, and some men wickedness,
By a fierce impulse given them at birth.
Should GOD for that hold them responsible,
And plunge them in a hell prepared before?
If that be justice, is it also love?
Is it not something rather contrary
To both?   This thought brings me perplexity,
From which I fain would be by thee unloosed.
Wilt thou, by aid which Scripture lends, bestow
Light to clear up the darkness of this theme?
Help me outside this labyrinth to pass!"

THE REPLY.

" Unto NEBRIDIUS, our brother loved,
And greatly honoured friend, ALYPIUS
Sends greeting in the LORD; in which AUGUSTINE
And all now with us join. We have received
Thy letter, and its questions read with care;
But by the weight of heavy matters pressed,
Which cannot be deferred, AUGUSTINE'S hand
Writes not to thee, but he will show thee soon
His Treatise on Free-Will, yet incomplete.
This will much profit.   But so well know I

[1] Mill's *Autobiography*, p. 40 *et post.*

T

His views, that I thy questions will resolve
By mine own thoughts, to which his words have led.[1]

"Of spiritual being, will the essence is:[2]
Therefore, when life to man by GOD was given,
Man had free-will, which GOD alone could give.
GOD could give that, else were Omnipotence
Under restrictions of necessity,
And not Omnipotent in truth.   This gift
The angels had before our world was made;
But some were fallen, who their eyes had turned
From GOD on self, and dislocation made
Between their wills and the Almighty's will.
Unless created beings had the choice
To follow or resist the will of GOD,
They had not been free agents, but no more
Than instruments, like things mechanical,
And not well suited, even when most good,
To give GOD pleasure; for which end alone
They were and are created and exist.
Can man complain of GOD because He made
Angels before our world had origin,
And gave free-will, a gift which some abused?
Can man complain of GOD because a hell
Grew then around the spirits reprobate
Of evil angels?   Evil had no share
In man's creation, which GOD's self called good;
But evil helped to mar, though not to make!

[1] Augustine's opinions on grace were not fully developed until after he had written his *Treatise on Free-Will*, which he completed at Rome; nor, indeed, until after he had been engaged in his controversy with Pelagius and his followers.   But in his later epistles his opinions are stated with great clearness. [See *Epistles*, Nos. 157, 186, 190.] Alypius, in this reply, somewhat forestalls them.
[2] See *De Pressigne*.

Man, a free being when from GOD'S hands fresh,[1]
And capable of evil and of good,
Used liberty obedience to transgress
And violate GOD'S law; therefore he fell,
Severed from his Creator, and became
The slave of passion and ignoble self,
His blessed nature gone, and free no more!
The origin of sin, which stands revealed
By Scripture in relation to mankind,
Seems clear to me, though hidden in a myth.
When EVE with ADAM walked in Paradise,
And both were innocent and beautiful,
A strict commandment GOD unto them gave,
The test of true obedience to His will.
But EVE, by curiosity o'ercome,
And the insidious tempting of a fiend,
Whose evil promptings, like a serpent's coils,
Writhed round her soul, into transgression slipped,
And her enticement led to ADAM'S sin,—
Sin which produced that earliest bastard, CAIN,
Fruit of unwedded and forbidden love!
The law, 'Thou shalt not,' ADAM'S will broke through;
Knowing and undeceived, he sinned and fell.
No light command had GOD on them imposed,
Nor one of arbitrary sort; for look
Around the world, recall its history,

[1] In his Epistle to Marcellinus (*Epistle* 143), Augustine himself says : "The soul of the first man did, before the entrance of sin, govern his body with perfect freedom of will, although that body was not yet spiritual, but animal ; but after the entrance of sin, that is, after sin had been committed in that flesh from which sinful flesh was thenceforward to be propagated, the reasonable soul is so appointed to occupy an inferior body, that it does not govern its body with absolute freedom of will. . . . It was only after the entrance of sin that bodies having this infirmity began to be produced ; for Adam was not created thus, and he did not beget any offspring before he sinned."

And say if this, the earliest sin, be not,
And hath not always been, the bane of man,
The source of hatred, murders, crimes, and woe !
If man, though warned, will beat his foolish head
Against hard rocks, can he with justice rail
When feeling pain, and cast reproach on GOD ?
Yet daily man doth this, and even worse !
The blood which in his veins with health ran pure
At his creation, he hath made corrupt,
Defiled it by incessant acts of sin,
Till now it flows a foul and tainted stream,—
Man's doing, and not GOD'S.   Free-will no more
Is the distinctive attribute of man.
That glorious gift is not the heritage
Of self-made slaves, in deep abasement sunk,
The tyrants and the terror of the world !
The bird whose flight was in the loftiest air,
And had the heavens for range, hath dashed herself
Against the cliffs, and now, with broken wings,
Limps a lame wretch imprisoned on the ground !
Yes, such is man, until CHRIST healeth him,—
A bird with broken wings that cannot soar !
Man groaneth now in bondage unto sin.
Let it be granted GOD all this foresaw,
Yet did create !   By that most gracious act,
Myriads of men, now blessèd saints in heaven,
Derived existence, and in glory dwell ;
To whom, from east and west, from north and south,
Shall countless throngs be added in each age,
To swell the number, not divide the joy.
Yes, from all nations, kindreds, peoples, tongues,
Shall multitudes in number numberless
Approach GOD'S throne, and stand before the Lamb,[1]

¹ Rev. vii. 9.

Clothed in white robes, and there salvation cry.
Should the elect in no such glory live,
Because, through sin, some others merit hell,
That endless torment of remorseful thoughts?
GOD, by His prescience, from eternity
Foresaw that man, when at creation made
And with free-will endowed, would surely fall
From innocence to sin, and would transgress
By an abuse of that most glorious gift
Which left him choice.   Yet GOD did not withhold
The gift itself, or make His creature thus
Less noble, though immaculate.   He gave
As none but GOD could give, and what He knew
Beforehand would be done, man's free-will did.
But GOD had, from eternity, ordained
That man, when fallen, should at last be saved
By JESUS CHRIST, who in His life should show
Obedience perfect, and should, by His blood,
Wash out transgressions, and for sin atone.
GOD did not by compulsion keep man good,
But by His Son He fallen man redeemed,
And made salvation easy unto all
Who CHRIST believe, and take on them His cross.
But what of them who do not?   What of them
Who never heard CHRIST'S name?   I answer thus : [1]
In the Lamb's Book of Life, shut close and sealed
With seven mystic seals, unbroken yet,
Are writ the names of those who shall be saved ;
But only He can ope that book and read.
None therefore now can know with certainty
The fate reserved for ignorance or guilt.
But the Lamb's other book, the Book of Works,
That faithful register of words and acts,

[1] Rev. v. 1, xiii. 8, xx. 12, xxi. 27.

Contains the account which each must answer for
At the great day, when all things shall be known.
Of this we glimpses have, but only guess
What names are written in the Book of Life.
The price which by His blood CHRIST paid for us
Was ample to remit the sins of all ;
But He Himself hath told us it was shed
' For us and many,' therefore not for all !
JUDAS is not sole traitor unto CHRIST ;
Others besides him are perdition's sons,
Their bodies in the Church, their souls without.
GOD'S prescience is a passive attribute,
That works not to effect what it foresees.
It does not take away or change in men
Free-will, but rather, on the contrary,
Supposes it, by knowledge of its acts.
They who make up the number of the damned,
Do so because of sin inherited,
Or sin themselves have done ; not because GOD
Foresaw their end.   But all of GOD'S elect
Are saved by grace, which in them operates
With force resistless.   Why they are elect,
And are like brands from the red flames plucked out,
Is unto us inscrutable ; the cause
Lies in GOD'S secret counsel.   There are none
Unto destruction forced as reprobates,
Though some, not all, are from destruction saved.
Grace is from GOD, and is of GOD the gift :
By it lost man created is afresh.
Grace precedes merit, and not merit grace : [1]
Grace finds not out, but maketh the elect : [2]
Gratuitous it is, not our just due. [3]

[1] Augustine's *Opera*, vi. 165 D ; x. 547 B, C.   [2] *Ib.* ii. 1003 B.
[3] *Ib.* x. 1573 A, B, 1575 B, C.

Grace, when it works with them for whom it works,
The wicked justifies, and helps the just.[1]
Whene'er it acts, it doth by mercy act ;
When it acts not, by justice it refrains.[2]
If some by grace are saved not, 'tis because
Their human will the will of GOD resists.[3]
GOD willeth not that any perish should,
But wills that all should to repentance come.[4]
By grace through faith are we (as PAUL saith) saved.[5]
Pray then for grace, and may thy prayer prevail !
Oh, may the grace of CHRIST, the love of GOD,
And HOLY SPIRIT'S blessed fellowship,
Now and for evermore, be with us all ! "

---

[1] Augustine's *Opera*, vi. 905 C.   [2] *Ib.* vi. 395 C.
[3] *Ib.* vi. 395 A.   [4] 2 Pet. iii. 9.   [5] Eph. ii. 8.

III.

WHAT GRAVE?

"THE ship is nearly ready ; soon we sail,"
　　ALYPIUS said to MONICA one day,
As on the shore she watched the bursting waves.
"Then," said EVODIUS, "we shall once more live !
For here our life is wearisome as death."
"Say not that death is wearisome, my friend,"
Replied the sweet, firm voice of MONICA ;
"This life it is which is so wearisome,
When the great objects which we would fulfil
Are all accomplished, and we yearn for rest.
Ah ! would that even now, this very night,
Death, whom so many dread, would visit me,
And thus my earthly pilgrimage might end !
Nay, look not on me with a face amazed,
Because I tell thee truly that I view
In death a blessing, but no cause of fear."
"What !" said EVODIUS, "would you wish to die
Far from Tagasta, from your native land,
And let this foreign soil receive your bones ?"
"Once felt I otherwise, I do confess,"
Was the reply ; "for, ere I left my home,
Some dim anxiety my mind disturbed
Lest I should find a foreign burial.
For I had built a tomb where I might lie
Beside the body of PATRICIUS,

That as our wedded lives were passed together
In an affection which increased each year,
And ended in such consolation true,
My children might, when my last hour had come,
Place my remains near his, and we might sleep
In death united, as in life we dwelt.
But now such wishes seem but vain and fond ;
For shall we not be near to one another
When both in ABRAHAM'S bosom shall repose ?
What place is far from GOD ?   How can I fear
That, when the world shall end, He will not know
The place whence He must raise me from the dead ?
Then, e'en in Ostia, content am I,
If here death visit me, to find a grave."
Thus spake she, and in silence to their home
They walked, EVODIUS wondering as he went.

MONICA MUSES.

" This earth, a charnel-house outspread,
        Is great and wide !
  Where shall I flee to, in my dread,
        To crouch and hide ?
  Where find a grave when I am dead,
        And there abide ?

" See yonder grave, where LAZARUS
        For three days slept ;
  JESUS stood there and prayed for us,
        JESUS there wept !
  Shall I the grave, much honoured thus,
        For mine accept ?

" Ah, no ! for though he once arose
  From out that grave,
And at the table sat with those
  Whom GOD forgave,
When MARY'S tears, with bitter throes,
  CHRIST'S feet did lave ;

" Yet sank he in the tomb again,
  Was once more tried,
Knew human sorrow, fears, and pain,
  Ate, drank, and died :
I would unbroken rest obtain,
  To him denied.

" Where can I find the rest I crave,
  But in one place ?
The sepulchre of CHRIST ! that grave
  So full of grace,
Wherein for all whom He shall save
  Is ample space.

" There would I lie, there take my rest
  In certain peace,
Until our GOD shall think it best
  That time should cease,
And shall, from tombs and graves, each guest
  At once release.

" Then should I from CHRIST'S grave uprise
  As out of sleep ;
See Him with gladness, love, surprise,
  And reverence deep ;
No more to gaze with darkened eyes,
  No more to weep.

"Oh ! in that sepulchre of Thine
    Find room for me ;
Let me there taste of rest divine,
    There wakened be ;
Thy resurrection make Thou mine,
    Change me like Thee !

" Let me behold Thy heavenly charms,
    Lean on Thy breast ;
Fold Thou me in Thy loving arms,
    My spouse confest !
And in Thy glory, safe from harms,
    Give me Thy rest ! "

IV.

THE DEPARTURE.

WHEN the trim vessel was at last equipped,
And waited only for the first fair breeze,
AUGUSTINE and his mother, quite alone,
Stood one night idly leaning on the sill
Of a high window, which looked down upon
The garden of their house in Ostia.
There, in seclusion from the din of men,
They rested as poor weary pilgrims rest,
Who, having just one tedious journey closed,
Must soon begin another. They discoursed
In mutual confidence, with no one near,
On truth whose presence here is that of GOD;
And, all forgetful of the things behind,
They reached forth to the things which are before.[1]
Then, in their interchange of thoughts, they next
Inquired between themselves what sort of life
The life eternal of the saints must be,
Which, as ST. PAUL declares, eye hath not seen,
Ear heard, nor hath it in the heart of man
E'en entered as a thought.[2] Yet for that life
They gasped with thirst, which longed to slake itself
In streams fresh-flowing from the fount of GOD,
That, thus refreshed, they might then meditate
In some way on a mystery so high.

[1] Phil. iii. 13.   [2] 1 Cor. ii. 9.

In their discourse they both of them agreed
That the chief pleasures earthly senses give,
The purest light of a material kind,
Could not in glory ever be compared
To light celestial, or deserve to be
E'en mentioned with it.   Raising, then, themselves
By love, which ever kindled more and more,
Towards the One, Self-same, Unchangeable,
They, in imagination, hurried through
All things material ; through Heaven above,
Whence sun, moon, stars, upon the earth shine down :
Then next, by inward musing, deep discourse,
And admiration of the works of GOD,
They soared still higher : unto their own minds
Came they as visitors, and went beyond,
That they might reach that region, fair and rich
With never-failing plenty, where GOD feeds
ISRAEL for ever with the food of truth,
And where the life is Wisdom's self, by whom
All things were made which are, have been, shall be ;
And yet this Wisdom was itself not made,
But is, and as it hath been will remain.
Thus, in their efforts struggling with spent breath
To reach that Wisdom, they at last attained,
By one whole effort of the labouring heart,
To touch it slightly, whereat pleased they sighed ;
But left the first-fruits of the Spirit bound
Where they had found them, and once more returned
From silent wanderings through the realms of thought
Back to the noisy clamour of the tongue,
Where a word spoken doth begin and end :
For what, O LORD our GOD, is like Thy Word,
Who in Himself continueth without change,
Yet He it is who all things doth make new ?

AUGUSTINE then spake thus to MONICA: [1]
"Oh! if to any favoured son of earth
Were silenced all the tumults of the flesh,
Silenced the images of earth, sea, air,
Silenced the poles, silenced the very soul,
Which, not self-conscious, should itself transcend ;
If dreams and pictures which from fancy come,
If every tongue and every sign, and all
Which transiently exist, were silent made,—
For, if one could but hear these things, all say,
'We have not made ourselves, but He us made
Who doth abide for ever!'—if, again,
When these had spoken thus, they should subside,
Having aroused the ear to list to Him
Who made them, and He then alone should speak,—
Not through these things which He created hath,
But by Himself, so that we heard His voice,—
Not through the tongue of flesh, through angel's speech,
Or by the thunder-cloud, or riddle dark
Expressed in language of similitude,—
But we should hear HIMSELF, whom in these things
We love, and should without these things Him hear,—
E'en as just now we heard, when, stretched in thought,
We in our rapid progress touched at last
Eternal Wisdom, which o'er all abides ;—
If we in such a vision could remain,
With other views of an inferior kind
Withdrawn from sight, and this one view alone
Should seize, absorb, and bury him who gazed
In inward joys, and one's life might remain
For evermore like to that moment gone
Of bright intelligence which late we felt,—
Oh! would not then these words be realized :

[1] See Appendix, Note Q; Augustine's *Confess.* lib. ix. c. 10.

'Into Thy LORD'S joy enter thou'?   Alas!
When shall that time be ours?   Will it not come
When we shall all arise?   But shall not all
Be changed alike?"—Thus did AUGUSTINE speak,
As with the earnestness of love he gazed
Upwards to heaven.   Then MONICA, who sank
Exhausted on a chair, looked up as well,
And both remained unconscious for a time
Of earth and its delights, which they despised.
But as a shiver, to November due,
Spread through the tender frame of MONICA,
She whispered to AUGUSTINE these few words:[1]
"My son, I do confess that in this life
Nothing there is in which I any more
Can take delight.   What here I have to do
Henceforth, and to what end I tarry here,
I know not; for the hope which in this world
I entertained is wholly realized!
One thing there was for which a little while
I wished to linger in this life, that I
Might, ere my death, see thee a Christian man
Of Catholic belief.   But this my GOD
Hath more abundantly performed for me;
So that I now behold thee, with a mind
Which scorns felicity of earthly sort,
Become His servant!   What more do I here?"
Then, as her son embraced her, she arose
And sought her chamber, laid her on her bed,
Where through the night she sighed for sleep denied.
There, ere five days had passed, she sank again
Sick of a fever, which consumed her strength;
Then, as her friends were weeping round her couch,
She had another vision of the joys

---

[1] See Appendix, Note R; Augustine's *Confess.* lib. ix. c. 10.

Reserved for saints in heaven, and on them gazed
With love ineffable, whilst, in a swoon,
Her mind was from the things of sight withdrawn.
At last, to consciousness returned, she looked
Upon her sons, who both stood close at hand,
And asked, "Where am I?" Then, when they,
        amazed,
Could not for grief reply, " Here," added she,
" Shall ye your mother bury." At these words
AUGUSTINE checked, from filial reverence,
His voice and tears ; not so NAVIGIUS,
Who stammered out a hope that she might yet
Enjoy a happier lot, and even die,
Not in a foreign, but her native land !
Whereat, with anxious look, she on him gazed,
As if she would reprove him with her eyes
For any thought which savoured of such things ;
And turning to AUGUSTINE, faintly cried :
" Lo, what he saith !" Then, soon, when strength
        availed,
To both gave this command :[1] " Lay anywhere
This body, but about it let no care
Disquiet thee. This only I request,
That ye will me remember, without fail,
At the LORD'S altar, wheresoe'er ye be."
Thus she besought them, that her memory
Might find a fitting shrine in holy thoughts,
As her best burial-place and sepulchre !
Nor did she further heed what should become,
After her death, of her remains on earth.
She spake no more, by weakness overcome ;
And when the fever had endured nine days,
She passed away from earth and entered heaven.

[1] See Appendix, Note S ; Augustine's *Confess.* lib. ix. c. 11.

AUGUSTINE closed her eyes ; and as he knew
Her soul had gone to bliss, he held his peace,
Checked the great sorrow swelling in his heart,
Which longed for vent in tears, and by his will
Dried up their fountain ; yet was full of woe,
Largely augmented by such inward strife.
Young ADEODATUS, knowing no restraint,
Burst forth into laments, and wept aloud.
He would have gone on weeping all the day,
But that his tears were checked by those who longed
With his to mix their own, but did not dare.
EVODIUS then stept forth, took in his hand
The psalter, and began to sing the Psalm,[1]
" Of mercy and of judgment will I sing
To Thee, O LORD," in which at once all joined ;
For they were well assured grief was unfit
For the departed, as for one quite dead,
Or one unhappy ; nay, they knew that she
Could not in death unhappy be supposed,
Or really dead, for she had passed through death
To life eternal.   Then came flocking in,
Some neighbours who had heard of the event ;
And after they a tender glance had given
At the calm, gentle face of MONICA,
On which a smile still lingered, all withdrew
Into another room, in which AUGUSTINE,
Putting a strong restraint upon his tears,
Addressed them in some few and solemn words,
Fit for the time, whereby he soothed the pain
Which had, by sharp attacks, near mastered him,
Although he seemed to those who heard him speak
As free from sorrow.   Thus he struggled on,
Feeling within him grief he must keep down,—

[1] Ps. ci. I.

U

Grief which, in the appointed course of things,
Will needs be present in hearts just bereaved,
And which he found with sorrow had such power,
Despite his judgment. Therefore with new grief
He grieved, because of grief which would not go,
And by a double sorrow was thus pained ;
But when this task was done, when all had gone,
And GOD alone was present to his heart,
He poured forth unto Him, in words like these,
The sorrowful effusions of his soul :[1]

" When I with all my heart to Thee shall cleave,
    No more with me will toil or pain abide,
And then my truly living life will heave,
    Filled to the full with Thy inflowing tide !
But since man filled by Thee Thou dost uplift,
Unfilled, a burthen to myself, I drift.

" My grievous joys with joyous griefs contend,
    Nor know I on which side stands victory.
O LORD ! Thy pitying eyes upon me bend ;
    My evil woe doth my glad good defy,
And where stands victory I do not know ;
Alas ! O LORD, Thy pity on me show !

" Behold ! my wounds from Thee I do not hide ;
    Physician art Thou, I a patient sick ;
Though Thou art mercy, I a wretch abide.
    Is not man's life on earth with trials thick ?
By whom are troubles and distress approved ?
Thou biddest them be borne, but not be loved.

[1] See Appendix, Note T ; Augustine's *Confess.* lib. x. c. 28.

" No man can really love the pain he bears,
 Though he may love to bear it. Be it true
That he e'en smile beneath his load of cares,
 Yet would he rather that no care he knew.
In mine adversity for good I sigh,
But dread, in happy times, an evil nigh.

" In what clear space between the two can we
 Find footing on some favoured spot, where may
Man's life no more a time of trial be ?
 Alas, woe ! woe ! once and again I say,
On earth's prosperity, which hath alloy
From dread of evil and decay of joy.

" Not once, nor twice, but three times, woe ! I cry
 On earthly sorrows, which for solace long :
For hard indeed is real adversity ;
 And its endurance, even to the strong,
Shipwreck oft brings. Then is not, I inquire,
Man's life on earth a constant trial dire ? "

THE BURIAL.

SOME hours elapsed, but ere the night arrived
   The corpse had to the earth to be consigned.
AUGUSTINE and his friends rose up from prayer,
And on their shoulders raised the precious load,
Then walking through the city with slow steps,
Bore it to where, in consecrated ground,
It was to rest—there gently set it down ;
But, ere 'twas lowered to its place in earth,
They knelt with reverence around the corpse,
And took with faith the holy sacrament,
Whereby, according to GOD'S ordinance,
They had communion with the saints on earth
And saints in heaven,—therefore with MONICA,
Through CHRIST, who is the food to nourish all.

They thought, when they her sepulchre had closed,
That her remains would rest there undisturbed
Till the last trump should sound ; for none surmised,
That when a thousand years and more had passed,
And true religion should from Rome have fled,
There would arise a shameless trafficking,
Which made foul merchandise of dead saints' bones ;
So that e'en MONICA'S remains, dug up
From where they were concealed beneath the ground,
Resting in peace, from curious eyes withdrawn,

Would as a sight be carried off to Rome,
To give occasion for a holiday!
But MARTIN, the fifth Pope who bore that name,
A dilettante Roman gentleman
Of the COLONNA family, did this!
He was the Pope who on his milk-white steed
Went through Rome's streets to church, while
    SIGISMUND,
The Emperor, held one bridle, and the other
Was lackeyed by the LORD OF BRANDENBURG.
But SIGISMUND ere long took his revenge:
For when Pope MARTIN, to some sinful act,
Condemned by Christian laws, desired to give
Beforehand the full sanction of the Church,
The Emperor reproved him in these words:
"Nay, Holy Father, thou the power hast
To pardon, but not authorize a sin!"
This MARTIN brought the corpse of MONICA
To Rome amidst the uproar of a mob,
And o'er it spoke, amidst immense applause,
A speech of pompous words, tagged round with lies.[1]
This done, he from the corpse tore off the head,[2]
And put it in a casket made of glass,
For his own keeping in the Vatican;
Her other bones he, as a boon, bestowed
Upon a chapelry of small repute,

[1] A copy of this speech may be seen in the Appendix to Bugeaud's *Hist. de S. Monique*, 4° ed. p. 599.

[2] Since this desecration of the dead by Martin v. in 1430, the remains of Monica have been subjected to further profanation, under the colour of doing them religious honour. In 1576 Gregory XIII. broke away a piece of the head, and sent it to Bologna. The rest of her corpse has fared no better. The sisterhood of St. Monica at Rome have had a bit given to them, and a rib has been given to Pavia by "la munificence des Papes." The Jesuits at Trèves also possess some fragments. The remains of St. Augustine himself have fared no better.

Whence they have since been shifted to a nook
In the great gilded church which now in Rome
Bears her son's name.   Few are the worshippers
Who kneel before her tomb ! but crowds are seen
All day just opposite, and throng around
A marble idol with a brazen foot,
Encircled by a row of silver lamps,
On whose cold bosom shines, to cheat the eye,
A gleaming breastplate of large coloured stones,
False as the worship which deludes men's souls.

AUGUSTINE wept not at the burial
Of MONICA, whom he so well had loved,
Nor through the day, though agonized by woe.
He sought relief in prayer, tried if a bath
Would soothe him, but his efforts were in vain.
The bitterness of sorrow could not thus
Exude from out his heart.   Soon as night came
He slept a broken sleep, which softer made
The hardness of his will ; then waking up,
Alone in midnight stillness, a few lines
Occurred to him of an Ambrosian hymn,
From which, in days at Cassiciacum
Lately so happy, MONICA had erst
Made a quotation.   Looking up to heaven,
AUGUSTINE then spoke out these words aloud :

" GOD, of all things Creator ! who
      Of this earth's poles the Ruler art,
Dost clothe the day in light's bright hue,
      And grateful sleep to night impart,—
Relax our weary limbs, that rest
      May faculty for work restore ;

Refresh our minds, by toil opprest,
   And give relief from sorrows sore."

Then came to memory his mother's face,
Her holy conversation towards GOD,
Her sacred tenderness for him, her son,
And all her family, now suddenly
Deprived by one fell stroke of so much love!
His overburdened soul could bear no more;
The pride he felt that she was now a saint
No longer gave support: his tears at last
Flowed forth unchecked; for Nature hath her rights,
And will assert them, struggle as we may.
Therefore AUGUSTINE in the sight of GOD
Wept like a child, and mingled sobs with tears;
Upon his tears his heart at length reposed,
And found therein sweet solace for his pain.

AUGUSTINE TO GOD.[1]

"O LORD our GOD! give peace to us from Thee!
   Giver of all things! give the peace of rest,—
That Sabbath peace—peace from eve's coming free!
   For all things good, in fairest order drest,
Their course being finished, pass unto their end;
On them both morn and eve alike attend.

"The seventh day hath no eve, nor is shade cast
   Thereon by sunset; it hath ever stood
Holy, and through Thee evermore will last;
   For when Thou madest all things very good,
Though Thou whilst doing so with peace wert blest,
Yet didst Thou on the seventh day take Thy rest.

[1] See Appendix, Note U; Augustine's *Confess.* lib. xiii. c. 35-38.

" Thy voice already to mankind hath told,
 In Holy Scriptures, which declare it true,
That when our works are done,—which we may hold
 Good works, since Thou didst give them us to do,—
We shall, on Thee reposing, free from strife,
Rest in the Sabbath of eternal life.

" Then wilt Thou in us rest, as now in us
 Thou workest ; through us shall Thy rest then be,
As through us now Thy works ; for Thou dost thus
 For ever rest and work ! Thou dost not see
Or move or rest in time ; yet from Thee come
Time's visions, time itself, and rest therefrom.

" The things Thou madest we can now descry,
 Because they are ; but they as things abide,
Because Thou seest them ! We view them lie
 Outside, since they exist ; also inside,
Since they are good; but Thou beheldst them made
When they, in embryo, to be fashioned stayed.

" We, being thereto moved, have some good wrought
 In days now past, after our hearts had free
Conception of Thy Spirit ; but we sought
 Evil in earlier days, forsaking Thee ;
Yet Thou, our one good GOD, didst never cease
The number of Thy blessings to increase.

" Some good works we have wrought by Thy grace blest,
 But they are not eternal.   All being done,
We hope to find ourselves in peaceful rest
 At Thy great hallowing! But Thou good from none
Dost need, being Goodness !   Thou must ever be
Tranquil, because Thine own tranquillity !

" What man can make a man this truth attain ?
    What angel, though by heaven's experience taught,
Can it to angel or to man explain ?
    Let it of Thee be asked, of Thee be sought,
With Thee be knocked for ; thus, and thus alone,
Shall it be had, be found, be open thrown !"

VI

CHRIST'S RESURRECTION.

PLATO'S stupendous intellect
   Could, without Revelation's aid
His search for knowledge to direct,
   Discover, by the things displayed
In nature, the great mystery,
And find in GOD a Trinity.

But PLATO did not comprehend
   That sin once done must sin remain
For ever, until time shall end ;
   And all who do it bear its stain,
Unless the Word should flesh assume,
And CHRIST'S own death avert the doom.

Nor could his proud philosophy
   Conceive beforehand the great plan,
Now told in sacred history,
   By which our LORD redeemed lost man,
For sin atoned, GOD reconciled,
And brought back home His erring child.

Not even CHRIST'S disciples, though
   He taught them what would Him befall,—
That He salvation must bestow
   By dying for the sins of all,—

Could understand the truths He said,
Or resurrection from the dead.

Upon the very day He died,
   When they had laid Him in the grave,
Apostles groaned and women cried,
   They cowered disheartened and dismayed ;
They all could weep, despair, and grieve,
But not their Master's words believe !

But when at last the third day came,
   Before the sun's light shone forth clear,
Lo, women whispering His name
   Before His sepulchre appear,
To find their tears and spices vain !
For risen had CHRIST to life again.

Before that day was turned to night,
   His weeping mother and His friends
Had seen and heard Him with delight !
   Their grief He blames, their faith commends :
Upon the fortieth day, with awe,
They CHRIST'S ascension wondering saw.

He chose for fallen man to die,
   To suffer scoffs, the cross, and pain ;
He chose within the grave to lie,
   And on the third day rise again,
Because from all eternity
GOD had decreed that this should be.

We now believe, but cannot yet
   Search out GOD'S deep things with our hand ;

Man's puny intellect may fret,
  But cannot all facts understand!
Suffice it that we give GOD praise,
Adore His love, revere His ways.

Suffice it if with CHRIST we share
  The mighty victory He won ;
Can think on death without despair,
  Rise from the grave, like GOD'S own Son ;
Be saved by Him, on high ascend,
To dwell in glory without end!

SAINT AUGUSTINE.

———◆———

BOOK VIII.

THE THREE TEMPTATIONS.

N.B.—The incidents related in this Book are imaginary, but they are
such as would, according to high probability, happen to Augustine during
the important year which he passed in Rome after his mother's death.
The opinions attributed to him are in accordance with passages in his works.

BOOK VIII.

———

I.

THE WORLD.

AUGUSTINE in the morning woke refreshed,
  Lighter in heart, and stronger in his will.
The ship had some days sailed for Africa
While MONICA was dying on her bed.
In Ostia's sickly harbour to remain
Would have been madness. "Quick, then, back to
    Rome!"
Cried out AUGUSTINE as the morning dawned;
His friends who heard, with swift and joyful haste,
Made needful preparations to depart.
Ere long they rode, a silent cavalcade,
Mounted on hirèd steeds, which slowly paced
Along the smooth-paved road; but ere they reached
The gates of Rome, AUGUSTINE from his horse
Alighted, and no more would ride. He sent
His party forwards, and walked on alone.
In melancholy silence crossed he o'er
Large undulating slopes of pasture land,
Until he reached the broad and reedy plains
Through which the Ostian road approaches Rome.
The winding Tiber made this region rich
With vegetation, but the dwellers there

Were few and fever-stricken.   On all sides
Large gardens flourished, full of fruits and flowers.
The vineyards, which extended far and wide,
Had their grapes gathered, but the leaves remained
Upon the vines despoiled, and glowed with hues
Of scarlet and rich brown.   Dark pomegranates
In clusters peeped above the jealous walls ;
The fig-trees spread luxuriantly their leaves ;
And here and there, as ornaments, were seen,
Uprising to the sky, the tufted heads
Of palm-trees, lately brought from Eastern climes.

    When close to Rome, AUGUSTINE some time stayed
At a basilica, which CONSTANTINE
Had raised with reverence above the spot
Where, ere the Church had peace, a Roman dame,
LUCINDA, had endured a martyr's doom
Rather than call the name of CHRIST accursed.
This church was destined to become ere long
A splendid pile, built at prodigious cost ;
For on its site ST. PAUL had suffered death,
When with more joy than fear his feet stepped o'er
The narrow strip of shade triangular
Cast by the tomb of CAIUS CESTIUS.
Back to that spot, where peace at last had come
And persecution ceased, his headless trunk,
Hidden for years among the Catacombs,
Was borne triumphantly, to find a tomb,
Its fit and ever honoured place of rest.
AUGUSTINE entered there and knelt him down,
To give CHRIST thanks that PAUL was, by His grace,
Made from a persecutor of the Church
A great apostle, chosen by Himself,
And by Him taught directly, not through men.

PETER was chosen first, that by his mouth
Gentiles should hear the gospel's precious truths,
And on the day of Pentecost believe.
But PETER kept not what this choice conferred ;
He gave the Gentiles up and chose the Jews : [1]
Then as apostle of the Gentile world
Did PAUL declare himself, and was thenceforth
Their chief apostle and their minister.
What GOD gave PETER to bestow on Jews,
The same for Gentiles gave He unto PAUL.[2]

Beneath the roof of that basilica,
Near where the saint reposed, were also laid
The bones of TIMOTHY, who has been called
PAUL'S own son in the faith ; who for that faith
Worked long with patience, charity, and meekness,
And unto CHRIST bore witness by his death.
Here, sheltered by that wayside humble church,
For then it was no more,[3] slept side by side
Those Christian saints in consecrated ground ;
And by their graves knelt down, with thanks to GOD,
One who, as their successor in the faith,
Hath never been, nor will he be excelled ;
Yet, like the Baptist, whom our LORD pronounced
More than a prophet, never ventured he
To claim men's credence by a miracle.
Sufficient unto him and for his work

---

[1] Gal. ii. 7, 8 ; Rom. xi. 13, xv. 16; 1 Cor. xv. 10; 2 Cor. x. 5, xii. 11.
[2] Augustine's *Opera*, vi. 2667 A.
[3] The church was called "San Paulo extra muros," and was first an oratorium erected by Constantine, A.D. 234. Valentine II. began to rebuild it in 386, and it was completed by Honorius. It has been burned down on several occasions. The present magnificent structure has recently been completed by Pius IX. from contributions collected from all parts of the world for the purpose.

Were answers made by GOD to fervent prayer.
AUGUSTINE rose refreshed and left the church,
Whose stones were hallowed by the sacred dust
Enshrined within it ; then to Rome walked on,
Entered the gate of Ostia, behind
Mons Aventinus, which from sight concealed
The gorgeous palaces and temples built
Around the Forum.   Dusty, hot, and tired
With his long journey, he that hill declined,
And turning to his right, soon reached the baths
Which bore their founder CARACALLA'S name.
There having bathed and rested, he became
Composed enough to look around, and gaze
With wonder on that famous edifice,
Which then existed in a splendour time
Had softened, not subdued.   It had been built
When the Imperial creed was Pagan still,
And every Emperor tried to mark his reign
By architectural prodigies in stone.
Rome at that epoch ruled by force the world,
And taxed at will all nations of the earth ;
Therefore their monarchs, proud and absolute,
Raised, in the very wantonness of wealth,
Huge structures built at unrestricted cost ;
Hoping to throw more awe about their creed
By cruel sacrifices offered up
In amphitheatres, where blood and tears
Of Christian captives and confessors stained
The horrible arena.   Policy
Found in religion a subservient tool,
And tyranny with superstition joined
In vain endeavours to postpone their doom,
And give a false coherence to decay.
Under such impulses this pile immense

Was planned by CARACALLA, a mean wretch,
Who by rebellion and ingratitude
First broke his father's heart, and afterwards
Slew GETA, his own brother, in the arms
Of JULIA, their mother, heeding not
Her shrieks of horror. In his pride he planned
These baths, to be his lasting monument,
And as a place of luxury for those
Who were his chief associates,—charioteers,
Eunuchs and boxers, gladiators, grooms,
And the vile crew which wait upon such men.
Under his auspices the structure vast
Rose from the earth amid the sighs of slaves,
Condemned in chains to work and groan in toil
Till death arrived to make a vacancy
For their successors, to the like fate doomed.
But CARACALLA'S low and scowling brow
Was never lighted up by smiles of joy
To see his baths completed ; for before
The building was half finished, he was killed
By an assassin's sword, and died unwept.
His cousin ELAGABALUS, the prince
Of every kind of low-lived luxury,
Continued the erection thus begun,
And lavishly on its adornment spent
Enormous sums, until he too was slain.
Then SEVERUS was left to crown a work
Which late should to posterity make known
The grandeur of the so-called ANTONINES !
It was a stately palace ; porticoes
Of porphyry, with marbles choice and rare,
Adorned the outside of the edifice,
Whose girth in circuit stretched beyond a mile.
The very earth was burthened by its weight,

And groaned beneath the too stupendous load.
Great was its splendour: buttresses of tile,
Sheathed in white marble from the isles of Greece,
Each strong enough to bear upon its back
A huge cathedral, held up in the air
Prodigious halls, palatial corridors,
And sumptuous chambers, carefully reserved
For the Imperial family, and those
Who formed as special favourites their train.
Below this costly labyrinth of rooms
Were spacious bathing places of all kinds,
Devoted to the common use of Rome,
Where sixteen hundred bathers easily
Could find accommodation at one time.
The Claudian Aqueduct, which brought to Rome
Fresh streams of water from the Alban hills,
Spanning for full ten miles with arches grand
The low Campagna, had its treasures drained
By a new conduit of the ANTONINES,
Which, crossing o'er the arch of DRUSUS, brought
Cool and pure water to the reservoirs
Of CARACALLA's baths.   The roofs and floors
Were covered with mosaics richly wrought ;
The lofty halls, chambers, and theatres
Were filled with sculptures of the finest art,
Obtained from Greece, whose fragments still are
      seen,
After the lapse of many centuries,
Among the wonders of the Vatican.
There FLORA, HERCULES, and VENUS strove,
Each with a beauty matchless of its kind,
To fill beholders' minds with ecstasy,
And prove to men the most incredulous
Their true divinity, if form alone

Is godlike, without spirit to give life.
There, too, were seen, in fighting attitudes,
Statues of gladiators, strong and fierce,
Who seemed prepared, should some great patron's voice
Give the command, to speak aloud the words
By which they hailed the Roman Emperor,
And bade him look on men about to die.
AUGUSTINE on these precious works of art
Looked with delight at first, which for some time
Absorbed his thoughts ; but when his eyes beheld
The gladiators' statues frowning there,
A shudder seized him, for he called to mind
That old imperial cruelty had formed
Within these baths arenas for the shows
Of gladiators trained, who savagely
Struggled to gain applause by shedding blood.
True, Christianity had long announced
The brotherhood of man and sacredness
Of human life, but had not yet o'ercome
The sanguinary wolfish taste which seeks
Horrors for food.   Therefore these bloody fights,
As in the Pagan times, took place there still !
Disgusted and admonished to withdraw
By such a thought, AUGUSTINE started up,
And would have sought at once some fitter place,
But as he reached the portal, lo, a voice
Called him by name ; when, looking round, he saw
Upon the stairs by which the privileged
Had access to the private rooms above,
The well-known countenance of MAXIMIN,
A former pupil in his class at Rome,—
One of the few who, when the rest proved false,
Had acted justly, and good faith maintained.
Young MAXIMIN was proud of his descent

From one of Rome's best, oldest families ;
And when new men came treading on his heels,
He with complacency bethought himself
Of his distinguished line of ancestors,
And how they all had from the earliest times
Clung with tenacity, which never swerved,
To the old faith which placed belief in JOVE.
Such was the fashion of great families
At Rome, until the time when ALARIC,
Twenty years later, captured with his Goths
This city gorged with plunder of the world,
And put the hunted Pagans to the sword,—
All but some few who fled, to save their lives,
To Christian churches, which the Arian spared.
MAXIMIN greeted with impetuous warmth
His late preceptor, hurried him up-stairs
Out of the crowd into a gilded room
Filled with rich furniture.   Its crimson walls
With frescoes were adorned of finest art,
Which illustrated in voluptuous scenes
The loves of MARS and VENUS.   Round the room,
Bronzes and cameos, gems of rarest kind
And costliest price, were in profusion spread ;
Nor was there wanting aught that could afford
To men most nice the highest luxury.
" Here can we quiet be," said MAXIMIN,
" Rest a short while, and interchange our thoughts.
Since we last met in Rome, three years ago,
Great changes have occurred ; for my rich sire,
Who kept me with such strictness to hard work,
Though I loved pleasure only, died last year,
And I, as heir, succeeded to his wealth.
His was the art to save, and mine to spend !
A sum which that old miser would have made

Last a whole year to keep his family,
Goes in one banquet when I entertain!
His jars of old Falernian, long stored up
In his deep cellars, now are brought to light,
And their contents must needs be excellent,
If their quick disappearance proves their worth!
Thou know'st the palace on the Cœlian Hill,
Which my good father let, to take the rent,
While he made me dwell with him in a house
As mean as penury;—well, there I live,
And there my friends, who know what things are
    good,
Are happy to attend and praise my wine.
Few men are now more popular than I!
The WORLD commends me, and I love the WORLD!
LUCIUS the poet reads his verses out,
When after supper we at ease recline;
And orators will sometimes speak so well
On subjects slight, that we applauding cry,
Great CICERO again hath come to life!
On choice occasions often will appear,
To grace my feasts and give them dignity,
The Prefect SYMMACHUS, thy friend and mine!
Loud rings his laugh, and loosely wags his tongue!
CREUGAS sits ever near my side, a man
Of herculean strength, of courage bold,
And the best boxer to be found in Rome.
Some of our gladiators now and then,
When they a crowning victory have won,
Are welcomed, as new lions, to my feasts;
But the same men not oft appear there twice—
The nature of their calling makes much change.
The prettiest girls of whom this city boasts—
Voluptuous beauties of no prudish kind—

Grace by their presence all our festive scenes,
Where songs and merriment, perfumes and flowers,
Dancing and laughter, feasting, dice, and love,
Make an Elysium, in which the nights
Are even ten times brighter than the days !
These friends of mine, perchance, might cheer thee
    up,
Although a mixed and somewhat noisy set,
Who snarl at times and quarrel o'er their cups ;
But they will always show civility
To me and those I specially protect.
This house and all I have, dear friend, are thine !
I know and honour what is excellent,
And in thee recognise that grand, calm strength
Which puts to shame the feebleness of fools.
Come to my palace, take up thine abode
In rooms which shall be thine, and thine alone.
Honour our pastimes, when thou feel'st inclined,
By being present.   Thou canst stay away
On days when privacy may be thy wish ;
And be thou sure that all which I possess,
With all that wealth and friendship can procure,
Are thine, if thou wilt come to be my guest."

  As thus he rambled on, AUGUSTINE heard
With half attention only ; for his heart
Was with his recent sorrow filled so full,
That he was scarcely conscious what was said.
But when young MAXIMIN next took his hand,
And cried exultingly : " Yes, thou wilt come ! "
AUGUSTINE shook his head, and, in few words,
Told him his late bereavement, and explained
That he at once must join his son and friends
Who were in Rome.   " But bring thy son as well,

And bring thy friends," responded MAXIMIN.
"The more the better! Now I think thereon,
Thy son is just of that green, shamefaced age
That would delight me. I could lead him out,
Teach him some little knowledge of the world,
And lavish on him more than brother's love!"
AUGUSTINE started, as if on his hand
He felt a viper's bite. "No!" he replied;
"Neither my son nor I will ever come
To join thy feasts, abhorrent unto GOD,
Or mix in pleasures Pagan and unclean.
Ours is a sterner but a wiser choice,
Which buys not the indulgence of a day
At price of life eternal. We to CHRIST
Have given ourselves, our bodies, and our souls."
"Oh!" MAXIMIN rejoined, "mistake me not.
True, I, like all our ancient family,
Worship great JOVE and Rome's old deities;
But only as a form. No word shall pass
From me to undermine thy Christian faith,
Or bring thy son round to embrace my creed.
I view these subjects as indifferent;
No dread of me need agitate thy mind."
"No dread have I of thee," AUGUSTINE said,
"Though I feel fear for your immortal soul,
Which on the brink of hell sports wantonly.
Be wise, ere 'tis too late, and sin no more.
But, as my answer, take these few plain words:
Rather than that my son with thee should live,
Mix with thy friends, and taste thy luxury,
I would prefer to place him in his grave.
Farewell! no more I linger in this place."
Then, rising, he embraced the foolish youth,
Who, by confusion crimsoned, hung his head.

AUGUSTINE swiftly hurried down the stairs,
Passed through the crowd, and reached the open
    air.
Then, as he threaded through the narrow streets,
To find the humble lodging of his friends,
He, in his mind, contrasted the small church
In which he had so lately prayed to GOD,
With that huge monument of human pride
He had just quitted.   " Great the difference
They now present," thought he ; "but greater far
Their difference will grow !   This last may stand
For some few centuries, until there come
An enemy, to cross yon lofty hills,
And subject Rome to miseries of war,
Break down those aqueducts, and leave the baths
Dry as Sahara's wilderness of sand ;
Doomed from that time to perish by decay,
Which, when it comes, shall never thence depart,
Those lofty arches, of their marbles stripped,
Shall break and fall ; those massive buttresses,
Which their proud builders fancied would endure
For ever, as a wonder and delight,
Shall crumble into dust, or only leave
Gigantic fragments, shapeless ruins foul,
Within whose confines shall be heard no sound
Except the screamings harsh of frightened daws,
Disturbed by footfall of the traveller.
But PAUL'S basilica shall, like the rocks,
Endure for ever.   Fire may burn it down,
But always from its ruins shall it rise
In an augmented splendour ; men will there
By honouring PAUL do honour unto GOD ;
The wealth of faithful men throughout the world
Is its endowment ; and though policy,

May strive to make it further worldly ends
By pageantry of histrionic kind,
Spoiling GOD'S truth by superstitious shows,
Yet in its sacred precincts pious hearts
Will ever congregate, to give CHRIST thanks."

II

THE FLESH.

AUGUSTINE dwelt in Rome beside the spot
    Where, near the Coliseum's ample shade,
Stood, in the days of the Apostle PAUL,
CLEMENT'S grand house.   Third bishop he of Rome ;
Though, even in AUGUSTINE'S time, doubts rose,
And none well knew if CLEMENT were a Jew,
Or Roman of great CÆSAR'S family ;[1]
But all agreed he was the friend by whom
PAUL was some time accompanied in Greece,
And that this CLEMENT, after his friend's death,
Acted in Rome as bishop some few years.
He was a man of consequence and wealth,
But by the Emperor's decree was soon
Banished to Kerson, whither as a slave
Contented went he, hoping he might spread
CHRIST'S gospel to all nations.   There he met,
Beyond the Euxine, with a martyr's death :
His body then was cast into the sea,
With a great anchor chained about its neck ;
Nor was the tale of its recovery
Told in AUGUSTINE'S age.   But men knew well
The spot where CLEMENT'S house had stood in
    Rome,

---

[1] *Saint Clement, Pope and Martyr, and his Basilica in Rome.* By Rev. Joseph Mullooly, O.P.   Rome, 1869.   8vo.

And on that spot, from reverence for one
Who was so holy, built they a new church,
And to ST. CLEMENT dedicated it.

.AUGUSTINE daily went to worship GOD
Within the walls of this basilica,
And stopped at times to look with curious eyes
On some mosaic pictures just set up,
Resembling those in Pagan temples seen.
One, which especially his wonder moved,
And won from men more notice than the rest,
Portrayed the BLESSED VIRGIN with our LORD,
Held in her arms as a young helpless child
Under her governance.   He often saw
Before this picture, bending to the ground,
Or kneeling abjectly upon the stones,
Two Christians, constant in attendance there,
And one of whom he knew was very rich.
This was the merchant CLAUDIUS, who had made
By trading speculations a vast sum,
Had bought up in bad years, when harvest failed,
Huge stores of corn, to sell at famine price,
And make large profits out of scarcity:
So, when the poor were dying in the streets
For lack of food, his garners sometimes burst.
Small scholarship was his; he seldom read,
Used no refined persuasiveness of speech,
But had the gift of calculating well,
And in his strong, retentive memory
Stored up results, which at his fingers' ends
Were ready when occasion promised gain.
Thrift was his occupation and delight:
Winning and saving, getting, hoarding up,
To make too great abundance something more!

But though he showed himself astute and wise
In all that appertained to gaining wealth,
Yet, when he was uplifted from the groove
Of mercenary thoughts in which he moved,
And placed on higher paths, to him most strange,
Lost was he utterly ! nor dared he stir,
Except where bolder men might lead the way.
He superstition took for godliness,
And in his weak bewilderment of mind
Was credulous as Empress HELENA,
That pious lady by false knaves befooled !
At times, when the display a stare would cause,
He gave to build or decorate a church
A hundred times as much as humbler men,
Who yet loved GOD a great deal more than he.
Large was his form, broad-shouldered, short, and
          square ;
Wide was his girth and heavy was his tread ;
His forehead, broad and low, had bright grey eyes,
Which twinkled in their tiny cavities ;
His beardless face was round and ever red,
Knotted by warts, and furnished with a chin
Which in its threefold massiveness hung down
Like a bull's dewlap, ponderous and huge.
Whenever CLAUDIUS, with his shambling gait,
Was seen approaching the basilica,
Attended by a swarm of well-dressed slaves,
A priest was his companion, on whose arm
He leaned to steady him, and in whose ear
He whispered sometimes confidential words.
This friend of CLAUDIUS was a Roman priest
Who held some paltry office in the Church,
Of small emolument.   He had received,
When DAMASUS THE FIRST was Pope, rebukes

Well merited and more than once renewed ;
Nor had he yet a good repute obtained.
His name was HARPAX ; no one knew his sire.
Large were his bones, bent inwards were his
    knees,
His elbows angular, with sharpened ends,
And from his wrists hung coarse, ill-shapen hands.
Lean in the flanks and narrow in the chest,
His body to a tube resemblance bore;
Whilst from his face, which mostly watched his
    feet,
And shunned the scrutiny of curious eyes,
A long thin nose projected furtively,
Like a rat's snout seen peeping from a drain.
His mouth was wide, awry, and cavernous,
With yellow tusks, protruding if he smiled,
As he was wont to do when some rich dish
Smoked on the table of his wealthy friend.
He was a stickler great for churchly forms,
Bowings and crossings, genuflexions low :
At every line in the Nicean Creed,
And sometimes, by mistake, at PILATE'S name,
He bowed his head to show his reverence.
Just as an itching calf in summer-time,
Tormented by impurity of blood,
Craves for some stone to rub against for ease,
So did this priest, of nature sensual,
Long for some statue, picture, reredos,
Or any likeness of a thing on earth
Or thing in heaven, to bow before and kneel ;
For he had hopes that such obeisance, made
On the outside and in the eyes of men,
Might help the want of holy thoughts within.
He found it easier of accomplishment

To dress his body in fantastic guise,
And with it curtsey, bow, and lowly kneel,
Than to adorn his soul with such rich pearls
As Faith, Hope, Charity, and make his heart
A holy altar, whereon, though unseen,
Bright fire should burn by Christian love inflamed.
Had HARPAX been a Jew in ancient times,
When CHRIST, our LORD, taught in Jerusalem,
He would have been a scornful Pharisee,
A bigot stern, intolerant of truth,
Wearing about him a phylactery
Of broadest fringe, paying with strictness tithe
Of mint and cumin, fair in outside show
As any other whited sepulchre,
But full within, alas! of dead men's bones.
When he, before the altar in the church,
Stood clad in vestments of rich silk and gold,
Which covered o'er his filthy gaberdine,
He in himself displayed, in union rare,
The wolf's fell hunger, the sly fox's craft,
The screech-owl's voice, the peacock's gaudy tail,
The panther's fawning mien and thirst for blood.

    This HARPAX in the house of CLAUDIUS
Had a small room, and lived there free of cost.
He acted as his almoner at times,
And undertook with ready cheerfulness
To go long rounds, dividing to the poor
Such contributions as rich CLAUDIUS gave ;
And this he did with so much secrecy,
That neither his right hand nor left could tell
On some occasions who the gifts received.
He argued that confession should be made
Not unto GOD Himself, but to a priest.

This he had long impressed on CLAUDIUS,
And knew so well, by what he learned of him,
His tricks in trade, the gains they brought him in,
And other matters of like nicety,
That CLAUDIUS feared him, and the priest obtained
More influence by the knowledge thus acquired.
The great solicitude which HARPAX showed
To have all sins without reserve disclosed
In the confessional was not confined
To CLAUDIUS only, but embraced as well
Some of the members of his family ;
And he would even longer time devote
To his friend's daughter, who was just eighteen,
Than to himself. He asked her of her acts,
Her feelings, wishes, hopes, her very thoughts ;
And if she faltered, he would ply her close
With questions which at one time made her blush.
But, as she grew familiar with his mode,
She minded less his drift, and, being bold,
Would sometimes stop his questions with a laugh.
HARPAX was pleased to find what great increase
Of consequence was his with fellow-priests
Since he had taken CLAUDIUS in hand,
And caused him to bestow rich largesses
Upon St. Clement's Church. All the expense
Of several large mosaics had been paid
By CLAUDIUS only, and his latest gift
Had been a picture of the VIRGIN'S self,
With her young child, placed upright in a niche.
It had been copied from another brought
From great Byzantium for sale in Rome,
And by the owner, a veracious Greek,
Declared to be the sole original
Of a true portrait painted by ST. LUKE.

Y

The VIRGIN sat upon a jewelled throne,
Strait-backed and cushioned ; strings of orient pearls

Hung in magnificence around her neck,
And in long rows were clustered on her head,
Hiding her hair and drooping o'er her ears
Until they reached the shoulders.   Her left hand
Was placed beneath the infant on her lap ;
The right one was upraised, as if to give
A benediction, as a bishop might.
Her child was not a child except in size ;
He rather seemed to be a tiny man,
And in one hand grasped fast a parchment scroll.
Around His head were lambent rays of light,
Which in three pencils, skilfully arranged,
Framed with the face itself a kind of cross
Within the nimbus.   He from neck to foot
Was in a dark robe clad, which contrast made
With the rich drapery His mother wore.
When the lean priest noticed AUGUSTINE stop
To view the picture and observe his friend,
He made the prayers he muttered audible,

And thus, with eyes upraised, cried out aloud:
"O HOLY MARY! listen to our prayers;
MOTHER OF GOD! speak for us to thy Son;
Do thou from hell itself deliver us."[1]
AUGUSTINE wondered, but he held his peace:
With great rapidity his mind ran through
All passages in Scripture which refer
Unto the BLESSED VIRGIN, but found none
Which called her by the name the priest had used,
Or could, directly or by inference,
Be made to give a colour to the thought
That she had power to liberate from hell,
Which is an attribute of Deity!
"Behold, I am alive for evermore,
And have the keys of hell and death,"[2] said CHRIST.
"This priest," mused he, "is one of those poor fools
Who ask the saints, instead of CHRIST, to do
Their Master's work, and intercede with GOD;
He and his friend, who kneeling worship here
Pictures, whose only use is to inform
Unlettered or forgetful men of facts
Which constitute the Christian history,
Must needs suppose that CHRIST, though now in heaven,
Pules as an infant in His mother's lap,
And is still subject to her, as He was
To JOSEPH also when at Nazareth.
Such was not His appearance to ST. PAUL,
When, near Damascus, he beheld that face
Whose brightness blinded him; nor thus looked He
Unto ST. JOHN, who saw His countenance
Was as the sun when shining in its strength,
His head as white as snow, His eyes like fire,

---

[1] See inscription over the portal of the church of Santa Maria Liberatrice, near the Forum at Rome.   [2] Rev. i. 18.

His feet like molten brass, and heard His voice,
As of the sound of many waters loud ! " [1]

   The priest and his companion soon arose
With much complacency, and left the church ;
Then, as AUGUSTINE followed, he discerned
About the ample cloak of CLAUDIUS
A number of small pictures, needle-worked,
Which, as was then the fashion with some men,
Depicted facts in Holy Writ described,—
CHRIST'S birth, His miracles, His life and death.
Just then EVODIUS met them, and at once
Saluted CLAUDIUS, who with cordial warmth
Returned the compliment, and grasped his hand ;
For CLAUDIUS was the banker unto whom
EVODIUS had letters brought when first
They came to Rome from Milan.   It much pleased
CLAUDIUS to meet AUGUSTINE, for his name
Already was familiar to his ears,
As one well known to him and greatly praised.
CLAUDIUS beheld the youthful Africans
With friendly smile some moments, and then said :
" To-morrow is the anniversary
Of CHRIST'S nativity ; we sup alone :
Come, then, my friends, and with us keep the feast."
EVODIUS answered yes ; and though AUGUSTINE
Shrank from distractions of society,
He could not well on such a day refuse.
ALYPIUS and NAVIGIUS had gone
With ADEODATUS, who loved history,
To see Mont Cavo in the Alban hills,—
The spot where HANNIBAL once fixed his camp.
They would be some days absent.   Therefore both

            [1] Rev. i. 14, 15, 16.

AUGUSTINE and EVODIUS gave consent.
CLAUDIUS went home to tell his wife the news :
" To-morrow," said he, " to our feast will come
EVODIUS of Carthage and a friend,
Less rich than he, who is AUGUSTINE called.
They are the friends of whom we late have heard
So much from our loved daughter, now away,
Even from JULIANA, who her life
Gives up to prayer, her wealth to charity,
And her chief thoughts to please such men as these.
Our coming guests are nondescript of kind ;
For though not priests, nor meaning to be priests,
They have resolved to consecrate to GOD
Their lives, and dwell secluded from the world.
A set of voluntary bachelors,
Who, though celibacy they have not vowed,
Will practise it, they say.   But mark my words !
Should a good chance arise, their minds will change.
They are like chary customers in trade,
Unwilling, seemingly, to deal at all,
But make it worth their while, and they are yours !'
HARPAX at this gave forth a boisterous laugh ;
The wife of CLAUDIUS smiled and turned her eyes
Upon her younger daughter, who there sat
In silence, wondering who the men could be
Of whom her married sister, JULIANA,
Had spoke so oft in terms of reverence.
On the next day, and at the hour named,
AUGUSTINE and EVODIUS went to sup
With CLAUDIUS at his house,—a pleasant home,
Rich in all comforts, but without a trace
Of any specimens of art, like those
Which had the house of VERECUNDUS filled.
CLAUDIUS received them gladly.   " Sirs," said he,

" This is my wife OCTAVIA ; " and he then
Presented them to a tall faded dame,
Whose haggard eyes had once been bright and fine.
" And this, my younger child, is LAURA named,
A maiden full of phantasy and fire."
She smiled at this description, raised her hand,
And pointed where AUGUSTINE should sit down
Close by her side, at which act HARPAX frowned.
But LAURA heeded not such men as he ;
She liked AUGUSTINE'S look, his splendid eyes,
His lofty air, his noble, handsome brow,
The tones of sweetness uttered by his voice,
And his distinguished elegance of form ;
But when, ere long, in some short argument,
In which he silenced HARPAX for a while,
She heard his fervid, manly eloquence,
A god, she thought, to visit them had come !
Then waywardly, without reserve or fear,
Toyed with the fascinating spell of love.

LAURA possessed in fullest brilliancy
The charms which have, from earliest times till now,
Given to Roman beauty its renown.
Luxuriant hair, black as the raven's wing,
Was wound in wavy tresses round her head ;
Beneath her forehead, low but broad and smooth,
With eyebrows finely arched and neatly trimmed,
Looked forth two eyes, black, lustrous, proud, and bold ;
Her nose was large, but finely formed and straight ;
Her olive-coloured face was ever pale,
Except when some emotion unrestrained
Stirred in her heart and flushed along her cheeks ;
Red as a cherry were her pouting lips,
And sweet the frequent smile that curved their lines ;

Her well-proportioned chin, which forward came,
Gave plainest evidence of strength of will ;
Her massive shoulders, neck, and rounded arms
Were almost herculean in their size,
But harmonized with her majestic bust.
The texture of her skin was in its grain
Finer than marble chosen by the eye
And fashioned by the hand of PHIDIAS.
Her step, though slow and firm, had no small grace ;
Her laugh was loud and merry ; but when vexed,
A cloud of passion gathered on her brow,
And in her eyes the vivid lightnings played.

   Ere the repast began, HARPAX arose,
And called on GOD, the VIRGIN, and the saints
To give a blessing on the feast there spread.
When that was done, and food was handed round,
He had some laudatory words prepared
As sauce for every dish. " Lo, here," he said,
"Is sturgeon from the Tiber's mouth, well stewed
In gravy, fit to make a hermit smile.
How rich these eels, fed in imperial ponds !
This beef is excellent as are the herbs
Which fatten oxen on Campagna's plains.
These ortolans are plumper than the grapes
Which, till the vintage, formed their dainty food.
Woodcocks are rare, but these are exquisite !
This porker's belly, stuffed with sausages,
Hath that strong taste of garlic which I prize ;—
We, who oft fast, know also how to feast !"
AUGUSTINE for a time in silence sat;
And as he watched the priest despatch with speed
The viands set before him, and imbibe
Deep draughts of wine to help them on their way,

His mind began in doubt to speculate
If he himself committed any sin,
When he perceived his palate take delight
In food of which he sparingly partook.
But soon fair LAURA, by whose side he sat,
Observed his silence, and began to speak :
"Good sir! you eat not; give me leave to ask
That you partake a little of this dish?"
Then, as he did so, her own hands poured out
A goblet of rich wine, which he must drink ;
Nor would she let him cease, but urged him on,
Until at length he firmly said, "Enough!"
LAURA herself was not abstemious,
And if she praised a dish, could show full well
The way it should be dealt with. She contrived
With ready wit to make AUGUSTINE talk ;
Asked of his son, expressing her regret
He should be absent; made her guest describe
His age, his tastes, his studies, and his gifts.
This was the topic upon which alone
AUGUSTINE was too weak, for he believed
His son to be a marvel ; and ere long
Informed the lady of a Dialogue [1]
Between himself and him,—one written down
From what had really passed between the two
During their stay at Cassiciacum.
"It showed," he said, "what gifts GOD had bestowed
On one so young!"   LAURA declared that she
Must see the book, nor did she rest content
Until AUGUSTINE promised he one day
Would read it to her. She felt sure, she said,
That she should ADEODATUS dearly love,
Nor could be happy until him she knew ;

[1] *De Magistro ;* Augustine's *Opera,* i. 887.

AUGUSTINE must present him to them all,
The moment he returned.   Thus talked she on,
And made AUGUSTINE talk, till grace was said.
All then, on couches ranged around the hall
In Roman style of luxury, reclined,
And o'er their hands were perfumed waters poured.
A slight pause then ensued ; but HARPAX soon,
Refreshed with the abundant share which he
Had had of everything which tasted nice,
Began to rouse himself to serious themes,
And in this way the conversation led:
" Glad was I yesterday to see how much
Our stranger friend, who now near LAURA leans,
Was struck with admiration at the mode
In which our church, by the munificence
Of CLAUDIUS, hath but lately been adorned,
And at the style of prayer which there I made,—
The last new style, as yet not general.
I think I may, with much humility,
Take credit to myself for what was seen,
As well as for the prayer AUGUSTINE heard ;
For thus, not long since, was it brought about.
We have in Rome a girl of holy life,
Whose parents are but poor ; they live to pray,
And have indeed no means for maintenance
Except the contributions of our church.
This girl hath discontinued to take food
For many months.   The fact I know as one
Supported by the solemn evidence
Of both her parents, who attest its truth.
She lies all day in bed, as in a trance,
And many neighbours go on her to gaze,
That they themselves may witnesses become
Of such clear proof of GOD'S almighty power.

Three times, whilst thus entranced, this girl hath seen
The HOLY VIRGIN come to visit her,
Descending queenlike from the clouds of heaven,
And holding in her arms a little child !
In memory of this great miracle,
And on the strong persuasion of myself,
The girl's confessor, CLAUDIUS hath caused
The picture in mosaics to be made;
And seldom hath a novelty done more
To crowd with worshippers St. Clement's Church !
I have myself not failed to do my best
To turn to good account this chance to pay
Honour to her who was, when first conceived,
Immaculate, was sinless in her life,
And whom I worship with that reverence
Which she, GOD'S Mother,[1] may with justice claim."
AUGUSTINE gladly would have held his tongue,
Rather than talk on topics such as those
At such a time ; but fearing, if he did,
His silence would be construed as assent,
Gravely replied : " The term thou hast just used ·
Is one unscriptural and full of risk.

[1] Augustine died before the Emperor Theodosius convoked a general council at Ephesus (A.D. 431) to decide upon the question then agitated so fiercely between Cyril and Nestorius, respecting the title of "Theotokos," or Mother of God, which Cyril had, with much vehemence of temper, insisted should be ascribed to the Virgin Mary. Both Nestorius and Cyril appear to have rushed, during their controversy, into deplorable extravagances. John, Patriarch of Antioch, took at one time a discreet view, when he recommended Nestorius not to persist in his rash attempt to solve the great mystery of the incarnation, and advised him to abstain from the further agitation of a question so inscrutable (*Hard. Concil.* tom. i. 1327). The term "Mother of God" is decidedly objectionable, as ignoring the human nature of Jesus Christ, in relation to which only was Mary His mother. In Ignatius we find this sentence : " For our God, Jesus the Christ, was born in the womb of Mary, according to the dispensation by God." In this sentence, the words "Jesus the Christ" are of great importance.

Mother of JESUS is her Scripture term,
And that is safest, and describes her best ;
Nor needs she other name.[1]
MARY was mother to the flesh of CHRIST. A prophetess
Holy in life was she, and hath a name
Which makes her blessèd more than all her sex.
But MARY'S fleshly body was conceived
By carnal concupiscence,[2] which itself,
Though not sin actual, is sin's origin,
The source whence acts of sinfulness proceed.[3]
But whether MARY sinned is a hard point,
Which, from due reverence for Him she bare,
I will not venture even to discuss.[4]
Although, by grace, MARY CHRIST'S flesh conceived,
And therefore is called blessèd, she was far
More blessèd when she first received CHRIST'S faith.[5]
Moreover, with her mind conceived she CHRIST
Before her body did so.[6] True, she was
The mother of His members in the flesh,
But spiritually, in the higher sense,
MARY herself was daughter unto CHRIST,
And of Him born.[7] This further must I add,
That the strange story HARPAX hath just told

---

[1] John ii. 1.

[2] " Quod Maria quidem mater ejus, de qua carnem sumpsit, de carnali con-
cupiscentia parentum, nata est."—Augustine's *Opera*, x. 2101 A, 1133 A.

[3] Rom. vii. 7, 8 ; James i. 14 ; Col. iii. 5.

[4] "Sancta virgine Maria, de qua propter honorem Domini multum
prorsus cum de peccatis agitur."—Augustine's *Opera*, x. 395 B. The
doctrine of the Greek Church is that the Blessed Virgin Mary was conceived
in original sin ; Dr. Pusey's *Eirenicon*, p. 407. Such also was the opinion
of Augustine, as appears by several passages in his works. [*De Gen. ad
Lit.* x. 18, 20 ; *De Pec. Mer. et Rem.* ii. 24 ; *Cont. Julian. Pelag.* iv. 122,
v. 15, vi. 22 ; *in Ps.* xxxiv. sec. 2 ; Pusey's *Eirenicon*, p. 176.]

[5] Augustine's *Opera*, vi. 580 B, C.

[6] "Prius mente quam ventre concipiens."—*Ib.*, *Serm.* 215, v. 1382 C.

[7] *Ib.* vi. 582 A, B. See Appendix, Note 3.

Appears to me a falsehood, which the girl
Hath framed to cheat the credulous; for food
The body must partake of, or soon die;
But that the dead to any one appear
Is merely superstition, false and vain.
Ah no! the dead return to us no more!
For if that power had been on them bestowed,
Never would any night have passed away
In which I should not with mine eyes have seen
My pious mother!—she, who through her life
Could not exist if from me separate;
She, who o'er sea and land my steps pursued,
And even into distant foreign climes,
Rather than quit me. It would not please GOD,
That, entering into life more blest than this,
She should in any measure love me less,
Or, when I suffer, should not come at once
To bring me consolation;—she, whose love
Was greater for me than I dare to say!"[1]
As thus he spake, remembrance of her loss
So overwhelmed him, that within his eyes
Large tears began to glisten: he arose
And took his leave; but, as from thence he went,

---

[1] "Si rebus viventium interessent animæ mortuorum, et ipsæ nos, quando eas videmus, alloquerentur in somnis; ut de aliis taceam, me ipsum pia mater nulla nocte desereret, qua terra marique secuta est ut mecum videret. Absit enim ut facta sit vita feliciore crudelis, usque adeo ut quando aliquid augit cor meum, nec tristem filium consoletur, quem dilexit unice, quem nunquam voluit mœstum videre. . . .

"Si autem parentes non intersunt, qui sunt alii mortuorum qui noverint quid agamus, quidve patiamur? Isaias propheta dicit: *Tu es enim pater noster; quia Abraham nescivit nos, et Israel non cognovit nos* (Isa. lxiii. 16). Si tanti Patriarchæ quid erga populum ex his procreatum ageretur ignoraverunt, quibus Deo credentibus populus ipse de illorum stirpe promissus est; quomodo mortui vivorum rebus atque actibus cognoscendis adjuvandis que miscentur?"—*De Cura pro Mortuis Gerenda;* Augustine's *Opera,* vi. 880, 881.

LAURA'S excited, sympathizing soul
Felt deep emotion, and she watched his form,
Which, leaning on EVODIUS for support,
Bent as doth one with anguish in his mind.
He vanished from her sight ; then silently
She sank again upon her silken couch,
To let her teeming fancy brood in peace.
But HARPAX came, and sought to take the place
Close by her side, at which the lovely girl,
Vexed that he checked her pensive reverie,
Turned round displeased, and motioned him away.

PETRONIUS PROBUS, after whose great name
His wife was called,—for, till their marriage day,
She was FALTONIA in her father's house,—
Had Consul and Prætorian Prefect been,
Commanded armies, ruled all Italy,
Selected governors of provinces,
And, when in office, patron had become
Of AMBROSE, then beginning his career :
Each for the other felt respect and love.
The good Archbishop had besought his friend
To show AUGUSTINE courtesy in Rome.
Such wish, when PROBUS knew it, was a law.
He had, when no more young, but ere old age
Had come, like winter's frost, to chill his blood,
Quitted the soldier's life, that he might wed.
The haughtiest houses his alliance sought ;
And he selected wisely, for his wife,
A noble heiress, rich and young, but wise,
Who would not vex him in his quietude,
And whose vast wealth brought splendour to his home.
PROBA'S descent was noble, but her mind
Was nobler than her lineage, and aspired

To saintly virtues, intellectual worth,
And the possession of that pure delight
Which a good mother, wife, or valued friend
Feels in her heart, although her tongue be mute.
Her tastes, despite the grandeur of her life,
Continued simple; all who merit had
With her found favour; some gained even more,
For her affections yearned for sympathy,
And would, on her perceiving in the crowd
Which fluttered round her the majestic presence
Of some great man, twine round him like a vine,
And cluster him with bounty.   To the poor
She was a benefactress never tired;
From her the weak had help, the timid praise,
The desolate a consolation sure,
But to the noble-hearted gave she love!
Imagination lent a brilliancy
To her reflections upon human life;
And when, in certain moods, emotions came
To stir impetuous fervour in her soul,
She shaped her fancies in melodious verse,
And as a Christian poetess won fame.
The greatest and the wisest men felt proud
To rank as PROBA'S friends; e'en JEROME'S self,
When he abode in Rome, for her conceived
Unwonted admiration, which endured
Throughout his life; and fortunate was she
To count besides, among her nearest friends,
AMBROSE, AUGUSTINE, and ALYPIUS.
Her fame extended even to the East,
Where she had great possessions; and in days
When her lost Roman grandeur brought eclipse,
The East yet sent her tokens of respect.
Great CHRYSOSTOM himself, the golden-mouthed,

Who from an advocate had hermit turned,
But, dragged from his seclusion, had received
The patriarchate of Byzantium,
Made PROBA'S virtues a choice theme of praise ;
And though he never lived to see her face,
Felt for her Christian love, which she returned.
She was the grandest lady of her day,—
Great in men's eyes, nor little e'en in GOD'S,
Yet not exempt from trials, pain, and woe.
A numerous progeny her care required ;
And ere the last had ceased to be a child,
Some had already into manhood grown.
Her eldest son, OLYBIUS, partook
More of his father's manly character
Than of his mother's meekness. Great his wish
As Consul, like his sire, to rule in Rome !
He scorned to wait for that inheritance
A father's death would bring in future years,
Nor in the interval was he content
To live on bounty, though parental hands
Dispensed it without stint. He took a wife
Of humble birth, but born to affluence,—
A merchant's daughter, JULIANA named,
Who was the elder of two heiresses
On whom the gains of CLAUDIUS would descend.
Her dowry made him rich, his rank her great.
The high-bred PROBA, first to please her son,
But soon to please herself, drew to her heart
The gentle girl, whose soul affectionate
Reciprocated kindness thus bestowed.
In the grand palace near the Capitol,
Where PROBUS lived, a stately senator,
Honoured by all men, by his wife revered,
Their children dwelt with them, and their son's wife,

In harmony perfect; nor could they,
With their attendants, family, and friends,
Half fill the chambers of the mighty pile.
Men of the highest station and repute
Came thither oft for hospitality,
To meet each other, and deep things discuss.
But none among the guests was honoured more
Than young AUGUSTINE, who when there felt pleased
To stand alone and from some nook observe
The soldier's frankness, the wife's piety,
And their warm, genial welcome to their friends.
He met there of the clergy many men
Of just renown; some, too, whose pushing arts
Had won, not note, but notoriety.
They clustered in the palace, as bees swarm
Within a garden full of honeyed flowers.
Some of all kinds were seen there, high and low,
From the pale face of proud AUFIDIUS,
Down through a multitude of smaller men
Even to HARPAX, who would go there oft
To gather doles, and feast at festivals,
Like a sharp sickle reaping ripened corn.
LŒTA, the child of PROBUS when grown old,
Was by him best beloved, yet not so much
As to provoke in others jealousy.
She was the playmate of all visitors;
Nor did AUGUSTINE fail to feel the spell
She spread around her by her winning ways,
The blissful charm of early innocence!
She drew him often to her father's house,
And made him tell her many wondrous tales,
Walk round the garden with her, hand in hand,
And teach her much; but while he did these things,
He took occasion in her soul to breathe

The fear of GOD, and love for CHRIST His Son.
The Lady PROBA was well satisfied
That LŒTA should have made so good a friend ;
Therefore she begged AUGUSTINE at their house
To spend such leisure hours as he could spare ;
And soon between him and the Roman dame,
Who was so kind, an intimacy grew
As close as that of long familiar friends.
In after times, when twenty years had passed,
And guilty Rome was taken by the Goths,
PROBA, a widow then, to save her life,
Flying from Italy, a refuge found
Beneath AUGUSTINE'S care in Africa.
She thither brought a portion of her wealth
Snatched from the pillage, and with her escaped
Some of her children ; but her two brave sons,
Who in one year had both as Consuls served,
Could not endure to see and to survive
Rome's fall ; one therefore at the prospect died,
The other sank and perished in its shame.
This lady, when affliction came with age,
Asked of AUGUSTINE and received advice
How, when in trouble, best to pray to GOD ;
And, for the guidance of her family,
Had counsel, in that day accounted wise.[1]
No contrast could be greater in all eyes
Than that between the gentle JULIANA
And her impetuous sister. There had been
Nearly a lustre's space between their births,
And she who was the elder had bestowed

---

[1] Augustine's *Opera*, *Epist.* 130, 131, 150, etc. Proba returned from Africa to Rome about A.D. 414, and she and her daughter-in-law, Juliana, were both buried there in the tomb of Probus.—*De Tillemont*, tom. xiii. 632–635.

On LAURA, from her infancy, a love
Almost maternal; but had never checked
Her will, or taught her temper discipline.
A strong affection, boundless and intense,
Repaid her kindness. LAURA wept for hours
When, to become a wife, her sister left
Their father's house; but afterwards she passed
Long mornings with her, and was gratified
With her grand palace and its courtly ways,—
With all, in truth, except the frequent prayers
And the decorum, which to one so young
Were wearisome, repulsive, and absurd.
Sometimes she saw AUGUSTINE, when he called
With his companion, young ALYPIUS,
But spake not to him much: she looked on him
With deep respect, not quite unmixed with fear;
But on his son, who had returned to Rome,
She scrupled not to lavish endless love.
On one occasion, when they all were met
In PROBA'S palace, and in silence sat,
She made AUGUSTINE read the Dialogue
Between himself and son, which he had named
At their first meeting. This she greatly praised,
But felt still more delight to hear his voice
Read out to them in deep, impressive tones
A portion of the Scriptures; then would ask,
If something seemed obscure, what that might mean.
Nor, though he wished to leave, would let him go,
Until what she required had been explained,
And PROBA and herself were satisfied.
An unextinguished, unseen fire which burns,
May, though well watched, be kindled into flame
To scorch or to consume. No danger ranks
In perils greater than the fire of youth,

Which like a fever lingers in the blood.
The will may check, but cannot drive it out ;
The body and the spirit are at war,
And while life lasts their struggles are renewed.
AUGUSTINE, in his search for holiness,
And in his wish to consecrate to GOD
His future life, had built around his heart
Icy entrenchments of strict chastity ;
Yet still within it and within his flesh
Were longings and rebellions unsubdued.
He had imposed upon himself a law,[1]
Forbidding him to entertain desire
For any woman, or to seek the charm
Of her companionship to sweeten life,
Much less to take her to his arms as wife ;
The very thought was banished from his soul !
Yet would at times the passion he repressed
Assert its power, and fill him with alarm,
When nature felt too strong and reason weak.
Then, as a frightened child flies to the arms
Of an indulgent parent, so to GOD
AUGUSTINE rushed with blushes on his cheeks,
And from Him help and consolation sought.

Thus passed some months, and LAURA every day
Became more pensive ; silently she sat,
Abstracted in deep thought, nor taking heed
Of those about her, but would start at times
If an unusual footstep in the street
Announced some coming visitor's approach,
Who yet stopped not, but onwards went his way.
AUGUSTINE seldom sought her father's house ;
Therefore she hated it, but knew not why.

---

[1] *Soliloq.* i. 17 ; Augustine's *Opera*, i. 609, 610.

Plunged in deep thought, she oft would muse for hours;
Impatience troubled her till evening came ;
Then, in seclusion, from all eyes withdrawn,
She to herself her burning thoughts would breathe.

LAURA MUSES.

" His face comes beaming on my eyes!
    His voice still sounds within my ears !
Though gone, the charm that in him lies
    Shines visible through blinding tears.
The world my secret ne'er shall know,
But he shall know it ere they go.

" Why is his speech so calm, so cold,
    When every word thrills through my heart ?
Why said he, he had now grown old ?
    Is that the truth, or was it art ?
Ah ! not too old for love's warm glow !
Yes, he shall know it ere they go !

" Oh ! if, encircled by these arms,
    His noble head reclined in rest,
How would I banish all alarms,
    And clasp him to my heaving breast !
The world my secret ne'er shall know,
But he shall know it ere they go.

" A fever wastes my very blood,
    Not even night can bring repose ;
Tears then burst forth, an unchecked flood,
    My hidden passion to disclose ;
I toss, I sigh in pain and woe:
Yes, he shall know it ere they go !"

The Roman mind is clear and positive ;
And LAURA had determined, with firm will,
That come what would, AUGUSTINE should be hers!
She told her sister so in plainest terms,
And made her promise to contribute aid,
If such were wanting, to obtain her wish.
The sister gave a smile incredulous
At the mere thought that aid could be required
To make a man, poor as AUGUSTINE was,
Espouse an heiress rich and beautiful,
The match just then most coveted in Rome!
Seldom they met except in PROBA'S house ;
But though the sister skilfully contrived
The very fairest opportunities,
And even gave at times some startling hints,
Which any wooer would have understood,
AUGUSTINE heeded not, but lived absorbed
Within himself, with views which seemed to them,
Who knew full well what projects he had formed,
The hazy obscurations of a dream,
Uneasy thoughts of things not possible.

'Twas on an eve in May, when sunshine warm
Had made the flowers bud forth, and happy birds
Warble soft notes, just as the zephyrs rose
To stir the fragrance of the balmy eve,
And Nature by her sweetness breathed delight,
That LAURA and her sister walked alone
Within the spacious gardens of the house
In which dwelt PROBA. By a chance not strange,
AUGUSTINE called, and joined them in their walk.
The exquisite creations of his GOD,
Whose colours, fragrance, freshness, and sweet sounds
Announced the welcome presence of the Spring,

Filled him with rapture, and his heart rejoiced
In bliss unwonted since his mother died.
The sternness of his mind felt softened then ;
The very accents of his voice proclaimed
His happiness and joy. As thus they walked,
Some household duties which had been forgot
Called LAURA'S sister hastily away,
And LAURA'S self was left at the far end
Of a secluded glade, with none but him
Whose presence made her tremble with delight
Mingled with fear. She leant upon his arm,
Spake in a whisper, sweeter than the notes
With which the birds made all the groves resound,
And answered every word which from him fell
With sympathy by tenderness enhanced.
He told her of the errors of his life,
Of his repentant and converted soul,
And, lastly, of his project to return,
Before the year was out, to Africa,
And in what strict privation and hard toil
He and his friends would live as celibates.
When this he said, a cry, as if of pain,
Came suddenly from LAURA'S ruby lips,
And with a voice but half articulate
She asked if he would leave and let her die ?
"Help me, AURELIUS," cried she, "or I sink!"
Her head in languishment sank down upon
His shoulder, and convulsively her hands
Grasped his firm arm, which, fearing she might fall,
Entwined the slender beauty of her waist.
Then, as he stooped, her blushing, crimson cheek
Touched his, and kindled all his blood with fire.
She sighed profoundly, and at every sigh
Her swelling bosom, which on him reclined,

Heaved like the waves of a tumultuous sea.
AUGUSTINE'S brain whirled round ; he sighed with her,
But ere his voice had time one word to speak,
HARPAX leaped nimbly from a bush hard by,
And in the half-light of the evening stood,
Livid with rage, before the pair surprised.
"What! thinkest thou, vile Carthaginian slave!
To play such pranks as these?" he hoarsely said ;
"Wouldst thou seduce the daughter of thy friend,
And thus his hospitality reward?"
AUGUSTINE staggered at the foul reproach,
Knew himself innocent, but saw not how
To make that clear which looked equivocal.
But LAURA was more prompt.   Upon her feet,
Leaving AUGUSTINE, she at once arose,
And to her utmost height drew up her form ;
Then looking HARPAX fully in the face,
While her clenched hand was raised as if to strike,
Thus she exclaimed : "How dar'st thou, paltry knave,
To come eavesdropping, and malignantly
Give vent to lies against my friend and me?
Begone! and if thou speak'st another word
To harm AUGUSTINE'S honest name or mine,
This hand shall lash thee for thine insolence.
Know, too, that LAURA hath at will the power
To chase thee humbled from her father's home!"
HARPAX stood overwhelmed, hung down his head,
Then sneaked away, inglorious and subdued.
AUGUSTINE followed with impetuous haste,
Thrust him aside, and left the house at once.
His soul recoiled with horror, as he thought
Upon the danger he had just escaped.
The noble purposes his mind had formed
Had almost melted in a damsel's sigh!

With blank astonishment he saw how near
His foot had slipped to fall to lower aims.
What! should he then relinquish as vain things
His life ascetic, and the deeds of worth
Which, by GOD'S grace, would yet by him be done?
Should he, who asked a life of poverty,
Cast it away or barter it for ease,
Become a rich man's heir, a spoilt girl's toy,
And pass his days in listening to the talk
Of CLAUDIUS on percentages and gains?
Should he such things complacently endure
Till the keen temper of his mind grew dull,
While every night, when glorious as a star
His soul shone brightest, it should idly sleep,
Lulled into languor by a woman's arms?
"Forbid it, Heaven!" he cried; "be it not so!
My mind shall rule my body, and the flesh
Be in subjection to the spirit held:
Wedded to CHRIST alone, I live and die!
Marriage is good; better virginity!
Oh, would that like ST. PAUL I had remained
In the pure state of virgin innocence!
But now must I, like PETER, be content
With humbler rank of widowed chastity.
A husband of his body hath not power,
But the wife hath.[1]   My flesh I crucify,[2]
With the affections and the lusts thereof."[3]

He hastened thence, and as he passed beneath
The Coliseum's walls, where beasts and men
So often in its wide arena fought,

---

[1] 1 Cor. vii. 4.   [2] Gal. v. 24.
[3] Augustine's *Opera: De Bono Conjugali; De Virginitate; De Bono Viduitatis.*

He heard, resounding in the silent eve,
The roaring of a prisoned lioness,
Which paced about the limits of her den
In fiery indignation and despair,
And tried to break the bars which held her fast.
AUGUSTINE reached his chamber out of breath,
Trembling to see how insecure was yet
The ground on which he stood. He yearned to
    find
In GOD a refuge, where to rest in peace.
Disconsolate, distracted, ill at ease,
He fervently implored that he might be
Free for the future from attacks like that
From which, by such a chance, he had escaped!
Then, with a voice in which despondency,
Self-condemnation, and complaint were mixed,
He thus poured forth to GOD his mournful prayers: [1]—

"Who then will grant me that in Thee I rest,
    That Thou shalt find within my heart a place,
And cheer it, so that every evil pest
    May be forgotten, and I Thee embrace,
Mine only good ?—LORD, what Thou art to me
In pity say, that I to speak am free.

"Say, what am I myself to Thee, O LORD,
    That Thou command'st my love, and dost, unless
This love I render, signs of wrath afford,
    With threats of mighty sorrows, deep distress ?
Is the loss little if I love not Thee ?
In pity say, LORD, what Thou art to me!

[1] Augustine's *Confess.* lib. i. c. v. See Appendix, Note V.

" ' I thy salvation am,'[1] say to my soul ;
  Speak so that I may hear.   Mine heart's ear see
Listening before Thee !   Open, make them whole.
  ' I thy salvation am : ' let these words be
Said to my soul.   After their joyful sound
Swift will I run, and hold Thee fast when found.

" Refuse, O LORD, from me to hide Thy face ;
  Yea, though I needs must die, let me then die
If I that face but see.   Narrow the space
  . My soul can for a house to Thee supply !
Widen its bounds, that Thou may'st enter there.
Ruined it is ; its ruined state repair.

" Alas ! I do confess and know too sure
  That there is that within which to Thine eyes
Must give offence ; but who will make it pure ?
  To whom but Thee should I direct my cries ?
Cleanse me from secret faults,[2] O LORD, and spare
Thy servant from the sins which others share."

[1] Ps. xxxv. 3.   [2] Ps. xix. 12.

III.

THE DEVIL.

AUGUSTINE had AUFIDIUS often met
    At PROBA'S house. He was an aged priest
Of great repute, high in the confidence
Of the then Pope SIRICIUS. His birth
Came of a noble family, whose chief
Had in the reign of CONSTANTINE embraced
The Christian faith ; from this time had all
To their new creed adhered. Their haughty names
Had in Rome's annals more than once been writ
When the Republic flourished. Some had held
Under the Emperors important posts ;
Nor had a generation passed away
Without distinction. From their ancient stock,
In after ages when the Popes bore sway,
The princely house of BORGIA took its rise.
Yet their prosperity some rude check met,
And they had persecution bravely borne
In DIOCLETIAN'S reign. AUFIDIUS
Himself had met hard usage at the hands
Of JULIAN, the apostate Emperor,
When he made efforts to arrest the course
Of Christianity, and vainly hoped—
Urged on by crafty schemes of policy·—
To make the Pagan creed again prevail,
And push back with his puny human strength

The progress of the Church.   He might as well
Have with his finger tried to stop the course
Of the revolving moon.   AUFIDIUS
Had firmly stood his ground, nor flinched one inch
Beneath the despot's threats ; and when the time
To Christianity was critical,
He gave such sage advice to all his friends,
Managed their measures with so much address,
And such ability and courage showed,
That he obtained an universal fame.
Age now had somewhat quelled his former fire ;
For nearly fourscore years of active life
Had calmed a man who laboured without rest.
Cold was his manner, haughty was his mien;
His face looked pallid, though from sickness free ;
His thin white lips, compressed as if by pain,
Were never seen relaxing to a smile ;
His keen grey eyes were like two balls of fire,
Scathing at times, and lurid with disdain ;
His lofty brow was nobly arched above,
But furrowed with the lines of age and care ;
Upon his temples hung some few grey hairs,
The scanty remnant of luxuriant locks ;
His shoulders, slightly bent, were stooped by age,
But more by weight of meditative thought ;
His voice was rather low than sweet, with tones
Which stirred the soul, but rather jarred the ear ;
His tall, spare form, majestical though slight,
Would, if some great emotion moved his heart,
Rise higher as he spoke, and into awe
Deepen the veneration for him felt.
Mostly he walked alone, with steps which changed
From fast to slow, then back from slow to fast,
Like the wild thoughts which sped across his brain.

He spake but little, and in words well weighed ;
Was feared, not loved, nor seemed to care for love,
If men but paid him the respect he claimed.
The self-indulgent, pampered multitude,
With whom at times he mixed in contrast strange,
Marvelled to see how cruel abstinence
Had to a skeleton his body worn,
And made his face a skull masked o'er with skin;
But when they, staring, marvelled at the man,
Little they guessed how in that tenement,
So thin and frail, there dwelt in silence close
A spirit of unbounded arrogance,
Restless ambition, overweening pride,
And stern self-will, unsoftened e'en by love !
When he walked out his dress was of the best,
But suited to his office of a priest.
He studied men, but read not much in books :
With some few words, directed to the point,
He cleared up doubts and made his views prevail.
All yielded to an influence felt by all ;
The priest was honoured, but none loved the man.
He came not to their feasts or happy homes,
But held himself apart ; drank sparingly ;
Ate, not with thankfulness, but as in scorn
That one like him should know the need of food.
He ever seemed as if some great design,
Concealed and cherished in his inmost mind,
Tormented him, and made each present hour
Irksome to one with hopes unrealized,
Who in some future lived, and for it longed.

AUFIDIUS, when AUGUSTINE on him called
As he through Rome had passed to Ostia,
Had read with care the letters by him brought

From Milan, pausing once or twice to cast
A glance on one who therein was so praised,
As if he would assure himself that words
Of such great weight had some foundation true.
With courtesy he welcomed him to Rome,
Asked of his journey, making some remarks
Best fitted to obtain from his guest's mouth
Descriptions of the things in Milan seen.
He listened with calm face to every word
By his dexterity elicited ;
Then, as the conversation further went,
And some bright sparks of intellectual fire
Were struck out in the course of argument,
The old man's manner warmed, though still reserved.
Soon afterwards he on AUGUSTINE called,
And had some talk with him ; but MONICA,
From a repugnance nothing could explain,
Held her son back.   It seemed that every time
AUGUSTINE saw AUFIDIUS, a fear,
As of some undefined calamity,
Harassed her soul, and she restrained her son
From intimacy close, which he desired.
Her fancies troubled not AUGUSTINE'S mind ;
So, when the latter had returned to Rome,
And MONICA no longer was a bar,
His conversations with AUFIDIUS
Became more frequent ; for the aged priest,
Who was at first so cold, turned cordial,
And even condescended to request
One who was much his junior to explain
Some problems too abstruse for common men.
In PROBA'S house the two friends often met
And interchanged ideas.   AUFIDIUS marked
The great respect felt for AUGUSTINE there,

And how much PROBUS always strove to please
His brilliant, youthful guest, whenc'er he came.
AUFIDIUS perused, in his quick way,
Some of AUGUSTINE'S writings, and at times,
When they walked out together, which was now
Nothing uncommon, would turn round and look,
With his bright, searching eyes, upon the face
Of his companion, seem about to speak
On some great topic, then his purpose change,
And on in silence and abstraction walk ;
Pausing, because the time had not yet come,
Or else because he doubted if AUGUSTINE
Were the right man to do what he desired.
AUGUSTINE soon felt flattered at the thought
Of one who had the reverence of all
Paying such marked attention to himself,
And showing for him such solicitude ;
For from AUFIDIUS did he often hear
Suggestions, nay, entreaties, that ere long
He would become a priest, and live in Rome.
But from the priestly office did AUGUSTINE
Excuse himself, declaring how he wished
To live and die a layman in Tagasta ;
Whereto AUFIDIUS would in peevish tone
Reply, "My friend, a priest thou needs must be ;
The most thy choice extends to is the time !
Think on it, therefore, and prepare thy mind."
Nor would he ever treat as possible
That one so fit should fail to be a priest.
He strove in conversation to impress
Upon AUGUSTINE'S mind the dignity,
The power, privilege, and holiness
Of sacerdotal rank, the reverence
Which every priest should, as his right, receive,

And can from churlish worshippers compel.
Not to AUGUSTINE, but to other men,
Who, like himself, were puffed up by the thought
That they, being priests, were to the laity
Not ministers, but masters spiritual,
Sometimes would he, in whispers, thus confide :
" We clergy are the Church !   The Christian priests
To CHRIST'S apostles are successors sole,
And with us, as He promised, will He be
To the world's end.   Our flocks, the laity,
Have, through us, close relation to the Church,
But are no part thereof : we form the whole.
According to our will they enter heaven,
Or, unabsolved by us, sink down to hell.
Great are a priest's prerogatives and power ! "
Once, when AUGUSTINE gave a half assent
To the opinion of AUFIDIUS,
That, though he might perchance postpone the time,
It was his certain fate to be ordained,
And from a bishop's hands commission take
Like that which the apostles once conferred,
His venerable friend was wild with joy,
And bade him mark how great a prospect then
Was to the clergy offered.   " View," said he,
" The aspect of the world in which we live !
The opportunity which now exists
Wants only a bold hand to grasp it firm.
The Pagan despots who once ruled in Rome,
Making the Senate their submissive slaves,
United in themselves imperial power
And sacerdotal sanctity ; for well
Knew they the art to govern.   They are gone !
The Christian princes who have, since their time,
Sat upon CÆSAR'S throne, were straightway shorn

Of sacred functions.   Emperor-priests no more
Are they, but simple laymen, who must look
To us, the clergy, for religious rites ;
And even were they wise,—not poor weak fools,—
Would have to stoop their pride and bate their breath
In presence of the prelates of the Church.
They have played ill their chances in the game ;
Intestine quarrels and ignoble tastes,
Vices of Oriental luxury,
The far removal to Byzantium,
The great division of the East and West
Which rent the Empire's purple robe in twain,
Habits unwarlike, sensual, and vile,
Have brought down Rome's Imperial family,
And temporal power lies now in disrepute !
All that is wanting to endow the Church
With power paramount, just slipped from hands
Too weak to hold it, is that some strong MAN—
A man as dexterous and wise as thou,
Who hath before him a long course of years
In which to dig and build, contrive and work—
Should as a priest and pope preside in Rome.
SIRICIUS hath proved of little use,—
A sickly Spaniard, dull and saturnine,
Who soon will leave this world, to swell the list
Of saints inserted in the calendar ;
For all our popes as yet take rank as saints !
Upon his death we must be prompt to act :
PROBUS will add his influence to ours,
If thou wilt undertake what must be done ;
Nor could we find a better time than now.
I, who can manage all, will make all safe !
See with what ease whate'er the world contains
May be made instruments to work our will !

We who have knowledge should rule men without ;
The mind directs the body ; we, who sway
The souls of men, can make their gifts our tools :
Painting and sculpture, music, and all arts
Which, through emotion, govern human souls,
Our handmaidens shall be ; the fierce and bold
Shall fight our battles and our foes destroy ;
Rebellion offered to the Church's will
Must be crushed down relentlessly by force,
Though rivers run with blood, the sea with tears,
And the loud winds swell big with captives' sighs.
Of small account is this world's agony
Compared with that of hell, and unto hell
Do we consign all sinful, baptized men,
Who, by resisting us, dishonour GOD !
All men who, after Christian baptism,
Of sin are guilty, are to hell condemned,
Unless to us, the clergy, they confess,
And absolution at our hands receive.
The power this gives, e'en fools may understand !
PETER called all who were by him baptized,
Though not ordained to any priestly office,
' A holy priesthood, which should offer up
Spiritual sacrifices of the kind
Acceptable to GOD by JESUS CHRIST.' [1]
But we, the clergy, no priests recognise
Except ourselves ; and what we offer up
Doth, though material, in our hands become
Miraculously changed ! Who dares that doubt ?
Therefore, as working miracles, we claim
Awe and obedience from the rest of men.
Behold the fulcrum for our use, whereby
We move the earth, and lift it where we choose !

[1] 1 Pet. ii. 5.

Imperial persons must be made to yield
To sacerdotal!   Soon the bishop here
Shall rule not only Rome, but all the world!
I am too old to act, but not to plan.
Reflect what mighty things, with aid like mine,
Thou may'st accomplish: thou canst make thy name
Great through all ages; by the laity,
By princes, kings, and emperors, be deemed
A kind of deity; may'st set thy foot
On their proud necks, while we stand looking on,
And all the clergy, still too much despised,
With thee as Pope supremacy shall gain!"
"I like not such a task," AUGUSTINE said;
"'Honour the king,' ST. PETER gave command;
Not humble him, and snatch his crown away."
"We will not snatch the crown from off his head,
But place it there," AUFIDIUS replied;
"But he from us will take the bauble then,
Which, if we please, we can, 'tis true, resume.
Think'st thou that priests, who are GOD'S chosen
    class,
The wisdom, worth, and virtue of mankind,
Can be content to carry on their necks
The yoke which brutal force would make them
    wear?
If thou hast sympathy with suffering,
And wouldst from wrong rescue thy fellow-men,
Who pine beneath oppression's iron hand,
Canst thou do better than with us unite,
Who would a milder system substitute,
And make the nobler principle of thought
Master the vulgar tyranny of strength?
Grasp, then, the keys, and wield the two-edged sword,
Which typifies a sway o'er earth and heaven!"

AUGUSTINE was embarrassed by these words,
Too plausible at first for prompt reply,
And in a doubting silence paced along.
His mind was conscious that a great thick cloud
Enwrapt it, like the mists which then began
To gather thickly round the setting sun.
AUFIDIUS now felt sure that he should win,
Without much more resistance, his assent ;
And when their feet had climbed the golden mount,[1]
In ancient times called the Janiculum,
Which stands above the Tiber's western bank,
He paused with his companion to survey
Rome's mighty city, stretched beneath their feet.
" Here," he exclaimed, " did PETER meet that doom
Which JESUS told him of in Galilee,
Saying : 'When thou wast young, thou didst thyself
Gird, and didst walk whither thou wouldest go :
But when thou shalt be old, thou shalt thy hands
Stretch forth, and some one else shall gird thee then,
And whither thou wouldst not shall carry thee !'[2]
When PETER died, he left unto the Church
The power to bind and loose, which he possessed ;
And who can claim that power with so much right
As the successors of his bishopric,
The prelates of the see of ancient Rome ?
This claim mankind seems willing to concede ;
Our Pope through PETER wields authority,
Which, as its consequence, will surely bring
That temporal sway which should by right be ours.
List, then, to me, and take at once such steps
As my mature experience shall devise."
" But," said AUGUSTINE, " if the temporal power
Is by the clergy seized, as thou wouldst have,

---

[1] Montorio.   [2] John xxi. 18.

And afterwards mankind, whose whims oft change,
Should tire of being longer ruled by priests,
Say, would not then some great catastrophe
Come to involve religion in its fall,
And do more harm to virtue, truth, and faith,
Than any ills which now the world can know ?
Our SAVIOUR in plain words to PILATE said,
' My kingdom is not of this world ;' but thou
Wouldst fain persuade me that the Church should say,
By one whom thou wouldst constitute its head,
' My kingdom *is* of this world, and shall be !'
Surely a scheme like that would fail at last."
" Talk not of failure," sternly said the priest ;
" Men, when in earnest, fail not easily,
And we have means all failure to repel.
The laity must take from us their creed,
And we will hide from their presumptuous eyes
The Scriptures, which we priests alone should read.
Through us, and with such dressing as we choose,
Shall they eat meat, else far too strong for babes.
They soon would cavil if they once knew all :
Therefore, when they shall tire of what they know,
The Church some dogmas new can promulgate,
And call the novelty development !
The temporal sway at which we boldly aim
Is nothing but a means unto an end ;—
That end is sovereignty, without control,
Over men's acts, their hearts, their consciences,
Their outward conduct, inward discipline,
Their hopes and fears, their bodies and their souls !
We, to attain that sway, will claim to know,
Through the confessional which we impose,
All sacred secrets of the family,
And e'en the thoughts which pass within men's minds :

Then, when the crowning work becomes complete,
The bishop whom we choose to be our Pope
Shall stand as CHRIST'S VICEGERENT on the earth,
And speak with voice infallible as His !
This privilege was PETER'S, and we claim
For PETER'S Church and his successors here
An equal, and indeed superior right ;
Because the Church can, through the Pope, proclaim
New revelations not to PETER known.
Our Pope of Rome shall rule from Urb to Orb ! [1]
His voice to men shall be the voice of GOD,
The living organ of His mind,—GOD'S mind
Incomprehensible !   Yes, he shall be
The instrument incarnate of GOD'S word,—
The teacher, sovereign and infallible,
Of the Almighty's wisdom and His will ! [2]
Men in the Holy Sacrament adore
JESUS, but they shall hear Him in our Pope,
Who is 'midst men the presence sensible
Of JESUS CHRIST, and, like his Master, stands
King, Pontiff, Host, or Holy Sacrifice." [3]

[1] "Urbi et Orbi"—to the city and to the world—is the address commonly assumed by the Pope in his letters intended for the public.

[2] The Rev. Don Pasquale de Franciscis, an intimate friend of Pope Pius IX., and editor of his speeches, has thus expressed himself : "Voce è senza dubbio ogni Papa, e voce di Dio; siccome colui che è da Dio costituito organo vivente della sua mente incomprehensibile, strumento incarnato della sua parola sustanziale, della sapienza è virtù sua maestro sovrana ed infallibile."—*Discorsi del Sommo Pontefice Pio IX.*, p. 14.   Roma, 1872.

[3] This passage, quoted by Friedrich in his *Tagebuch Während das Vaticanischen Concils* (p. 320), is from a picture in the Exposizione of Ecclesiastical Art, held in Rome during the Council ; the picture being a portrait of Pope Pius IX., with two burning candles before it, and crowned with a *crown of thorns* passing into a royal diadem above.—*The Modern Jove*, by Wm. Arthur ; London, 1873.   Since this chapter was written, the article in the *Quarterly Review*, "Speeches of Pope Pius," by the Rt. Hon. W. E. Gladstone, M.P., has appeared, and is strongly corroborative of what is here represented as the views of the High Papal party.

"What!". said AUGUSTINE, "wouldst thou take from
   men
The Scriptures, which our SAVIOUR bade them search,
And by whose means alone I found out truth?
Wouldst thou thy bishop's chair set up on high
Above GOD'S altar,[1] and presumptuously
Deceive the foolish and distress the wise?
If PETER founded here a church which shall
Become what thou wouldst make it, well might CHRIST
Inquire of him who did it represent,
'Lovest thou me?' and thrice repeat the words!
Well might He also add, 'Feed thou my sheep,'
And 'Feed my lambs;' for He the danger saw
That such a church might, wolf-like, tear the lambs,
And shear too close the fleeces of the flock.
To any Pope who acts as thou dost plan,
I would declare, as CHRIST to PETER said,
'Thou savourest not the things that be of GOD,
But those that be of men, and SATAN art!'[2]
How would the heart of PETER swell with grief,
Did he but know, where he in peace doth dwell,
Rejoicing in the bliss he finds with CHRIST,[3]
By what misconstruing perversity
The powers which JESUS to him gave, when he
Confessed Him first as CHRIST, should e'er be made
The basis of a Roman prelate's pride!
Never will I be used to work such ends.
Perish ambition and the wiles of priests,
Perish the dignity and name of POPE,

---

[1] In the Basilica of St. Peter at Rome, the so-called chair of St. Peter
is placed *above* the altar in the Tribune. Pope Pius IX., the promulgator
of infallibility, has also placed there a mosaic portrait of himself imme-
diately *above* the celebrated bronze statue of St. Peter, whose foot is kissed
by so many worshippers.

[2] Matt. xvi. 23.   [3] Augustine's *Opera*, v. 1376 C, D.

Rather than such a sad catastrophe
Should to perdition bring CHRIST'S Holy Church!"
" Nay, perish thou, and all such men as thou!"
Replied AUFIDIUS, as his eyes flashed fire;
" From the deep bottom of my heart I hate
Such cowards as thyself, who have the gifts
Whereby to do great things, but lack the will,
And waste away their miserable lives
In poring over or in writing books.
Just such was JEROME,[1] that Dalmatian rude,
A man of genius, though misunderstood
By shallow groundlings of the Curia;
He, when in Rome, but four short years ago,
As guest of DAMASUS, the offer had
Which I, with stronger hopes, have just made thee.
But when I daily pressed him to consent,
He, wanting courage, fled from Italy,
And now, instead of sitting on a throne,
Lives as a hermit on a sandy waste,
Crouches half-naked in the Syrian den
Of a huge lion, tamed to be his friend,
And like a savage shuns society.
There let him hold companionship with brutes,

---

[1] The following passage is from Villemain's *Life of Gregory the Seventh* (vol. i. p. 53):—"St. Jerome calls the Roman clergy a pharisaical senate, an ignorant faction. 'Read,' he exclaims, 'the Revelation of St. John; read what is foretold of the woman robed in scarlet, and of the blasphemy written on her forehead, of the seven hills, the great waters, and the ruin of Babylon. There is there figured, doubtless, a holy church, with the triumphs of the apostles and martyrs, but ambition and power pervert many.' St. Jerome speaks like Luther. It is remarkable," Villemain adds, "that this same saint, though attached to the faith of the Romish Church, and even during a long period secretary to Pope Damasus, did not admit the supremacy of the Roman Pontiff. 'If we seek authority,' says he, 'the universe ought to prevail over a city. Wherever one is bishop, be it Rome or Eugubia, Constantinople or Rhegium, Alexandria or Thanis, one holds the same rank in the priesthood' (*Epist. ad Evagrium*)."

Who might have governed emperors and kings!
Go thou, too, to thy native Africa;
Find in Numidia some city small;
There live and die in fit obscurity,
For thou unworthy art to undertake
An enterprise majestic as is mine;
The lot I offered is for thee too great.
But dream not that the scheme, which hath been
    planned
With so much care and thought, will therefore fail.
Reject it if thou wilt; but other men,
Of more ambition and with scruples less,
Will some day do the work which shall be done.
True, I may not survive that time to see,
But soon or late the pride of intellect,
Moving a class which knows and feels its power,
Will trample every obstacle to dust,
Its glorious destiny at last achieve,
And put the fears of timid fools to shame!"
Thus saying, in a rage he tore away,
Stern as grim death stalked slowly down the hill,
And from that day ceased further intercourse.
The sacerdotal scheme his mind had planned
For planting priestly feet on laymen's necks,
And subjugating to the Pope mankind,
In after ages had accomplishment!
Rome then was once more Mistress of the World!
Her clergy for a thousand years enjoyed
Absolute sway, yet found it often hard
To quell rebellious heavings of brave hearts,
Repress the growth of freedom, stifle thought,
And an usurped authority maintain.
To do this work their means were merciless,
For their familiars used without remorse

Dungeons and chains, torture and massacre :
Their doves of innocence were Jesuits,
Those black persistent poisoners of truth ; [1]
The Holy Inquisition was their child!
The spotless whiteness of the LAMB of GOD
Did they by brutal cruelty defile,
Wiping their gore-stained fingers on His fleece.
The earth yet reeks with blood of slaughtered saints,
Shed by their hands ; the ever restless air
Yet echoes sighs and groans of prisoned men,
Who died when pining in their noisome cells.
What fruits, by Time's hand gathered, do we find
As harvest of their culture ?   Were they figs,
And fit for food ? or thistles, to be burned ?
Religion spiritual they soon debased,
By turning it to one material
In·doctrine, ordinance, and daily life,—
A thing of wafers, relics, images,
Idolatrous, repugnant to GOD'S word ;
So that a rival was made possible,
Which took the simple faith of ABRAHAM
For its foundation, but divorced from what
The Law, the Prophets, and CHRIST'S self had taught,
As well as from idolatry accurst !
A new religion thus gained mastery,
Unbroken yet, o'er countless ruined souls.
The Pope and clergy tried what force could do,
And at their instance millions lost their lives
In mad crusades to win Jerusalem
Which is on earth, forgetting that in heaven !
In Christendom itself they failed, because
They bartered heavenly treasure for the dross

---

[1] *Lettres Provinciales*, par Blaise Pascal ; "The Jesuits "— *Quarterly Review* for October 1874 and January 1875.

Of this world's grandeur and supremacy ;
Forbade the Bible to the laity,
Nor made sufficient use of it themselves ;
For money vile professed to pardon sin,
And by indulgences dispelled its dread.
As flowers will blossom in a wilderness,
So, despite Papal barrenness of soil,
GOD'S Spirit, fertilizing human souls
With power resistless, brought forth some great men,
Whose genius, learning, holiness, and love
Deserve remembrance yet with gratitude :
Exceptions few in twice five centuries,
When priests in temporal things were governors.
Under their rule, licentiousness and vice
Flourished, like rankest weeds in summer days,
Among the great and wealthy of the world !
Whom scheming priests, devoid of piety,
Taught to bow down and kneel to images,
Parade in grand processions with the host,
And from their lips deliver by the score
Prayers unaccompanied by heart or mind ;
While the untaught and grosser mass of men,
Shut out from Scripture's light, and left to grope
In superstition's dark and dreary caves,
Remained, like lava of Vesuvius,
Stagnant and crude, except at intervals,
When, molten by hell-fire, they have surged up
In violent eruptive overflow,
To burn or stifle with their sulphurous heat
The rich, who left them in neglect so long,
And basked, like dogs, in false security !
Frightful this lesson ! but far worse the fact
That millions now of sullen men exist,
Content themselves to be the slaves of priests

And minions of their will, who still desire,
Urged on by zealots of perversion new,
To try if methods old suit modern times,
Though meanwhile they can speak in humble tones,
And walk about with feline, stealthy steps,
Biding their time to make the fatal spring!
A new crusade to reinstate the Pope,
Under the banner of the Sacred Heart,
Already stirs the hopes, and fears of men ;
While vultures, by unerring instinct taught,
On the horizon loom, and wait their prey.
Hath Italy itself no talisman
To save mankind in this emergency ?
Small things have often great results produced,
When by GOD'S loving grace effectual made ;
As BALAAM, when he hurried on his way
To honour BALAK, but GOD'S truth suppress,
Was by his ass's voice reproved, so PETER,
When he from craven fear denied his LORD,
And in His presence swore he knew Him not,
Was chastened by the crowing of a cock!
Then the LORD turned and looked with mournful eyes
On PETER, who, repenting, fled and wept.
Oh, would that CHRIST would turn now, and regard
With looks of startling, stern admonishment
The Church which boasts itself of PETER'S chair,
But brings by promulgation and support
Of error, verging upon blasphemy,
The Universal Church to grief and shame!

IV.

MYSTIC BABYLON.

AUGUSTINE watched AUFIDIUS as he strode,
  With back turned round upon the blood-red sun,
Along the slope which led him down to Rome:
Before him moved his shadow, thin and black
As a tall cypress.   Then AUGUSTINE stood
And meditated much on the events
Which had of late his fortitude so tried.
"O GOD!" he cried, "but lately I renounced,
When I accepted the baptismal rite,
The WORLD, the FLESH, and DEVIL; yet they come
Dogging my footsteps in my daily walks,
And tempting me to evil!"   Then he looked
On the vast city spread before his eyes,
And saw the view on which, tradition says,
The dying PETER for some moments gazed
In his last agony, when, on the cross
Head downwards, he expired;—for so he begged
His executioners that he might die,
In token of his true humility
And penitence for having CHRIST denied!
On his left hand, AUGUSTINE gazing saw
Mons Vaticanus, where would one day dwell
The Roman Popes in royal luxury,
And where now rises to the sky the dome
Which rests its weight on the basilica
Called by ST. PETER'S name,—a monster pile,
Cumbrous outside, ugly but vast within!

AUGUSTINE, on his right hand, where the stream
Of Tiber makes a broad and sudden bend,
Beheld the church where PAUL and TIMOTHY
In blessed union side by side repose :
But PAUL'S bones, like his faith, are outside Rome!
Right opposite to where AUGUSTINE stood,
Across the city and beyond its walls,
Appeared the distant, gleaming Alban hills,
On which his Carthaginian countrymen
Were posted once, when every Roman heart
Shuddered with indignation and dismay.
The setting sun upon those eastern heights
Cast clear transparency, which brought to view
Cities and villages of ancient note,
Built on their sides or nestling in their clefts.
Thence in a circle, bending to the north
Far as Soracte's lofty mountain-top,
An amphitheatre of hills ran round,
And formed the wide horizon.   Close below,
Resting on seven hills of lesser height
But more renown, was Rome itself outspread !
There, on the Capitol, AUGUSTINE'S eye
Rested awhile, then scanned with hurried glance
Mont Palatine, with palaces adorned
And temples consecrate to heathen gods ;
Near which, as an appendage to their pride,
On lower ground the Coliseum stood.
HADRIAN'S huge mausoleum next he saw,
Striving to vie with structures of more worth,
But winning for itself but notice slight,
Because, still more in front, and placed between
The Palatine and the Janiculum,
The FORUM'S site was seen, dimly discerned
Among the porticoes and palaces,

Arches of triumph, temples, and all else
Which crowded round that focus of old Rome.
There erst the GRACCHI, full of fiery zeal,
Denounced the rich, who trembled when they spake ;
And there each brother, by patricians slain,
A victim fell, to welter in his gore ;
There King JUGURTHA stood in cruel bonds,
Ere in his dungeon cast to starve and die ;
There once the eloquence of CICERO
Awakened echoes, which in human hearts
Will still reverberate till time be done ;
There ANTONY harangued the populace,
And stirred them up because of CÆSAR'S death ;
There did ST. PAUL once walk, a prisoner
Greatly despised, and to a soldier chained ;
There passion, genius, faction, falsehood, truth,
Battled for centuries with varied aims,
While on the issue of their contests hung
Of an expecting world the weal or woe !
AUGUSTINE on the Forum looked with awe,
Thinking what scenes had passed, what scenes might come
Upon that theatre of struggling life.
He gazed with hands uplifted, full of grief,
Until his heart no longer could restrain
Emotions, which in words expression found : [1]

"O CITY ! stained with blood on every stone !
    Founded by one whose hand, like that of CAIN,

[1] " Romulus, Caini imitator, fratrum occidit, ut totam dominationem habiret unus " (Augustine's *Opera*, vii. 610, 611) ; "Roma quasi secunda Babylonia" (vii. 775, 806) ; "A Cain cœpit civitas Babylonia" (iv. 846, 847) ; "Roma primordia, facinorum asylum, Romuli fratricidium" (iii. 1254). Augustine, in his Epistle to Marcellinus (*Epist.* cxxxviii.), quotes with approbation from Sallust the passage in which Rome is thus spoken of : "O venal city, and doomed to perish speedily, if only it could find a

His brother slew, that he might reign alone ;
   Where vice finds luxury, and virtue pain ;
   Cruel, impure, idolatrous, and vain !
Thou concentrated scum of lies and fraud,
By GOD abandoned and by man abhorred !

" Stronghold of Pagan rites, which are thy breath,
   E'en Christianity shalt thou debase !
O mystic Babylon ! which hell and death
   Tend with deep love, felt for no other place !
   A pestilential mist around thy face
Hangs like a veil, and underneath its shade
Corrupt things flourish and the healthy fade.

" Deception in thy palaces is rife,
   Reigns in thy temples, desecrates thy shrines;
Thy aim is empire, and not holy life ;
   Thy heart to SATAN, not to CHRIST, inclines ;
   Pride swelters in thee, but true merit pines ;
Sharp soon must be thy scourge, heavy thy rod,
Thou CITY OF THIS WORLD, and not of GOD ![1]

" Why longer in thy streets do I abide ?
   Behold, my native country calls me home !
There will I go, and GOD shall be my guide !
   No more will I within thy precincts roam,
   With feet defiled by thy disgusting loam ;

purchaser ;" also some celebrated lines, condemnatory of Rome, from the
6th book of Juvenal. He adds : "Rome had more reason to regret the
departure of its poverty than of its opulence ; because, in its poverty, the
integrity of its virtue was secured, but through its opulence, dire corruption, more terrible than any invader, had taken violent possession, not of
the walls of the city, but of the mind of the State."

[1] In an Epistle to Paulinus and Terasia (*Epist.* xcv.) Augustine says :
" We seek the interest of those who are citizens and subjects, not of
Rome, which is on earth, but of Jerusalem, which is in heaven."

My soul feels stronger since she lately swore
To quit thee soon, nor ever see thee more.

" I cannot pry into futurity ;
 But if it be GOD'S will that I should live
In thickest shades of dull obscurity,
 And, as an undistinguished layman, give
 My peaceful hours to thoughts contemplative,
I am content ! I bow to GOD'S decree ;
As He would have me, gladly would I be !

" But if it be His will that heavier toil
 Should fall upon me ere this world I leave,
And in activity and its turmoil
 My knees should tremble and my bosom heave,—
 Which comes if I a bishopric receive,—
I will submit, and make hard work my cheer,
Stedfast till death, and feel for death no fear.

" Dark clouds with storms now threaten all the world,
 Ruin impends, disasters are at hand,
Empires must fall and be to ruin hurled ;
 Yea, even thou, great Rome ! besieged, shalt stand
 A monument of woe in this fair land !
Barbarian hordes in their triumphant joy
Shall sack thy city, and thy sons destroy !

" But greater are the evils I foresee
 From error sapping at the Church's root,
Religion shifting into policy,
 And poisoned shafts which unbelief will shoot !
 Teachers of heresy, whom none refute,
Will walk the earth, and eagerly combine
The structure of GOD'S truth to undermine.

2 B

" Against these evils, imminent and dire,
   Which slay men's souls that cannot from them fly, —
Against the ruthless traitors who conspire
   Our faith to weaken and GOD'S Son deny,
   My aim shall be to struggle till I die,
Till He who gave me life my work shall close,
And bless His weary servant with repose!"

APPENDIX.

APPENDIX.

———

NOTE a.—PAGE 192.

SAINT AUGUSTINE'S TOMB AT PAVIA.

(See Frontispiece.)

THIS exquisitely sculptured tomb of white marble forms the subject of a splendid work, published at Pavia in 1832.[1] The frontispiece to the present work, which represents a portion only of the tomb, is taken from one of the engravings which illustrate it, as is also the vignette at the end. In giving a brief history of this tomb, Sacchi is my principal authority.

The Vandals, who took Hippo in the year following St. Augustine's death, showed great respect for his memory, by carefully preserving from injury his library, his works, and his body. When the Catholic bishops of Africa were, half a century afterwards, driven out of their native country by Thrasamond (A.D. 500), they took St. Augustine's body with them to Sardinia, where it remained about 200 years. At the expiration of that period the Saracens were ravaging the shores of the Mediterranean, and the rage for relics was at its height in Christendom. Luitprand, king of Lombardy, therefore took advantage of the opportunity to purchase St. Augustine's remains for a large sum; and he had them (about A.D. 724) conveyed from Sardinia to his capital city, Pavia, then in its highest splendour, and there

———

[1] *L'Arca di Sant' Agostino*, monumento in marmo del secolo XIV. Ora esistente nella Chiesa Cattedrale di Pavia. Disegnato ed inciso da Cesare Ferreri, colle illustrazioni di Defendente Sacchi. Pavia, 1832. Folio.

placed in the Church of San Pietro. In A.D. 1027, according to William of Malmesbury,[1] the tomb was opened by the monks, to make over to Agelnoth, Archbishop of Canterbury, an arm, which had been sold to him by the Pope for the sum of 100 talents (*i.e.* 6000 lbs. weight) of silver and one talent (*i.e.* 60 lbs. weight) of gold.

This sale by the Pope is probably the reason why the friars who were the custodians of the relics hid what remained to them in the crypt of San Pietro. That this arm of St. Augustine was brought to England is confirmed by the testimony of the English chronicler, but we have no historical account of what afterwards became of it. If it were deposited in the Cathedral of Canterbury, its fame would for centuries before the Reformation have become quite eclipsed in the minds of worshippers there by the paramount glory of Thomas à Becket's remains ; just as, at the present time, ninety-nine persons out of one hundred who go to pray in the Cathedral of Pavia may be observed to kneel before the altar of St. Carlo Borromeo, the fashionable saint of North Italy, while the tomb and altar of St. Augustine, where his body lies buried, are left unnoticed. When the Reformation took place in England, there was a great scattering to the winds, and unsparing destruction, at Canterbury and elsewhere, of all relics used for superstitious purposes, and St. Augustine's arm seems to have fared no better than less worthy objects. At all events, every trace of it has disappeared ; but it may be a gratification to some minds to know that a portion of the dust of the great Augustine consecrates the soil of England.

The "arca" or monument in honour of St. Augustine, now in the Cathedral of Pavia, was begun in December 1362, and in 1365 the base was laid in the sacristy of San Pietro. Galeazzo, Duke of Milan, made provision in his will for the monument being finished by his heirs ; but this was not done, and finally recourse was obliged to be had to subscriptions. Sacchi is of opinion that, in 1380, it was in the finished state in which we now see it. At all events, an iron railing was placed to protect it in 1383 (p. 17),

---

[1] *De Gestis Regum Anglorum*, lib. ii. c. 1.

and Sacchi supposes it to have been actually finished in 1370. The remains of St. Augustine were intended by those who constructed and erected the monument to have been placed inside it, but this has never been really done down to the present time.

In 1339, Balduccio, of the school of Pisa, constructed the arca or monument of St. Pietro Martire in Milan. The arca of St. Augustine at Pavia bears some resemblance to this, but is greatly superior. Balduccio formed a school of sculpture in Milan, and had many pupils. There is a little village called Campione on the shore of Lake Lugano, and from it, in the thirteenth and fourteenth centuries, issued a troop of sculptors, who dispersed themselves over Italy to find employment, and several of them lent a helping hand and gave counsel in the construction of the Cathedral of Milan. Among them was BONINO. They were named after their native village, Campione, and were sometimes called Tedeschi, because that village was on the confines of Switzerland. They originally engaged themselves as masons to sculptors, and eventually made excellent artists. Balduccio is believed to have engaged some of these Campionesi. In the ducal cemetery of La Scala at Verona is the tomb of Cansignorio, constructed in 1375 by Bonino da Campione, whose name is inscribed on it as the sculptor.[1] Sacchi is of opinion that the arca of Cansignorio at Verona, the arca of Azzo Visconti at Milan, and the arca of St. Augustine at Pavia were all by one and the same artist; and that this is proved by the striking points of resemblance which exist between them,— the general position of the figures, the expressions, the postures, the cut of the eyes, the turn of the hair, the clothing, and other particulars; and that we may be certain of the artist's name, because we find it engraved on the first of these three Lombard monuments.

The monument of St. Augustine has experienced several vicissitudes since its erection. It has already been mentioned

---

[1] "Hoc opus sulpsit et fecit Boninus de' Campiliono, Mediolanensis Diocesis."

that the remains of the saint were never placed within it. In 1695, a mason at work in the crypt of San Pietro broke an urn erected behind the altar of St. Augustine, and inside this urn was found a marble shrine with the inscription "AUGUSTINUS," and inside this shrine was a "silver casket," containing bones or ashes. This was removed for security to the Cathedral for a short time. The friars and the bishop pronounced the contents of the casket to be the bones of the saint, but a dispute arose on the subject, which had to be settled by a Papal bull. Then it was determined to remove the monument into the tribune of the basilica, that it might be erected above the spot where the relics of the saint had been found, and this was done. In 1738 a new altar to St. Augustine was erected in the Church of San Pietro, and in the same year the "arca" was placed upon this altar, and the casket was brought from the Cathedral and placed under the altar, but not within the tomb. Towards the end of the eighteenth century the Eremitani Friars had to withdraw from Pavia to Milan, and they carried with them St. Augustine's remains, and also the "arca," which was taken to pieces for convenience of removal. It remained in that condition in Milan for thirteen years. In 1799, the Augustine order of friars having been abolished, the remains of St. Augustine were brought back to the Cathedral at Pavia, and the "arca" also; but the latter narrowly escaped being sold in pieces and dispersed by the administration charged with the alienation of national property. But the chapter of the Cathedral at Pavia obtained the concession of the monument for the Cathedral, and there it was deposited in pieces in the chapter-house. At last, in 1831, a new chapel was erected in the Cathedral for the monument, and it was set up there in 1832; but it was not placed upon a lofty altar, according to the plan before adopted, nor upon the ground, according to what Bonino intended, but upon a square marble structure, which resembles in front a drawing-room chimney-piece, and which still lifts the monument so much above the eye that the principal figures cannot be conveniently seen unless the spectator stands on a chair. This square

marble structure can be used as an altar, and underneath it is a hollow chamber which contains the casket of relics. This chamber has a metal grid in front, through which the casket can be seen when the moveable screen which hides the chamber from sight is taken away.

In 1871 the author personally examined the monument with great admiration, and had the screen taken away, and saw the " silver casket " through the grid. It appeared to be a wooden box, on each side of which some thin plates of metal, which are said to be silver but look like tin, have been fastened by rows of little nails or tacks in the roughest fashion. This casket stands, however, upon a modern silver tray, with chased border and feet. Why may not the remains of the saint be at last suffered to rest within the magnificent tomb which 500 years ago was constructed to contain them? Possibly it is because they are wanted in order to be shown for sensational purposes on certain fête days. The present state of things is most unsatisfactory to minds which feel a true reverence for the great man whose memory the monument was intended to honour.

WORSHIP OF THE VIRGIN MARY.

DR. PUSEY, in his *Eirenicon*,[1] has collected from the writings of various distinguished members of the clergy of the Church of Rome, a body of quotations which demonstrate the blasphemous nature of the worship now offered up in that Church to the Virgin Mary. This worship has been greatly encouraged in consequence of Pope Pius IX. having promulgated the dogma of her " Immaculate Conception." Dr. Newman, in a recent letter,[2] has given a summary of the opinions so collected by Dr. Pusey, and he does not attempt to deny that they are the utterances of persons of great ability, some of whom are members of the Roman hierarchy. This summary is as follows :—

" That the mercy of Mary is infinite ; that God has resigned into her hands His omnipotence ; that (unconditionally) it is safer to seek her than her Son ; that the Blessed Virgin is superior to God ; that He is (simply) subject to her command ; that our Lord is now of the same disposition as His Father towards sinners, viz. a disposition to reject them, while Mary takes His place as an advocate with Father and Son ; that the saints are more ready to intercede with Jesus than Jesus with the Father ; that Mary is the only refuge of those with whom God is angry ; that Mary alone can obtain a Protestant's conversion ; that it would have sufficed for the salvation of men if our Lord had died, not to

[1] *The Church of England a Portion of Christ's one Holy Catholic Church, and a means of restoring Visible Unity. An Eirenicon.* By E. B. Pusey, D.D. Oxford, 1865. 8vo.

[2] *A Letter to the Rev. E. B. Pusey, D.D., on his recent " Eirenicon."* By John Henry Newman, D.D. London, 1866. 8vo.

obey His Father, but to defer to the decree of His mother; that she rivals our Lord in being God's daughter, not by adoption, but by a kind of nature; that Christ fulfilled the office of Saviour by imitating her virtues; that as the Incarnate God bore the image of His Father, so He bore the image of His mother; that redemption derived indeed from Christ its sufficiency, but from Mary its beauty and loveliness; that as we are clothed with the merits of Christ, so are we clothed with the merits of Mary; that as He is Priest, in like manner is she priestess; that His body and blood in the Eucharist are truly hers, and appertain to her; that as He is present and is received therein, so is she present and received therein; that priests are ministers of Christ, so of Mary; that elect souls are born of God and Mary; that the Holy Ghost brings into fruitfulness His action by her, producing in her and by her Jesus Christ in His members; that the kingdom of God in our souls, as our Lord speaks, is really the kingdom of Mary in the soul, and she and the Holy Ghost produce in the soul extraordinary things; and when the Holy Ghost finds Mary in a soul, He flies there."

Dr. Newman, addressing Dr. Pusey, adds: "Sentiments such as these I never knew of till I read your book, nor do I think that the vast majority of English Catholics know them. They seem to me like a bad dream," etc. etc. (p. 119).

But there are other passages in the writings of distinguished members of the Roman clergy, besides those thus summarized, which have been called to our attention by Dr. Pusey's *Eirenicon.* Thus Father Faber, who complains that in England Mary is not half enough preached, adds: "Thousands of souls perish because Mary is withheld from them" (p. 118). The Archbishop of Cuba especially distinguishes himself by the following extravagances :—
"The Virgin Mother of God, helping our infirmities, will entreat her Son for us, *with groanings which cannot be uttered*" (p. 143). The assumption of the Blessed Virgin Mary as now understood means, "the taking of her body up into heaven without seeing corruption," whereas it originally denoted only the removal of her soul to heaven (p. 150). She is accounted to be "placed by God

between 'Christ and the Church" (p. 151). She is "Mediatrix with the Redeemer," and our "Co-Redemptress" (*ib.* and p. 154). Of Mary it may be said, "So Mary loved the world, that she gave her only-begotten Son" (p. 156). "She bears, together with Christ, all the names and titles which are wont to be ascribed to Christ, and is rightly called Redemptress, Pastoress, Mediatress, Authoress, and Cause of our salvation" (pp. 157, 158). We may say that, by dying, "Christ obeyed not only His Father, but also His mother" (p. 158). "As Christ, both as God and Man, bore the image of the eternal Father, so it was meet that, God and Man, He should bear the character of His mother" (p. 161). The priest is "minister of Christ" and "minister of Mary." On this teaching of Oswald, Dr. Pusey observes: "'They seem to assign to her an office, *like that of God the Holy Ghost,* indwelling in the soul. They speak of souls born not of blood, nor of flesh, nor of the will of man, but of God and Mary," etc. (p. 164). She is called "the Complement of the Trinity" (p. 167).

After many more extracts of the same kind, Dr. Pusey says : "This system is, I understand, developing" (p. 168).

Mary in her office of advocate is named "Omnipotency kneeling," or "interceding Omnipotency;" and this, Oswald observes, is "saying not too much, but too little" (p. 182). Oswald further says: "Ascending the ladder to heaven leads first to the mother; from the mother to the Son; from the Son to the Father" (p. 183, note).

Dr. Pusey adds: "Faber anticipated 'an Age of Mary,' in comparison to which all previous devotion to her should be slight" (p. 333). If educated persons thus express themselves, the blasphemous idolatry in which the vulgar indulge can excite no wonder. Dr. Newman expresses in his letter much surprise at and disapproval of these opinions. Nevertheless he has attempted to justify much of that which cannot without risk be extenuated ; for there is reason to fear that these errors will lead before long to serious consequences—such, indeed, as are neither anticipated nor desired by those who will be answerable for them. In God the Father of Christ we have the Father of God, and in Mary we

have one who, according to the theology current at Rome, is the "mother of God!" The extracts given above show what deductions are capable of being made from the term "mother of God," and what it is considered to imply. Opinions are now being expressed by important members of the Roman Church, and eagerly received by the ignorant, which must in the course of time lead to attempts being made to identify the Virgin Mary with the Third Person in the Trinity!

We know that at an early period of Christian history the Holy Ghost was occasionally spoken of as the "mother of Christ." It is generally agreed that the original Gospel of St. Matthew was written in Hebrew, or rather Aramæan, and Jerome found in the hands of the Nazarenes a book represented to be a copy of it, but the text of which was evidently corrupted. According to him, the Saviour is in this Aramæan gospel introduced as saying, "Just now my mother, the Holy Ghost, laid hold of me by one of my hairs" (Modo tulit me, *mater mea, Spiritus Sanctus*, in uno capillorum meorum[1]). Origen also refers in one of his works to this same book, and quotes from it a passage containing the same expression : "My mother, the Holy Ghost."[2] It is obvious that this is readily capable of misconstruction ; and considering the tendency exhibited in the passages cited by Dr. Pusey, there is great danger that we may before long be favoured with a new dogma from Rome of an incarnation earlier than that of Christ. He quotes a long passage from St. Irenæus, in which the latter draws in rhetorical language a contrast between Eve and her disobedience, and Mary, "who, being obedient, became both of herself and to the whole human race the cause of salvation." " And so," says Irenæus, "the knot of Eve's disobedience received its unloosening through the obedience of Mary ; for what Eve, a virgin, bound by incredulity, that Mary, a virgin, unloosed by faith" (*Adv. Hær.* iii. 22-34). And again, Irenæus, in another passage quoted by Dr. Newman, says : "As Eve by the speech of

[1] *Comment. in Mic.* vii. 6.
[2] *Comment. in Joann.* vol. iv. p. 63, ed. Delarue. See Davidson's *Introduction to the New Testament,* vol. i. pp. 19 and 27.

an angel was seduced, so as to flee God, transgressing His word, so also Mary received the good tidings by means of the angel's speech, so as to bear God within her, being obedient to His word. And though the one had disobeyed God, yet the other was drawn to obey God; that of the virgin Eve the virgin Mary might become the *advocate.* And as by a virgin the human race had been bound to death, by a virgin it is saved, the balance being preserved, a virgin's disobedience by a virgin's obedience " (*Ibid.* v. 19). Now upon this last passage Dr. Newman makes the following comment :—"It is supposed by critics, Protestant as well as Catholic, that the Greek word for advocate in the original was *paraclete;* it should be borne in mind, then, when we (*i.e.* the Romanists) are accused of giving our Lady the titles and offices of her Son, that *St. Irenæus bestows on her the special name and office proper to the Holy Ghost.*" Dr. Newman, without intending it, has contributed his share to the development now in progress, for at p. 37 of his letter he says : "But it is certain Irenæus never intended to ascribe to the Blessed Virgin 'the name and office proper to the Holy Ghost,' though he may, for rhetorical effect, have expressed himself incautiously." In consequence, however, of the distortion of his real meaning given by Dr. Newman's gloss, Irenæus may henceforth be quoted, by persons whose blasphemy would have been abhorrent to him, as an early supporter of their false opinions. It is impossible to say what results may not follow from Pius IX.'s new dogmas of the Immaculate Conception and of the Pope's Infallibility. The floodgates of error have been opened in a high place, and we already hear the distant rumbling of the approaching torrent, but cannot tell beforehand what will be carried away by it when it comes, or what will be saved. What security is there any longer that the dogma of the Incarnation of the Holy Ghost in the person of the Virgin Mary will not, before long, be promulgated from Rome, and be accepted by the Roman Church? All that is necessary is that there should again be a Pope of intense personal vanity, who wishes to make his name conspicuous in ecclesiastical history through all future ages, and who is not afraid

to do so by embodying the gross belief of ignorance and superstition in a new dogma, to be promulgated by himself *ex cathedra* and with professed infallibility. The notion that the Roman Curia, composed for the most part of obsequious Italian priests, is any guarantee against such a contingency, is preposterous.

LATIN NOTES.[1]

NOTE A.—PAGE 19.

"Alia erant quæ in eis amplius capiebant animum : colloqui et corridere, et vicissim benevole obsequi ; simul legere libros dulciloquos, simul nugari, et simul honestari ; dissentire interdum sine odio, tanquam ipse homo secum, atque ipsa rarissima dissensione condire consensiones plurimas ; docere aliquid invicem, aut discere ab invicem ; desiderare absentes cum molestia, suscipere venientes cum lætitia : his atque hujusmodi signis a corde amantium et redamantium procedentibus per os, per linguam, per oculos, et mille motus gratissimos, quasi fomitibus conflare animos, et ex pluribus unum facere.

"Hoc est quod diligitur in amicis, et sic diligitur, ut rea sibi sit humana conscientia, si non amaverit redamantem, aut si amantem non redemaverit, nihil quærens ex ejus corpore præter indicia benevolentiæ. Hinc ille luctus, si quis moriatur ; et tenebræ dolorum, et versa dulcedine in amaritudinem cor madidum, et ex amissa vita morientium mors viventium. Beatus qui amat te, et amicum in te, et inimicum propter te. Solus enim nullum charum amittit, cui omnes in illo chari sunt, qui non amittitur. Et quis est iste, nisi Deus noster, Deus qui fecit cœlum et terram, et implet ea, quia implendo ea fecit ea? Te nemo amittit, nisi qui dimittit : et qui dimittit, quo it, aut quo fugit, nisi a te placido ad te iratum? Nam ubi non invenit legem tuam in pœna sua? Et lex tua veritas, et veritas tu."— AUGUSTINE's *Confess.* lib. iv. cc. 8 and 9.

---

[1] Title of St. Augustine's works from which the Latin notes are taken :— *Sancti Aurelii Augustini Hipponensis Episcopi Opera Omnia. . . . Editio Parisina altera, emendata et aucta. . . .* Parisiis, apud Gaume Fratres, Bibliopolas. MDCCCXXXVI.

NOTE B.—Page 38.

"Nam et superbia celsitudinem imitatur; cum tu sis unus super omnia Deus excelsus. Et ambitio quid nisi honores quærit et gloriam; cum tu sis præ cunctis honorandus unus et gloriosus in æternum? Et sævitia potestatum timeri vult: quis autem timendus nisi unus Deus? Cujus potestati eripi aut subtrahi quid potest? quando, aut ubi, aut quo, vel a quo potest? Et blanditiæ lascivientium amari volunt; sed neque blandius est aliquid tua charitate, nec amatur quidquam salubrius, quam illa præ cunctis formosa et luminosa veritas tua. Et curiositas affectare videtur studium scientiæ; cum tu omnia summe noveris. Ignorantia quoque ipsa atque stultitia, simplicitatis et innocentiæ nomine tegitur; quia te simplicius quidquam non reperitur. Quid te autem innocentius, quandoquidem opera sua malis inimica sunt? Et ignavia quasi quietem appetit: quæ vero quies certa præter Dominum? Luxuria satietatem atque abundantiam se cupit vocari: tu autem es plenitudo et indeficiens copia incorruptibilis suavitatis. Effusio liberalitatis obtendit umbram; sed bonorum omnium largitor affluentissimus tu es. Avaritia multa possidere vult; et tu possides omnia. Invidentia de excellentia litigat: quid te excellentius? Ira vindictam quærit: te justius quis vindicat? Timor insolita et repentina exhorrescit, rebus quæ amantur adversantia, dum præcavat securitati: tibi enim quid insolitum? quid repentinum? aut quis a te separat quod diligis? aut ubi, nisi apud te, firma securitas? Tristitia rebus amissis contabescit, quibus se oblectabat cupiditas; quia ita sibi nollet, sicut tibi auferri nihil potest.

"Ita fornicatur anima, cum avertitur abs te, et quærit extra te se, quæ pura et liquida non invenit, nisi cum redit ad te. Perverse te imitantur omnes qui longe se a te faciunt, et extollunt se adversum te. Sed etiam sic te imitando indicant creatorem te esse omnis naturæ; et ideo non esse quo a te omni modo recedatur."—Augustine's *Confess.* lib. ii. c. 6.

2 C

"Veni Carthaginem ; et circumstrepebat me undique sartago flagitiosorum amorum. Nondum amabam, et amare amabam, et secretiore indigentia oderam me minus indigentem. Quærebam quod amarem, amans amare, et oderam securitatem, et viam sine muscipulis. Quoniam fames mihi erat intus ab interiore cibo teipso, Deus meus, et ea fame non esuriebam ; sed eram sine desiderio alimentorum incorruptibilium : non quia plenus eis eram, sed quo inanior, eo fastidiosior."—AUGUSTINE's *Confess.* lib. iii. c. 1.

" Invoco te, Deus meus, misericordia mea, qui fecisti me, et oblitum tui oblitus non es. Invoco te in animam meam, quam præparas ad capiendum te ex desiderio quod inspiras ei : nunc invocantem te ne deseras, qui priusquam invocarem prævenisti et institisti crebrescens multimodis vocibus, ut audirem de longinquo et converterer, et vocantem me invocarem te. Tu enim, Domine, delevisti omnia mala merita mea, ne retribueres manibus meis in quibus a te defeci ; et prævenisti omnia bona merita mea, ut retribueres manibus tuis quibus me fecisti : quia et priusquam essem, tu eras ; nec eram cui præstares ut essem ; et tamen ecce sum ex bonitate tua præveniente totum hoc quod me fecisti, et unde me fecisti. Neque enim eguisti me, aut ego tale bonum sum quo tu adjuveris, Domine meus et Deus meus ; non ut tibi sic serviam quasi ne fatigeris in agendo, aut ne minor sit potestas tua carens obsequio meo ; neque ut sic te colam quasi terram, ut sis incultus si non te colam ; sed ut serviam tibi et colam te, ut de te mihi bene sit, a quo mihi est ut sim cui bene sit."—AUGUSTINE's *Confess.* lib. xiii. c. 1.

NOTE E.—PAGE 125.

" Magnus es, Domine, es laudabilis valde : magna virtus tua, et sapientiæ tuæ non est numerus. Et laudare te vult homo, aliqua portio creaturæ tuæ ; et homo circumferens mortalitatem suam, circumferens testimonium peccati sui, et testimonium quia superbis resistis : et tamen laudare te vult homo, aliqua portio creaturæ tuæ. Tu excitas, ut laudare te delectet ; quia fecisti nos ad te, et inquietum est cor nostrum, donec requiescat in te. Da mihi, Domine, scire et intelligere utrum sit prius invocare te, an laudare te ; et scire te prius sit, an invocare te. Sed quis te invocat, nesciens te ? Aliud enim pro alio potest invocare nesciens te. An potius invocaris, ut sciaris ? Quomodo autem invocabunt in quem non crediderunt ? aut quomodo credent sine prædicante ? Et laudabunt Dominum qui requirunt eum. Quærentes enim invenient eum, et invenientes laudabunt eum. Quæram te, Domine, invocans te ; et invocem te, credens in te : prædicatus enim es nobis. Invocat te, Domine, fides mea quam dedisti mihi, quam inspirasti mihi per humanitatem Filii tui, per ministerium prædicatoris tui.

" Et quomodo invocabo Deum meum, Deum et Dominum meum ? Quoniam utique in me ipsum eum vocabo, cum invocabo eum. Et quis locus est in me quo veniat in me Deus meus ? quo Deus veniat in me, Deus qui fecit cœlum et terram ? Itane, Domine, Deus meus, est quidquam in me quod capiat te ? An vero cœlum et terra quæ fecisti, et in quibus me fecisti, capiunt te ? An quia sine te non esset quidquid est, fit ut quidquid est capiat te ? Quoniam itaque et ego sum, quid peto ut venias in me, qui non essem, nisi esses in me ? Non enim ego jam in inferis, et tamen etiam ibi es. Nam etsi descendero in infernum, ades. Non ergo essem, Deus meus, non omnino essem, nisi esses in me. An potius non essem, nisi essem in te, ex quo omnia, per quem omnia, in quo omnia ? Etiam sic, Domine, etiam sic. Quo te invoco, cum in te sim ? aut unde venias in me ? Quo enim recedam extra cœlum et terram, ut inde in me

veniat Deus meus, qui dixit, *Cœlum et terram ego impleo?*"—
Augustine's *Confess.* lib. i. cc. 1 and 2.

NOTE F.—PAGE 141.

" Et inde admonitus redire ad memetipsum, intravi in intima
mea, duce te ; et potui, quoniam factus es adjutor meus.   Intravi,
et vidi qualicumque oculo animæ meæ, supra eumdem oculum
animæ meæ, supra mentem meam, lucem incommutabilem ; non
hanc vulgarem et conspicuam omni carni : nec quasi ex eodem
genere grandior erat, tanquam si ista multo multoque clarius
claresceret, totumque occuparet magnitudine.   Non hoc illa
erat ; sed aliud, aliud valde ab istis omnibus.   Nec ita erat supra
mentum meam sicut oleum super aquam, nec sicut cœlum super
terram ; sed superior, quia ipsa fecit me, et ego inferior, quia factus
sum ab ea.   Qui novit veritatem, novit eam ; et qui novit eam,
novit æternitatem.   Charitas novit eam.   O æterna veritas, et
vera charitas, et chara æternitas ! tu es Deus meus ; tibi suspiro
die ac nocte.   Et cum te primum cognovi, tu assumpsisti me, ut
viderem esse quod viderem, et nondum me esse qui viderem.
Et reverberasti infirmitatem aspectus mei, radians in me vehe-
menter, et contremui amore et horrore ; et inveni longe me esse
a te in regione dissimilitudinis, tanquam audirem vocem tuam de
excelso : Cibus sum grandium ; cresce, et manducabis me.   Nec
tu me in te mutabis, sicut cibum carnis tuæ ; sed tu mutaberis
in me.   Et cognovi quoniam pro iniquitate erudisti hominem, et
tabescere fecisti sicut araneam animam meam ; et dixi : Numquid
nihil est veritas, quoniam neque per finita, neque per infinita
locorum spatia diffusa est ?   Et clamasti de longinquo : Imo
vero, *Ego sum qui sum.*   Et audivi sicut auditur in corde, et
non erat prorsus unde dubitarem ; faciliusque dubitarem vivere
me, quam non esse veritatem, quæ per ea quæ facta sunt, intellecta conspicitur."—Augustine's *Confess.* lib. vii. c. 10.

NOTE G.—Page 159.

"Obsurdesce adversus immunda illa membra tua super terram, ut mortificentur. Narrant tibi delectationes, sed non sicut lex Domini Dei tui.

"Tu non poteris quod isti, quod istæ? An vero isti et istæ in semetipsis possunt, ac non in Domino Deo suo? Dominus Deus eorum me dedit eis. Quid in te stas, et non stas? Projice te in eum; noli metuere non se subtrahet ut cadas: projice te securus, excipiet et sanabit te."—AUGUSTINE'S *Confess.* lib. viii. c. 11.

NOTE H.—Page 185.

"Accipe sacrificium confessionum mearum de manu linguæ meæ quam formasti et excitasti, ut confiteatur nomini tuo; et sana omnia ossa mea, et dicant: Domine, quis similis tibi? Neque enim docet te quid in se agatur qui tibi confitetur; quia oculum tuum non excludit cor clausum, nec manum tuam repellit duritia hominum; sed solvis eam, cum voles, aut miserans aut vindicans; et non est qui se abscondat a calore tuo. Sed te laudet anima mea, ut amet te; et confiteatur tibi miserationes tuas, ut laudet te. Non cessat nec tacet laudes tuas universa creatura tua; nec spiritus omnis hominis per os conversum ad te, nec animalia nec corporalia per os considerantium ea; ut exsurgat in te a lassitudine anima nostra, innitens eis quæ fecisti, et transiens ad te qui fecisti hæc mirabiliter: et ibi refectio et vera fortitudo.

"Eant et fugiant a te inquieti et iniqui: et tu vides eos, et distinguis umbras; et ecce pulchra sunt cum eis omnia, et ipsi turpes sunt. Et quid nocuerunt tibi? aut in quo imperium tuum dehonestaverunt, a cœlis usque in novissima justum et integrum? Quo enim fugerunt, cum fugerunt a facie tua? aut ubi tu non invenis eos? Sed fugerunt, ut non viderent te videntem se, atque excæcati in te offenderent; quia non deseris aliquid eorum

quæ fecisti : in te offenderent injusti, et juste vexarentur ; sub-
trahentes se lenitati tuæ, et offendentes in rectitudinem tuam, et
cadentes in asperitatem suam.　Videlicet nesciunt quod ubique
sis, quem nullus circumscribit locus, et solus es præsens, etiam
iis qui longe fiunt a te.　Convertantur ergo et quærant te, quia
non sicut ipsi deseruerunt creatorem suum ita et tu deseruisti
creaturam tuam.　Ipsi convertantur et quærant te ; et ecce ibi es
in corde eorum, in corde confitentium tibi, et projicientium se in
te, et plorantium in sinu tuo post vias suas difficiles : et tu facilis
tergens lacrymas eorum ; et magis plorant et gaudent in fletibus,
quoniam tu Domine, non aliquis homo caro et sanguis, sed tu,
Domine, qui fecisti, reficis et consolaris eos."—Augustine's
Confess. lib. v. cc. 1 and 2.

NOTE K.—Page 188.

"Sero te amavi, pulchritudo tam antiqua et tam nova ! sero te
amavi !　Et ecce intus eras, et ego foris, et ibi te quærebam ; et
in ista formosa quæ fecisti, deformis irruebam.　Mecum eras, et
tecum non eram.　Ea me tenebant longe a te, quæ si in te non
essent, non essent.　Vocasti, et clamasti, et rupisti surditatem
meam.　Coruscasti, splenduisti, et fugasti cæcitatem meam.
Fragrasti, et duxi spiritum, et anhelo tibi.　Gustavi, et esurio,
et sitio.　Tetigisti me, et exarsi in pacem tuam."—Augustine's
Confess. lib. x. c. 27.

NOTE L.—Page 193.

"Non dubia sed certa conscientia, Domine, amo te.　Percus-
sisti cor meum verbo tuo, et amavi te.　Sed et cœlum, et terra,
et omnia quæ in eis sunt, ecce undique mihi dicunt ut te amem,
nec cessant dicere omnibus ut sint inexcusabiles.　Altius autem
tu misereberis cui misertus eris, et misericordiam præstabis cui
misericors fueris ; alioquin cœlum et terra surdis loquuntur laudes

tuas. Quid autem amo, cum te amo? Non speciem corporis, nec decus temporis, nec candorem lucis ecce istis amicum oculis, non dulces melodias cantilenarum omnimodarum, non florum et unguentorum et aromatum suaveolentiam, non manna et mella, non membra acceptabilia carnis amplexibus. Non hæc amo, cum amo Deum meum; et tamen amo quandam lucem, et quandam vocem, et quemdam odorem, et quemdam cibum, et quemdam amplexum, cum amo Deum meum, lucem, vocem, odorem, cibum, amplexum interioris hominis mei; ubi fulget animæ meæ quod non capit locus, et ubi sonat quod non rapit tempus, et ubi olet quod non spargit flatus, et ubi sapit quod non minuit edacitas, et ubi hæret quod non divellit satietas. Hoc est quod amo, cum Deum meum amo.

"Et quid est hoc? Interrogavi terram, et dixit, Non sum; et quæcumque in eadem sunt, idem confessa sunt. Interrogavi mare et abyssos, et reptilia animarum vivarum, et responderunt: Non sumus Deus tuus; quære super nos. Interrogavi auras flabilis, et inquit universus aer cum incolis suis: Fallitur Anaximenes; non sum Deus. Interrogavi cœlum, solem, lunam, stellas; Neque nos sumus Deus quem quæris, inquiunt. Et dixi omnibus iis quæ circumstant fores carnis meæ: Dixistis mihi de Deo meo quod vos non estis, dicite mihi de illo aliquid. Et exclamaverunt voce magna: Ipse fecit nos. Interrogatio mea, intentio mea; et responsio eorum, species eorum. Et direxi me ad me, et dixi mihi, Tu quis es? Et respondi, Homo. Et ecce corpus et anima in me mihi præsto sunt; unum exterius, et alterum interius. Quid horum est unde quærere debui Deum meum, quem jam quæsiveram per corpus a terra usque ad cœlum, quousque potui mittere nuntios, radios oculorum meorum? Sed melius quod interius. Ei quippe renuntiabant omnes nuntii corporales præsidenti et judicanti de singulis responsionibus cœli et terræ et omnium quæ in eis sunt dicentium: Non sumus Deus, sed ipse fecit nos. Homo interior cognovit hæc per exterioris ministerium; ego interior cognovi hæc, ego, ego animus per sensus corporis mei. Interrogavi mundi molem de Deo meo, et respondit mihi: Non ego sum, sed ipse me fecit.

"Nonne omnibus quibus integer sensus est, apparet hæc species? Cur non omnibus eadem loquitur? Animalia pusilla et magna vident eam, sed interrogare nequeunt: non enim præposita est in eis nuntiantibus sensibus judex ratio. Homines autem possunt interrogare, ut invisibilia Dei, per ea quæ facta sunt, intellecta conspiciantur; sed amore subdunter eis, et subditi judicare non possunt. Nec respondent ista interrogantibus nisi judicantibus; nec vocem suam mutant, id est speciem suam, si alius tantum videat, alius autem videns interroget, ut aliter illi appareat, aliter huic; sed eodem modo utrique apparens, illi muta est, huic loquitur: imo vero omnibus loquitur; sed illi intelligunt qui ejus vocem acceptam foris intus cum veritate conferunt. Veritas enim dicit mihi: Non est Deus tuus cœlum, et terra; neque omne corpus. Hoc dicit eorum natura videnti: Moles est; moles minor est in parte quam in toto. Jam tu melior es; tibi dico, anima; quoniam tu vegetas molem corporis tui, præbens ei vitam, quod nullum corpus præstat corpori. Deus autem tuus etiam tibi vitæ vita est."—Augustine's *Confess.* lib. x. c. 6.

NOTE M.—Page 204.

"Quando autem sufficio lingua calami enuntiare omnia hortamenta tua, et omnes terrores tuos, et consolationes, et gubernationes quibus me perduxisti prædicare verbum, et sacramentum tuum dispensare populo tuo? Et si sufficio hæc enuntiare ex ordine, caro mihi valent stillæ temporum. Et olim inardesco meditari in lege tua, et in ea tibi confiteri scientiam et imperitiam meam, primordia illuminationis tuæ, et reliquias tenebrarum mearum, quousque devoretur a fortitudine infirmitas. Et nolo in aliud horæ diffluant, quas invenio liberas a necessitatibus reficiendi corporis, et intentionis animi, et servitutis quam debemus hominibus, et quam non debemus et tamen reddimus.

"Domine Deus meus, intende orationi meæ, et misericordia tua exaudiat desiderium meum, quoniam non mihi soli æstuat, sed usui vult esse fraternæ charitati: et vides in corde meo quia sic

est. Sacrificem tibi famulatum cogitationis et linguæ meæ; et da quod offeram tibi. Inops enim et pauper sum; tu dives in omnes invocantes te, qui securus curam nostri geris. Circumcide ab omni temeritate omnique mendacio interiora et exteriora labia mea. Sint castæ deliciæ meæ Scripturæ tuæ; nec fallar in eis, nec fallam ex eis. Domine, attende; et miserere, Domine Deus meus, lux cæcorum et virtus infirmorum, statimque lux videntium et virtus fortium, attende animam meam, et audi clamantem de profundo. Nam nisi adsint et in profundo aures tuæ, quo ibimus? quo clamabimus? Tuus est dies, et tua est nox: ad nutum tuum momenta transvolant. Largire inde spatium meditationibus nostris in abdita legis tuæ, neque adversus pulsantes claudas eam. Neque enim frustra scribi voluisti tot paginarum opaca secreta; aut non habent illæ silvæ cervos suos recipientes se in eas et resumentes, ambulantes et pascentes, recumbentes et ruminantes. O Domine, perfice me, et releva mihi eas. Ecce vox tua gaudium meum, vox tua super affluentiam voluptatum. Da quod amo: amo enim; et hoc tu dedisti. Ne dona tua deseras, nec herbam tuam spernas sitientem. Confitear tibi quidquid invenero in Libris tuis; et audiam vocem laudis et te bibam, et considerem mirabilia de lege tua, ab usque principio in quo fecisti cœlum et terram, usque ad regnum tecum perpetuum sanctæ civitatis tuæ.

"Domine, miserere mei, et exaudi desiderium meum. Puto enim quod non sit de terra, non de auro et argento et de lapidibus, aut decoris vestibus, aut honoribus et potestatibus, aut voluptatibus carnis, neque de necessariis corpori, et huic vitæ peregrinationis nostræ, quæ omnia nobis apponunter quærentibus regnum et justitiam tuam. Vide, Domine Deus meus, unde sit desiderium meum. Narraverunt mihi injusti delectationes, sed non sicut lex tua Domine. Ecce unde est desiderium meum. Vide, Pater, aspice, et vide, et approba; et placeat in conspectu misericordiæ tuæ invenire me gratiam ante te, ut aperiantur pulsanti mihi interiora sermonum tuorum. Obsecro per Dominum nostrum Jesum Christum filium tuum, virum dexteræ tuæ, filium hominis, quem confirmasti tibi mediatorem tuum et nostrum,

per quem nos quæsisti non quærentes te, quæsisti autem ut quærercmus te ; Verbum tuum per quod fecisti omnia, in quibus et me ; Unicum tuum per quem vocasti in adoptionem populum credentium, in quo et me : per cum te obsccro qui sedet ad dexteram tuam et te interpellat pro nobis, in quo sunt omnes thesauri sapientiæ et scientiæ absconditi.   Ipsos quæro in Libris tuis.   Moyses de illo scripsit : hoc ipse ait ; hoc Veritas ait."—Augustine's *Confess.* lib. xi. c. 2.

NOTE N.—Page 229.

"Quem invenirem qui me reconciliaret tibi ? Ambiendum mihi fuit ad Angelos ? Qua prece ? quibus sacramentis ? Multi conantes ad te redire, neque per seipsos valentes, sicut audio, tentaverunt hæc, et inciderunt in desiderium curiosarum visionum, et digni habiti sunt illusionibus.   Elati enim te quærebant doctrinæ fastu, exerentes potius quam tundentes pectora, et adduxerunt sibi per similitudinem cordis sui, conspirantes et socias superbiæ suæ potestates aeris hujus, a quibus per potentias magicas deciperentur, quærentes mediatorem per quem purgarentur, et non erat.   Diabolus enim erat transfigurans se in Angelum lucis.   Et multum illexit superbam carnem, quod carneo corpore ipse non esset.   Erant enim illi mortales et peccatores ; tu autem, Domine, cui reconciliari superbe quærebant, immortalis et sine peccato.   Mediator autem inter Deum et homines oportebat ut haberet aliquid simile Deo, aliquid simile hominibus : ne in utroque hominibus similis, longe esset a Deo ; aut in utroque Deo similis, longe esset ad hominibus, atque ita mediator non esset.   Fallax itaque ille mediator, quo per secreta judicia tua, superbia mereretur illudi, unum cum hominibus habet, id est peccatum ; aliud videri vult habere cum Deo, ut quia carnis mortalitate non tegitur, pro immortali se ostentet. Sed quia stipendium peccati mors est, hoc habet commune cum hominibus, unde simul damnetur in mortem.

"Verax autem mediator quem secreta tua misericordia

demonstrasti humilibus, et misisti ut ejus exemplo etiam ipsam discerent humilitatem, mediator ille Dei et hominum homo Christus Jesus, inter mortales peccatores et immortalem justum apparuit; mortalis cum hominibus, justus cum Deo. Ut quoniam stipendium justitiæ vita et pax est, per justitiam conjunctam Deo evacuaret mortem justificatorum impiorum, quam cum illis voluit habere communem. Hic demonstratus est antiquis sanctis, ut ita ipsi per fidem futuræ passionis ejus, sicut nos per fidem præteritæ, salvi fierent. Inquantum enim homo, intantum mediator; inquantum autem verbum, non medius, quia æqualis Deo, et Deus apud Deum, et simul cum Spiritu Sancto unus Deus.

"Quomodo nos amasti, Pater bone, qui Filio tuo unico non pepercisti, sed pro nobis impiis tradidisti eum! Quomodo nos amasti pro quibus ille, non rapinam arbitratus esse æqualis tibi, factus est subditus usque ad mortem crucis; unus ille in mortuis liber, potestatem habens ponendi animam suam, et potestatem habens iterum sumendi eam; pro nobis tibi victor et victima, et ideo victor quia victima; pro nobis tibi sacerdos et sacrificium, et ideo sacerdos quia sacrificium; faciens tibi nos de servis filios, de te nascendo, nobis serviendo! Merito mihi spes valida in illo est, quod sanabis omnes languores meos, per eum qui sedet ad dexteram tuam et te interpellat pro nobis; alioquin desperarem. Multi enim et magni sunt iidem languores mei, multi sunt et magni; sed amplior est medicina tua. Potuimus putare Verbum tuum remotum esse a conjunctione hominis, et desperare de nobis nisi caro fieret et habitaret in nobis.

"Conterritus peccatis meis et mole miseriæ meæ agitaveram in corde meditatusque fueram fugam in solitudinem; sed prohibuisti me, et confirmasti me, dicens: *Ideo pro omnibus Christus mortuus est, ut qui vivunt, jam non sibi vivant, sed ei qui pro ipsis mortuus est.* Ecce, Domine, jacto in te curam meam ut vivam, et considerabo mirabilia de lege tua. Tu scis imperitiam meam et infirmitatem meam: doce me, et sana me. Ille tuus Unicus in quo sunt omnes thesauri sapientiæ et scientiæ absconditi, redemit me sanguine suo. Non calumnientur mihi superbi: quoniam cogito pretium meum, et manduco, et bibo, et erogo, et pauper

cupio saturari ex eo inter illos qui edunt et saturantur, et laudant Dominum qui requirunt eum."—Augustine's *Confess.* lib. x. cc. 42, 43.

NOTE O.—Page 234.

" Gratias tibi, Deus noster, tui sumus ; indicant hortationes et consolationes tuæ : fidelis promissor, reddes Verecundo, pro rure illo ejus Cassiciaco, ubi ab æstu sæculi requievimus in te, amœnitatem sempiterne virentis paradisi tui, quoniam dimisisti ei peccata super terram, in monte incaseato, monte tuo, monte uberi."—Augustine's *Confess.* lib. ix. c. 3.

NOTE P.—Page 256.

" Dum in die Pentecostes esset refecta refectione illius panis qui de cœlo descendit, post sumptionem sacramenti ; tanta satietate repleta fuit, quod per diem ac noctem absque corporali cibo perseveravit (Boll., die 4 Maii).

" Tanta ebrietate Spiritus sancti rapiebatur, quod in ea fere per totem diem quiescens, dum esset Rex in accubitu sui cordis, neque vox neque sensus in ea audiebatur. Neque mirum ; quia illa pax quæ exuperat omnem sensum, sepeliebat viduæ sensus corporalis, in tantum ut vix matronæ nostræ et etiam vicinæ eam pungentes excitare valerent (Boll., die 4 Maii)."— L'Abbe Bugeaud, p. 441.

NOTE Q.—Page 302.

" Fili, quantum ad me attinet, nulla jam re delector in hac vita. Quid hic faciam adhuc, et cur hic sim nescio, jam con- sumpta spe hujus sæculi. Unum erat propter quod in hac vita aliquantum immorari cupiebam, ut te Christianum catholicum

viderem, priusquam morerer. Cumulatius hoc mihi Deus meus
præstitit, ut te etiam, contempta felicitate terrena, servum ejus
videam : quid hic facio?"—AUGUSTINE's *Confess.* lib. ix. c. 10.

NOTE R.—PAGE 303.

" Dicebamus ergo : Si cui sileat tumultus carnis, sileant phan-
tasiæ terræ et aquarum et aeris, sileant et poli, et ipsa sibi anima
sileat, et transeat se non se cogitando, sileant somnia et imagi-
nariæ revelationes, omnis lingua et omne signum, et quidquid
transeundo fit, si cui sileat omnino ; quoniam si quis audiat,
dicunt hæc omnia, Non ipsa nos fecimus, sed fecit nos qui
manet in æternum : his dictis si jam taceant quoniam erexerunt
aurem in eum qui fecit ea, et loquatur ipse solus, non per ea,
sed per seipsum, ut audiamus verbum ejus, non per linguam
carnis, neque per vocem angeli, nec per sonitum nubis, nec per
ænigma similitudinis ; sed ipsum quem in his amamus, ipsum
sine his audiamus, sicut nunc extendimus nos, et rapida cogita-
tione attigimus æternam Sapientiam super omnia manentem ; si
continuetur hoc, et subtrahantur aliæ visiones longe imparis
generis, et hæc una rapiat et absorbeat et recondat in interiora
gaudia spectatorem suum, ut talis sit sempiterna vita, quale fuit
hoc momentum intelligentiæ, cui suspiravimus ; nonne hoc est,
Intra in gaudium Domini tui? Et istud quando? An cum
omnes resurgemus, sed non omnes immutabimur?"—AUGUSTINE's
Confess. lib. ix. c. 10.

NOTE S.—PAGE 304.

" Ponite, inquit, hoc corpus ubicumque ; nihil vos ejus cura
conturbet ; tantum illud vos rogo, ut ad Domini altare memi-
neritis mei ubi ubi fueritis."—AUGUSTINE's *Confess.* lib. ix. c. 11.

NOTE T.—Page 306.

" Cum inhæsero tibi ex omni me, nusquam erit mihi dolor et labor ; et viva erit vita mea, tota plena te. Nunc autem quoniam tu imples, sublevas eum ; quoniam tui plenus non sum, oneri mihi sum. Contendunt lætitiæ meæ flendæ cum lætandis mœroribus ; et ex qua parte stet victoria nescio. Hei mihi, Domine, miserere mei. Contendunt mœrores mei mali cum gaudiis bonis, et ex qua parte stet victoria nescio. Hei mihi ! Domine, miserere mei. Hei mihi ! ecce vulnera mea non abscondo : medicus es, æger sum ; misericors es, miser sum. Numquid non tentatio est vita humana super terram ? Quis velit molestias et difficultates ? Tolerari jubes eas, non amari. Nemo quod tolerat amat, etsi tolerare amat. Quamvis enim gaudeat se tolerare, mavult tamen non esse quod toleret. Prospera in adversis desidero, adversa in prosperis timeo. Quis inter hæc medius locus, ubi non sit humana vita tentatio ? Væ prosperitatibus sæculi, semel et iterum, a timore adversitatis, et a corruptione lætitiæ ! Væ adversitatibus sæculi, semel et iterum et tertio, a desiderio prosperitatis ! et quia ipsa adversitas dura est, et naufragat tolerantia : numquid non tentatio est vita humana super terram sine ullo interstitio ? " — AUGUSTINE'S *Confess.* lib. x. c. 28.[1]

NOTE U.—Page 311.

" Domine Deus, pacem da nobis (omnia enim præstitisti nobis) ; pacem quietis, pacem sabbati, sabbati sine vespera. Omnis quippe iste ordo pulcherrimus rerum valde bonarum modis suis peractis transiturus est ; et mane quippe in eis factum est, et vespera.

" Dies autem septimus sine vespera est, nec habet occasum,

[1] See translation by Rev. J. G. Pilkington, published by T. and T. Clark, page 264.

quia sanctificasti eum ad permansionem sempiternam; ut id quod tu post opera tua bona valde, quamvis ea quietus feceris, requievisti septimo die, hoc præloquatur nobis vox Libri tui, quod et nos post opera nostra, ideo bona valde quia tu nobis ea donasti, sabbato vitæ æternæ requiescamus in te.

"Etiam tunc enim sic requiesces in nobis, quemadmodum nunc operaris in nobis; et ita erit illa requies tua per nos, quemadmodum sunt ista opera tua per nos. Tu autem, Domine, semper operaris, et semper requiescis. Nec vides ad tempus, nec moveris ad tempus, nec quiescis ad tempus; et tamen facis et visiones temporales, et ipsa tempora, et quietem ex tempore.

"Nos itaque ista quæ fecisti videmus, quia sunt: tu autem quia vides ea, sunt. Et nos foris videmus quia sunt, et intus quia bona sunt: tu autem ibi vidisti facta, ubi vidisti facienda. Et nos alio tempore moti sumus ad benefaciendum, posteaquam concepit de Spiritu tuo cor nostrum; priore autem tempore ad male faciendum movebamur deserentes te: tu vero, Deus une bone, nunquam cessasti benefacere. Et sunt quædem bona opera nostra ex munere quidem tuo, sed non sempiterna: post illa nos requieturos in tua grandi sanctificatione speramus. Tu autem bonum nullo indigens bono, semper quietus es; quoniam tua quies tu ipse es. Et hoc intelligere quis hominum dabit homini? quis angelus angelo? quis angelus homini? A te petatur, in te quæratur, ad te pulsetur: sic, sic accipietur, sic invenietur, sic aperietur. Amen."—AUGUSTINE'S *Confess.* lib. xiii. cc. 35, 36, 37, 38.

NOTE V.—PAGE 361.

"Quis mihi dabit acquiescere in te? Quis mihi dabit ut venias in cor meum, et inebries illud, ut obliviscar mala mea, et unum bonum meum amplectar te? Quid mihi es? Miserere, ut loquar. Quid tibi sum ipse, ut amari te jubeas a me, et nisi faciam irascaris mihi, et mineris ingentes miserias? Parvane ipsa est, si non amem te? Hei mihi! Dic mihi per misera-

tiones tuas, Domine Deus meus, quid sis mihi. *Dic animæ meæ : Salus tua ego sum.* Sic dic, ut audiam. Ecce aures cordis mei ante te, Domine ; aperi eas, et *dic animæ meæ : Salus tua ego sum.* Curram post vocem hanc, et apprehendam te. Noli abscondere a me faciem tuam : moriar, ne moriar, ut eam videam. Angusta est domus animæ meæ quo venias ad eam ; dilatetur abs te. Ruinosa est ; refice eam. Habet quæ offendant oculos tuos ; fateor et scio : sed quis mundabit eam ? aut cui alteri præter te clamabo, *Ab occultis meis munda me, Domine, et ab alienis parce servo tuo ?* Credo, propter quod et loquor ; Domine, tu scis. Nonne tibi prolocutus sum adversum me delicta mea, Deus meus ; et tu dimisisti impietatem cordis mei ? Non judicio contendo tecum qui veritas es ; et ego nolo fallere meipsum, ne mentiatur iniquitas mea sibi. Non ergo judicio contendo tecum ; quia si iniquitates observaveris, Domine ; Domine, quis sustinebit."— AUGUSTINE'S *Confess.* lib. i. c. 5.

The Works of St. Augustine.

EDITED BY MARCUS DODS, D.D.

SUBSCRIPTION:

Each year's Volumes One Guinea, *payable in advance* (24s. when not paid in advance).

FIRST YEAR.

THE 'CITY OF GOD.' Two Volumes.

WRITINGS IN CONNECTION WITH the Donatist Controversy. In One Volume.

THE ANTI-PELAGIAN WORKS OF St. Augustine. Vol. I.

SECOND YEAR.

LETTERS.' Vol. I.

TREATISES AGAINST FAUSTUS the Manichæan. One Volume.

THE HARMONY OF THE EVANgelists, and the Sermon on the Mount. One Volume.

ON THE TRINITY. One Volume.

THIRD YEAR.

COMMENTARY ON JOHN. Two Volumes.

ON CHRISTIAN DOCTRINE, ENCHIRIDION, ON CATECHIZING, and ON FAITH AND THE CREED. One Volume.

THE ANTI-PELAGIAN WORKS OF St. Augustine. Vol. II.

FOURTH YEAR.

'LETTERS.' Vol. II.

'CONFESSIONS.' With Copious Notes by Rev. J. G. PILKINGTON.

ANTI-PELAGIAN WRITINGS. Vol. III.   } In 1876.

LIFE BY PRINCIPAL RAINY.

The Series will be completed in the above Sixteen Volumes. Subscription price, Four Guineas.

Each Volume is sold separately, at Ten Shillings and Sixpence.

THE series of St. Augustine's works, as originally announced by Messrs. CLARK, being now nearly completed, the Publishers desire to invite attention to it more in detail. They trust they may hope to receive the support of all who value the writings of the great Fathers, especially as the larger portion of those writings contained in this series have not been hitherto translated.

The series appropriately begins with the greatest of St. Augustine's works, 'THE CITY OF GOD,' which has hitherto only been accessible to the English reader in a very old and feeble version.

THE CITY OF GOD.

In Two Volumes.

The propriety of publishing a translation of so choice a specimen of ancient literature needs no defence. There are not a great many men now-a-days who will read a work in Latin of twenty-two books. Whilst there have been no fewer than eight independent translations into the French tongue (one of which has gone through *four* editions), only one exists in English, and this is so exceptionally bad, so inaccurate, and so frequently unintelligible, that it is not impossible it may have done something towards giving the English public a distaste for the book itself.

'Dr. Dods has evidently achieved his task in a spirit of loving reverence for his Master, and has provided a spirited, racy, and elegant translation of what Dr. Waterland describes as "a most learned, most correct, and most elaborate work."'

'An idiomatic translation like this speaks highly for the powers of its authors. The English reader who has been before only familiar with the crabbed versions of St. Augustine will be delighted to get hold of so great a treasure, which reads like an original English work, and that of the best style.'—*Church Review.*

'We have already exceeded the limits within which we proposed to restrict our observations on this very remarkable book, for the reproduction of which, in an admirable English garb, we are greatly indebted to the well-directed enterprise and energy of Messrs. Clark, and to the accuracy and scholarship of those who have undertaken the laborious work of translation.'—*Christian Observer.*

'This famous book is still of historic and present value. It was wise to issue the "City of God" as the first volume of the series, that being the most representative of Augustine's works. It is the embodiment not of the writer only, but of the age in which he lived. With all its faults, it is the *great* work of a great man.'—*Record.*

THE LETTERS OF ST. AUGUSTINE.

Translated by Rev. J. G. CUNNINGHAM, M.A.

In Two Volumes.

'St. Augustine's Epistles are delightful reading. They will teach more Church History, if read together with St. Jerome's and with the Canons of contemporary Councils, than any professed historian can do, for they put the reader in contact with one of the great primitive minds of Christendom. The translator has rendered the original into simple and perspicuous English.'—*Churchman.*

'We can speak strongly as to the care and fidelity, and also readableness, of this translation; we wish that any words of ours could persuade young students (or older ones for that matter) to take advantage of such helps as these.'—*Literary Churchman.*

'A great boon to English readers, as no other translation in our language has yet appeared.'—*Rock.*

'St. Augustine's correspondence embraced all who were eminent in philosophy, literature, politics, religious and social life; everybody found his way to the Bishop of Hippo.'—*British Quarterly Review.*

'A most valuable contribution to a wider acquaintance with St. Augustine.'—*British and Foreign Evangelical Review.*

'An invaluable supplement to and commentary on his larger works, and furnishing a lively picture of the theological movements of the times.'—*Daily Review.*

'If the reader has any taste for the acquisition of knowledge, he cannot fail to be interested and instructed. We advise students rather to deny themselves of, or postpone their acquaintance with, many modern writers, than to neglect this mighty man of old.'—*Watchman.*

WRITINGS IN CONNECTION WITH THE MANICHÆAN HERESY.

TRANSLATED BY REV. RICHARD STOTHERT, M.A.

In One Volume.

In this Treatise, in finding his way through the mazes of the obscure region into which Manichæus led him, he, once for all, ascertained the true relation subsisting between God and His creatures, formed his opinion regarding the respective provinces of reason and faith, and the connection of the Old and New Testaments, and found the root of all evil in the created will.

'At first sight the reader might suppose these treatises to be antiquated and dull; but let him "take up and read," and if he has any taste for the acquisition of knowledge, he cannot fail to be interested and instructed.'—*Watchman.*

ON THE TRINITY.

TRANSLATED BY REV. ARTHUR HADDAN, B.D.,

HON. CANON OF WORCESTER, AND RECTOR OF BARTON-ON-THE-HEATH.

In One Volume.

One of the most valuable portions of this volume is the eloquent and profound exposition given of the rule of interpretation to be applied to Scripture language respecting the person of our Lord.

'In giving this work to the English reader, Canon Haddan has left us another of those rich legacies which endear his memory as a scholar and real divine.'—*John Bull.*

'This treatise is valuable, apart from every other value, as an intellectual exercise to the student. The thought is often so delicate and profound, that it requires the most patient investigation to grasp *all* its meaning; and it possesses that unmistakeable quality of genius, that it is continually bringing out into form ideas that have often flitted through the reader's mind when he was unable to stop them for analysis.'—*Church Review.*

'In these times of rash and irreverent speculation, when there is such a strong propensity to exalt reason and to depreciate faith, it is well to see how one of the most colossal and majestic intellects of which the Church could ever boast, bowed meekly and implicitly to the authority of the word of God.'—*Methodist Recorder.*

THE SERMON ON THE MOUNT EXPOUNDED,

AND THE

HARMONY OF THE EVANGELISTS.

TRANSLATED RESPECTIVELY BY

REV. W. FINDLAY, M.A., AND REV. S. D. F. SALMOND, M.A.

In One Volume.

St. Augustine himself looked on the 'Harmony' as one of his most exhaustive works; he speaks of the themes here dealt with as matters which were discussed with the utmost painstaking.

'This translation is about the best substitute for the original that skill and labour could produce. Most undoubtedly they are much *pleasanter* reading than St. Augustine's Latin.'—*Church Review.*

'A wonderful monument of genius and learning consecrated to the noblest ends, and the more we read, the more we admire.'—*Baptist Magazine.*

WRITINGS IN CONNECTION WITH THE DONATIST CONTROVERSY.

TRANSLATED BY J. R. KING, M.A.,

VICAR OF ST. PETER'S IN THE EAST, OXFORD, AND LATE FELLOW AND TUTOR OF MERTON COLLEGE, OXFORD.

In One Volume.

'His Donatist Lectures are not only intrinsically valuable, but they present a vivid picture of the times, and throw great light on the conditions of thought and life in the Church.'—*British Quarterly Review.*

'It is a great advantage to English-speaking Churchmen to be enabled to study the works of so great a mind as Augustine's, who lived in an age which called forth all his powers, and whose writings are still suitable for some of the chief controversies of our own times.'—*Record.*

ON CHRISTIAN DOCTRINE;

THE ENCHIRIDION,

BEING A TREATISE ON FAITH, HOPE, AND LOVE;

ON THE CATECHIZING OF THE UNINSTRUCTED;

ON FAITH AND THE CREED.

TRANSLATED BY PROFESSOR J. F. SHAW AND REV. S. D. SALMOND.

In One Volume.

This Volume comprehends four most important Treatises, all of which have their own special value.

'I cannot express, my beloved son Laurentius, the delight with which I witness your progress in knowledge, and the earnest desire that you should be a wise man,—not one of those of whom it is said: "Where is the wise? where is the scribe? where is the disputer of this world?" but one of those of whom it is said: "The multitude of the wise is the welfare of the world," and such as the apostle wishes those to become whom he tells: "I would have you wise unto that which is good, and simple concerning evil." . . . I will, therefore, in a short discourse, unfold the proper mode of worshipping God.'

'A valuable book for the theologian. In the four treatises which it contains he will find, ready to hand, in a very excellent translation, the teaching of the great Augustine on questions which are fermenting in the world of religious thought at the present day, and challenge discussion at every turn. He will also meet with practical suggestions so fresh in tone, and so directly to the point, that they might have been the ideas of a contemporary speaking in view of existing creeds.'—*Church Bells.*

'The translation flows with quite remarkable ease.'—*Church Review.*

THE ANTI-PELAGIAN WORKS OF ST. AUGUSTINE.

Translated by PETER HOLMES, D.D., F.R.A.S.,

DOMESTIC CHAPLAIN TO THE RIGHT HON. THE COUNTESS OF ROTHES.

In Three Volumes 8vo (Vol. 3 in preparation).

'It is a privilege of genius to be adapted to the future as well as to the present. This is finely exemplified in the Christian genius of the Bishop of Hippo.'—*Record.*

'No man can understand the history of doctrine without understanding the works of St. Augustine, and especially his writings against Pelagianism. We are therefore happy to see that these are to be published in our own language.'—*Bibliotheca Sacra.*

'Extremely well translated, with scholarly ability and with excellent taste.'—*Union Review.*

'No uninspired treatise on the subject of sin and grace is better fitted to bring to view the true issues, the seed-truths, and the largest wealth of suggestive thought on this subject, than these great treatises.'—*Princeton Review.*

LECTURES & TRACTATES ON THE GOSPEL ACCORDING TO ST. JOHN.

Translated by Rev. JOHN GIBB and Rev. JAMES INNES.

In Two Volumes.

'Of great and perpetual interest.'—*Guardian.*

'Beautifully printed and got up; the translation is careful, accurate, and readable.'—*Church Bells.*

'In reading this Commentary we are reminded of the frequency with which the sayings of St. Augustine have been repeated by modern interpreters of the Bible.'—*Bibliotheca Sacra.*

'We regard the Lectures as a capital illustration of the principles laid down in the treatise on "Christian Doctrine." They display the real greatness of the author's mind, his profound spiritual insight, his vast knowledge of human nature on all its sides, and his rare power of moulding the minds of others after the pattern of his own; it is both refreshing and re-invigorating to come thus into contact with him.'—*Baptist Magazine.*

THE CONFESSIONS OF ST. AUGUSTINE.

An entirely new Translation.

With copious Notes, Historical and Explanatory, by

Rev. J. G. PILKINGTON, M.A., VICAR OF ST. MARK'S, DALSTON.

In One Volume.

In Twenty-four Handsome 8vo Volumes, Subscription Price £6, 6s. od.,

Ante-Nicene Christian Library.

A COLLECTION OF ALL THE WORKS OF THE FATHERS OF THE CHRISTIAN CHURCH PRIOR TO THE COUNCIL OF NICÆA.

EDITED BY THE

REV. ALEXANDER ROBERTS, D.D., AND JAMES DONALDSON, LL.D

MESSRS. CLARK are now happy to announce the completion of this Series. It has been received with marked approval by all sections of the Christian Church in this country and in the United States, as supplying what has long been felt to be a want, and also on account of the impartiality, learning, and care with which Editors and Translators have executed a very difficult task.

The Publishers do not bind themselves to *continue* to supply the Series at the Subscription price.

The Works are arranged as follow :—

FIRST YEAR.

APOSTOLIC FATHERS, comprising Clement's Epistles to the Corinthians; Polycarp to the Ephesians; Martyrdom of Polycarp; Epistle of Barnabas; Epistles of Ignatius (longer and shorter, and also the Syriac version); Martyrdom of Ignatius; Epistle to Diognetus; Pastor of Hermas; Papias; Spurious Epistles of Ignatius. In One Volume.

JUSTIN MARTYR; ATHENAGORAS. In One Volume.

TATIAN; THEOPHILUS; THE CLEmentine Recognitions. In One Volume.

CLEMENT OF ALEXANDRIA, Volume First, comprising Exhortation to Heathen; The Instructor; and a portion of the Miscellanies.

SECOND YEAR.

HIPPOLYTUS, Volume First; Refutation of all Heresies, and Fragments from his Commentaries.

IRENÆUS, Volume First.

TERTULLIAN AGAINST MARCION.

CYPRIAN, Volume First; the Epistles, and some of the Treatises.

THIRD YEAR.

IRENÆUS (completion); HIPPOLYTUS (completion); Fragments of Third Century. In One Volume.

ORIGEN: De Principiis; Letters; and portion of Treatise against Celsus.

CLEMENT OF ALEXANDRIA, Volume Second; Completion of Miscellanies.

TERTULLIAN, Volume First; To the Martyrs; Apology; To the Nations, etc.

FOURTH YEAR.

CYPRIAN, Volume Second (completion); Novatian; Minucius Felix; Fragments.

METHODIUS; ALEXANDER OF LYcopolis; Peter of Alexandria; Anatolius; Clement on Virginity; and Fragments.

TERTULLIAN, Volume Second.

APOCRYPHAL GOSPELS, ACTS, AND Revelations; comprising all the very curious Apocryphal Writings of the first three Centuries.

FIFTH YEAR.

TERTULLIAN, Volume Third (completion).

CLEMENTINE HOMILIES; APOSTOlical Constitutions. In One Volume.

ARNOBIUS.

DIONYSIUS; GREGORY THAUMAturgus; Syrian Fragments. In One Volume.

SIXTH YEAR.

LACTANTIUS; Two Volumes.

ORIGEN, Volume Second (completion). 12s. to Non-Subscribers.

EARLY LITURGIES AND REMAINing Fragments. 9s. to Non-Subscribers.

Single Years cannot be had separately, unless to complete sets; but any Volume may be had separately, price 10s. 6d.,—with the exception of ORIGEN, Vol. II., 12s.; and the EARLY LITURGIES, 9s.

LANGE'S
COMMENTARIES ON THE OLD AND NEW TESTAMENTS.

Translations of the Commentaries of Dr. Lange and his Collaborateurs on the Old and New Testaments.

Edited by Dr. PHILIP SCHAFF.

There are now ready (in imperial 8vo, double columns), price 21s. per Volume,

OLD TESTAMENT, Eight Volumes:

COMMENTARY ON THE BOOK OF GENESIS, in One Volume.
COMMENTARY ON JOSHUA, JUDGES, AND RUTH, in One Volume.
COMMENTARY ON THE BOOKS OF KINGS, in One Volume.
COMMENTARY ON THE BOOK OF JOB.
COMMENTARY ON THE PSALMS, in One Volume.
COMMENTARY ON PROVERBS, ECCLESIASTES, AND THE SONG OF SOLOMON, in One Volume.
COMMENTARY ON JEREMIAH AND LAMENTATIONS, in One Volume.
COMMENTARY ON MINOR PROPHETS, in One Volume.

The other Books of the Old Testament are in active preparation, and will be announced as soon as ready.

NEW TESTAMENT (now complete), Ten Volumes:

COMMENTARY ON THE GOSPEL OF ST. MATTHEW.
COMMENTARY ON THE GOSPELS OF ST. MARK and ST. LUKE.
COMMENTARY ON THE GOSPEL OF ST. JOHN.
COMMENTARY ON THE ACTS OF THE APOSTLES.
COMMENTARY ON THE EPISTLE OF ST. PAUL TO THE ROMANS.
COMMENTARY ON THE EPISTLES OF ST. PAUL TO THE CORINTHIANS.
COMMENTARY ON THE EPISTLES OF ST. PAUL TO THE GALATIANS, EPHESIANS, PHILIPPIANS, and COLOSSIANS.
COMMENTARY ON THE EPISTLES TO THE THESSA- LONIANS, TIMOTHY, TITUS, PHILEMON, and HEBREWS.
COMMENTARY ON THE EPISTLES OF JAMES, PETER, JOHN, and JUDE.
COMMENTARY ON THE BOOK OF REVELATION.

'Lange's comprehensive and elaborate "Bibelwerk." . . . We hail its publication as a valuable addition to the stores of our Biblical literature.'—*Edinburgh Review.*

The price to Subscribers to the Foreign Theological Library, St. Augustine's Works, and Ante-Nicene Library, and Meyer's Commentary on the New Testament, or to Purchasers of Complete Sets of the Commentary (so far as published), will be

FIFTEEN SHILLINGS PER VOLUME.

Dr. LANGE's Commentary on the Gospels and Acts (without Dr. SCHAFF's Notes) is also published in the FOREIGN THEOLOGICAL LIBRARY, in Nine Volumes demy 8vo, and may be had in that form if desired. (For particulars, see List of Foreign Theological Library.)

MEYER'S
Commentary on the New Testament.

M ESSRS. CLARK beg to announce that they have in course of
preparation a Translation of the well-known and justly esteemed

CRITICAL AND EXEGETICAL
COMMENTARY ON THE NEW TESTAMENT,
By Dr. H. A. W. MEYER,
OBERCONSISTORIALRATH, HANNOVER,

Of which they have published—

FIRST YEAR.
ROMANS, Two Vols.
GALATIANS, One Volume.
ST. JOHN'S GOSPEL, Vol. I.

SECOND YEAR.
FIRST ISSUE.
ST. JOHN'S GOSPEL, Vol. II.
PHILIPPIANS AND COLOSSIANS, One Vol.

The Subscription is 21s. for Four Volumes, Demy 8vo, payable in advance.

In order to secure perfect accuracy, the Publishers have placed the whole
work under the editorial care of Rev. Dr. DICKSON, Professor of Divinity in the
University of Glasgow, and Rev. Dr. CROMBIE, Professor of Biblical Criticism,
St. Mary's College, St. Andrews.

Each Volume will be sold separately at (on an average) 10s. 6d. to Non-
Subscribers.

Intending Subscribers will be kind enough to send their orders either
direct to the Publishers at 38 George Street, Edinburgh, or through their
own Booksellers.

'I need hardly add that the last edition of the accurate, perspicuous, and learned commentary of Dr. Meyer has been most carefully consulted throughout; and I must again,
as in the preface to the Galatians, avow my great obligations to the acumen and scholarship of the learned editor.'—BISHOP ELLICOTT *in Preface to his 'Commentary on Ephesians.'*

'Meyer has been long and well known to scholars as one of the very ablest of the
German expositors of the New Testament. We are not sure whether we ought not to
say that he is *unrivalled* as an interpreter of the grammatical and historical meaning of
the sacred writers. The publishers have now rendered another seasonable and important
service to English students in producing this translation.'—*Guardian.*

'The ablest grammatical exegete of the age.'—PHILIP SCHAFF, D.D.

www.ingramcontent.com/pod-product-compliance
Lightning Source LLC
Chambersburg PA
CBHW030948110726
47900CB00004B/1172